Acclaim for the authors of
CHRISTMAS WEDDING BELLES

NICOLA CORNICK

"Readers will relish this sensual and emotional love story."
—*Romantic Times BOOKreviews* on *Lord of Scandal*

"A rising star of the Regency arena."
—*Publishers Weekly*

MARGARET McPHEE

"A nicely written and captivating high-seas adventure."
—*Romantic Times BOOKreviews* on *The Captain's Lady*

"McPhee's story combines sensuality, an innocent heroine
and a rakish viscount…in a touching, poignant novel."
—*Romantic Times BOOKreviews* on *The Wicked Earl*

MIRANDA JARRETT

"Miranda Jarrett continues to reign as the queen
of historical romance."
—*Romantic Times BOOKreviews*

"A marvelous author…each word is a treasure,
each book a lasting memory."
—*Literary Times*

NICOLA CORNICK

became fascinated with history when she was a child and spent hours poring over historical novels and watching costume drama. She still does! She has worked in a variety of jobs, from serving refreshments on a steam train to arranging university graduation ceremonies. When she is not writing she enjoys walking in the English countryside, taking her husband, dog and even her cats with her. Nicola loves to hear from readers and can be contacted via her Web site at www.nicolacornick.co.uk.

MARGARET McPHEE

loves to use her imagination—an essential requirement for a trained scientist. However, when she realized that her imagination was inspired more by the historical romances she loves to read rather than by her experiments, she decided to put the ideas down on paper. She has since left her scientific life behind, retaining only the romance—her husband, whom she met in a laboratory. In summer, Margaret enjoys cycling along the coastline overlooking the Firth of Clyde in Scotland, where she lives. In winter, tea, cakes and a good book suffice.

MIRANDA JARRETT

considers herself sublimely fortunate to have a career that combines history and happy endings, even if it's one that's also made her family far-too-regular patrons of the local pizzeria. Miranda is the author of over thirty historical romances, and her books are enjoyed by readers the world over. She has won numerous awards for her writing, including two Golden Leaf Awards and two *Romantic Times BOOKreviews* Reviewers' Choice awards, and she is a three-time Romance Writers of America RITA® Award finalist for best short historical romance. Miranda is a graduate of Brown University with a degree in art history. She loves to hear from readers at P.O. Box 1102, Paoli, PA 19301-1145, or MJarrett21@aol.com.

CHRISTMAS
Wedding Belles

NICOLA CORNICK

MARGARET McPHEE

MIRANDA JARRETT

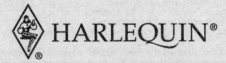

HARLEQUIN®

TORONTO • NEW YORK • LONDON
AMSTERDAM • PARIS • SYDNEY • HAMBURG
STOCKHOLM • ATHENS • TOKYO • MILAN • MADRID
PRAGUE • WARSAW • BUDAPEST • AUCKLAND

ISBN-13: 978-0-373-29471-8
ISBN-10:   0-373-29471-9

CHRISTMAS WEDDING BELLES
Copyright © 2007 by Harlequin Books S.A.

The publisher acknowledges the copyright holders
of the individual works as follows:

THE PIRATE'S KISS
Copyright © 2007 by Nicola Cornick

A SMUGGLER'S TALE
Copyright © 2007 by Margaret McPhee

THE SAILOR'S BRIDE
Copyright © 2007 by Miranda Jarrett

CONTENTS

THE PIRATE'S KISS

Nicola Cornick

Author Note

From the time that I first started reading—and loving—romance novels, books with pirate heroes have been amongst my very favorites. Georgette Heyer's Beauvallet possessed all the heroic qualities I most admire—courage, daring, integrity and honor. The mysterious Frenchman in Daphne du Maurier's *Frenchman's Creek* and the dashing Rory Frost in M. M. Kaye's *Trade Wind* ran off with my heart. I owe all of those writers a huge debt for the inspiration and enjoyment that they have given me over the years.

A couple of years ago, when I was researching my family tree, I discovered that two of my husband's ancestors had been smugglers and pirates in Dorset at the end of the eighteenth century. Escaping from the authorities, they were last heard of in the Bahamas!

The lure of the pirate hero is a difficult one to resist— what could be more appealing than a man who lives outside the law and yet has his own code of honor and courage? In *The Pirate's Kiss** Daniel had loved and lost Lucy years before. Now they meet again and find that the attraction between them has never died. But can they find love again, or is it too late?

This story is dedicated to all the readers who wrote to me after they had read *The Rake's Mistress,* asking for Daniel de Lancey to have a story of his own. Here it is—just for you.

Nicola

*Linked to Nicola Cornick's *Bluestocking Brides* trilogy

Chapter 1

Suffolk, England, November 1808

NOTHING ever happens here…

Lucinda Melville sighed and put down her pen. The casement window of her bedroom was open, allowing crisp winter air to flood in. It brought with it the scent of cold sea mixed with the fragrance of pine, and carried the distant sound of breakers on the shore and the hoot of owls down in the forest. A full moon shone bright in the black sky. It was a night made for romance, but Mrs Melville had no time for that sort of thing.

She picked up her pen again.

Nothing ever happens here… But pray do not think that I am complaining, dear Rebecca. I am more than grateful to you for finding me this position with Mrs Saltire. Indeed, I think that when Eustacia marries, as she is set to do in the New Year (to the dull but worthy Mr Leytonstone, just as I predicted), I will seek another governess's post in this locality. Wood-bridge is a charming town. We take tea at the assembly rooms and visit the theatre, provided that the entertainment is not

*too racy, of course. It is all entirely delightful, and very proper
for a governess companion.*

Lucinda paused again, thinking. There had been a time in her life
when matters had not been so staid and unadventurous, but that had
been a very long time ago and was soon dismissed again.

She dusted the letter down and closed the writing box. As nothing
else had happened she had no more to tell her childhood friend,
Rebecca Kestrel. Besides, Rebecca and her husband, Lucas, were to
join their party in a couple of months' time, for Christmas at Kestrel
Court, so she would save the rest of her news, such as it was, until then.

Lucinda went across to the window and leaned her arms on the
sill, resting her chin on her hand as she stared out into the dark. When
she had first heard from Mrs Saltire that they were to spend autumn
in the Midwinter villages she had been quite concerned, for everyone
knew that there had been the most scandalously diverting occur-
rences at Midwinter a mere five years before, when the members of
a dangerous spy ring had been captured. It was not at all the type of
environment that Lucinda thought appropriate for her young charge.
Miss Eustacia Saltire was a sweet girl, but she was deplorably
romantic in her inclinations, and Lucinda was very concerned that
Stacey would become quite over-excited by her proximity to people
who had actually been *involved* in the shocking events of those times.

Balanced against the danger of encouraging Stacey's wayward
imagination, however, had been the possibilities provided by a
family connection to the Duke of Kestrel. Mrs Saltire had the good
fortune to be distantly related to the Duchess of Kestrel, and it had
been the Duchess who had suggested that Mrs Saltire might like to
bring Stacey to Midwinter for a few months. Mindful of the fact that
the Duke still had several eligible relatives unmarried, and also that
Stacey simply had not *taken* during her first season in London, Mrs
Saltire had eagerly agreed. The journey had been accomplished,
made all the smoother by the attentiveness of the ducal servants, and
they had now been situated at Kestrel Court for eight weeks.

Lucinda sighed again. It would soon be time for her to start applying for a new post, for Stacey was now betrothed to the worthy but dull Samuel Leytonstone, who had a solid fortune and a manner to match. Secretly Lucinda thought that Stacey could aim higher than a young man who behaved as though he were already in flannel vests, but she kept the unworthy thought to herself. Mr Leytonstone was steady and rich and reliable, and one had to count such matters above trifling things such as passion and gallantry. Lucinda knew all about the dangers of rash youthful passion, and if a tiny part of her still craved excitement she usually managed to ignore it.

Lucinda knew all about Making Do too. In her youth her looks had been no more than tolerable—dark blonde hair and cool blue eyes had been unfashionable at the time—and her parents, an indigent vicar and his social climbing wife, had been delighted when she had become engaged straight from the schoolroom. But then the plan had gone awry.

She had been betrothed for four years to her childhood sweetheart—a man who, humiliatingly, appeared to have forgotten her existence as soon as she was out of his sight, a man with dash and brilliance and the prospect of a glittering naval career. Eventually the most appalling of news had filtered its way back to her, conveyed by the gossips and scandalmongers who made it their business to upset as many people as possible. Her betrothed was a criminal. He had abandoned his promising naval career and had taken up instead as—*whisper it*—a pirate.

That was the moment Lucinda's heart had broken. So she had married the first man who asked, had been widowed two years later, and now here she was, at nine and twenty, earning her own living and putting youthful folly firmly where it belonged—in the past.

Lucinda spotted a moth that was coming dangerously close to the candle flame. She trapped it gently in her cupped palms and released it out of the window, worrying as soon as it was gone that the night would be too cold for it and it would perish.

As she turned to close the casement a flicker of movement caught her eye, away on the edge of the woods that bordered the garden at Kestrel Court. She stopped, staring into the shadows. The leaves rustled in the slight breeze and the scent of pine mingled with the fresher, salty smell of the sea and the crispness of the frosty night. Lucinda paused, her hand on the window latch. There was no one there. The skipping shadows and her imagination were playing tricks.

At least she hoped so.

But a nasty suspicion had lodged in her mind and would not be shifted. What if it was Stacey, making an assignation with a young man? What if—perish the thought—Stacey was planning an *elopement*?

Before the dull but rich Mr Leytonstone had proposed, a certain Mr Owen Chance, the Riding Officer stationed in Woodbridge to catch smugglers, had asked Mrs Saltire's permission to pay his addresses to Stacey. Mrs Saltire had refused graciously, politely, but very finally. She had pointed out elegantly that Mr Chance had good birth but no money, and precious little prospect of making any in a backwater like Midwinter. But Owen Chance was a good-looking man, with a charm to match, and, being fair, Lucinda could see that he quite eclipsed poor Mr Leytonstone. One could not imagine Mr Chance in a flannel vest. In fact Lucinda could tell that Stacey had imagined Mr Chance more as a knight on a white charger, and her mother's refusal to countenance his suit made him all the more attractive.

There had been tears when Mrs Saltire had pointed out the financial realities of their situation to her daughter, and then Mr Leytonstone had proposed and been accepted. Stacey had gone very quiet and suspiciously biddable, but Lucinda was not convinced...

If Stacey was regretting her betrothal and making midnight assignations with the dashing Mr Chance... Well... Lucinda shook her head. It would be very foolish because, apart from any issues of propriety, she would catch her death of cold out on a night like this.

It was past twelve and time for bed. Lucinda heard the clock at the bottom of the stairs chime the quarter-hour. Mrs Saltire would be asleep by now, tucked up with her laudanum, and Stacey, whom Lucinda had caught reading *Ivanhoe* earlier in the day, was probably dreaming of romantic heroes, not creeping out into the grounds of Kestrel Court to meet one.

Nothing ever happens here...

Lucinda put up a hand to pull the curtains shut, then paused as the flicker of movement caught her eye again. A man on horseback was riding very slowly down the track that bordered the gardens of Kestrel Court. Lucinda could see his outline in the moonlight. It looked disturbingly like Mr Chance, on the raking bay mare upon which he had caught Stacey's eye in the first place.

A floorboard creaked on the landing, and then there was the sound of a step on the stair. With a sharp sigh Lucinda snatched her cloak from the chairback where she had left it earlier, and flung it about her shoulders. She grabbed the candle from beside her bed, and hurried out into the corridor. It was not the first time that her role as governess had involved her in counselling against an improvident love affair. She did not want Stacey to ruin herself in a foolish elopement and then rue it for the rest of her days when the love was gone and there was no money on which to live.

The house was silent. A lamp burned in the porch, but the night porter was not at his post, though the front door was unlocked. Deploring such laxity on the part of the servants, Lucinda turned the handle and went outside, down the steps and onto the gravel sweep. Her candle flickered and went out, doused by the sharp sea breeze. For a moment she blinked in the sudden darkness, but then her eyes adjusted to the moonlight and she could see a figure slipping between the trees in the lee of the park wall. At the same time she heard the sound of hooves on the frosty ground. Could that be Mr Chance, coming to carry off his bride? Lucinda screwed up her face as she imagined Mrs Saltire's hysterics when she discovered that her little ewe lamb had thrown herself away on a pauper.

She hastened after the fleeing figure, but Stacey—if it were she—had already lost herself amongst the trees that bordered the park. The night was quiet now. Suspiciously so. Lucinda held her breath, straining to hear any sound that might give her quarry away, but there was nothing except the wind in the top of the pines and the distant beat of the waves on the shore.

Perhaps she had been mistaken. Perhaps Stacey really was tucked up in bed. It was a servant she had heard on the stair and she was out here chasing shadows. The cold was eating deep into her bones now. It was no night for an elopement. Feeling foolish, Lucinda turned to go back to the house.

The moon went behind a cloud, but in the moment before it disappeared Lucinda clearly saw a man crouching in the lee of the park gates—and in the same instant she saw what he could not: the menacing shadow of the Riding Officer moving silently along the wall, coming closer all the time. She caught her breath on a gasp, and the hidden man turned his head at the sound. With a shock of recognition Lucinda knew him.

Terror and amazement jolted through her. Past and present collided violently. Lucinda started to tremble. She could see that the man had spotted her and was about to speak; she saw too that Owen Chance was urging his horse forward silently, every sense alert for the slightest sound.

Lucinda acted on instinct. She raised a finger to her lips in a beseeching gesture and saw the fugitive pause, and then she was beside him in one silent move, clapping her hand over his mouth. She pulled him deeper into the shadow of the gate and leaned forward to whisper in his ear.

'Be silent! There is an excise man on the other side of the wall.'

Touching him as she was, she could feel the tension that ripped through his body at her words. Every muscle he possessed was taut and ready for flight—or fight. He moved slightly, silently, to grasp the pistol in his belt.

Lucinda eased her hand from his mouth and rested it warningly on his shoulder. They were both utterly still. She could not even hear his breathing. But she was more aware of him than she had ever been of any other person in her life. She was pressed against the unyielding lines of his back. She could feel the warmth of his skin and she could *smell* him, a scent of fresh air and salt and leather that went straight to her head and made her senses spin, and also made her wonder, quite outrageously, if he tasted of the sea as well.

The tension spun tight as a web and seemed to last for ever, and then there was a chink of harness. She heard Owen Chance swear softly, and the horse snorted as he pulled on the rein. The shadows shifted and the horse and rider turned towards the Woodbridge road to be were swallowed up in the darkness. The frost glittered on the road behind them. Lucinda released the man and stood up slowly, every muscle in her body protesting at being clenched so tight.

The man got to his feet and they stood looking at each other in the moonlight. Lucinda felt breathless—a natural enough condition, she assured herself, since she had forgotten to breathe during the entire encounter. Twelve long years slipped away as though they had never been, and she was a young girl again, fathoms deep in her first love. She had thought never to see this man again…

'So…' he said. His voice was smooth. 'I must thank you for saving my skin. I had no notion that he was there.' He shook his head ruefully. 'Muffling the horse's hooves is an old trick. I cannot believe it almost caught me.'

'You should be more careful,' Lucinda said. She was glad that her voice sounded so calm when inside she was trembling. Did he not recognise her? Had she changed so much? It seemed impossible that he would not know her when she had known him instantly. A spasm of bitterness twisted within her. Perhaps it was not so surprising. He had, after all, forgotten her as soon as he had walked out of her life. Why would he remember her now?

She saw his teeth flash white as he smiled. 'I will take your advice in future. But you, mistress… What made you decide to help me when ninety-nine of one hundred females would have screamed loud enough to bring every last Riding Officer in the vicinity down on me?'

Lucinda regarded him steadily. She was not entirely sure why she had helped him when she had reason enough to wish him dead. But instinct, as old and deep as time, had made her save him rather than condemn him, and she did not want to question why.

'I did it for the sake of your sister, Daniel de Lancey,' she said, reaching for an acceptable half-truth. 'Rebecca would not wish me to condemn you to hang if I could save your neck.'

He went very still. 'Do I know you?'

'You did once,' Lucinda said.

He took her chin in his hand and turned her face up to the moonlight, and Lucinda took the opportunity to study him as candidly as he was scrutinising her. He had not changed so much from the young man she had last seen twelve years before. He still had intensely dark hair, untouched with grey, and dark eyes that had once bewitched every young lady in the county—eyes so black she had once imagined fancifully that they were darker than midnight. Differences were there, though. His face was leaner than she remembered, hardened, perhaps, by experience and adversity—the line of the jaw harsh, the mouth firm. And he was no longer the lanky youth he had once been, but had filled out with hard muscle beneath his coat, so that his shoulders were broad and he seemed taller, tougher, altogether more dangerous.

Her skin prickled with awareness beneath his fingers. Emotions stirred. Old memories… She had been so young, only seventeen, but there had been nothing childish about her feelings for Daniel de Lancey. He had been her first love—her only love, if she were honest. And she had never forgotten him, not even when humiliation and pride had flayed her alive, and common sense and practicality and every sound, rational reason she could ever come up with had prompted her to let his memory go.

He pursed his lips into a soundless whistle.

'Lucy Spring… By all that's miraculous…' There was something in his eyes, something of nostalgia laced with a wickedness that made her heart turn over. But she was a sensible widow now, not a lovestruck young girl who would fall for his shallow charm a second time.

'Lucinda Melville,' she corrected primly.

His hand fell. 'Of course. I heard that you had wed. You did not wait for me as you promised.'

Emotion raked Lucinda suddenly, as raw and painful now as it had been eight years before, when she had heard of his betrayal. 'You did not come back for me as *you* promised.' The hot words tumbled from her lips before she could help herself. 'How dare you reproach me? You left me without a word. I waited four years, Daniel! And then I heard that you had abandoned me—abandoned everything you had previously held dear!' There was a wealth of bitterness and humiliation in her voice. 'Did you expect me to wait for ever?'

It seemed a long time before he replied. His face was in shadow and she could not read his tone. 'Yes,' he said, at last. He shifted a little. 'Yes, I suppose that I did.'

'I never received anything from you,' Lucinda said. 'No word, no letters… Did you write to me at all? Did you even think of me?'

There was a silence. She could still remember the stifling conventionality of the vicarage drawing room where, over tea each and every day, her mother's visitors would press her gently on whether she had heard from her fiancé yet and commiserate maliciously with her when she was forced to admit she had not.

'It was a long time ago,' Daniel said, and Lucinda's heart wrenched to have her suspicions confirmed. He had not written. He had not cared.

'So it was,' she said. 'And now I am a widow and you are a pirate, so I hear.'

She saw him grin. 'You heard correctly.'

She looked at him. In boots and a tattered old frieze coat he looked more like a yeoman farmer—except for the pistol and sword at his belt.

'You do not look much like a pirate,' she said. 'How disappointing.'

Daniel tilted his head on one side. 'How do you know what a pirate looks like? Have you met any others to compare me with?'

'No,' Lucinda conceded. 'I was basing my judgement on literature only.'

'Ah. Blackbeard?'

'And Calico Jack.'

'Neither had any style, so I hear.'

'They are both dead,' Lucinda said repressively. 'It is not a career with good prospects.'

Daniel laughed. 'You always were the practical one.'

'And you were reckless and dangerous,' Lucinda said.

'So, no change there. Which is why I am a pirate. We both made our choices, did we not, Lucy? Mine to be wild and irresponsible and yours to marry for money.'

'I am a governess,' Lucinda snapped, 'not a rich widow.'

'I heard,' Daniel said. 'Fine justice that you threw me over for Leopold Melville and then he turned out to be penniless.'

The anger and hurt that Lucinda had spent years repressing jetted up. 'By what right do you say that, Daniel de Lancey? I waited and waited for you, but you never came, did not even send word!' Her voice rose. 'Do you think it was right that I should be obliged to wait on the whim of a man who did not care enough to send just one letter?' She glared at him. 'You were an arrogant, selfish, *heartless* boy, and you are no better now as a man! I wish I had not saved your skin just now.'

Daniel had listened to her outburst without a word, but now he took a step towards her. He put his hand on her wrist. Neither of them was wearing gloves. His touch scalded her.

'Will you give me away, then?' he demanded. 'Run back to the house and raise the alarm?'

'Of course not,' Lucinda said contemptuously. 'What good would that do? You would be long gone before the militia were out.'

His fingers tightened. 'But you would like me to be caught?'

Lucinda shrugged angrily. 'You deserve no sympathy from me.'

'Perhaps not. But you helped me, all the same. Why was that, Lucy? If you bear such a grudge against me?'

Lucinda shivered a little, for beneath the anger that smouldered in both of them she sensed something else, something much more perilous. Old passion as hot and brittle as burning sticks.

Daniel was rubbing his fingers over the tender skin on the underside of her wrist, sending ripples of sensation cascading along her nerves. 'Why?' he asked again, softly this time.

Lucinda tried to snatch her hand away but he held on to her. 'And what,' he continued, 'were you doing out here in the dark? Meeting a lover?'

'Mind your own business,' Lucinda snapped, seizing on his second question so she did not have to answer the first, more difficult one. 'If you must know, I was out here looking for Miss Saltire. She has a *tendre* for Mr Chance, the Riding Officer, and I was afraid that she had made a foolish decision to elope.'

Daniel smiled a little. 'You would not approve of that, of course.'

'No, indeed. I know how misleading youthful passions can be.'

'But instead of Miss Saltire it is her governess who is out meeting a gentleman in the moonlight.'

'You are no gentleman.'

'That's true. Which probably makes me even more dangerous to tryst with.'

'Then I shall leave.'

'Very wise,' Daniel said. His tone became contemplative. 'Last time we parted you kissed me goodbye.'

There was a short, sharp silence. 'I remember,' Lucinda said, adding crushingly, 'It was not a very good kiss, was it?'

She remembered that it had been sweet, though, despite their lack of experience. And, truth to tell, she had little more knowledge of kissing now than she had had then. One could not count Leopold's fumbling attentions as adding to her experience. It had been endurance rather than passion that had been her companion in the marriage bed. Leopold had accused her of coldness and had turned from her in fury.

She suspected that Daniel's experience with the opposite sex, in contrast to her own, had increased in leaps and bounds—a suspicion confirmed when he said, 'No doubt we could do better now.'

Lucinda's stomach muscles clenched with a mixture of nervousness and longing. She tried hard to ignore it.

'No doubt we could,' she said. 'But such things were over between us a long time ago, Daniel.'

'Then consider it no more than an expression of thanks.'

'Most people,' Lucinda said, 'would make do with a handshake.'

Daniel smiled. 'But not me.'

He drew her in to his body and the shadows merged and shifted as his arms closed about her. His lips were cold against hers. Lucinda had imagined that she would resist him, but now she found that she did not want to do so. Their bodies fitted together as though they had never been apart, as though the intervening years had never existed.

Lucinda parted her lips instinctively and felt his tongue, warm and insistent, touch hers. She had wondered how he would taste, and now she knew: he tasted of the sea and the air and something clean and masculine and deliciously sensual. She felt shocked and aroused, and shocked by her own arousal. It had been such a long time. She had thought that her wild, wanton side was gone for ever. Sensible Lucinda, who advised debutantes against unruly passion, should not feel hot and dizzy and melting in a pirate's embrace.

She drew back a little on the thought, and felt him smile against her mouth—a smile that turned her trembling insides to even greater disorder. She was afraid that her legs might give way if he let go of her now.

'Was that better than last time?' he whispered.

'I… It was…' She grasped for words, grasped for any kind of coherent thought.

'You do not sound very sure.'

He sounded wickedly sure of himself. Before she could protest he had tangled a hand into her hair and tilted her face up so that his mouth could ravish hers with a thoroughness that left her dazed. She found that she was clutching his forearms, seeking stability in a world that spun like a top.

Have some sense. Push him away...

Instead, she drew him closer, sliding her hands over his shoulders, feeling the broadcloth of his coat rough against her cold fingers. His jaw grazed her cheek; that too was slightly rough with stubble, and the way it scored her sensitive skin made her shudder with helpless desire.

'Lucinda...' His lips were against her neck, sending the goose-bumps skittering across her skin. She felt cold, but her head was full of images of a summer long ago. She could smell the flowers and the scent of hot grass, hear the buzz of the bees, and see Daniel's hands trembling slightly as he unlaced her petticoat, his skin tanned brown against her pale nakedness.

Memory was powerfully seductive. She let go of all sense and pressed closer, arching to Daniel as his hand slipped beneath her cloak to find and clasp her breast, his thumb stroking urgently over the sensitised tip. She could feel how aroused he was, feel the strong, clean lines of his body moulded against every one of her curves. She opened her lips again to the demand of his, and for one timeless moment they stood locked together before he released her and stepped back with a muffled curse.

'Devil take it, you always could do this to me, Lucy. I thought that after twelve years—' Daniel stopped and Lucinda drew in a long, shuddering breath. Common sense was reasserting itself now, like a draught of cold night air. She felt tired and bitter, and aching with a sense of loss for what might have been, for all the golden, glorious promise that long-ago summer had held.

'This is foolish,' she said. Her voice shook. 'It was all over long ago. I must go, Daniel.'

He did not try to stop her. And because she was never going to see him again Lucinda raised her hand to touch his cheek in a fleeting caress before she turned away and walked towards the house. She did not mean to turn and look back, but when she did he had gone.

Chapter 2

THE path down to the creek was treacherous in the dark and the frost, but Daniel had walked there sufficient times in the past to leave at least a part of his mind free to think on other matters—and tonight that other matter was Lucy Spring. He could still feel the soft imprint of her body against his, and smell the flower perfume of her hair, a summery fragrance, lavender or rose or jasmine. Daniel was not sure which it had been. It was a long time since he had had the luxury of strolling in an English country garden, but the scent and the memory of her still filled his senses.

He ached for her, his body still alive and sharp with arousal. He could think of nothing but the taste of her and the need to take her to bed. It was frightening, as though all the years they had been apart were cancelled out, counting for nothing, as though the youthful passion that had fired his life then had reawoken and was concentrated solely in her.

She had saved him from capture. Fatally, he had not been paying attention. His mind had been distracted. The day before he had had the melancholy duty of visiting Newmarket, to tell the mother of one of his crew that the lad—a boy of fourteen—had died of a fever contracted in Lisbon back in the autumn. Breaking the news had been a dreadful experience. The woman had looked at him with so much grief in her eyes, but had said no word of reproof. Daniel had wanted to pour it all out—how he had nursed the boy himself, praying desperately for his recovery, how they had thought he was improving only to see him slip away from them so quietly that the moment of his death had come and gone in a breath. He knew there were no other children to support her or comfort her through her grief. He had left a big bag of gold on the table, knowing that it was not enough, that it could never replace the only son who had run away to sea and died on a pirate ship.

He ran a hand over his hair. On the way back to the coast he had ridden hard, trying to outrun his demons, but they had stayed with him at every step. When the winter fog had come down as he reached the outskirts of Woodbridge, he had stabled the horse at the Bell and sought to drown his sorrows in ale. He had sat alone in the bar. No one had approached him. Either they'd known who he was, in which case they would not have dared speak to him, or they'd thought he looked too grim to be good company. For that was the truth of it. Once it had been enough to know that he was doing the King's work, even if he was doing it outside the law, but now he felt old and sick of the fight. He had not seen his sister, his only family, for two years now. He was damnably lonely. And seeing Lucinda, holding her close in his arms, feeling her warmth as he pressed his mouth to the softness of her hair… That had almost been the undoing of him. He had not wanted to let her go again. He had watched her walk away, and it had been the hardest thing he had ever done.

It had been such a long time. He'd thought he had forgotten her. Now the vividness of his memories and the ache of his body told him it was far from over, no matter what Lucinda said.

But there was such bitterness between them. Daniel pushed the dark hair back from his forehead. She had called him selfish, and it was true. He had not thought, in his arrogant, youthful carelessness, what it must have been like for Lucy, left at home in the stifling atmosphere of the vicarage, fending off those spiteful tabbies who would be enquiring every day as to when he was returning to make her his bride. As the weeks had slid into months, and the months into years, with no word from him, what must she have thought? How must she have felt, sitting at home waiting for him? Could he really reproach her for breaking their betrothal and accepting Leopold Melville instead?

Daniel paused, listening for sounds of pursuit, but the night was silent. Not even the call of an owl penetrated the dark woods.

The worst thing was that Lucy's reproaches were well founded. He had assumed that she would always be there for him. He had been complacent, certain of her love for him. For a while after he had joined the Royal Navy the sea had become his mistress, to the exclusion of all other loves. She was demanding, imperious, dangerous, exciting. She pushed all other thoughts from his mind. And then the Admiralty had approached him to leave the relative security of the Navy and strike out as a privateer, gathering information, working beyond and outside the law. It was made clear to him that he would be denounced as a pirate from the start, in order to give his apparent betrayal more credibility. The idea had appealed to his recklessness, and he had not thought then of Lucy, or home, or anything beyond the excitement of the moment. He had been a damnable fool. He had thought that one day he could go back for her and everything between them would be as it had been.

Eventually word had come to him that she was married, and the shock of it had brought him to his senses. He had realised what he had lost. But it was too late. Now he knew they could never go back.

The challenge came out of the darkness and he gave the password. One of the crew stepped onto the path in front of him. Even though the *Defiance* was a privateer, his men were drilled as on a regular Navy ship, disciplined and sound.

'Welcome back, sir.' Daniel's deputy, Lieutenant Holroyd, sounded relieved. The crew were jumpy as cats when he was ashore. 'There is someone to see you.'

The *Defiance* was berthed in a deep, wide tidal pool, close under the trees of Kestrel Creek. The tide was high and Daniel could step aboard from the bank. It was one of his favourite moorings, but it was a dangerous one given the length of time it took to sail out of the creek to the open sea. But then nowhere was safe for a pirate. That was one of the things that had attracted him to the life in the first place— The freedom and the sense of risk. He had been young then, and dangerously wild. These days he realised that he valued a cool head as much as reckless courage.

There was a lamp burning in his cabin, spilling warm golden light across the papers on his desk and illuminating the still figure of the man who sat waiting for him.

'I heard that the Riding Officer was out,' Justin, Duke of Kestrel said, rising to greet him. 'I am glad to see you made it safely back.'

Daniel shook his hand. He had worked with Kestrel for the last five years, providing the Admiralty with intelligence on French shipping movements during the Wars, chasing the French from British shores, smuggling refugees from Napoleon's regime. Daniel liked Justin; he was tough but fair. They were also linked by the marriage of Daniel's sister Rebecca to Justin's brother Lucas, but they seldom referred to their family connection. Their relationship was strictly professional.

'Chance almost caught me,' he said now. 'He's good, but I think someone tipped him off.'

Justin Kestrel's brows snapped down. 'Norton?'

'It must be.' Daniel threw his damp coat across the back of a chair and loosened his stock. Many people thought that John Norton, the infamous pirate and French spy, had died alongside his mistress in the wreck of his ship five years before, but Daniel knew better. He had seen the ravages of Norton's piracy along the Suffolk coast of late, and knew that Norton was using Daniel's own name to cover his tracks. He had sworn to bring Norton to justice once and for all.

'We are trying to catch him,' Justin said.

Daniel's mouth set in a grim line. 'So am I,' he said. 'Before he sullies my name for ever with his cruelty.' He shot Justin Kestrel a look. 'That might seem strange to you, Kestrel,' he said, with a lop-sided smile. 'Honour amongst thieves…'

Justin shifted in his chair. He was a big man, and the cabin seemed almost too confined for him. He looked at Daniel directly with his very blue eyes.

'There was another matter that I wished to discuss with you, de Lancey. You may not have heard that your cousin, Gideon Pearce, has died.'

Daniel absorbed the news and found that he felt nothing at all. Years ago his cousin had denounced him as a traitor and a disgrace to the family name. The only family that mattered one whit to him was Rebecca.

'As you know, he was childless,' Justin Kestrel continued. 'You are now Baron Allandale.'

Daniel's mouth twisted derisively. 'I am no such thing. He disinherited me.'

'No, he did not. At the end, it seems, blood was thicker than water.'

Daniel raised his brows. That had surprised him. 'Nevertheless,' he said, 'I cannot inherit as a wanted criminal.'

Justin Kestrel put the brandy glass down. The lamplight shone on the richness of the amber. 'The government wishes you to take up your title. They think it is time you came in to port. They are willing to grant a public pardon. Should you wish to continue a career at sea they will offer you another commission in the Royal Navy, as a commodore.'

'A promotion?' Daniel said dryly. 'Is the Home Secretary also willing to state that I have been working in secret for the government the whole time?'

Justin Kestrel shifted. 'With some persuasion, perhaps. Spencer is a reasonable man, and he has served at the Admiralty so he understands your role.'

Daniel grimaced. The government was notoriously and understandably reluctant to reveal the names and activities of their spies. He knew they would far prefer that he disappear quietly to live in the country.

'They must want me to turn respectable very much,' he murmured. 'I wonder why?'

Kestrel seemed to be choosing his words carefully. 'You are a peer of the realm now, and you are seen to be flouting the King's laws. If you were to carry on as a privateer after this you would be beyond pardon. Already some of your activities—the smuggling, for example—place you technically outside the law, no matter that you engage in it in order to obtain information.'

Daniel laughed. 'I engage in it in order to obtain good French brandy,' he said.

'Precisely.'

There was a silence.

'There is a very fine estate in Shropshire,' Kestrel continued, 'and another in Oxfordshire.'

'It is a long way from the sea.'

'Perhaps you might wish to settle down, though—marry, even…?'

Daniel's thoughts flew instinctively to Lucinda. Where had that idea come from? Two hours before he would have said that marriage was the very last thing he would ever contemplate. Marriage and piracy were fundamentally opposed. Yet here was Justin Kestrel with the suggestion that he might be married off and settled in Shropshire with a wife and family—the 28th Baron Allandale, respectable at last. And he was getting into dangerous waters, for he was thinking of Lucinda in his life and in his bed, her warmth thawing the cold loneliness that had ambushed him of late, her love fending off the darkness that threatened his soul.

He shook his head sharply. He was mad even to think of it. Lucinda hated him for his callous disregard for her feelings all those years ago, and anyway, respectability bored him. It was deadly dull.

He thrust his hands into his pockets. 'And if I refuse?'

Kestrel raised his brows. 'Are you going to?'

'Yes, I think I am. I like my way of life too much to give up now.'

Kestrel grimaced. 'Think about it before you turn us down. It's a good offer. If you refuse, then Spencer will cut you loose and in the end you will surely hang.'

'Despite my service to the Crown over the years?'

'Despite that.' Kestrel nodded towards the brandy bottle. 'Officially you are outside the law, de Lancey.'

'You drink my brandy,' Daniel said. 'You *order* my brandy.' All the same, he knew Justin was right. In his dealings with spies and smugglers and criminals he had, inevitably, blurred the line. If he refused to conform now, to come into port and accept his barony, he knew the government would deny he had ever worked for them—and he could not prove it. He would be cast adrift.

'I do drink your brandy,' Justin Kestrel agreed. 'I am a hypocrite. I like your brandy. I like you, de Lancey. Too much to see you hang. Think of your sister if you won't do it for any other reason.'

That, Daniel thought, was below the belt. If anything was likely to sway him it was the thought of all that Rebecca had suffered for him in the past. But now she was settled with Lucas and their growing family. Would his return add so much to her happiness? He knew that the answer was probably that it would. He knew it, but then he thought of the stifling tedium of life on land and he shook his head. He could never go back to that now.

'It is too late. The answer is no.'

Justin Kestrel's expression was impassive. 'I am sorry for it, but I am not surprised.' He held out a hand to shake Daniel's one last time. 'You are on your own then, de Lancey. Goodnight.'

After he had gone, Daniel lay down in his bunk with his hands behind his head and thought about Justin Kestrel's offer. He cared nothing for having a title, and he had thought that he would care nothing for the estates, but conscience, which had hardly troubled him these ten years past, stirred uncomfortably, reminding him of all the people whose livelihoods depended on him now. He could not simply neglect his estates and let them go to ruin, taking people's future with them. With the title came responsibilities—responsibilities he did not want to be burdened with. Was that not what he had always done, now he came to think of it? Had he not run from those who depended on him? Run from his duty? He had preferred the reckless excitement of the hunt to facing up to his responsibilities at home.

He thought of Lucinda, waiting for him in vain all those years and telling him in no uncertain terms that very night that the love that had been between them was long gone, even if they both knew that the flame of their wild passion was scarcely extinguished. If there had been a way back from that... But there was not. There was no way back to the past. He knew that. Nor could he see himself settling to the life of village squire. But he would write to Rebecca and see if there was a way she might help the people of Allandale on his behalf.

And tomorrow he would take the *Defiance* out to sea and outrun his memories. He would hunt down John Norton. And he would make sure that he never saw Lucinda again. This time he would make sure that he forgot her.

Chapter 3

'LADIES, ladies,' the Duchess of Kestrel said reproachfully. 'Your concentration is wandering today.' She closed her copy of *King John* and placed it on a side table. 'I know that Shakespeare's histories may not be the most romantically engaging of his works,' she added, with a slight smile in Eustacia Saltire's direction, 'but I thought it was the type of *improving* book that would suit our little reading group. My dear Mrs Melville—' here Lucinda jumped guiltily '—pray tell me, what do you think of the piece?'

Lucinda gulped. She had not been thinking about Shakespeare's *King John* for the past ten minutes, for her thoughts had been occupied by a far more compelling character—that of Daniel de Lancey. Truth to tell, she had been thinking about him from the moment she had left him the previous night until she had fallen into a restless sleep at about three in the morning. Then she had dreamed about him: disturbing, passionate, heated dreams, full of half-remembered desire that even now caused her limbs to tingle and a burning and undeniable ache to fill her.

She realised that Sally Kestrel was still looking at her, a flicker of concern in her very green eyes.

'You look a little too warm, Mrs Melville,' she murmured. 'Are you sure you are not running a temperature? Have you taken a chill, perhaps?'

'I…no, I do not believe so.' Lucinda struggled to push away the mental images of herself entwined in naked consummation with Daniel. She felt hot and bothered and aroused. She had prided herself on her cool common sense for years, and now she realised that she was afire with lust—and for a man she did not even like any more. It was maddening. It made her furious. And it was typical of Daniel de Lancey that he could do this to her.

'I do find the room rather stuffy,' she excused. 'I think I shall take a walk down to the cove and take some fresh air.' She turned to Eustacia. 'Would you care to join me, Stacey?'

Miss Saltire, a lively brunette, looked glum.

'For my part I would adore it, Mrs Melville, but Mama has forbidden me to go out whilst the weather is so inclement. She thinks that I might turn my ankle or catch an infection of the lungs or ruin my looks with frostbite.'

Lucinda caught the Duchess of Kestrel's eye. 'Dear Letitia is very careful,' the Duchess observed wryly. 'Perhaps if you took the gig, Mrs Melville, then the groom could drive and Stacey could wrap up in warm blankets?'

Stacey looked even gloomier. 'It is a capital plan, cousin, but Mama would not approve. She fears a carriage accident in icy weather.'

Lucinda nodded. She understood Mrs Saltire's concerns. There were so many things to be afraid of in her world, especially when Eustacia was her only defence against penurious old age. Lucinda knew that Mrs Saltire could not bear for Stacey to lose her looks or run off with an unsuitable man, or do anything that might risk their futures. But she also saw the slump of Stacey's shoulders, and wished that Mrs Saltire might allow her daughter a little more latitude—or Stacey would rebel with the very behaviour her mother dreaded.

She went up to her room to wrap up warmly and fetch bonnet and gloves. Although it was not much past two in the afternoon, the sun was already beginning to sink in the west as she made her way

along the track that led from Kestrel Court down to the cove. The
path plunged deep into the pinewoods and the air was fresh with the
sharp scent and loud with the song of the birds. Lucinda walked
quickly, glad to feel the crisp chill of the breeze on her face. She
had been active all her life, loving to walk and ride, and sometimes
the determined staidness of life in the Saltire household chafed at
her. Out here, in the open air, she felt a lift of spirits.

She had gone only a little way along the track when she heard
the sound of hoofbeats and, turning the corner, espied Owen Chance
on his bay mare, making his slow way towards her from the direction of the cove. Remembering the events of the previous night
Lucinda immediately felt guilty for her part in helping Daniel evade
capture. She liked Owen Chance. It was a pity that instinct and an
older loyalty had set her against him.

There was a deep frown on Owen Chance's forehead. The sort
of frown, Lucinda thought, that a man might well wear when he had
failed to capture a notorious pirate. Nevertheless, his expression
lightened when he saw her, and he reined in, removing his hat and
bowing with a flourish.

'Good afternoon, Mrs Melville! I trust you are well?' He looked
around. 'Miss Saltire does not accompany you on your walk?'

Lucinda smiled at the transparency of his interest. It was clear
that the poor man was as besotted with Stacey's dark prettiness as
she was taken with his charm and dashing character. It was only a
shame that the whole affair could come to nothing.

'Not today, I fear,' she said, and saw his handsome face fall with
disappointment. 'I am going to the cove,' she continued, with determined cheerfulness. 'Are you travelling from that direction, sir?'

Owen Chance frowned again. 'I am, ma'am, but I would urge
you against such a walk today. It will be dark within a couple of
hours, and there is talk of the smugglers being out tonight. If you
could take word back to Kestrel Court and ask them to lock all the
doors safely at dusk…?'

Lucinda's heart jumped. Could the smugglers be Daniel's men?

She had no illusions, and knew that Daniel's shady business would necessarily involve him in smuggling as well as piracy and goodness only knew what other nefarious activities. And Chance had almost caught him the previous night. If he planned a trap tonight then he might achieve what he had singularly failed to do before and take Daniel prisoner. She could not, for the life of her, repress the flicker of apprehension that ran through her body at the thought.

She cleared her throat. 'How vastly frightening,' she said, hearing the false brightness in her own voice and hoping that Owen Chance would ascribe it to excitement rather than nervousness. 'I expect they are a desperate bunch?'

'Criminals,' Chance said contemptuously. 'They deserve to hang.'

Lucinda's heart battered against her ribs. 'I am sure you are correct,' she said. 'There was once an infamous privateer in these parts, was there not? I suppose he is long gone, though.'

'You suppose incorrectly,' Owen Chance said. His voice was cold. 'He still smuggles with the worst of them, and spies for France. It will be my great pleasure to bring him to justice.'

The cold crept along Lucinda's neck and slithered down her spine. Surely he must be speaking of Daniel? Could it be true? She could hardly condone smuggling, for it was against the law—even if half the gentry in the county turned a blind eye and Justin Kestrel himself cheerfully admitted to buying French brandy. But spying for the French was another matter. Had Daniel turned traitor during the long years of the war? Was it all a matter of money to him, and patriotism counted for nothing? She felt sick even to think of it.

'I think I will go back, as you suggest, sir,' she said, aware that her voice was not quite steady. 'And I will warn them up at the house. Good wishes for your hunting.'

Chance touched his hat and cantered away up the path, and Lucinda stood for a moment alone beneath the pines. She did not wish to return yet to the stuffiness of the overheated house. Owen Chance's words had disturbed her deeply. She could not believe that it was true. Yet what was it that Daniel had said the previous night?

'*We both made our choices... Mine to be wild and irrespon-sible...*'

But a traitor? She did not want to believe it of him. And yet she did not know the man he had become. He might well consider that his country's secrets were just commodities to sell, like brandy or French lace.

In her agitation she realised that she had left the main path and plunged off down a narrow track to the right. It forced its way through the trees, downwards towards the river. No doubt in summer it was completely impassable, but now the grasses and bracken underfoot had died back a little, and Lucinda thought that if she followed the path down to the water's edge she could walk back to Kestrel Court that way. She knew there was a very pretty trail that followed the course of the stream until it reached the gardens.

Nettles brushed Lucinda's skirts, and thorns clutched at her as she passed. Overhead the chatter of the birds had died away, and the pale winter light barely penetrated, but then she caught the flash of water ahead of her. The trees were thinning now, and suddenly she was on the edge of Kestrel Creek, with the water still and dark before her. She had come out further along the stream than she had intended, almost out in the bay—precisely where she had promised Owen Chance she would not walk. She had better turn for home at once.

The tide was ebbing. An oystercatcher pattered across the mud, leaving little footprints, then, as it saw her, it rose into the air, giving its piping call.

Lucinda smiled and wrapped her cloak more closely around her against the salty breeze. She could taste the tang of the sea here, but she knew she should not linger.

She went on, coming to a place where there was a sharp turn in the creek, and then she stopped, drawing back instinctively into the trees. The creek had widened into a deep pool and there, beneath the overhanging trees, hidden from the open river and the sea beyond, lay a ship at anchor. Lucinda's breath caught painfully in her throat as she took in the snarling dragon figurehead on the prow and the name: *Defiance*.

All night she had lain awake, knowing that Daniel was nearby, imagining his ship riding at anchor out in the bay, perhaps, but never thinking that he was so close by, in this hidden mooring deep in Kestrel Creek. Suddenly the truth of his identity and his whole way of life hit her anew with the force of a blow. He was a criminal, a wanted man, very likely a traitor. The Daniel de Lancey she had known was gone for ever. There was nothing for her here.

She turned to go, stumbling over tree roots in her haste, and in the same moment a figure stepped out onto the path before her and a sack, thick and suffocating, was thrown over her head. She struggled, felt her arms pinioned to her sides, and then she was picked up as easily as though she were a sack of flour, thrown over the man's shoulder, and carried off.

It was Daniel. Lucinda could tell from the feel and the scent of him, and from the disturbing familiarity of his hands on her body. He held her impersonally, and yet she burned with awareness. It made her angry to be at his mercy. She managed one well-placed and satisfying kick that landed somewhere soft and caused him to swear, and then his arms tightened about her so painfully that she could scarcely breathe, let alone move.

Being upside down completely disorientated her. There was the sound of voices, she was passed from hand to hand like a parcel, and then, finally, she was placed back on her feet and the sack pulled roughly from her head. She stood there, panting and glaring about her.

'What were you doing spying on my ship?'

Daniel's voice, measured and hard, snapped Lucinda's attention straight back to him. She was standing in a well-appointed cabin that was lit by the rays of the sinking sun. The refection from the water outside made patterns on the wooden panelling and she could hear the gentle slap of the water against the stern of the ship. Daniel was sitting at a fine cherrywood desk and was toying with a quill between his fingers. A book lay open on the top of the desk, and a half-finished letter beside it. It was so peaceful, and so utterly removed from what Lucinda had expected, that for a moment she could not speak. The pristine cleanliness was a far cry from the smelly darkness she had anticipated, with a roaring drunk crew knocking back the rum and dallying with quayside whores.

'Well?' Daniel sounded slightly bored, as though he found stray women spying on the *Defiance* every day of the week. Lucinda felt prickles of resentment run along her skin that he should treat her with such disdain.

'I was not spying,' she retorted. 'I was walking back from Kestrel Cove and took a wrong turn on the path.'

Daniel raised one dark, disbelieving brow. 'You got lost? I see.'

Lucinda ran a hand over her hair and tried to smooth it down. There were stray pieces of straw—no doubt from the sacking—sticking to her cloak. She smelled faintly agricultural. Catching sight of herself in the small mirror on the bulkhead, she realised that she also looked a complete fright.

Daniel, in contrast, looked deplorably elegant, and she hated him for it. He had always been able to wear his clothes with careless aplomb, and now, with his dark well-cut jacket and snowy white linen, he looked hard and tough, with no soft edges. He was still watching her with cold impassivity, and she felt colour flood her cheeks as hot and embarrassing as though she had been a young girl. She knew he thought she had gone there deliberately to see him, and that the more she protested the less he would believe her.

'You can believe what you like,' she said, 'but I did not seek you out.'

Daniel shrugged. His face was set in hard lines. 'So you say.'

'It's true!' Pride and embarrassment compounded Lucinda's anger. 'What, do you think yourself so dashing, so irresistible—the gallant pirate captain!—that every female in the neighbourhood must want to throw herself at you? Do you think I was so bowled over to meet you again last night that I could not keep away?'

Daniel's firm mouth lifted in a slight smile that was not quite reassuring. He stood up. 'I don't know, Lucy. Were you?'

'No, I was not. And stop calling me Lucy!'

'I forgot. You are—you always were—Lucy to me.' He had come to stand before her, and suddenly the spacious cabin seemed very small and very airless. Lucinda caught her breath. She tilted her head to glare up at him.

'And you always were *so* arrogant! Believing that I came here solely to—' Lucinda stopped abruptly.

He was so close to her now, perilously close, his body all but pinning her against the door. She found that she was watching his mouth, that *tempting* mouth, as he said softly, 'Yes?'

Lucinda ran her tongue over her lips. 'To…um…'

'You are somewhat inarticulate for a governess. I noticed it last night.'

He put his hands flat against the door on either side of her head and leaned in. Their breath mingled for a moment and then his mouth captured hers. Only their lips touched, but that was more than enough.

The kiss was ruthless in its intensity. The swift current of desire raced between them, leaving Lucinda breathless and unable to think of anything other than the undeniable pleasure of his embrace. He lingered over her mouth as though he were learning her all over again, and when he stood back she could barely breathe, barely think. Her lips felt soft, and a little bruised, and she pressed one hand to them and saw that she was shaking.

'This is not—' She stopped, cleared her throat. 'This is not what I want.'

'No?' Daniel had turned away, and she could not see his face, but she thought that his voice sounded strained. 'Well, this isn't a game, Lucinda. Do not come down to my ship looking for trouble, or you will surely find it.'

Lucinda's anger—the anger he could always arouse in her, along with that uncomfortable attraction—jetted up.

'I play no games,' she said. 'You are the one who hides out in the wood playing at pirates, abducting people, smuggling, *spying* for the French, so I hear! You are the one who never grew up!'

Daniel moved so quickly that she jumped back. But it was too late. He had caught her wrist in a grip that did not hurt, but which she could not break. His expression was grim, but just for a moment, and for the first time in her life, she saw a bleak unhappiness in his dark eyes before his face was impassive once again.

'What do you mean?' He spoke very quietly, but there was an undertone to his words that made her shiver.

'I met Mr Chance in the woods just now,' Lucinda said. 'He told me that the smugglers would be out tonight and he would be hunting them.' Daniel's fingers tightened a little and her voice faltered. 'He said that you are a criminal, Daniel, and a spy and a traitor—'

Daniel dropped her wrist as though he had been burned. 'Did he mention me by name?'

'No,' Lucinda said. She suddenly felt chilled. Could she have made a mistake? 'But who else could he mean?' she whispered.

For a long moment they stared into one another's eyes, and then Daniel turned away in what felt like a gesture of repudiation.

'Dearest Lucy, always thinking the worst of me!'

'Well, it did not require a great leap of imagination!' Lucinda said, stung by his accusing tone. 'After all, you told me yourself that you were a pirate, and I thought…I assumed…'

'You assumed that I was a traitor as well.' He slammed his fist against the panels of the door. 'You would have trusted me once. You loved me once.'

'That is all in the past,' Lucinda said. She felt bitter and sick at what had become of that love, what had become of him.

He turned back to her suddenly, almost violently. 'You are telling me that you feel nothing for me now?' He raised a hand and trailed the back of it down her cheek. His touch seemed to burn her. She could feel her blood heating beneath the skin. The same treacherous attraction he could always arouse in her flared up, but was quenched in bitterness.

'I cannot deny that I respond to you,' she said, unflinchingly honest. 'But it is nothing more than physical attraction. I do not trust you, Daniel, and I cannot respect you.'

For a moment she thought he was going to pull her into his arms and kiss her senseless, as though in defiance of all the love that had been lost between them, and her perfidious heart leapt to think of it. But then his hand fell to his side and he stepped back, turned on his heel and walked out of the cabin.

Lucinda stood still for a moment, trembling a little with the intensity of the storm of emotion within, and then suddenly recollected where she was and hastened after him.

'Daniel! Wait! I want to get off the ship—'

He was standing at the end of the companionway, but now he turned and looked at her. One long, unreadable look.

'You cannot,' he said. 'You should have thought of that before, Lucy. The tide has turned and we have sailed.'

Daniel strode up on deck, his hands clenched in tight fists at his side.

'I do not trust you... I cannot respect you...'

He had been within an ace of grabbing Lucinda, throwing her down on the floor and making love to her there and then—as though that would enable him to wipe out all the anger and bitterness between them and conjure the old love in its place. Devil take it, he must be going soft in the head. What did it matter what she thought of him? He could have explained it all to her if he had wanted her good opinion. But it was far too late for that. Lucinda was right. They could never go back.

The *Defiance* was slipping down Kestrel Creek very slowly, towards the open sea. He heard the patter of feet on the deck behind him, and then Lucinda had grabbed his sleeve and pulled him around to face her. Her blue eyes were blazing. She looked furious.

'What do you think you are doing? Turn the ship around! Make it stop! I want to get off!'

Daniel was aware that all the crew were covertly watching, under cover of going about their tasks. He put his hands on his hips and smiled down into Lucinda's infuriated face.

'Can't do that, Mrs Melville,' he drawled. 'We sail on the tide. It doesn't wait.'

Lucinda's eyes narrowed to angry slits of blue. 'You mean that I am stuck here with *you*? For how long?'

Daniel had only been intending to take the ship out for a night, to hunt Norton along the coast and remove himself from the threat of Owen Chance's men finding him, but now he shrugged lightly.

'A week? Two? Who knows? You can share my cabin if you like,' he added with a mocking smile. He took a step closer to her. 'It might not be love between us any more, Lucy, but it could still be pleasurable…'

He thought for a moment that she was going to strike him, but then she turned on her heel and ran across to the side of the ship. They were still very close to the bank as the *Defiance* slid almost imperceptibly out of the creek, and Lucinda did not even hesitate. She grabbed the rigging, pulled herself up onto the rail, and stood there, poised to jump.

Daniel swore violently. Anger and fear collided within him, and he covered the deck faster than he had ever run before, grabbing her about the waist and dragging her backwards into his arms in the very second she was about to launch herself over the side.

'Are you insane?' he shouted. 'You could *kill* yourself trying a trick like that!'

She struggled like a demon in his arms, kicking him, beating him with her fists, and calling him some colourful names that Daniel felt vaguely shocked she even knew. Her tomboyish behaviour reminded him of their childhood, when she would scramble through the fields, losing her bonnet and tearing her dress, an utter hoyden. Evidently she still had that same wild spirit. His crew were looking highly diverted, trying to smother their grins, and Daniel picked Lucinda up bodily and dragged her behind the mainmast for a little privacy. The man working there moved discreetly away.

Daniel held Lucinda tightly until she went soft and quiescent in his arms, then he gently pushed the tumbled hair away from her face.

'Do you hate me so much, Luce, that you would risk your very life to get away from me?'

They stared at one another for what seemed like hours, and then Lucinda dropped her gaze. 'No,' she whispered, 'but I wish I had never met you again, Daniel.'

Something wrenched Daniel deep inside.

'I'll take you back,' he said shortly.

She looked annoyed. 'There is no need for you to come. I can manage perfectly well on my own.'

Daniel smiled. 'I know, Luce, but I insist.'

After a second she gave him a faint, hesitant smile in return. 'Owen Chance might catch you.'

'I doubt it.'

She smoothed her tattered gown 'You are *so* reckless.' She raised her gaze and gave him a proper smile this time, and it made his heart lurch. But there was sadness in her eyes as well, and it hurt him to see it.

'I wish I did not feel I know you so well,' she said, 'when I do not really know you at all.'

For a moment Daniel was desperate to tell her the truth. The temptation was so strong that he could feel the words jostling to come out. He had never previously cared for any man's good opinion, but now he found he wanted to regain Lucinda's trust and respect. He wanted it more than anything else in the world. He drove his hands into his pockets in a gesture of repressed rage. He could tell her he was on the side of the angels, but in the end what good would it do? He could neither take her with him, nor make up for the damage he had done to her in the past. So it was better that he kept his peace and let her go.

The anchor was lowered and a rope ladder thrown over the side. Lucinda insisted on climbing down it herself, just as Daniel had known she would. He instructed Holroyd to take the ship out beyond the bay and stand by to pick him up at Harte Point whilst he walked back with her through the woods to Kestrel Court.

They walked in silence, though every so often he would hold back branches from her path, or pull aside brambles, and she would thank him politely. It was only as they were approaching the edge of the parkland that she spoke.

'Does it suit you, Daniel, this business of being a pirate?'

'Most of the time,' Daniel said. He raised his brows. 'Does it suit you to be a governess?'

She shot him a look from beneath the battered edge of her bonnet. 'Most of the time,' she said. There was an undertone of humour in her voice. 'It is better than marriage, at any rate.'

'That would surely depend on who you were married to?'

There was a pause. The wind sighed through the pines. 'I suppose so,' Lucinda said. 'I made a bad mistake with Leopold. I was running away from my feelings for you, I suppose. And I was angry, so I took the first offer I received.'

The pain and guilt in Daniel tightened another notch.

'We all make mistakes,' he said, 'and mine have been the greater.'

He saw her smile. 'So what were your mistakes, Daniel?'

Daniel turned to look at her in the gathering dusk. 'Leaving you,' he said. 'Arrogance, complacency, thoughtlessness... Oh, and cheating a Portuguese pirate at cards and almost paying for it with my life.'

Lucinda gave a peal of laughter.

'And wishing,' Daniel said softly, watching her face, 'that I could change the past.'

The laughter died from her eyes. 'That *is* a mistake, Daniel.' She looked over her shoulder. 'We are almost at the park wall. You may leave me here. I shall be quite safe.'

She put a hand against his chest and stood on tiptoe to kiss him.

Her lips were cool and they clung to his, and he wanted to pick her up and carry her off to make love to her under the trees of the pine forest. But he knew that some things could never be, and already he had let matters go far too far.

'Goodnight,' she whispered, and he knew that she meant goodbye.

'Tell them to lock the doors fast tonight,' Daniel said.

She raised her chin. 'Because you and your scoundrel crew will be out smuggling?'

The frustration, the wanting, poured through him and almost swept everything else aside. He caught her shoulders, pressing her back against the trunk of the nearest tree.

'Ah, Lucy, what a shockingly poor opinion you have of me,' he muttered, his mouth harsh against hers. He wanted to forget her anger and her scorn and find the sweetness beneath—the sweetness he was sure was still there for him. He plundered her mouth like the pirate he was—taking, demanding, asking no permission. He held her hard against the unyielding wood as he stole the response he wanted from her, his kiss fierce and insistent, until he was panting for breath and she was too, and he knew from the touch and the feel of her that she was his for the taking.

Her eyes were a hazy blue in the moonlight, dazed with sensual desire, and her mouth was soft and ripe and he ached for her. But he knew that if he made love to her now she would hate him in the morning. Because although he could wrench this response from her body she mistrusted him, and detested what he had become, and once she thought about what had happened she would despise herself and him too.

With an oath he set her away from him.

'You had better go, Lucinda,' he said, deliberately cruel. 'Go before I forget what little honour I have left and treat you like the pirate I am.'

He saw her flinch at his harshness, and then she gathered her cloak to her and hurried away. He felt a cold desolation that had nothing to do with the winter night.

Chapter 4

THE middle of December brought the final Woodbridge Assembly before Christmas. The Assembly Rooms were icy cold that night. A wind was whistling in from the sea, finding all the gaps between the windows and setting the candle flames dancing in the draught. Lucinda drew her shawl more closely about her and shivered on her rout chair. Company was light that evening—a few local families, and some of the officers from the Woodbridge barracks—but amidst the small crowd Miss Stacey Saltire shone like a jewel.

Lucinda had observed that it was often the way when a young lady was engaged: all the gentlemen who had been wary of approaching her when she had been husband-hunting now felt free to pay attention to her, knowing she was promised to another. And none was more assiduous in his attentions than the Riding Officer, Mr Owen Chance, who was even now dancing with Stacey, the two dark heads bent close to one another as they indulged in intimate conversation.

Lucinda sighed. Not only was she concerned by what she saw— as was Mr Leytonstone, glowering from across the other side of the floor but too cowardly to intervene—but she felt for a moment a wave of envy so sharp that it that shocked her. Envy for Stacey, and for the way that Owen Chance was looking at her, and for her own lost youth and her lost love.

She had not seen Daniel since the night he had kissed her in the woods. She had run from him then—run from his harshness and the feelings he could still stir in her. More than anything she had run from the fact that he was not the man she wanted him to be, and her heart ached that she had loved him once and now he was a stranger to her.

She had kept away from the creek, just as Daniel had demanded, and had taken her walks in less dangerous places. Sometimes as dusk was falling she would stand by her bedroom window and scour the wide expanse of the bay for a scarlet and black ship with a snarling dragon on the prow, but the horizon was always empty, and she would draw the curtains together with a sigh and feel her heart plummet to her slippers. If only she had never met him again. But she had, and memory, reawakened, was difficult to dismiss. It taunted her at every turn with the restless passion and excitement of that distant summer when she and Daniel had been young. And the knowledge that he was a different man now, supposedly a criminal and a traitor, tortured her.

She had asked questions about him of Sally Kestrel, and had listened to Midwinter gossip with avidity. Although she knew she should forget Daniel, she found she could not help herself. His name was mentioned frequently, but the stories were as insubstantial as smoke, and at the end it was impossible to tell the truth from the myth. Intriguingly, many of the legends painted Daniel de Lancey as a hero—a man secretly in the pay of the government rather than the renegade he pretended to be. Lucinda found she ached for it to be true, but thought it probable that she would never know.

'My dear Mrs Melville, you look blue-devilled!' a warm female voice beside her commented, and Lucinda turned to see the Duchess of Kestrel smiling sympathetically at her. She followed Lucinda's gaze to the couple on the dance floor.

'Matter for concern, do you think?'

'As a chaperon, I would say most definitely,' Lucinda said. She hesitated. 'As someone who would wish to see Miss Saltire happy, perhaps not.'

Sally Kestrel's green eyes focused shrewdly on her face. 'You think that Miss Saltire will be making a mistake in marrying Mr Leytonstone?'

Lucinda shrugged a little awkwardly. She was acutely aware that in her youth Sally Kestrel had chosen the rather more solid merits of Stephen Saltire above the dashing brilliance of Justin Kestrel, and that it had been twenty years before they were reunited. Their glowing love for one another now was plain for all to see, and was something else that made Lucinda feel even more cold and alone.

'I think that Stacey should marry for love, not money,' Lucinda admitted reluctantly. 'Though it contradicts my duty to say so.'

Sally Kestrel smiled understandingly. 'We do not wish to see others make the same mistakes that we did,' she said. 'I have already tried to speak to Cousin Letitia, but she is adamant. They have no money and Mr Leytonstone is very rich.'

'And Mr Chance, I suppose, is not?'

Sally Kestrel shook her head. 'He is better born, but he has no fortune. And I fear that Cousin Letitia values fortune above all things.'

Lucinda glanced towards the doorway, where the Master of Ceremonies was announcing a late arrival. The knot of people gathered by the doorway parted to allow the newcomer entrance.

'Mr Jackson Raleigh!'

Lucinda's breath caught in her throat. She dropped her fan and had to rummage under the rout chair to find it again. She felt hot and cold all at the same time, shaking as though she had a fever. Raleigh, she remembered, was the name that her good friend Rebecca de Lancey had used when she had lived in London before her marriage. It was the name of a famous sailor whom some might say had been a privateer…

She straightened up. Daniel De Lancey was coming directly across the room towards her. He looked spectacular, in evening dress of a stark severity that emphasised the breadth of his shoulders and the hard, strong lines of his body. His step was light, and his demeanour one of confident charm that, Lucinda sensed, drew the eye of every woman in the room.

She tried not to look at him, afraid that if she did it would in some way give him away. She was surely the only one present who knew his identity. A little flicker of anger heated her blood to think that Daniel was taking her silence for granted, that he believed that she would not betray him. He had the audacity of the devil himself, and a part of her thought he richly deserved a fall. Another part of her was terrified that he would be found out.

'My dear Mrs Melville,' the Duchess of Kestrel was saying. 'You have gone very pale. Are you quite well?'

'I am very well, thank you,' Lucinda said, recovering. 'I feel a little chilled. It is a cold night.'

'You should dance, you know,' Sally Kestrel said, smiling. 'Just because one is a chaperon…'

'Oh, I do not dance these days,' Lucinda said.

'Not even when the most handsome man in the room is intent on asking you?' the Duchess enquired.

Lucinda looked up. Daniel was now cutting a very determined path through the small crowd towards her. He was looking straight at her, with a mocking challenge in his eyes. He was taunting her, daring her to denounce him. Lucinda drew herself up a little straighter in her chair.

'Madam,' he was bowing over her hand now. 'Allow me to introduce myself to you—'

'I remember you,' Lucinda said, before he could finish. 'We have met before.'

She savoured the first faint sign of wariness that she saw in his dark eyes and smiled. 'How do you do, Mr Raleigh?'

He raised her hand to his lips in an old-fashioned gesture and pressed a kiss against it—a real kiss rather than a formal brush of the lips. Her skin tingled, and she tried to withdraw her hand, but he held her fast for a long moment.

'I am flattered that you remember me, madam,' he said.

'Oh, I had all but forgotten you until you walked in,' Lucinda said airily. 'But then I thought that you seemed vaguely familiar. Pray permit me to introduce you to Her Grace the Duchess of Kestrel. Your Grace, may I introduce Mr Raleigh?'

Daniel bowed, smiling, and Sally Kestrel looked delighted. 'Mrs Melville! You did not vouchsafe the fact that you and Mr Raleigh were already acquainted. How do you do, sir? What brings you into this part of Suffolk?'

'Business,' Daniel said promptly. He smiled at Lucinda, a smile of cool confidence, and to her annoyance she could feel herself blushing like a schoolroom miss.

'But when I saw Mrs Melville across the room,' Daniel added, 'I was tempted to renew our old acquaintance and mix business with pleasure.'

'A capital idea,' Sally Kestrel said promptly. 'I was remarking to Mrs Melville only a moment ago that it is an evening for dancing...'

'My sentiments precisely, Your Grace,' Daniel said. He held out a hand to Lucinda. 'If you would do me the honour, madam?'

'I am here to chaperon Miss Saltire, not to dance myself,' Lucinda began, but Sally gave her a gentle little push with her fan.

'I will watch over my cousin, Mrs Melville. What could be more appropriate? You and Mr Raleigh must have a deal of news to catch up on.'

Daniel's fingers were insistent against hers. 'Come, Mrs Melville. It is the waltz, I believe, and I am sure that you were given permission to dance it many years ago.'

'More than I care to remember,' Lucinda said. She allowed him to draw her onto the floor and into his arms. 'You are insufferable!' she added in an undertone, as the music struck up. 'Why not tell me I am at my last prayers and have done with it?'

Daniel smiled broadly. 'Oh, I do not believe the case to be quite as bad as that.' He sobered, though the smile was still in his eyes. 'Truth to tell, you look very beautiful tonight, Lucinda.'

Lucinda stamped down hard on the little quiver of awareness that his words caused within her.

'Truth, is it?' she said coldly. 'I thought the truth was that you had no desire ever to see me again? You certainly went to a great deal of trouble to make me believe so when last we met.'

The smile died from Daniel's eyes. 'Oh, I had the desire to see you,' he said quietly.

Lucinda met his eyes very directly. 'Then why try to drive me away?'

A rueful smile twisted his lips. 'I was trying to do the right thing for once, Luce. Belatedly, cruelly and probably pointlessly, but for the right reasons all the same.'

His use of her old nickname tugged at her heart. 'Because…?' she whispered.

'Because you know it is too late.' Daniel's eyes were very dark, his tone a little rough. 'You said it yourself, Lucy. It was over a very long time ago.'

Lucinda swallowed hard. 'So why are you here tonight?'

'I came to say goodbye.'

Lucinda had almost been expecting it, but now that he had said the words she felt swamped by a loss and a loneliness that made her catch her breath.

'You are insane to take such a risk,' she whispered.

'I know.'

'Why did you do it?'

'I had to.' Daniel's eyes were very dark. 'I wanted to see you one last time.'

Lucinda's heart was beating fiercely in her throat. 'There is no point,' she said harshly. 'Ever since we met we have known that what was once between us cannot be rekindled. Why risk all for one last meeting?'

Daniel shrugged. 'Because I like the danger? And because I…' He hesitated, and for one mad moment Lucinda thought he was going to tell her that he loved her.

'And for one last dance,' he said, drawing her closer. His cheek brushed hers. She could feel the beginnings of his stubble and it sent a long, cool shiver through her.

'The least you could do was shave if you were planning on attending a social gathering,' she said sharply, to cover her feelings, and he laughed and rubbed his cheek against hers again.

Lucinda struggled with her emotions. The intimacy of their encounter, here in a ballroom with fifty other people, seemed extraordinary. She was aware of nothing other than the touch of Daniel's hands as he steered her through the waltz, the brush of his body against hers, the smile that was for her alone.

'For the duration of this one last dance, then, the least you can do is tell me the truth,' she said, and felt him stiffen a little.

'The truth?'

'Yes.' Lucinda looked up into his eyes. 'Surely the truth is not so alien to you that you cannot recognise the concept? Since we are not to meet again—' she threw down her challenge '—the least you owe me is to answer one question honestly.'

'What is the question?'

She could feel the tension in him as he waited for her to speak.

'Since I saw you last I have heard things,' Lucinda said. She looked around, keeping her voice low. 'I have heard that it is Sir John Norton who is the traitor and French spy whom Owen Chance currently seeks, not the notorious Daniel de Lancey—though de Lancey is still a wanted man. And some say—' she lowered her voice still further '—that de Lancey is not even a pirate, but a privateer secretly in the pay of the government.' She glanced up and caught the look of brilliant intensity in his eyes. 'What do you say to that, sir?'

Daniel's hands tightened on her waist for a moment and he bent his head close to hers. 'I say that you should forget you heard those words,' he said softly. 'It might have been true once, but not now. Not any more. Now I am a wanted man.'

Their eyes met. His were restless and heated, and there was something there that stole her breath.

'Don't ask any more questions about me,' he said. 'It is too dangerous.'

Lucinda's heart pounded. 'But I have to know—'

He touched a finger to her lips in a fleeting gesture, and she felt the echo of that touch through her whole body.

'You are too loyal,' he said, 'and too passionate, Lucy.'

Lucinda shook her head. 'No! If I have misjudged you—'

He did not let her finish. 'You did not,' he said. 'Not in any way that matters. I am sorry, Lucy, but I am not the man you would wish me to be.'

Lucinda understood at once what he meant. She had wanted to exonerate him, to think him true and good and honourable. But he was refusing to allow that, and she knew there was no going back for them—no matter what the truth was. Too much had changed.

'But for tonight,' Daniel said, 'I wish it were not so. I never thought to say it, but I wish I could turn back the clock.'

His words silenced Lucinda for a moment, bringing a longing so potent that she could not speak. It was madness, yet instinct deeper than reason, deeper than sense, made her want this man with every bone in her body. She fought the primitive urge that beat in her blood. The touch of his hands burned her through the silk of her dress, the brush of his thighs against her skirt distracted her, making her want to press closer with a shameless, wanton longing. She almost missed her step, and his hands tightened for a second.

In this moment, she thought, in this one dance, she would forget all that had come between them and give herself up to the here and now. Soon, she knew, Daniel would be gone, and this brief time would be no more than a dream. She closed her eyes and allowed the music to sweep her up, and thought of nothing but the pleasure of being in his arms.

'Why do you wear that foolish turban?' he asked softly, his breath brushing her ear. 'I want to see your hair, touch it like I did that night in the moonlight…'

Lucinda's heart raced. She could feel herself shaking a little. 'I wear it because, as you so rightly pointed out when we first met again, I am a respectable widow, not a flighty girl. You should remember that too.'

He laughed. 'You are still the wild country girl I knew all those years ago, Luce. You may hide it well most of the time, but I saw you trying to jump ship. I know you are still a hoyden.' He ran his fingers caressingly over her wrist where the pulse beat erratically. 'I know you,' he repeated softly.

'You knew me,' Lucinda corrected, against the fierce beating of her heart. 'Like you, I have changed.'

'Not so much as you pretend.'

Lucinda looked at him and felt swamped by the same hopeless rush of feeling she had felt upon first meeting him again. She knew that there was a wanton, sensual and reckless side to her character. Daniel was the only one who could arouse it in her. She had locked it away for so long, but now he had awakened those feelings again and they troubled her and gave her no peace. But soon he was to be gone again, vanishing from her life again like the spectre he was. So it was easier by far to be angry with him and keep those other treacherous, terrifying emotions out—for this Daniel was a man to the boy he had once been, and she knew he could demand a response from her that was every bit as fierce as the one she had given him all those years ago when they had been young.

'De Lancey!'

The shout cut through the web of emotion that had engulfed them, causing them both to jump violently. The music wavered and died. Lucinda saw Daniel swing round on instinct—but there was nothing surprising in that. Everyone in the Assembly Rooms had frozen at the sound of that name, then spun around to confront the person from whom it had come. Searching feverishly through the shocked faces of the crowd, Lucinda saw Owen Chance striding forward. He had what looked like a letter in his hand, and he was making directly for them.

'You are Daniel de Lancey,' he said.

Lucinda felt all the blood drain from her face. For a moment she thought that she was about to swoon for the first time in her life. It was purely emotional, purely instinctive. She felt terrified at the danger Daniel was now in. No one in the Assembly Rooms had ever seen him before, so she knew someone must have informed on him. She looked at the letter in Owen Chance's hand, and then up into his face with a sort of despair.

Daniel was made of sterner stuff, she realised. Her face looked pale and stricken in the long mirrors that lined the ballroom, but he was standing there with the cool of the devil himself, one brow raised in polite enquiry, a look of amused tolerance on his face as he confronted Owen Chance.

'I beg your pardon,' Daniel said, 'but I fear there is some mistake. I am Mr Jackson Raleigh, of Ludlow in Shropshire.'

The room had erupted into a torrent of whisper and speculation. Someone had moved to the door as though to guard it. Out of the corner of her eye Lucinda saw one of the redcoat captains draw his men closer. She saw the easy amusement in Daniel's eyes turn to calculation as he looked around for an exit. Her heart swooped into her satin slippers as she realised that there was nowhere for him to go. There was no escape.

Their eyes met for a long second, and in that moment she knew exactly what he was going to do.

'I am sure that Mrs Melville will vouch for me,' he said. He held Lucinda's gaze very directly. 'She knows me well. We were children together.' He looked around the circle of amazed faces. 'In fact she is my betrothed.'

Chapter 5

'OF ALL the unpardonably dirty tricks!'

The door of the room was locked and the guard's footsteps receded along the corridor. Lucinda grabbed Daniel by the lapels of his jacket and shook him hard, her weight carrying them both backwards onto the dirty pallet bed in the corner of the room.

He went down with a thud, banging his shoulder against the wall, all the breath knocked from his body. Lucinda was no lightweight. Now she was sitting on top of him, just as she had when they had fought as children, in the days before their youthful feelings had turned to something deeper. Daniel shifted beneath her. No. On second thoughts it was not quite as it had been when they were children. Now Lucinda's silk-clad legs were pressing against the side of his body, the warm juncture of her thighs was brushing a rather delicate and responsive part of his anatomy, and as she leaned forward, her wrathful face only a few inches from his, he caught a tantalising glimpse of the curve of her breasts beneath the silk ballgown.

He did the first thing that came into his mind.

He seized the hateful turban from her head and threw it into a corner of the room. Lucinda's hair tumbled down to her shoulders, sticking out from its pins in charming blonde disarray. Daniel smiled.

'That's better.'

Lucinda made a noise like an enraged kitten and beat her fists against his chest.

'Beast! Hateful, lying, deceitful, manipulative, *traitorous* beast!'

Daniel laughed out loud. 'Don't hold back, Lucinda!'

'I hate you! You ruined my life once before, and now you have ruined *me*! I detest you!' Her voice broke. To his amazement, Daniel realised that she was on the very edge of tears, his indomitable Lucinda. He had never, ever seen her cry—not even when her pet slow-worm had died when she was thirteen.

His hands gentled on her shoulders. He felt a huge wave of remorse, sobering him, humbling him. He got into—and out of—situations like this every day of his life, but Lucinda did not. In his careless, selfish disdain for her feelings and her future he had indeed ruined her.

'I am sorry,' he said slowly.

Her eyes were very bright with unshed tears as she looked down at him.

'Why did you do it?'

Daniel shrugged uncomfortably. 'It wasn't supposed to be like this. We weren't supposed to be locked up. I thought that Chance would believe me. My plan was for him to back down and apologise, and for everyone to congratulate us, and then we would simply walk out of there—'

'And you would walk out of my life. Again. Leaving me to explain—again—the disappearance of my fiancé.'

There was a silence.

'Something like that,' Daniel admitted.

Lucinda straightened, moving away from him. Daniel swung his legs over the side of the bed and sat next to her. They were in a hastily converted office on the first floor of Woodbridge Gaol, detained at His Majesty's pleasure whilst Owen Chance sent to Shropshire for urgent confirmation of Mr Jackson Raleigh's identity. The door was locked, and a soldier was on guard at the end of the corridor. The Riding Officer had been apologetic but firm. Clearly he had not thought he could consign to the filthy cells a couple who might just possibly be all that they seemed—outraged gentry caught up in a case of mistaken identity. Even so, their situation was not a comfortable one. The room had one pallet bed, a desk, a wooden chair, a bucket, and that was all.

Daniel could not see Lucinda's face. The unruly strands of hair that he had released now masked her expression from him.

'You have never cared about anyone else in your life,' she said slowly. 'It is all of a piece.'

When he did not reply she glanced sideways at him.

'Why do you not answer?'

Daniel shook his head. He felt cold within. 'I have no defence against your words. You are correct. I thought only of myself and how I might escape.'

'You abandoned me without a word when I was seventeen,' Lucinda continued. 'Tonight I almost forgot all of that, and was nearly seduced into caring for you all over again. But you—you care for no one but yourself, Daniel. You always have and you always will.'

Daniel made an abrupt movement of pain and frustrated rage. Until recently he had been his own sternest critic. Sometimes in the dark hours he struggled with his guilt, but that fight was his alone and he never spoke of it. That had changed when Lucinda had burst into his life again. She had confronted him and made him face up to the hurt he had dealt her in the past. And now he had hurt her all over again.

'Why did you not denounce me?' he said now. 'Why did you lie to save me? Why did you not tell them at once that I was using you?'

She shot him a look from her very blue eyes. A tinge of colour touched her cheek. She caught her lush lower lip between her teeth.

'Because I find that I am not as ruthless as you.' She knitted her fingers together. 'I did not want to see you hang.'

'Thank you.'

She glared at him. 'Oh, I *wanted* to denounce you for ruining me. Don't mistake me. It is simply that I do not have the necessary hardihood.'

Daniel winced. 'Well, thank you anyway.'

Lucinda turned her head slightly towards him. 'Is there someone in Ludlow who can vouch for you?'

'Of course not.'

'Nor anyone else who will come to our aid?'

'No.'

'The Duchess of Kestrel might try, for my sake.'

'She cannot do anything to help.' Daniel rubbed his brow. 'I dare say she realises that I am indeed de Lancey, but she will not intervene. I have worked with Justin Kestrel for the past five years, but he cannot save me now. He offered me a pardon only a few weeks ago and I turned him down. It is understood that if I am captured I am on my own.'

Lucinda was staring. 'You have worked with Justin Kestrel?'

'Yes.' Daniel paused for a moment, but he knew that this was hardly the time to keep any further secrets from Lucinda. 'You mentioned tonight that you had heard I worked for the Admiralty. Well, it is true. I am no traitor, Luce. I have worked for this government throughout the war.'

'Then you are no spy?'

'I spy for the British, not the French.'

'And the piracy?'

'I certainly harry the French fleet as much as I can.'

'And the smuggling?'

'I have helped smuggle fugitives from Napoleon's regime.' Daniel shrugged. 'And I also smuggle good French brandy, so it is absolutely true that I am a criminal.'

'Oh, Daniel!'

For a moment he thought Lucinda was going to throw herself into his arms, but being the woman she was she swallowed hard and glared at him instead.

'Why did you not tell me the truth before? Why did you want me to think the worst of you?'

Daniel shifted a little. He took her hand. 'Because I had to drive you away, Luce. It is not as simple as you think. I may have worked for the Admiralty, but I have crossed the line many times. By any definition I am a criminal now. That was what I meant when I said that you had not misjudged me.' His grip tightened on her hand. 'All the things of which you accuse me—the selfishness and the reck-lessness and the love of danger—they are all true.'

Lucinda's eyes flashed. 'But it is iniquitous for the Admiralty to treat you so when you have worked for them! Justin Kestrel should be ashamed if he leaves you to hang!'

Daniel's lips twitched. 'Your sense of fair play is admirable, Lucy,' he said quietly. 'But in your haste to acquit me do not forget that I have ruined you. I am as bad as you have painted me.'

'That's true,' Lucinda agreed. 'You are still a lying, deceitful and manipulative beast, even if you are not a traitor.'

Daniel smiled at her. 'Thank you.'

Lucinda fidgeted and looked away, though she allowed her hand to remain in his. 'So, if Justin Kestrel will not come to our aid, we have a couple of days of this…this purgatory…until they get word that you are not Mr Jackson Raleigh and then we are both hanged.'

'That's about the size of it.' Daniel's squeezed her fingers. 'But we shall escape before that.'

Her eyes flew to his. 'Shall we?'

'Of course. In fact we are about to do so. It is always best to escape early on, with the element of surprise.'

Lucinda raised her brows. 'I see. And I admire your confidence. So how is this cunning plan to be achieved?'

'I am not sure yet,' Daniel admitted. 'But I know I will think of something.'

Her shoulders slumped slightly. 'How reassuring.'

He put his arm about her. 'Whatever happens, Lucy, you are coming with me. You have to now.'

She looked down her nose at him. 'I have to do no such thing. Why should I?'

'Because, as you so succinctly pointed out a few moments ago, I have ruined you,' Daniel said calmly. He had had no time to think anything through beyond an absolute certainty that he had to put matters right for Lucinda. It was the one good thing that he *could* do—even if it would be the last. 'You will come with me and you will marry me.'

'What makes you think that I will have you?' Lucinda said, with a flash of hauteur. 'You are no great catch.'

Daniel grinned. 'Being married to me will be better than trying to marry off the brats of the nobility for a living. Trust me on that.'

'You always had an inflated opinion of your own charms,' Lucinda commented. 'I cannot believe that you are using the opportunity of us being locked up together to press your suit. I will *not* marry you, Daniel, and that is final. You are the least reliable man on earth, and I would have to be mad or desperate or both to accept you.'

Daniel was thinking quickly. He was sure that if the worse came to the worst he could barter information for Lucinda's freedom. Justin and Sally Kestrel could help her, if not him. She could go to Allandale, do the work that he had been too weak and too wild to do. At least she would be safe...

'Marry me,' he said again. 'Please, Lucy. It is the only way in which I can put matters right.'

'I have no wish to be a pirate's wife,' Lucinda said. 'If we escape I would be obliged to sail with you, and I am the world's worst sailor. Merely sitting in a rowing boat makes me sick. It is a miracle I was not ill aboard the *Defiance*.'

'You were too busy quarrelling with me to notice,' Daniel said ruefully. He spread his hands. 'You need not sail with me. I inherited Allandale from my cousin just a month ago. You could live there—'

'You are Lord Allandale now?' Lucinda's eyes widened.

'Yes. Which is why I need to know there is someone I can trust to take care of the estate.'

Lucinda's gaze snapped onto him. 'You need an estate manager, not a wife!' She hesitated for a moment, and then looked at him very directly. Her tone changed, turned sad. 'I cannot wed you, Daniel. Do not press me to it. Oh, I care for you.' She laced her fingers together a little awkwardly. 'And 'tis true that I respond to you—' Here she blushed, and he wanted to kiss her very much. 'But I do not trust you. You will always put yourself first. You always have and you always will. And I could not bear for you to break my heart again.'

She stood up, smoothing her skirts, and crossed to the window. She stood with her back turned to him, her arms folded tight about her as though she was cold, and though Daniel wanted to take her in his arms, to hold her and comfort her, he knew she would not let him touch her. What could he say? That it would be different this time? That he cared for her and would never hurt her? He knew it was true, but trust had to be earned and he had forfeited the right to hers.

'Look!' Lucinda said suddenly. A note of excitement had crept into her voice. 'It is snowing outside!' She paused. 'You will have observed that there are no bars at the window, Daniel?'

Daniel had already noticed. 'Given that there is a drop to the ground of about twelve feet,' he pointed out, 'I cannot see that it benefits us.'

Lucinda ignored this. 'We are at the back of the building, and all it faces is a wall,' she continued. 'And this door is solid, so the guards cannot see what we are doing in here—and anyway, they are away down the corridor…'

Daniel smiled. 'An intriguing thought, Lucy. You are putting ideas into my head.'

'Try thinking of escape rather than seduction,' Lucinda snapped. 'Mr Chance has been lamentably lax in leaving us so ill-guarded.'

'I think he was rather trusting to the fact that you are a respectable widow,' Daniel murmured dryly, 'and that I might actually have been telling the truth when I said you could vouch for me.'

Lucinda cast him a look. She was ripping a length of material from her skirt, wincing at the tearing noise it made, and then another, which she knotted to the first. This left her with her gown bodice still intact, but nothing but petticoats below. Daniel stared at her shapely garter-clad legs, feeling his throat dry.

'What the devil are you doing?' he managed.

Lucinda edged the sash window up.

'If the guard comes in, hit him over the head with the chair,' she instructed. 'Only try not to hurt him too much. I do not wish to be accused of murder as well as conspiracy!'

Daniel raised his brows. 'Lucinda—'

She gave him a fierce frown. 'Hush!'

She tied the end of the makeshift rope to the desk and gave it an experimental tug. Then, before Daniel could protest, she had thrown the other end of the rope out of the window and climbed out. Forgetting his duty with the chair, Daniel rushed to the window and looked down. Lucinda was standing in the snow, her breast heaving slightly with the exertion of her climb down the rope, her face upturned to his. Flakes of snow were settling on her eyelashes and she brushed them away. Her impatient whisper floated up to him.

'Do you intend to join me, or do you prefer to wait at His Majesty's pleasure?'

The silk gave way when he was halfway to the ground, depositing Daniel in the snow with a rather sharp bump. Before he knew what was happening, Lucinda had grabbed his arm and hauled him to his feet, dusting him down with brisk, impersonal hands. Daniel flinched.

'Ouch! There is no need to be so rough.' He looked her over. With snowflakes in her blonde hair she looked entirely charming. 'Clearly I have underestimated you, Luce,' he said. 'You have a natural bent for criminality. I should have invited you to join my crew years ago.'

She gave him a glare from those glorious blue eyes. 'Are we

going to stand here chatting whilst we await discovery? Or are we going to hire some horses at the Bell around the corner?'

'Surely you mean steal some horses?' Daniel said mildly.

She gave him another glare, holding her wrist up to show her reticule, still dangling there. 'I have some money. There is no need to make matters worse by adding theft to our list of crimes.'

'Absolutely,' Daniel said. He grabbed her, gave her a brief, fierce kiss. 'Lucy, you are a wonderful girl.'

For a moment she stood still in his embrace, and he thought he felt her lips soften beneath his.

'It astounds me that you have been at liberty as long as you have, Daniel, given your lack of resourcefulness and your penchant for wasting time,' she said, a little breathlessly.

She was shivering. Daniel shrugged out of his jacket and placed it about her shoulders, watching as she drew it close with shaking fingers. For all her bravado he knew that she was half-shocked, half-elated by what they had done.

'Wait in shelter whilst I get the horses,' he began—but even as he spoke Lucinda recoiled with a gasp and, looking past her, Daniel saw a figure rear up out of the tumbling snow at the corner of the alleyway.

He had already moved to place himself between her and this latest threat when he recognised the man and saw that behind him was a carriage drawn up in the snow. No, it was not a carriage—it was a covered horse-drawn sleigh.

'Evening, sir—ma'am,' Lieutenant Holroyd said, coming forward to shake his hand. He grinned. 'Good to see you again. Transport compliments of the Duchess of Kestrel. What kept you, sir?'

Chapter 6

IN THE sleigh, beneath the fur-lined rugs that Sally Kestrel had so thoughtfully provided, Lucinda sat shivering and shivering in her torn evening gown and petticoats. The sleigh was a splendid affair— a little coach on runners, with a hood lashed down on all sides so that it was very snug inside. Sally Kestrel could not have sent anything better suited to their purpose, and the fact that she *had* sent it led Lucinda to hope that matters might be all right, for if ever she needed help it was now.

Despite the thick furs and the cloaks that Holroyd had passed to them, Lucinda was trembling as though she would never be warm again. She knew that it was reaction to her situation, rather than cold, that was making her shake like this. She had escaped from Wood-bridge Gaol with Daniel—no, she had engineered their escape—and she was ruined, a fugitive and a criminal. No doubt her face would be appearing on the 'wanted' posters soon. And the shocking, inex-cusable and truly extraordinary thing about the whole experience was that she felt stirred up, alive, free for once from the stifling re-strictions and endless petty rules that had governed her existence as a governess and chaperon. Oh, she was half appalled at her own be-haviour, but she was excited as well.

She must be mad.

She must be in love.

She closed her eyes in denial of the thought. It could not be true. But she knew it was. She thought back to that terrible moment in the ballroom when she had known with blinding certainty that she could not have borne them carrying Daniel off to gaol and seeing his lifeless body swinging on the end of a rope. She knew he was all of the things she had said he was. He was unreliable and reckless and dangerous. But it made not one whit of difference because she had loved him when she was seventeen and she loved him still, after all these years.

Which still did not mean, of course, that she would agree to marry him. Daniel had said that they must be married to save her reputation—as though marrying an outlawed pirate would not be the most monstrous scandal in itself. She imagined her parents, the good vicar and his wife, positively spinning in their graves. And it simply would not serve. Daniel did not want a wife. His way of life was completely opposed to it. Besides, were not women supposed to be bad luck at sea? Lucinda had the conviction that if she went to sea it would be very bad luck for all concerned. If she felt sick sitting in a rowing boat, then once a ship began to move she would probably be horribly unwell the entire time.

So there was no possibility of her becoming Daniel's wife. And it was not simply a practical matter of seasickness. She could, as Daniel had suggested, go to live at Allandale. But she had no wish to sit at home wondering where Daniel was and what he was doing. That was not her idea of marriage.

The truth was that she knew if she were to marry Daniel she would be an encumbrance to him rather than the person he had chosen to share the rest of his life. It would be a marriage borne of necessity rather than desire. For how could he want a wife when his way of life was so unsuited to marriage? And she was old enough and proud enough not to want to be second-best to a ship. Time and again Daniel had proved that the lure of the sea and the wild life he lived outside the law were more important to him than all else. She loved him, but she could not trust him not to hurt her again.

The smooth running of the sledge over the snow slowed a little, and then they came to an abrupt halt. Lucinda heard Daniel jump down, and then his voice, speaking low. There was a chink of harness and then the creak of the sleigh as he lifted the hood and slid in beside her, shaking the snow off him like a dog.

'The snow is too deep to continue,' he said. 'Holroyd has set off back to the ship on foot.'

Lucinda scrambled up. 'We should do the same—'

Daniel put a hand on her shoulder, pressing her back into the furs. 'Lucinda, the snow is already two foot deep and drifting, and you are clad in nothing but your petticoats and evening slippers. We stay here until the snow stops.'

Lucinda hastily slipped her stockinged legs back under the covers. 'But we cannot simply sit here! They will be looking for us.'

'What is bad for us is also bad for our pursuers,' Daniel said. He shrugged out of his jacket, then started to pull off his boots. 'No one will be out whilst the snow falls like this. I have found an empty byre where the horse will be safe, and we shall be snug in here until we can make the last few miles down to the creek. We are near Midwinter Mallow, so there is not far to go.'

He raised the edge of the fur covers as though to slip underneath.

'What are you doing?' Lucinda asked, scooting across to the other side of the sleigh.

Daniel paused. 'I am coming in there with you. What do you expect me to do? Shiver all night in a snowdrift?'

'But…' Lucinda grabbed the rugs up to her chin. 'Surely you should go with Holroyd back to the ship? I will be quite safe here.' She took a deep breath. This might be her best opportunity to explain to Daniel the half-formed plan that she had made concerning the future.

'I have been thinking,' she said. 'I have a plan, Daniel, which means that neither you nor I need be trapped into anything we do not wish. I thought that if you were to return to the *Defiance* now, without me, someone would be bound to find me before too long.

And when they do I will simply pretend that you coerced me at the ball and that I am blameless of all crime…'

Her voice trailed away as she sensed the rather ominous silence that greeted her words. She could not see Daniel clearly in the near-darkness, but she could feel his outrage.

'Let me understand you,' he said, after a long moment. 'Having taken me to task for abandoning you in the past, you are now suggesting that I should behave like a complete scoundrel, leave you here at the mercy of whoever should stumble out of the storm and find you, and that I should run back to my ship, make my escape, and leave you to take all the consequences?'

Lucinda had seldom heard him so angry. Not since she had been in her teens, when an irate farmer had shouted at her for trying to free his exhausted ploughing team and Daniel had practically threatened to run the man through.

'Well,' Lucinda said, through suddenly chattering teeth, 'I thought it was a good plan.'

'It is the stupidest plan that I have heard in an age,' Daniel said, in the same hard, insulted voice. 'For once in my life, Lucy, permit me to do the *right thing*.'

These last words were hissed through his teeth.

'But—'

'I will stay with you,' Daniel continued, as though she had not spoken. 'When the snow ceases we will finish the journey back to the ship, and there I will marry you.'

Lucinda sat bolt upright. 'Now, just a minute! That will not be necessary, Daniel. I have already said that I will not marry you.'

'You *will* marry me. As ship's captain I have the right to conduct marriage services, and the first one I shall perform is my own.'

'That is definitely illegal,' Lucinda said, hoping she was right.

Daniel ignored her. He slid beneath the blankets and his body grazed against hers. Lucinda felt the long, hard length of him, felt his legs entangle with hers beneath the petticoats, and tried to shift away as far as she could. Her throat was dry, and her heart was thundering in her ears, a counterpoint to the soft swish of the snow against the roof of the sleigh. A moment later he had put out a negligent hand and pulled her into his arms. Her hands came up against the hard, warm barrier of his chest.

'You are cold and you are suffering from shock,' he said against her hair. 'You need to stop worrying about what is going to happen and allow me to warm you.'

Lucinda was shivering violently, but not with either cold or shock now. 'I do not need you to warm me,' she argued. 'I certainly do not need you to marry me, and I *cannot* permit you to do the right thing.'

She felt him smile. His cheek was pressed to hers, his lips resting in the little, sensitive hollow beneath her ear. He reached with his free hand and pulled his jacket towards them, delving in the pocket.

'Take some of this brandy, Lucy, and please stop arguing with me. You know I can be at least as stubborn as you, if not more so.'

Their fingers touched as Lucinda took the small flask of brandy from him. 'Is this the brandy that you smuggle?' She enquired.

'It is. Drink it up.'

'I hate brandy.' Even so she tilted it to her lips, more out of curiosity than anything else.

Daniel smiled. 'I might have known you wouldn't care for it.'

But a rosy glow was spreading from Lucy's stomach down to her toes and up to her face. She felt curiously warm, and suddenly a great deal more relaxed. 'Actually,' she admitted, 'it is rather pleasant.'

'Good.'

'But I still won't marry you, so don't think to try and get me drunk in order to persuade me.'

Daniel did not reply. Very deliberately he took the empty flask from her hand, placed it back in his pocket, and threw his coat into a corner of the sleigh. Then he turned back to her.

'Is there anything else you wish to say on the subject?' he enquired.

Lucinda was starting to feel strangely light-headed. She knew there were lots of good reasons she wanted to give him for refusing his proposal of marriage, but they kept slipping out of her mind, and all she seemed capable of thinking about was how her body burned at every point of contact with his.

'You don't want a wife,' she said, a little forlornly.

'I want you,' Daniel said. His lips grazed hers. 'I want you very much, and I am determined to persuade you to my point of view.'

His hands stroked up from her waist, caressing the tender skin on the side of her breasts beneath the shreds of her silk gown. Lucinda gave a little involuntary moan and was shocked to hear it. What had happened to her? Her head was spinning and her body was aching with a fierce desire. Suddenly the atmosphere in the sleigh felt as hot as a summer day—the sort of long, sultry day she remembered from her girlhood.

'You put something in the brandy,' she said, trying to sound accusatory but instead sounding breathless and tempted. She heard Daniel laugh.

'I hardly need brandy to seduce a woman.'

'Why, you arrogant—'

The words were lost in his kiss. There was no warning, no gentle seduction. It was a deep kiss, and the sweep of his tongue against hers made her tremble. He tasted her, branded her, *knew* her, and she was helpless beneath his touch as the same wild, wanton, wicked feelings he could always arouse in her stormed through her blood and set her entire body alight. She gasped against his lips and he plundered her mouth again, the kiss at once ruthless, demanding, insistent on a response.

Once more his hand came up to brush away the shreds of silk that covered her bodice. She felt his fingers at the laces. One tug and they were undone. Her bodice parted and she relaxed gratefully, remembering how tightly it had been laced beneath her ballgown. That seemed centuries ago—the respectable chaperon in her tasteful blue silk dress, preparing for an evening's entertainment. This was hardly the entertainment she had anticipated, and yet now that she was lying here with Daniel she wanted nothing more than to feel his body upon and within her; the strength of him, the hardness of him, the sheer, smooth masculine power. Her gown was completely gone now, ripped apart in their escape, and then the scraps that had been left brushed aside by his impatient hands. Lucinda felt as though her own fears and inhibitions had been cast away with them.

It was so dark in the sleigh that she could see nothing of Daniel's face, nor her own shocking state of undress. He had pushed back the fur-lined rugs now, and laid her on top of them, and she could feel the cold breath of the night air against her skin. Her bodice was unlaced, parted, pushed back from her bare breasts. Her nipples peaked tightly as she waited in an agony of desire and anticipation for him to touch her.

Lucinda gave another moan of desperation, and then he swooped down, his mouth warm at her breast at last, and she actually screamed as he took her nipple between his lips and bit down gently on it before soothing away the delicious hurt with his tongue. He kissed the underside of her breast, and her sensitive skin puckered into tiny goosebumps as she writhed on the covers.

'Daniel…'

She rolled over and raised a hand to Daniel's cheek, felt his stubble rough beneath her palm, then pressed her fingers against the nape of his neck to bring his head down to hers so that she could kiss him again. She tangled her fingers into his hair and kissed him with all the pent-up wildness of those lost years. She slid her hands under his shirt and ran them over the hard planes of his chest and upper arms, exulting in the solid muscle and smooth, warm skin. Her whole body was a mass of sensation as she tore the shirt from his back and pressed her nakedness against him, wanting to bind him closer than ever before.

'Lucinda… Sweetheart, slow down.' Daniel's voice was scarcely recognisable, so slurred with emotion that she had to strain to hear his words. 'I don't want to hurt you.'

'You won't,' Lucinda said. Her body hummed, waiting, demanding. 'I'm not a virgin,' she said. 'Leopold was an old man but he… we….' She stopped. A pang of nervousness took her by surprise, threatening all the excited arousal that had built up within her. She bit her lip. How stupid of her to think of Leopold now, of those demeaning fumbles that had left her humiliated in mind and body. She could feel all the pleasure draining from her like water down a drain.

She felt Daniel shift a little beside her. 'What is it, Lucinda?'

'It was horrible,' Lucinda said in a rush. 'I hated it when he touched me. I had to try to endure it, but I felt repulsed. He told me I was cold.'

'The man was a fool.' Daniel sounded angry, but his hand at her breast still stroked with seductive gentleness, his palm a little rough against her skin. 'You are not cold by nature. You are very, very passionate, Luce…'

He punctuated the words with little kisses scattered across the soft skin of her belly and Lucinda shivered. 'We must make sure that you don't feel repulsed now,' he whispered. 'You must tell me what you want.'

His hands moved caressingly across her bare stomach and she felt the muscles there jump and tighten.

'Do you like that?' Daniel asked softly.

Lucinda gulped. 'Yes,' she whispered. Tiny quivers were running along her nerves as his lips followed his fingers, teasing, stroking.

'And that?' His voice was a low murmur.

'It is tolerable,' Lucinda managed. The hot excitement was building within her again, but she sensed that Daniel would not let her hurry. He had reached for the ruined skirts of her petticoat, deftly rolling them up so that his hand could skim the top of her stocking and settle in sly caress on the soft skin of her inner thigh.

'I protest,' Lucinda said weakly. 'You are a practised seducer.'

She heard him laugh in the darkness. 'Acquit me. I never had the time to practise. This is all for you, Luce. Only for you.'

Lucinda caught her breath as his fingers grazed the secret place at the juncture of her thighs. Pleasure, tantalising and sublime, swept through her. He paused just long enough for her to worry that he had stopped altogether, and then his fingers resumed their gentle slide back and forth, a teasing motion that would soon, she knew, have her begging aloud.

'Daniel—'

'Yes?'

She could tell he was enjoying tormenting her, damn him.

'Please…'

He did not reply, but she could almost feel his smile, there in the hot darkness. He shifted, and she sensed him moving lower, and then she felt his hand on her bare stomach again, this time below the petticoats, and the tip of his tongue instead of his fingers at the very core of her.

She shrieked, arched upwards, and felt his free hand on her hip, warm through the petticoats, holding her down so that his mouth could plunder her at will. It was blissful, agonising. Her legs were quivering now, the muscles of her stomach tight beneath his palm, her fingers clenched in the fur-lined blanket. The rub of the material against the back of her thighs was blissful torment. Never, ever had she felt like this. The incandescent sensations grew and exploded irresistibly in a cluster of light, and she felt as though her whole body had shattered too.

But only for a moment. He did not give her time to think about what had happened. He slid back up her body and took her mouth again, and she moved beneath him and gave a little moan. The sensations he had aroused had not gone away. They thrummed through her like the vibration of an instrument. Her skin felt hot with a passion she had never experienced before.

'Please,' she said again, and hardly recognised her own voice.

There was a brief moment of cold as he withdrew from her, but then he was back, the whole of his long, hard body matching and fitting perfectly against her. But when he eased himself inside her at last it was so slow and gentle that she almost screamed with frustration.

'Damn you, Daniel.' Temper flared in her. 'Don't *tease* me so…'

He laughed. 'My impatient Lucinda.'

The controlled, smooth friction was driving her to near madness, and suddenly she wanted to know her own power, to show him he could not always dictate to her. She dug her fingers into his back and bit his shoulder, and she felt his body jolt as his restraint broke at last and he plunged into her, hard and fast, all gentleness fled, and in its place a driving masculine possession that almost consumed her.

His kiss had a savage urgency; she heard him cry out her name and then the exquisite shudders racked her body again, primitive and intense. She felt the force of his climax sweep them both away and held on to him desperately as the only sure thing in a tumultuous world. Gradually her senses started to settle, and she shifted into the circle of his arms. They held one another close as the bitterness of lost love was finally wiped out by all the bright promise of the future.

Later on Lucinda lost the petticoats, and with them the very last shreds of her modesty and inhibitions. The snow had stopped falling and they had run out into it, naked in the moonlight, Lucinda squealing as Daniel tumbled her into a snowdrift and kissed her until she forgot the cold and clung to him with the blood racing hot again through her veins.

'Make love to me here,' she whispered to him, as the snow melted against her flushed body, stinging her skin with its exquisite, shocking cold.

This time his possession was slow and erotic, and she writhed beneath his deliberate caresses.

Tell me what you want…

Oh, she wanted this pleasure. With his hands and his mouth he drove her to heights she had not even guessed existed, and he made love to her with a passion that made her feel she might die from the sheer bliss of it.

At last, when the coldness finally drove them back to the shelter of the sleigh, Daniel took her in his arms and wrapped her tightly in the fur-lined rugs. Lucinda rested her head against his chest and listened to the steady beat of his heart, and she thought perhaps that she had been a little hasty in rejecting the idea of marriage out of hand if it had such benefits as these.

'I do believe that I would give up everything else in my life just to have you,' she whispered, wondering if he could hear her or if he was asleep.

He made a soft sound of contentment and his arms tightened about her. 'And I would gladly take you barefoot and journey with you to the world's end,' he murmured against her hair. And she fell asleep, dreaming of tall ships and distant horizons.

Chapter 7

DANIEL found that he was whistling as he went to forage for fresh hay for the horse and to pick up the provisions that Holroyd had so thoughtfully left with them the previous night. The sky was a bright, cold, piercing blue, the sun was shining and the snow was fresh and crisp, blindingly white. It felt to Daniel as though the whole world was newly made, and all because he had woken with Lucinda curled up in his arms.

Lucinda, the only woman he wanted. The only woman he had ever loved.

He found that he was smiling. She had refused his proposal of marriage last night, but he was sure that this morning he could persuade her. He was sure that she loved him. He knew that he had hurt her badly before, and that now he had to earn her trust, but suddenly that felt like the most exciting challenge in the world. He felt his heart swell with a mixture of pride and hope and sheer happiness.

He found a bale of old hay in a corner of the outhouse where he had stabled the horse. The grey mare seemed less than impressed with the offering, but snorted her disdainful way through a few mouthfuls. Daniel broke the ice on the water trough, patted her on the nose, and scooped up the bag with bread, slightly stale now, and ham and a bottle of cider, and made his way back to the sleigh.

All was quiet. Lucinda must still be asleep. Humming softly under his breath, Daniel lifted the hood. The bright morning light flooded inside.

The sleigh was empty. Lucinda's clothes—what was left of them after the ravages of the previous night—had disappeared, along with her ruined dancing slippers.

Daniel's first thought was sheer incredulity that she would have run from him after all they had shared the previous night. She would not. She could not.

Then he remembered her saying that he should leave her behind—that she would be able to persuade people that she was innocent and he had coerced her into helping him. He felt a sickening lurch of disillusion to think that she had acted upon her word. But then, hot on the heels of that thought, he saw the knife-cut through the material of the hood.

He leaped out of the sleigh. The snow was scuffed up, showing confused signs of footprints and perhaps a struggle. He spun around. There was no one in sight and no sound at all. The empty, bright morning mocked him. Fear clutched at his heart now, driving out the disillusion. What a fool he had been to doubt her. And a greater fool to have left her unprotected. He had allowed himself to become distracted again. He had not been paying attention because he was happy and in love, and blind, deaf, thoughtless to all else. And John Norton—for it must be he—had been watching him and waiting, and had taken the one thing that mattered more to Daniel than life itself. He had taken Lucinda for revenge.

A moment later Daniel realised that that had not been the full extent of Norton's treachery. He spun around as he heard the thunder of hoofbeats on the snow. A posse of soldiers, with Owen Chance at their head, was spilling into the clearing and surrounding the sleigh. Chance had a pistol in his hand. The soldiers had rifles and they were all pointing at him. There was nowhere to run—no way in which he could help Lucinda now. This time it really was all over.

'Daniel de Lancey, I arrest you in the name of the King!' Chance jumped down. He looked about him. 'Where is Mrs Melville? What have you done with her, you traitorous bastard?'

'Norton has taken her,' Daniel said.

Two of the soldiers grabbed him roughly by the arms, forcing him to his knees. He felt the manacles snap about his wrist, but he ignored them, concentrating desperately on Owen Chance.

'For God's sake, man, we have to find her!' He said. 'Norton has carried her off. You must let me go after him!'

Chance's handsome face looked as though it was carved from stone. He did not even look at him. 'If what you say is true,' he said, 'then we will find her.'

Fear, fury and frustration swept through Daniel in equal measure. 'No! You don't understand!'

Chance was walking away. The soldiers were already dragging Daniel towards the nearest horse, in preparation for chaining him to the saddle and hauling him back to Woodbridge Gaol—the wanted criminal, the pirate, captured at last.

'Norton will get clean away!' he shouted. 'Even now he is probably halfway back to his ship. I have to stop him!'

A sharp tug on the chains sent him sprawling in the snow, in danger of being trampled by the horses, but he did not care about the indignity of it. Fear for Lucinda roared through him. 'Don't you understand, man?' he yelled, towards Owen Chance's unresponsive back. 'She will be raped and murdered before you even have the first idea where to look for her! It is Norton's crew that has been ravaging the coast these six months past! For pity's sake—'

For the first time Owen Chance turned and met his gaze, and Daniel could see that he was thinking about what he had said. For a moment his hopes hung in the balance. But then Chance's jaw set and he shook his head. 'We will find her,' he said again.

Daniel would have put his head in his hands if he had been able. He knew it was hopeless. Perhaps it was already too late. He could beg and plead, but Chance would never let him go to rescue Lucinda. Probably he did not believe his story anyway, seeing it as just another ruse in order to try and escape. Chance had his prize now: the pirate he had been hunting through years of failure and frustration and humiliation. He would never risk losing him again.

The chains tightened again, jerking Daniel to his feet. He spread his manacled hands wide in a last gesture of appeal.

'Please… I swear on my life that if you let me find her I will turn myself in and surrender to you as soon as she is safe.'

Chance looked at him. And laughed. 'Do you think I would take the word of a pirate and a traitor, de Lancey? Take him away!'

The soldiers remounted and the little procession formed up. But they had gone less than a hundred yards towards the Woodbridge road when a lone horseman came galloping towards them and reined in sharply, in a showy but beautifully controlled circle. The rider—and it was a slender young woman, with long dark hair—tumbled from the saddle and ran across the snow towards Owen Chance, who jumped down from his own horse and caught her in his arms.

'Miss Saltire! Eustacia! What on earth are you doing here?'

'They've taken Lucinda!' the girl cried, grabbing his arm. 'Owen, you must do something to stop them. Sir John Norton holds her to ransom!'

Daniel's heart lurched with a mixture of hope and despair. If Norton was planning on ransoming Lucinda there was the smallest chance that he might not hurt her. But it seemed unlikely. He knew Norton's tricks of old. He would take the woman, rape her, abuse her, and then throw her back to her relatives and friends once they had paid up, as though she mattered less than a side of meat. He faced the thought of that happening to Lucinda and felt a mad, murderous rage mixed with his fear, and a furious frustration at his own inability to do anything to help her.

'For God's sake, Chance!' he shouted, his voice breaking with the emotion that was inside him. 'Will you stop wasting time here and just go and get her?'

Chance shot him a look. The girl—Eustacia—grabbed Chance's arm again. 'Owen, please! Lucinda has been the truest friend to me that I could ever have asked for. You must help her!'

'I'll call the Navy out—' Chance began.

'There's no time,' Daniel said.

Chance looked down at Eustacia's white, pleading face, and back at Daniel. 'How do I know you are not in league with Norton and this isn't all a trick, de Lancey?'

'You don't,' Daniel said. Despite the cold, sweat was trickling down between his shoulderblades now. 'I love her, Chance,' he said. He looked at Eustacia. 'If you have any understanding or sympathy for that, then I beg you to help.'

There was a long silence.

'We'll take the *Defiance* then,' Owen Chance said. He came across to Daniel. 'Do we still have a bargain, de Lancey? We free Mrs Melville and then you surrender to us?'

'I swear on my life,' Daniel said.

They looked at one another for a long moment, and then Chance nodded slowly. 'Take his manacles off,' he said. There was a flicker of amusement in his dark eyes. 'I never thought to be doing this, de Lancey…'

'Oh, thank you!' Eustacia Saltire looked radiant. She stood on tiptoe to kiss Owen Chance's cheek—a kiss that turned into something rather more passionate as Chance caught her in his arms and returned the kiss in full measure.

The soldiers shifted, trying not to grin, and Daniel tried not to feel too impatient.

'Time for that later,' he said, and Stacey turned within the circle of Owen Chance's arms and gave him a dazzling smile.

'Good luck!' she said.

Chance, still looking vaguely stunned by the kiss, let her go at last.

'Well,' he said, 'what are we waiting for?'

Lucinda had never felt so ill in all her life—nor been so abjectly grateful for feeling so. As soon as she had set foot on John Norton's ship she had started to be sick, and she had barely stopped since. It was the only thing that had saved her. Norton, at first so delighted to have the woman he had termed 'de Lancey's doxy' in his power, had been utterly disgusted to discover that she was so poor a sailor, and had had her thrown into a festering little cabin in the bowels of the ship and had left her alone.

'Don't think de Lancey will be coming for you,' he had sneered. 'I tipped off those useless redcoats—again—and this time the Riding Officer will have him in chains.' He'd leaned against the cabin doorway and his insolent bloodshot gaze had appraised her from head to foot. 'Perhaps you'll be more use to me financially than you are for anything else,' he'd said. 'The crew can have their pleasure with you once you've stopped throwing up, and then I'll sell you back to your friends.'

After that Lucinda was happy to be as sick as she possibly could.

She had no idea of how much time had passed, but eventually the seasickness abated and she started to feel a little less faint. In her head, round and around, drummed the thought that Daniel must have been captured this time, taken by Owen Chance's men, and she did not know what made her feel more despairing, the thought of what might happen to him or the certainty of what was going to happen to her. She lay down on the bare wooden floor and curled up tightly, trying desperately to think of a way out of her hideous situation. Norton had said that she might be more use to him financially than any other way, and that could only mean that he intended to ransom her—but who would pay? Who would pay for the return of a penniless governess who was already ruined by running off with a notorious privateer?

It was a little while before her misery receded sufficiently for her to realise that the ship was not merely at anchor but actually underway. Although there were no portholes in her little prison, she could tell that the movement of the ship was different, and some kind of urgency seemed to have come over the crew, different from the drunken lassitude she had glimpsed when Norton had first dragged her on board. The *Saucy Helen* was no well-drilled ship like the

Defiance, and Lucinda could hear the sound of running steps overhead, and shouting that became ever more agitated. And then the door of her noisome cabin was flung open and Norton burst in, cursing and swearing.

'Come on, you little doxy! I care not how sick you are—*now* we have a use for you!'

The wind, cutting as a knife, buffeted Lucinda as she stumbled up the steps on to the deck. She blinked in the bright winter light, dashed the hair out of her eyes and caught her breath. Away to the west the coast was no more than a dark smudge on the skyline. The grey water heaved beneath them, the ship creaking with each slap of the waves against its hull. The wind ripped through the mainsail above her head. It felt wild and exhilarating, and suddenly, for the first time, Lucinda could understand the irresistible lure of the sea. She took a deep breath of fresh, salty air.

'We can't outrun them, Captain,' the helmsman was saying, leaning on the wheel with increasing desperation. 'The *Defiance* is too fast—faster by far than we are. He's going to come around and block us.'

Norton swore. 'How in hell did he get away this time? Damn him, I *told* them where to find him—'

Lucinda spun around, ignoring the way Norton's hand tightened with such bruising intensity on her arm. Sure enough, the *Defiance* was there, just off the starboard bow, so close she could see the snarling dragon's head at the prow, drawing closer all the time with an inevitability that was causing fear to flare in Norton's eyes. And surely she could see Daniel—and was that not Owen Chance *with* him on the deck? Her spirits soared from misery to pure elation, and she laughed aloud.

Norton growled his anger and raised a hand to strike her, but before he could there was a whistling overhead, and a shout from one of the crew, then a terrible, splintering crash as the mainsail was struck squarely and started to fall like a tree felled in one blow. The ship checked, shuddered, and lost power, and the *Defiance* came alongside, almost close enough for her to jump from one ship to the other.

Norton, a knife in his hand, made a grab for Lucinda but she was too quick for him. She clutched at a coil of rope, tripping him up, and dived for cover behind a stack of crates. Bits of broken mast were falling all about them, and a second later she heard the helmsman's terrified squeal, 'Grenades! Glass grenades!'

There was the crack of gunpowder and the billow of smoke, followed by the smack of gunshot. Lucinda put her arms over her head, curled up, and prayed for her life. The *Saucy Helen* juddered again as the *Defiance* came closer alongside, and Daniel's crew lashed the two ships together before pouring over the sides to board.

Norton's pirates were fighting for their lives now, hand to hand, but against Daniel's crew and a company of soldiers they stood no chance. Peering around the edge of her hiding place, Lucinda saw Norton take a bullet in the chest, and covered her eyes.

'A clean death was too good for him,' a voice said beside her, and then she was in Daniel's arms, and he had wrapped a cloak about her, and she was clinging to him as he said, in a hard voice she hardly knew, 'Did he hurt you, Lucy? Tell me the truth. If any of these men so much as touched you then I swear I will kill them myself—'

'No,' Lucinda said, unsure if she was laughing or crying. 'No, I promise... I was too sick, and they were too drunk and... Oh, Daniel, I thought Chance had arrested you. I am so happy to see you...'

'Sorry about the grenades,' Daniel said. 'I saw you escape Norton and hide, so I thought we could risk it.'

'I don't mind,' Lucinda whispered. She pressed her face to the curve of his neck. 'I love you.'

Daniel took a breath to reply to her, but then she felt him stiffen slightly and, looking up, saw that Owen Chance had come across them.

'Mrs Melville.' He bowed. 'You are well?'

'Tolerably well, I thank you, Mr Chance.' Lucinda tried not to

laugh at the incongruity of greeting the Riding Officer as though
they were at a social occasion.

Chance nodded. 'Good. Norton is dead and the crew have sur-
rendered. Topsham is taking the ship into Felixstowe. I take it that
Holroyd will captain the *Defiance* in your absence, de Lancey?'

Daniel nodded. Watching, Lucinda sensed some sort of message
that she did not understand pass between the two men. Daniel loosed
her a little.

'Lucinda, sweetheart. I must go and help Chance sort matters out.
Do you wish to go below until we reach port?'

Lucinda shuddered. 'No, thank you! I shall stay here. I will be
quite well.'

Daniel gave her a quick kiss and walked away, and for the remainder of the time sailing into port she sat and watched the soldiers
round up the pirates, shackle them, and line them up on the deck
with admirable efficiency, ready to march them away to prison
when they landed. The lines to the *Defiance* were cut, and the little
black and gold ship slipped away from them, disappearing along the
line of the coast as they neared harbour. Daniel stayed on the *Saucy
Helen*, and Lucinda wondered a little at it, just as she wondered how
he had evidently come to some sort of agreement with Owen
Chance. But she was too tired and relieved to wonder too much, and
mostly she was content to sit there and watch him as he worked the
ship, admiring the grace and economy of movement with which he
undertook whatever job was required, a natural sailor, she now
realised, and in his element.

They came into Felixstowe, and the prisoners were disembarked
and marched away. Lucinda saw with a glad lift to her heart that the
carriage from Kestrel Court was drawn up on the quay. She stood
up, surprised to realise how stiff and cold she felt. She had been so
happy inside that she had not felt the discomfort outside, and mere
cold could certainly not quench her contentment. If matters were
now settled between Daniel and the authorities, as indeed they must
be, perhaps they could all return to Kestrel Court together. She re-

membered that Daniel's sister Rebecca and her husband Lucas were
due to arrive shortly, for the Christmas season, and her heart gave
a little skip of excitement. She knew that Rebecca had not seen
Daniel in years, but now, surely, all that might change? And she and
Daniel had much to discuss…

He was coming towards her now, to escort her onto the quay, and
she smiled with such vivid happiness to see him that she was sure
all the love and excited anticipation within her must show on her
face and she did not care who saw it.

Then she became aware that Daniel was not smiling in return.
Immediately behind him was Owen Chance, and behind him three
of the redcoats.

Something was very wrong. The smile faded from Lucinda's
eyes. Slowly, painfully, she looked from Daniel to Owen Chance's
stony face and back again. The soldiers were standing, waiting.

Daniel said to Chance, 'Please give us a moment,' and Chance
nodded and motioned with his head to the soldiers to stay back.

Daniel took Lucinda's hands in his.

Understanding burst on Lucinda, shattering all the hope and the
happiness and the excitement within her in one huge explosion of
grief.

'No,' she said, before Daniel could speak. 'No!'

She thought that she had shouted, but it came out as a whisper.
She knew now what was going to happen—but she did not *want* to
understand, did not want to accept it.

'No,' she said again. 'Tell me it isn't true.'

Daniel's face was ashen. She thought he looked so tired, and she
wanted to take him in her arms and hold him and comfort him, but
she could not. She knew she would never be able to now.

'It was the only way,' Daniel said. 'It was the only way I could
save you. I am sorry, Lucy. I have failed you again, but I have to
leave you. I gave Chance my word.'

'Don't say that,' Lucinda said fiercely. 'Don't say that you failed
me.' She felt so cold, so numb. She clung to his hands as the only

thing left to warm her. 'You offered your life to save mine,' she said. 'What more could you give me?'

'You are to have Allandale,' Daniel said. 'It is agreed. Listen to me, Lucy.' He drew her closer to him. He was dirty, and he smelled of smoke and gunpowder and sweat, and she went willingly into his arms, holding him tightly, as though to defy anyone ever to take him from her. He spoke softly, for her alone.

'I love you, Lucy. I will love you always. You are my wife in every way that matters, and you are to have Allandale and do the work there that I cannot. And even when I am gone you will know that I am with you—'

Lucinda made a small sound and buried her face against his shirt. She tried to draw strength from the feeling of his arms about her, for she was not at all sure that she would ever be strong enough to do as he asked and let him go.

'No,' she said brokenly. 'It isn't fair.' Anger rushed through her in a fierce tide. 'It isn't *fair* for them to condemn you as a criminal! Not when you have done so much to help them—'

'I have done plenty of things that were wrong,' Daniel said. 'And in the end that is what counts.' He kissed her hair. 'Now I have to go, sweet.'

He loosed her, gently but firmly, and she saw in his eyes the devastation and misery, and understood that this was the hardest thing he had ever had to do in his life and that he was not even sure he could do it. And she knew then that she had to help him. She straightened up and let him go, and the soldiers stepped forward to put him in chains. Cold loneliness ripped through her, leaving her heart in tatters, and she thought that she would never, ever be whole again.

Later she could not even remember how they got her off the ship, but down on the quayside Sally Kestrel was waiting with the carriage, to take her back to Midwinter. The Duchess said nothing at all, merely wrapping Lucinda in a thick cloak and bundling her inside. Lucinda was profoundly grateful that she was not expected to talk. Later, perhaps, she could speak to Sally about how she felt and what she was going to do with the rest of her life. She had a feeling that the Duchess of Kestrel would be the most understanding person in the world when it came to talking about lost love and lost hope, and how one might somehow forge something from the ruins and find a reason to live again. But not now. Not yet. She could not talk about it yet.

Early night was falling fast, and the winter blue had drained from the sky to leave it dull and grey. The journey back seemed interminable, but finally they were there. The flaring lights in the house made her eyes sting, and Eustacia was waiting, pale and questioning. Lucinda saw Sally shake her head, just once, and Stacey's face fell and she looked as though she wanted to cry.

There was the sound of voices, and Lucinda stopped and looked questioningly at Sally Kestrel.

'Is that—Rebecca?'

Sally nodded. 'They arrived this afternoon.'

Lucinda squared her shoulders. Rebecca was her oldest friend, but now she shrank from telling her what had happened to Daniel. She felt a huge, smothering guilt that she should be the cause of his capture and death. She could not bear to see Rebecca's grief.

Rebecca came into the hall, and for a moment they just stared at one another. To Lucinda she looked heartbreakingly like Daniel—both so dark, both with the same courage and gallant spirit. She could see that Rebecca had been crying, but now her eyes were dry, and there was resolution and acceptance in her face—as though she had always known it would come to this, that one day she would hear that Daniel was dead, or captured. Lucinda understood suddenly that it was news that Rebecca had always dreaded and yet somehow expected to hear.

And as Lucinda waited, terrified she would lose her friend as well as her lover all in the same day, Rebecca hurried forward, and caught her up in a hug that was so fierce Lucinda could not help but gasp.

'He did the right thing,' Rebecca whispered. 'Stacey told us what happened. Dearest Lucy, I am so sorry.'

And in the face of such generosity Lucinda felt her own grief break at last, and they clung to one another until Lucas Kestrel, with the presence of mind for which he was renowned, pushed a glass of brandy into each of their hands.

'Drink it up,' he said tersely. 'We know that Justin is up in London and will do what he can.' He raised his own glass in a toast. 'To Daniel de Lancey. The game is never over until the last counter has been played.'

Chapter 8

IT WAS Christmas Eve and another bright, clear winter's day, with a frost on the ground. Early in the afternoon, Lucinda was roused by the sound of a carriage clattering up the drive, and then Justin Kestrel's voice was heard in the hall and Sally called out to him in joyous greeting.

Lucinda, who had been sitting at the desk in her room, vainly trying to read, sat up a little straighter and smoothed the skirts of her gown with fingers that were shaking a little. In the fortnight since Daniel had been captured she had slept little and spent a great deal of time talking with Rebecca, and even more time hoping against silent hope that Lucas was right and there was something, anything, that Justin Kestrel could do to help Daniel's situation. But it did not look good. She knew there was no clemency for pirates. Justin had offered Daniel a pardon once before and Daniel had turned it down. This was not going to be a happy Christmas.

She heard laughter, quickly stilled, and the excited chatter of voices, and then running footsteps on the corridor outside her room before Sally and Rebecca burst in like a pair of excited schoolgirls.

'He's escaped!' Rebecca said. Her face was flushed pink with excitement, happy tears in her eyes. She grabbed Lucinda and danced her around the room. 'He escaped two days ago, apparently, whilst they were taking him to London for his trial!'

Lucinda, her heart soaring, glanced at Sally for confirmation. 'It's true,' Sally said. 'Don't ask how. I think that Owen Chance might have let him go, though he will never admit it if he did.' She laughed. 'Mind you, I think that Stacey would not have forgiven him had he not, so the poor man was caught whatever he did!'

Lucinda bit back an irrepressible grin. 'I hope that Mrs Saltire will relent now of her refusal to permit them to wed.' Stacey had been in shocking disgrace since breaking her engagement to Mr Leytonstone, and in even more trouble when rumours of a rather passionate embrace with Owen Chance had started to circulate in Woodbridge.

'She will,' Sally said. She gave her mischievous smile. 'I reminded her this morning that Mr Chance is related to the Olivers and also has a very rich uncle who has no direct heirs…'

'But never mind about Mr Chance for now!' Rebecca besought. She caught Lucinda's hand and pulled her down to sit on the bed. 'What are you going to do, Luce? Do you think Daniel will come looking for you? If he did, would you go with him?'

Lucinda sat down a little abruptly. In the soaring euphoria and relief of hearing about Daniel's escape she had had no thought for the future, but now she realised with a little lurch of dread that Daniel was still a fugitive and a condemned criminal, and that no doubt he would be sought all the more urgently now that he had escaped yet again.

'I hope he does not come back to find me,' she said, with a little shiver. 'I could not bear for him to risk capture just for me.'

Rebecca's face fell. 'But, Lucy, what will you do?'

Lucinda looked from Rebecca's face to Sally's. 'I will do as Daniel asked me,' she said, 'and go to Allandale, if I may.' She saw the understanding in Sally's face, for only that morning she had confided in the Duchess the secret that she had been hugging to her heart—that she was now almost certain she was going to have

Daniel's child. Sally had been immensely comforting, extremely practical, and not in the least judgemental, but she had agreed with Lucinda that she should be well away from Midwinter when the pregnancy started to show.

'I am sure that can be arranged,' Sally Kestrel said, clearing her throat. 'I know it was one of the matters Justin was attending to in London, Lucy, so perhaps you would wish to speak to him of that? He has asked to see you anyway, when you are ready. He has something to give to you.'

Left alone, Lucinda scrubbed at her eyes to wipe away the smudges of her own tears, and moved over to the window to stare out into the dark. She remembered the night—was it only six weeks before?—when she had gone out to look for Stacey and instead saved Daniel from capture by Owen Chance. She wondered where, in all that dark night and darker sea, he was now.

As she walked slowly down the stairs to see the Duke, she reflected that no doubt Justin had done his best to secure leniency for Daniel, but that it was probably irrelevant now that he was once more a fugitive from justice.

Justin Kestrel stood up as she was shown into the library, and gestured towards the decanter on the table.

'Would you care for a glass of brandy, Mrs Melville?'

Lucinda smiled and shook her head. 'No, thank you, Your Grace. I think I may need to keep a clear mind.'

Justin inclined his head. 'I hope you do not object if I do?'

'Of course not.'

Justin raised his glass to her. 'To…the future, Mrs Melville? You have heard, no doubt, that Lord Allandale has escaped custody?'

Lucinda nodded. It felt strange to hear Daniel referred to thus. Her throat felt dry. 'I have heard.'

Justin reached for a packet that was resting on the desk in front of him. 'There is something I should like you to have,' he said. He appeared to be weighing his words. 'Should you ever see Lord Allandale again,' he said, 'I would like you to give it to him.'

Sensation pricked between Lucinda's shoulderblades suddenly, excitement vivid and alive in her blood. She looked at the Duke. He was watching her with a faintly quizzical smile, and his eyebrows lifted in slight but unmistakable question.

'Of course,' she said. 'I will do my best. But... I am not sure that is very likely, Your Grace. Lord Allandale is still a wanted criminal, after all.'

'Of course,' Justin agreed affably. He got to his feet and went over to the long windows that led out onto the terrace and faced the sea.

'Where, after all,' Lucinda continued, 'could such a man be sought? It would be well-nigh impossible to find him.'

Justin drew back the heavy red velvet curtains and gazed out thoughtfully into the night. 'Who can say?' he concurred. 'A man would have to be mad—or in love, perhaps, which almost amounts to the same thing—to go back to the very same place he frequented before.' He turned to look at her. 'The tide turns very soon, I believe.'

Lucinda got to her feet. 'Then if you would excuse me, Your Grace?'

'Naturally.' Justin Kestrel smiled. 'Do not forget the packet. A Christmas present—or a wedding present, perhaps?'

Lucinda blushed. 'Thank you,' she said. 'If you could give my thanks and best wishes to everyone, I should be most grateful.'

On impulse she reached up and kissed him. He seemed pleased.

'I hope it will not be too long before we all meet up again,' he murmured.

Excitement sped Lucinda's feet as she hurried up the staircase. She had to trust Justin Kestrel now, even if she did not quite understand what he was entrusting to her. But he had made his instructions quite plain, and now she had to have the courage to fulfil them.

Once in her room, she dragged a heavy portmanteau out from under the bed, but then stood looking at it in a sort of despair. If she were to go it would be with nothing at all. She had no time.

The clock in the hall struck the quarter. The door of the drawing room opened and she heard a snatch of conversation.

'Where is Lucinda? I thought she might join us this evening…'
The door closed.

In sudden desperation Lucinda grabbed her writing box. Rebecca, Sally and Stacey particularly—they all deserved something more than to be abandoned so abruptly. For who could tell when she would see them again? But if she left a note there could be no going back.

For a moment she hesitated. She was running away to an uncertain future—running away from the life she knew and from all that was familiar. Almost she did not dare. And yet… And yet…

If she had understood Justin Kestrel aright, Daniel might even now be waiting for her—and surely a life with him, whatever form it might take, was a thousand times better than any life without him?

'I do believe that I would give up everything else in my life just to have you,' she had said to Daniel that night he had held her in his arms and their child had been conceived. Yet now she hesitated, unsure of her courage, unsure of his love.

Go, she thought, suddenly fierce. *He said he would love you for ever. He loves you now.*

Anger overtook her then—anger at her own weakness and her lack of faith. She jumped up and grabbed the quill.

Two minutes later and it was done. She ran down the stairs, leaving the note on the silver tray in the hall and taking a lantern from the sconce. The door slammed behind her. The snow of the drive crunched beneath her slippers. Within a minute her feet were soaking and frozen. No matter. Daniel had told her that he would take her barefoot, and now she was asking him to do precisely that.

Branches snagged at her hair, pulling it loose from its pins, as she ran down the path to the creek. Dusk was falling already, the short winter day fading into dark. Her heart was thumping painfully now, her breath coming in short gasps as much from fear as exertion. If the tide had already turned… She could not bear to think of it.

The path narrowed as it reached the creek, trees pressing close. She stopped on the edge of the pool. The tide was full and the *Defiance* was gone.

Catching her breath on a sob, Lucinda sped along the path that bordered the water. The frosty air stung her cheeks. Her shawl caught on a bramble and she let it go. The creek was widening, a shining ribbon that caught the last white winter light and momentarily dazzled her eyes. A heron rose, flapping from the reed beds. As the trees fell back and Lucinda came out into the bay she saw the ship at last, a quarter of a mile out, its riding lights pinpricks against the dusk.

It was stupid, it was pointless, it was *hopeless*, but she ran out into the bay until the water reached her waist and the sudden cold knocked all the breath out of her body.

It was then that she realised she could not swim, and that if she carried on she would soak whatever was in the packet Justin Kestrel had given her.

She stumbled, the muddy seabed catching her ankles, trying to pull her down. A little wave buffeted her, then a stronger one, and she staggered.

This was so foolish. A part of her was watching, incredulous that she was going to die running after a pirate ship on a dark night in December. Would they ever find her body? And if they did, what would they say?

She always seemed so sensible... Who would have thought it?

This time when the wave hit her she went down, flailing, and the water closed over her head and she thought it was the end.

But something—someone—caught her tightly and dragged her, kicking and struggling, to the surface. A hook tangled in her gown, pulling her in the most undignified and unceremonious way possible into a longboat.

'What the *devil* are you doing here?'

Daniel. She felt so weak with relief that she almost cried.

'I was coming to find you.'

In the light of the ship's lantern she could see that he looked furious. And then, miraculously, he looked so happy she almost cried again. 'And I was coming to find you,' he said.

He was pushing the wet hair away from her face. She noticed that his hand was not quite steady. 'You must be mad for trying to swim, Lucy. You could have drowned! You *were* drowning!'

'I know.' Foolishly, she smiled. 'Thank you for saving me.'

He kissed her, and she was aware of nothing but the warm beat of his blood against hers and a heady relief and happiness so acute that she wanted never to let it go.

Daniel released her gently. 'We have to get you back to the ship, Lucy, before you die of the cold.'

That foolish smile was still on her face, she knew. 'I feel very warm,' she said. 'I am absolutely fine.'

Daniel laughed, but he turned and gave an order and there was the rattle of a chain and the splash of an oar as the longboat turned. The boat rocked dangerously. Lucinda felt sick, and wondered if she would ever be cured of it or if the rest of her life would be spent retching in a chamber pot. She found she did not care. Daniel was here, and his arms were about her, and he was holding her as though he would never let her go, and that was enough.

The cold was starting to bite now. Her teeth were chattering so much that she could not stop, and when someone wrapped a blanket about her, her fingers were so numb she let it slip away. Daniel took the blanket and rubbed her hard with it until her arms felt raw.

'Ouch! Stop! I will have no skin left.'

Daniel did not reply. He pulled her close, so that his chin was resting on the top of her head and she could hear the steady beat of his heart. He did not need to speak. They held one another in wordless contentment.

Once on the ship, in the privacy of the cabin she had seen once before, Daniel poured hot soup down her throat rather than brandy, and she remembered at last the packet of papers that Justin Kestrel had given her.

'The ink will have run,' she said ruefully, passing over the sopping bundle. 'I am so sorry, Daniel. I do not know what was in them.'

'He wrapped them in oilskin,' Daniel said. His eyes were gleaming. 'He must have known that you were going to come looking for me.'

'Well,' Lucinda said, 'he did rather encourage me.'

There was a crackle as Daniel unwrapped the papers. Then he went very still. Lucinda looked up. In the candlelight Daniel's face was grave.

'What does it say?'

'It is a Royal Pardon,' Daniel said, a little gruffly. 'And an offer of a commission in the Navy.' He cleared his throat. 'His Majesty writes that he needs good sailors, and it would be a monstrous waste wilfully to lose one, so he hopes that I will have reconsidered the offer that Justin made me.' He gave a reluctant laugh. 'He also states that it reflects badly on the country for a peer of the realm to be an attainted criminal, and urges me to take up my title and lands and choose a wife.' A smile lit his eyes. 'And as a final sign of goodwill he asks for a bottle of what he calls my "rather fine French brandy" before I give up my former ways.'

Lucinda put her soup spoon down slowly. 'Then I do not understand,' she said. 'If the Duke of Kestrel knew that you were going to be pardoned, why did he not tell Mr Chance, so that you did not have to go to the trouble of escaping?'

Daniel smiled ruefully. 'The last time Justin Kestrel offered me a pardon I turned him down flat, because I thought I could not give up my way of life.' He held out Justin's note to her. 'He says that this time he wanted me to have a choice. He knew that abandoning my life as a privateer would be difficult for me after all this time, but even so, I think he knew what my final choice would be.'

Lucinda was still, captured by the look in his eyes.

'And what is your choice?'

Daniel thrust his hands into his pockets and turned away. 'I won't pretend that it will be easy for me, Luce,' he said. 'I have lived like this for over ten years, and a part of me is desolate to think of giving it up, but…' He turned towards her. 'I love you, and I would give my life for you, and you are too precious and important to live the life of a pirate's wife. So…will you be the wife of a Navy captain instead?'

'Yes,' Lucinda said. A tear sparkled on her lashes and fell into the soup. 'No doubt I will feel sick every moment I spend on a ship, but I will do that for you. And in between our travels we will have Allandale, so at least I shall spend some of my life on dry land!'

'My poor darling!' Daniel came across to her. 'Do you feel ill now?'

'No,' Lucinda said, smiling radiantly. 'But we are not moving at the moment, are we?'

Daniel looked at her quizzically. 'I hate to contradict you, sweetheart, but we have been sailing from the first moment you stepped onto my ship.'

'Oh!' Lucinda raised her eyebrows. 'Then perhaps I am cured!'

'I hope so.' Daniel took her hand. 'You know this will not be easy, Luce. A lot of people will disapprove that I have been pardoned, and will talk scandal even once it is spread abroad that I worked for the Crown. I do not want the gossips to hurt you.'

'It will be a great deal easier for me to deal with if I have you at my side,' Lucinda said. 'To have had to raise our son or daughter on my own would have been a horrid fate, and that really would have given the scandalmongers cause for comment.' She stopped, smiling mischievously as she saw the thunderstruck look in his eyes. 'Oh, did I not mention it, Daniel? I do believe that I am expecting our child—' She caught her breath on a gasp as he grabbed her and kissed her hard, and then put her from him with sudden care, as though she were spun china.

'You need not fear to kiss me—if you wish it,' she added. 'I will not break.' She smiled radiantly at him. 'And I am very happy.'

'I must get Holroyd to marry us at once,' Daniel said. 'He has captained this ship, so he is permitted to perform the ceremony.' He stood up, and would have strode across to the cabin door at once to summon his lieutenant, but Lucinda caught his hand and pulled him back down beside her on the bunk.

'I would be delighted to be married at sea,' she murmured. 'It is only appropriate. And I am relieved that you wish to make an honest woman of me sooner rather than later, Daniel. But could you… perhaps…make a dishonest woman of me first?'

She watched the amusement light his eyes as he leaned closer to kiss her.

'What did you have in mind?' he asked, his lips a hair's breadth away from her own.

Lucinda put a hand on the nape of his neck and brought his mouth down to meet hers.

'This,' she whispered.

The Duke and Duchess of Kestrel and their guests were taking dinner when the butler brought Lucinda's note in on a silver tray.

'A message for Miss Saltire,' he said, blank-faced.

Stacey unfolded it, perused it swiftly, and let out a piercing and unladylike shriek.

'How famous! Cousin Sally! Mama! Lucinda has run away. She has gone to sea with Daniel de Lancey!'

Mrs Letitia Saltire fainted dead away, and had to be revived with smelling salts. Lucas kissed Rebecca, and Justin Kestrel and his wife exchanged a smile of quiet satisfaction.

Sally Kestrel took the note that Stacey proffered, a slight smile on her lips.

'She was certainly in a hurry. I can barely read her hand.'

'Oh, Sally,' Mrs Letitia Saltire said brokenly. 'What a terrible scandal! How could she? Once was bad enough, but at least we were able to *pretend* she was blameless that time. I cannot think what has come over her! She always seemed so sensible! Who would have thought it?'

The Duchess laughed. 'I, for one,' she said.

Mrs Saltire shook her head. 'Eloping! At her age! Nine and twenty, and a widow into the bargain! *What* can one say? What can one *think*?'

The Duchess smiled at her husband. 'I found eloping to be rather fun,' she said, giving Justin a little secret smile. 'And I know what I think. Good for Lucinda!'

'And a very Happy Christmas to them both,' Justin added.

'Oh,' Sally said, 'I think they are like to be *very* happy.'

She got to her feet, crossed to the window and drew back the curtain. The moon was full, and its light turned the water in the bay to silver, illuminating the tiny ship in shades of black and white. Then the wind caught its sails and the *Defiance* turned and slipped away, and the night was still.

* * * * *

A SMUGGLER'S TALE

Margaret McPhee

Author Note

Christmas is a time of year when we think of our families and those we love. We want to spend time with them and for them to be happy. We would do a lot for our families, especially at Christmas. It was with this in mind that I found myself thinking of a story in which a woman and a man find themselves caught up in a dangerous situation in a tiny Devonshire harbor in the dead of a December night. Both are there because they are trying to help their families, albeit in very different ways. I wanted to give the woman, whose life is filled with responsibility and hardship, something special for Christmas. I also wanted the man, from the opposite end of the spectrum who has experienced the hedonistic excesses of life and the misery that it can bring, to find happiness. So weaving these strands together created Francesca and Jack's story.

The sea has always held a fascination for me. Inadvertently, I think that it manages to sneak its way into most of my books. But for Francesca and Jack there was no sneaking required for the sea plays a critical part in their story, in which they become involved in the murky underworld of smuggling. Francesca and Jack's is a tale of a long-ago Devonshire Christmas, of smuggling and the sea, but most of all of love—a smuggler's tale that I hope brings a little happiness to you.

With very best wishes for a Merry Christmas and a Happy New Year.

Margaret

Chapter 1

Devon, December 1803

THE night was cold and dark as Francesca moved stealthily through the shadows. Every now and again the tiny sliver of the new moon was revealed behind the drifting cover of cloud. A smugglers' moon. Francesca shivered at that. Her worst suspicions of her brother were growing stronger by the minute. She followed him right down into the harbour, hiding herself behind a great pile of lobster pots that had been stacked close to the tall stone harbour wall, and watched Tom head down the walkway that led to where the boat was moored. She did not need to read the *Swift*'s name to know Tom's game. She knew one of the Buckleys' luggers when she saw it. There could be little dispute as to his intent now. She moved to stop him. A noise sounded behind. She made to turn, but a hand snaked round to clamp firm against her mouth. She felt herself hauled backwards, her back pressed hard against a man's body, her arms pinioned to her sides.

His breath tickled against her ear. 'Shh, hold quiet, now. I mean you no harm.' She could smell the clean scent of him.

Francesca's heart raced. Shock had momentarily paralysed her, and now fear trickled icy through her veins. He was stepping slowly backwards, retreating from the walkway and the boats, dragging her with him. She threw herself back hard against him, trying to off-balance him while simultaneously struggling to free her arms, but her assailant was too big, too strong. Nothing she did seemed to make any difference other than to make him move faster towards the iron gate that was cut within the harbour wall. She tried to scream, but his hand tightened and all that came out were muffled mews.

'Quiet, girl,' he whispered, 'if you want to live.'

In a matter of seconds they would be through the gateway and out on to the road that lay beyond and the dark, desolate landscape that surrounded it. She increased her struggles, and as he adjusted his grip to hold her she bit the hand that was gagging her mouth, and tasted warm metallic blood on her tongue.

'Hell's teeth!' she heard him curse, and just for a second his hand was gone.

A second was all that Francesca needed. Tom would hear her. Tom would come to save her. She did not think any further than that. She cried her brother's name as loud as she could—or at least that was what she tried to do. 'To—'

The hand stifled the word before it was even formed. There was nothing but the wind and the distant roar of the sea and the rhythmic rush of nearby waves. Francesca thought that her cry had not been heard, that the stranger would drag her out of the harbour to disappear for ever, and no one would be any the wiser. She could not believe that this was happening—that a man could have crept so silently upon her without her hearing. Then she heard it: the clatter of men's boots running, the sound of voices, Tom's amongst them, and she knew that she would be saved after all. Relief flooded through her and she thanked God.

'Came from over 'ere,' said one.

'Can't see anything,' said a voice she recognised as her brother's.

'Well, bloody look harder!' said another.

A dark shape emerged from around the pile of lobster pots. She saw the glint of silver as a cloud drifted to expose the pale light of the moon.

'What have we here, then?' The quietness of the voice did not detract from its menace. She could see that the man who spoke was tall and thin, with white hair. In his hand was a black walking cane topped in silver.

Francesca felt the sudden stillness in the man's body against which she was pressed. His hand gripped tighter over her mouth, and suddenly he was walking her forward, towards the lobster pots and the men that had come to stand silently by the side of the pile to watch. 'Look what I've found,' he said, and this time it wasn't a whisper. She noticed how well spoken he was. It was an educated voice, a gentleman's accent.

Four men stood looking at her, Tom amongst them, his face pale in the moonlight. Her eyes locked to his, imploring. He looked younger than his eighteen years, and the shock in his expression was plain to see.

'Dispose of her,' said the man with the cane. 'We haven't got time for this. The tide's right to sail now.' His voice was polished, another gentleman, and she wondered exactly with what Tom had got himself involved.

'No!' Tom said, a little too forcefully.

Francesca saw the man with the cane turn his gaze to her brother.

Tom was looking nervous. 'She's just a girl; she won't say anything.'

'Not with her throat slit, she won't,' said a small, fierce-eyed man.

'Mr White's right and so's Weasel,' said another man at the back of the group. 'We can't risk anythin' muckin' this up. This is the Christmas haul. There's too much at stake.'

'Too much at stake, indeed,' said the man with the cane.

Tom took a step towards her and suddenly Francesca was more afraid than she had ever been—for she knew that it was not only her own life that was at risk now, but Tom's too. 'You can't do that. She's—'

But the man whose arm was still wrapped around her, holding her in place, did not let Tom finish. 'The last thing we need is for the constable to start nosing about down here.'

'Then what do we do?' asked the small man who went by the name of Weasel.

'Let her go,' said Tom.

'So she can tell everyone what she's seen? I think not,' said the man with the walking cane. 'I'm getting the feeling that you might be in the wrong game here, Linden. This is for men, not lily-livered boys.'

'The solution is simple,' said the voice behind Francesca. 'We take her with us.' Francesca swallowed hard.

'A woman aboard ship is bad luck,' someone muttered.

'And the riding officer waiting here on our return isn't?' said the man holding her, and she could hear the sarcasm in his tone.

Weasel sniffed and the contents of his nose rattled. 'What do you want to do, Mr White?' He turned expectantly to the man with the cane.

The man leaned heavily upon his cane. 'As Mr Black said, we take her with us. Let us move, gentlemen, if we are to catch our tide.' He gestured his cane towards Francesca and the man who held her. 'After you, Mr Black.'

'Thank you, Mr White,' said Mr Black. It was as if they were playing out some foolish game.

Francesca found herself being half walked, half carried down the gangway towards the *Swift*. She did not struggle; she was wise enough to realise the futility in that. Instead she conserved her energy for whatever might happen aboard the *Swift*. She had the horrible feeling that she was going to need every last ounce of it.

Almost as soon as they were on the boat, the *Swift*'s ropes were untied and she slipped quietly out of Lannacombe's tiny harbour. The tide was high. The wind was in their favour. Up on deck men were busy at the sails and the helm. Below deck, where the others took her, a half-closed lantern swung from the low ceiling, casting shadows all around. In the centre was a shabby table that had been bolted to the floor, around which had been placed boxes and half-casks as makeshift chairs. It was on to one of these boxes that Francesca found herself dumped.

Mr White stood opposite, leaning on his cane, watching her. She could see now that despite his cane he was not an old man at all. His face was thin to the point of being gaunt, but unlined, his eyes were pale but alert, his hair not white but blond. In the background two or three of the crew hovered.

'Bind and gag her, and stick her through there. We'll deal with her once we're clear of the coast.'

She heard the man standing behind her move.

'Not feeling squeamish over manhandling a woman, are you, Mr Black?'

She heard a low laugh behind her. 'I've felt many things over women, squeamish, however, is not one of them.'

The man with the cane laughed.

'You did promise me an especially entertaining night.'

'I did indeed,' said the man with the cane.

'And a good return on my investment.'

'A very good return, Mr Black. Mark my words.'

'I'll do that,' said Mr Black, and then he moved round to stand before her, a piece of rope dangling loose in his hands.

She saw him then for the first time, this Mr Black. He was in his mid to late twenties, his hair dark and straight and cut short, his face clean-shaven. Beneath the dim flicker of the lantern light her eyes travelled swiftly over his features, which were strong and regular and intensely masculine: a chiselled chin, cut square in the strong line of his jaw; a hard mouth, high cheekbones, and eyes so dark as to appear black. He wore an air of lazy arrogance. Undoubtedly a man of the *Ton,* a man of wealth, despite the shabby attire in which he was clothed. Undeniably handsome, in a roguish sort of way. And he was a villain—a part of this group of thugs into which her brother had fallen. She shivered.

'Come along, our little spy,' he said, and took hold of her elbow. He guided her through to what seemed to be some kind of large cabin, leaving the door open behind him so that the light spilled through from where Mr White sat, twiddling his cane. Then he set about tying her wrists together behind her back, checking that the rope was not so tight as to cut into her flesh. He sat her down, bound her ankles, and produced a clean white handkerchief from his pocket, which he began to fold to form a long strip.

Francesca's eyes opened wide at that. 'There is no need to gag me. I will not cry out.'

'You should have thought of that back in the harbour.'

'I shall not be able to breathe with that around my mouth.'

'You shall breathe very well, I assure you.'

'Please.' It was bad enough being trussed like a chicken. The thought of being gagged brought a feeling of panic.

He looked at her then, with those black eyes of his, and for a moment she thought that he would heed her plea. 'You have very sharp teeth, miss,' he said, 'I would not risk you biting me again.'

His voice was arrogant and uncaring, a stark contrast to what she read in his eyes and the touch of his hands. His fingers were gentle beneath her chin as he unfastened the ribbons of her bonnet and set it down on the floor by her side. They were gentle too against her cheek as he tied the handkerchief around her mouth. He looked at her a moment longer, then he rose and walked away towards the lantern light and the room beyond. The door shut behind him, leaving Francesca sitting alone in the darkness, worrying over her mama who, tomorrow morning, would find not only her son gone but her eldest daughter too. Worrying too that, instead of saving her brother, she had just made things a whole lot worse.

Mr Black, or Lord Jack Holberton as he was in truth, sipped from his hip flask of brandy, knowing that this evening had come close to ruin because of a slip of a girl who had shown up spying on them at Lannacombe Harbour. Ten months' work almost lost and a girl's life with it too, and the night had barely begun. He raked a hand through his hair at the thought.

Lord Edmund Grosely, or Mr White, as he was calling himself, waited until the other men had disappeared up the ladder that led to the upper deck. 'Mr Black.' He glanced towards the retreating foot-steps. 'Feeling lucky?'

'Naturally,' said Jack with his usual arrogance. 'Am I ever anything but?'

Edmund laughed. 'That's what I like about you,' he said. 'That and your money.'

Jack smiled and lounged on a half-cask.

'What do you think of the clothes?'

Jack surveyed his shabby fisherman's attire. 'They make a change from Cork Street or Savile Row, I suppose.'

'If we're stopped tonight then we stay in the background and keep our mouths shut. Weasel knows what to do.'

Jack cocked an eyebrow.

'One word from our mouths and the game's up. There's no fish-erman that sounds like us.'

'True.' Jack gave a half-smile and took another swig of brandy from his silver patterned hip flask. 'But venturers do.'

'Exactly.' Edmund drank from his own flask. 'They would know us for what we are. I don't normally come out on the trips—Buckley's trustworthy enough to do the run himself—but, as I said, the good captain seems to have taken himself off to God only knows where. Weasel can sail the vessel well enough, but I don't trust him with the rest of our business.'

'Hence our little jolly this evening.'

'I'd hardly call it that.'

'What, then, would you call it?'

'A necessity. I don't like risking my anonymity, but I like risking my money even less.'

'Life's a bore without risk.' Jack examined his nails.

'It's even more of a bore without money.'

'I wouldn't know about that,' said Jack. 'Besides, I thought when it came to money that Harrow funded you well enough—better than my father does me.'

'My father's a tight-fisted bastard, hoarding it all to pass on to my brother. David will inherit the lot. I'll get nothing. But then you know all about the injustice of primogeniture, don't you?'

Jack gave a small cynical smile. 'You might say that.'

'And life's little pleasures all come at a cost.'

'Especially in Mayfair,' said Jack.

'You heard about that, then?' said Edmund.

'The whole of London has heard.' Jack laughed, then looked at Edmund slyly. 'Three thousand and a house in Mayfair is a lot to spend on an opera singer, even if she is a pocket Venus. She must be good.'

'She's very good indeed.'

'Doesn't Harrow ask any questions?'

'The old man thinks I'm lucky on the tables.'

'He's not wrong. I saw you clean out young Jenkins in Brooks's last week.'

Edmund nodded. 'Jenkins is a fool.' He smiled at Jack. 'There's more money to be made in this game than at the gaming tables.'

'And more risk,' said Jack.

'They'd not imprison me. The old man would see to that. He might hate the ground on which I stand, but he'll not see a blight on the family name. If it came to it he'd pull every string he could. I'd get a slap on the wrist and nothing more.'

'And what of the men here?'

'The Buckleys look after their own.' Edmund smiled. 'And *you've* no need to worry, because for all that you're quite the worst son a man might wish for, Flete'll not see anything happen to you. He'd hush it up as much as my father.'

'No doubt he would,' said Jack, and something of the arrogance slipped from his face.

'You needn't look like that, Holberton.'

Jack looked up sharply at the use of his real name.

'Forgive me,' muttered Edmund. 'Besides, *Mr Black*—' he stressed the name '—we're not about to be caught. We'll pick up the brandy, get it off our hands as soon as we get back, and have a lovely bloody time at Christmas spending it. I'm taking Jeanette to Yorkshire. You're welcome to come and spend Christmas with us. Bring one or two little ladybirds.'

'A Christmas of drink and lightskirts?' said Jack.

'Unless you'd prefer to spend it with Flete and the rest of your family?'

'Not likely.' Jack yawned. 'Did you mean it when you said I was the worst son a man might wish for?'

'Afraid so,' said Edmund. 'You make *me* look good, and that's saying something.'

Jack took another swig of brandy and looked rather pleased. He raised the hip flask to Edmund. 'Here's to errant sons and a Christmas to remember.'

'I'll drink to that,' said Edmund.

The two men laughed.

Francesca wriggled her hands against the ropes that bound them. The man they called Mr Black had not tied them that tight. She reckoned that she might even be able to free herself from them eventually. She peered around the hold, trying to see through the darkness, but it was useless. The thin rim of yellow light that surrounded the door did not extend far enough to illuminate her surroundings. From beyond the door came the hum of voices and the occasional laugh. She strained to listen, but the talk was little more that a low-pitched murmur that was not discernible over the slap of the waves against the body of the boat and the howl of the wind. The stench of fish and damp and tar surrounded her. The floor was dank and hard. She leaned to her right-hand-side, resting against something large and solid and wooden. She thought she had seen fishing nets heaped over in the far corner before Mr Black had closed the door behind him, and she wondered if that was where the smell was coming from.

The rope around her wrists was now loose enough that she managed to pull it lower and work her fingers into the knots. She was still busy with the knots when she heard the doorknob turn. Francesca froze.

The door creaked slowly open. She held her breath and stared at the sudden flood of light. A figure crept quietly through the door, a half-shielded lantern in his hand, a small blade glinting in the other. Her heart began to beat fast and hard. The door closed quietly behind him.

'Tom!' She tried to call, but the word just came out as a muffled noise behind the handkerchief.

'Shh!' he whispered, and came quickly towards her.

He set the knife down upon the floor and pulled the gag from her mouth.

'Untie me.'

'No.' He shook his head. 'There's not much time,' he said. 'There's no way off this boat—at least not alive, Fran—until we're back at Lannacombe. If I untie you they'll know I did it, and we'll be in even more trouble than we are already.'

'Oh, Tom, what on earth were you thinking of, getting involved with the Buckleys? And who are those gentlemen?'

A closed look came over his face and he answered only her first question. 'We need the money, Francesca—especially with Christmas coming.'

'Lord, Tom! They're villains. You're risking too much. What do you think it would do to Mama were you to end up with a knife in your back?'

'It would all have been fine if you hadn't showed up at the harbour. Damn it, Francesca, you've no idea what you've done.'

'Tell them I'm your sister. No matter what I think of the wrongs of this evening, I'm not about to report my own brother to the Revenue. They'll see the truth in that.'

Tom rubbed an agitated hand against his chin. 'It isn't quite as simple as that.'

'What do you mean?'

'I would that you had not followed me on this night above all others.' He sighed, and the soft yellow lantern light showed the worry on his face.

'Tom,' she said softly. 'We will get through this.'

Tom wrapped an arm around her. 'I only hope that you're right, Fran. I only hope that you're right.'

They heard no noise, nothing to warn them before the door was thrown open. The man simply stepped into the hold and shut the door quietly behind him.

'Well, well, well,' he said softly. 'Very cosy.'

Tom jumped back in fright, his fingers instinctively snatching up his knife.

Francesca looked up to see the tall dark figure of Mr Black walking towards them. Fear rippled through her.

On seeing Mr Black, Tom sheathed the knife and seemed to relax.

'Who is she, Linden? Your sweetheart? Your lover?'

'No!' Francesca and Tom said in unison.

The colour that flooded Tom's cheeks was evident even in the lantern light. 'Nothing like that.'

'Then what?'

'My sister,' Tom said with a sigh. 'Francesca's my sister.'

'What the hell was she doing in the harbour?'

'I wanted to stop him getting himself into any kind of trouble.' Francesca met Mr Black's gaze from her position on the floor.

Tom glanced rather sheepishly at Mr Black. 'She's always been rather over-protective of me.'

'He means that I can tell when he's up to no good,' said Francesca.

Tom ignored her. 'I swear she knows nothing of this night.'

'She does now,' said Mr Black.

'If you think that I'll speak of what I've seen, then you're mistaken. I give you my word that I'll say nothing, sir.'

'Your word?' Mr Black raised one eyebrow. 'And you think that makes everything all right?'

She felt her anger rise at his mocking tone. 'If I say anything of this then I will be implicating Tom. Why would I do that? I'm not about to put my own brother at risk.'

'I'd say you've already done a good job of that, Miss Linden.' Mr Black made no effort to mask his irritation.

'What shall we do, sir?' Tom rubbed at his chin. 'Tell Mr White about her?'

'You think that telling White will protect her?' There was an edge to Mr Black's voice.

'I hoped…'

'You've not a hope in hell,' he snapped. 'If you go to White with your story, you're both as good as dead. And you'll jeopardise other issues, Linden. You don't need me to tell you that.'

'What else can we do?' Francesca could hear the desperation in her brother's voice.

'We can buy your sister time.'

Francesca and Tom waited for an explanation.

'I'll keep her from White and the others.' All trace of Mr Black's lazy drawl had vanished. 'No matter that it may appear otherwise, she'll be safe. And for God's sake don't show the slightest regard for her welfare, if you don't want White guessing the truth. Do you understand?'

'Yes, sir,' said Tom.

'Now, get out of here before your absence is noticed.'

Tom hesitated. 'The rest of this night…'

'Proceeds as planned,' finished Mr Black.

Tom glanced towards Francesca. 'Do as he says, Fran.'

'Go,' Mr Black commanded.

Tom turned and hurried from the hold.

The door shut with a quiet click, leaving Francesca alone with Mr Black.

'Now, Miss Linden,' he said. He crouched down close before her. 'Have you no sense in your head? What did you think would happen, following him alone in the dead of night to the harbour?'

He sounded angry, and nothing like he had when he had spoken to Mr White.

His words touched a chord in Francesca, but she wasn't about to admit any such thing. She stared at him defiantly. 'I would have stopped him had it not been for you.'

'So your predicament is my fault, is it?' His voice was hard and his eyes blazed into hers.

Francesca looked away. 'No. But had you not tried to abduct me in the harbour…'

'*Abduct* you?' He raised an eyebrow at that. 'Was that what I was doing?'

She ignored his question and regarded him suspiciously. 'Why would you help us, sir, if Mr White is your friend and you are involved in this…this…'

'Gentlemen's revenue trip,' he supplied.

She said nothing.

'Let's just say, whatever my interests are, they do not stretch to slitting young women's throats and throwing them overboard.'

Francesca felt a spasm of fear at his words but she kept her face impassive. 'What do you propose to do, sir?'

'Have my wicked way with you, Miss Linden,' he said smoothly.

She could not prevent the gasp that escaped her. 'This is no time for jests.'

'I'm not jesting.' He looked at her straight-faced.

'Do not be ridiculous, sir!' She felt the shock rolling over her in waves.

'You will not play the harlot even to save your life and that of your brother?'

She stared at him in disbelief. 'You will trade our lives to bed me?' she said slowly, and it seemed that her throat was constricting.

'No.'

'No? Then what…' Her voice raised in anguish.

'Shh!' he said. 'It will be a pretence only—a play-act.'

'But…'

He laid one finger gently against her lips. 'It's the only chance, Miss Linden…for you and for Tom.'

Her eyes held his.

'All we need do is convince White that matters between us are intimate, and then we will be left quite alone.'

'Why—?'

'No time for questions, Miss Linden,' he said. 'Do I save you or not?'

What choice did she have? Play Mr Black's game, or risk Tom's life and her own? Her only alternative was to throw herself on Mr White's mercy—but she had heard what had been said of that, and Tom had seemed to trust this man. She thought of Mr White's cruel pale gaze and looked up into the dark eyes of the man before her. In them she thought she could see compassion and urgency and truth. Something tightened in her stomach, and in that instant she made her decision. She nodded.

He untied her hands and ankles, stuffing the rope in his pocket, then reclaimed the handkerchief that was hanging loosely around her throat.

A noise sounded: the tread of feet coming down the ladder. Mr Black took her hand and helped her to her feet.

'Truly a knight in shining armour,' she said, the irony heavy in her tone.

The footsteps walked across the floor, coming ever closer.

'Hardly,' he murmured and, reaching across, pulled her against him.

One hand slid against her waist, the other secured the nape of her neck. His mouth swooped over hers, and he kissed her as she had never been kissed before. This was no peck on the cheek. Indeed, it was barely a kiss at all, but a ravishment—a possession, almost. His lips were enticing and insistent and demanding all at once. Francesca was completely and utterly shocked.

She thrust her hands against his chest, intent on freeing herself, but the embrace in which she found herself was unyielding. The blood surged through her with a frenzy, her heart beating so hard and fast that she was sure it would leap from her chest. His mouth continued its sensuous massage against hers, luring her against her will, beguiling her, stripping the very soul from her body. She tried to turn her face away, but the hand cradling the back of her head prevented that escape.

His hand slid down, caressing the swell of her hip. Francesca gasped at his audacity. His fingers stroked and teased…and all the while the kiss continued. His breath was her breath, his scent hers. The stubble on his chin rasped rough against her face. It was as if he was awakening something deep within her—something that she did not understand.

Just as the footsteps paused outside the door she felt the flicker of his tongue within her mouth, and his hand close over her breast. Her nipples hardened. Francesca panicked.

The door was thrown open just as she raised her knee and thrust it into Mr Black's groin.

She saw the flare of shock in his eyes, heard the gasp he could not smother, and his hands released her. He staggered back.

'This must be a first—a woman who is positively averse to your amorous advances. Must be losing your touch, Mr Black.'

Although Francesca's heart was thumping loud enough to echo in her ears she could hear the amusement in Mr White's taunt.

Mr Black recovered himself quickly. He shot her an unfathomable look before turning and presenting a very different face to White. A cold smile curved his mouth, and even Francesca, innocent as she was, could see the lust in his eyes. Everything about him bespoke a man who was used to taking what he wanted exactly when he wanted it. This was not the Mr Black who had spoken so rationally with Francesca and her brother only minutes earlier. This was a predator, a rake. A shiver rippled down her spine and she backed away, increasing the distance between them.

'We'll see, Mr White,' he said in the same drawl she had heard him use before. 'As I said, I like a challenge.' His gaze flickered towards Francesca. 'And Francesca here is proving to be just that.'

Mr White smiled.

'Quite a challenge indeed,' said Black, and that frightening half-smile was there again. 'How long do we have before the rendez-vous?'

'An hour.'

Black's smile deepened. He slid his eyes to Francesca. They roamed over her, head to toe, evaluating her in the most base of manners.

Her anger flared at his bold appraisal. She faced him squarely, her eyes seeking his, but Black's gaze was not on her eyes: it was positioned lower, lingering over her breasts. 'How dare you?'

White chuckled. 'There's a blanket next door. I'll fetch it for you.' He disappeared for all of two minutes, returning with a folded grey woollen blanket, which he threw at Black. 'Catch.' He smirked. 'I take it you'll have need of it.'

'Thank you kindly, Mr White,' said Black, and Francesca again had the notion that they were playing a game.

She watched White walk away. He was over the threshold, the door closing in his hand. Almost gone. Almost.

'Oh, and Mr Black,' White stuck his head back through, 'I'll take my turn of her next…once you've blunted her claws.' The door closed with a click.

Chapter 2

THE semi-smile that curved Jack's mouth was gone as soon as the door shut. His expression altered in an instant. The lascivious rake was gone, in his place a man whose look was closed and hard and determined.

The girl's eyes were filled with anger and disgust. She faced him, saying nothing, waiting. Her face was pale in the lantern light, her skin smooth. She looked young, too young to be involved in this mess, and he already knew that she was an innocent. He thought again of that kiss. His blood was still hot from it. She was such an unexpected delight, even for a man as jaded as him. He pushed the thoughts away. He wasn't here to play games. Those days were done.

Tonight had been a long time in coming. So carefully planned. So much riding on it. The girl's very presence risked it all. And yet he knew he couldn't let White have her—even had she not been Tom Linden's sister. Jack had not lied. If White and the Buckleys had their way she'd finish this night in Davy Jones's locker, after an orgy of rape. He began to unfasten his coat.

Her eyes were fixed to where his fingers loosed the buttons. Her eyes still blazed with indignation, but he could see the wariness that lay beneath. She opened her mouth to speak.

He touched a finger to his lips and gave a slight shake of his head, gesturing with his eyes towards the room next door. He let the blanket drop from his hands. Then he shrugged off his coat and laid it on the floor.

Her eyes followed his every move, and although she seemed composed he could sense the chaos of her emotions. Yet Francesca Linden did not shout or scream or weep, she just stood there, dignified and silent, and watched him. When she finally spoke, the anger in her voice almost masked the fear.

'What on earth did you—?'

He stepped closer.

She tried to back away, but realised there was nowhere left to go. The wooden wall was already pressed against her spine.

He leaned down to whisper in her ear, and with a lightning reflex intercepted her palm just before it landed on his cheek.

'You are despicable, sir!'

He shrugged and released her hand. 'White has gone. I only wish to speak with you.'

Her eyes were filled with suspicion. 'What—?'

His mouth touched almost to her ear. 'Have a care over the volume of your voice, Miss Linden. We may be heard through the door.'

She stared at him unconvinced, but finally gave a tiny movement of her head, which he took to be assent.

There was barely a foot between them, but he did not touch her. He could see the high colour in her cheeks and her kiss-swollen lips. He ran his eye briefly over the high-necked brown woollen dress and the matching cloak that dangled precariously from her shoulders and neck. Although clean, both garments were worn, and showed the evidence of numerous repairs. The styles were those that had not been fashionable for a good number of years. He knew from when he had tied her ankles together that she was wearing darned woollen stockings, and sturdy brown leather boots whose soles were thin. The dark brown bonnet she had worn was the only thing that did not look as if it had come from the Parish. It sat proudly on the wooden decking at her side, where he had placed it earlier that evening. Her reddish blonde hair was scraped primly back in a chignon. In spite of all that was shabby, there was an air of gentility about Tom Linden's sister.

He sighed inwardly, knowing that what had just happened was nothing to that which would have to be done for this illusion to work. If she balked at his kiss she certainly would not like the rest of it. Would not like? That was the understatement of the century. Most young ladies would have a fit of the vapours at the mere suggestion, but, for all she was clearly a young lady, Francesca Linden did not look to be in danger of succumbing to such hysteria. There was something in her expression and the defiant stance of her body that bespoke an underlying strength of character that he had not before seen in a woman. Apprehension prickled at the prospect of what lay ahead. He almost laughed at the irony of the situation. Jack Holberton's reputation as a dissolute was legendary, even if he was still only twenty-six years of age. But all the women he had known had been experienced, and as keen to be bedded as he had been to bed them. This was different. Francesca Linden was different. This whole situation was damnably ridiculous.

He raked a hand through the ruffle of his hair.

'You said it was to be a play-act,' she said in whispered accusation.

'And so it was.'

'That was an act?'

'Believe me, Miss Linden, you would know the difference were I to kiss you properly.'

Her whisper grew louder. 'You had no right to kiss me at all, or to touch me as you did!'

'What would you have White interrupt us doing? Quietly conversing? Playing cards? Do you think that either of those activities would convince him that we must spend time in here alone?' His expression was one of amusement.

'No, but you might have warned me what you were about to do.'

'I wanted to provoke a convincing reaction from you—I had not anticipated quite how vigorous that would be.' He could still feel the tenderness between his legs where she had struck with unswerving accuracy. 'Who taught you the manoeuvre with the knee?'

'My brother.'

He was gaining the rapid impression that he had misjudged Tom Linden's sister. 'Perhaps I should have told you of my intention, but I couldn't risk that you would give the game away.' He raked his hair again. 'I'll warn you of the rest.'

'The rest?' Her eyes widened.

'To put it bluntly, there is more to bedding a woman than mere kissing. And we must convince White that a bedding is taking place in here.'

She swallowed.

'It is merely a strategy to keep White and the Buckleys away from you. Do you understand, Miss Linden?'

She held her head up and looked him directly in the eye. 'Are you asking me to play the whore?'

Their eyes held.

'I'm not asking you to be one, and there is a very great difference in that.'

'I suppose that there is.' But the tone of her voice suggested otherwise.

'I'm not going to bed you. It will be a pretence only.'

'Like the kiss?'

There was a small silence between them.

'Do you have any better suggestions, Miss Linden?'

'No.' She glanced away, and her hands gripped a little more tightly together.

Jack ignored that small sign and pushed on with the matter in hand. 'White will not knock and wait by the door. He might enter at any time, and if he does we must ensure he sees that which he is anticipating.' He looked at her expectantly.

'Mr Black,' she said, 'I must inform you that I have no knowledge of…' she hesitated, her gaze flickering down '…of such
affairs.' Her eyes raised to his once more, steady, with just a flare
of defiance. 'But I have agreed to do what is necessary to save my
brother's life.'

'And your own.'

'My own as well.' She took a deep breath. 'You had better tell
me exactly what it is that I'm to do, sir.'

Under different circumstances Jack might well have desired to
hear just such a phrase from Francesca Linden's lips. But not here,
not like this. 'Give me your cloak.'

He noticed the slight tremble in her fingers as they fumbled with
the ties of her cloak. The drab cloth was soon in his hands. He folded
it to form a pillow and laid it down on the floor on top of his own
shabby coat. 'Now, turn around,' he said, 'that I might unhook your
dress.'

'My dress?'

'Your dress, Miss Linden.'

There was a hesitation, and he thought for a moment that she
would refuse him. But then she did as he asked. His fingers worked
their way down, separating each hook from its corresponding eye,
and her dress opened like a fan in their wake, gaping to reveal the
layers of material that made up her petticoats, her stays and her
shift…and the soft skin at the nape of her neck.

'Can you slip your arms free?'

She shook her head. 'It does not unfasten far enough to allow
that.'

Jack soon remedied that problem. The material tore easily
beneath his hands, opening the garment right down to the small of
her back. The dress was falling from her shoulders before he had
even finished.

He could see the slight rise and fall of her shoulders with each
breath. She did not look round. 'Free yourself from the bodice and
arms only. It will serve us better if you keep your skirts in place.'

He was standing directly behind her, so close that he could smell the faint perfumed aroma from her. 'Your stays will also have to be removed.'

She craned around and peered at him with a scowl. 'Is this really necessary?'

'I would not ask were it not so.'

Her gaze held his for a few seconds longer before she faced ahead once more, presenting him with her back, standing still, waiting patiently. When his fingers touched to the top fastening of her stays he felt her jump. He worked quickly, steadily unfastening the ties until the stays lay abandoned on the floor beside the cloak and coat. 'You can turn around now.'

She hesitated, then with her head up slowly turned to face him, gritty control upon her face. From the waist down she was still fully dressed. From the waist up only the thin gauze of her shift covered her nudity—that and the strategic positioning of her arms.

He did not stare, but quickly pulled the pins from her chignon, unwinding the roll of hair, loosening it, so that it tumbled long and free in a curtain of curls down her back. He resisted the urge to tangle his fingers within it and rapidly averted his gaze.

'Take off your boots and lie down on my coat.'

He turned away and began to untie his tatty neckcloth, dispensing with it on top of her stays. He pulled his shirt off over his head. From the corner of his eye he could see that Miss Linden was sitting down upon his coat. Her boots sat in a neat pair next to the pile of clothing. He unfastened the fall on his breeches and moved to where she was sitting like a mermaid with her flowing hair and her skirts wrapped around her legs. He knelt down on the edge of the coat.

'Lie down.'

She stayed sitting, her forearm shielding her breasts, her hair spilling over her shoulders.

'If White comes in again I will have to lie on top of you.'

'You will squash me, sir.' She was finding it harder to disguise her uneasiness now.

'Rest assured, I shall not.' He leaned a little closer. 'Now, lie down.'

She looked up at him with quiet defiance.

'Miss Linden?' he prompted.

The sound of laughter drifted through from beyond the door.

Mr White laughed again. 'Such a feisty little thing. It's little wonder that she's keeping Mr Black occupied for so long.'

The men grinned at White's crudity.

Tom gritted his teeth and tried to ignore the lecherous smirks of the men around him, knowing full well that it was his sister of whom White was speaking.

'Lucky bugger,' said one.

'Can we have her when you're finished?' said another.

'If the job goes well you can have what you like,' said White.

'I'd like to get my hands around her bubbies,' said Weasel. 'What about it, Tom? You up for a bit?'

Tom dug his nails hard into his palms and squeezed, trying to force some measure of a smile, but his lips would not form the curve.

'Or maybe Tommy boy's got other preferences. Is that why you're lookin' so pale about the gills?'

Tom's body was rigid with anger and fear and worry for Francesca. The sound of his sister's shouts had rattled him, and he had the urge to run back there, but that, he knew, would ruin everything.

'Eh, Tommy boy, is that it?' Weasel thumped him on the shoulder.

'Leave the lad alone,' said Ginger. 'He's just green. Probably never had a lass. Ain't that right, lad?'

Tom nodded, not trusting himself to speak.

White laughed. 'Well, you're in the right company, Linden. You can have the girl last. There'll be no fight left in her by then. She'll take you meekly enough. And if you ask nicely Mr Black might give you some advice. He's considered something of an expert in such matters.'

Tom knew precisely Jack Holberton's reputation up in London. It was not a thought on which he wished to dwell, given that his sister was alone in there with the man.

'You feelin' all right?' asked Ginger.

'Looks a bit strange to me,' said Weasel.

Tom gave another nod, but did not meet their eyes for fear that they would guess the truth.

'What the hell's the matter with you tonight?' Weasel stared at him.

'Nothing.' Tom pulled himself together.

'Lad's just nervous with all that talk of shaggin',' said Ginger. 'Leave him be.'

'Nervous or not, he had best be ready when we meet the contact. I won't tolerate any mistakes,' said White. 'Do you understand?'

The men nodded.

No sound came from the cabin. Tom was careful not to look in that direction. He pushed his mind to think of the real reason he had joined the *Swift*'s crew. Francesca would be safe with Lord Holberton. Tom had to trust in that.

There was the scrape of boxes being pushed back, and the sound of men moving, of voices that sounded too close. In an instant Francesca found herself lying flat on her back with Mr Black stretched out by her side. Protected only by the thin material of her shift, her breasts were precariously close to the bare skin of his chest, and he had bundled her skirts in an indecent fashion somewhere up around her thighs. His face was hovering close to hers.

He spoke quietly. 'When he enters you must protest—although with perhaps not quite as much fervour as you did the last time.'

She gave the smallest of nods, trying not to move, or even to breathe. She was excruciatingly conscious of the overwhelming proximity of the man and his masculinity.

'You shall expire if you hold your breath much longer.'

She looked at him; his face was barely a few inches away from hers. The light of the lantern served only to emphasise its shadows and planes, and set soft hues in the darkness of his eyes. She released her breath and inhaled another. Her cheeks grew uncomfortably warm. She averted her gaze. 'How long must we stay like this?'

'You wound me with your impatience. Surely you cannot find me so very unpleasant?'

'On the contrary, sir, you greatly overestimate your appeal. And you have not answered my question.'

His smile was one of resignation. 'For as long as it takes to reach our rendezvous point, Miss Linden.'

'The rendezvous where you pick up the goods to be smuggled?'

He made a gesture of agreement.

'And after we reach the rendezvous point?' she demanded.

'You will be safe.'

'But what of Mr White? You heard what he said.'

'He'll not touch you, none of them will.'

'How can you be so sure?'

He just looked at her, the certainty in his eyes more convincing than any words.

'Then what do we do in the meantime?'

He crooked an eyebrow suggestively.

She glared at him fiercely.

He gave a soft laugh. 'My dear girl, you need not look at me so. I merely meant that we shall converse.'

She relaxed a little, but still watched him with wary eyes.

'Tell me something of yourself, Miss Linden.'

They might have been standing in an assembly room, such was Mr Black's polite tone. It was ridiculous when they were lying practically naked beside each other. Her heart was beating too fast, and she could feel the throb of her pulse in her throat. She took a deep breath, and was immediately reminded of how very close Mr Black's chest was to hers. She felt embarrassment flood her cheeks, and kept her eyes carefully averted from his so that he would not see the measure of her vulnerability. Francesca was used to being strong and unfazed—or at least pretending to be. It was she, after all, who had held her family together since her mama's illness. And if ever Francesca had needed to appear strong it was now.

'Miss Linden?' Mr Black's voice had gentled.

She struggled to contain her emotions, determined not to show any weakness. When at last she looked at him again, she was certain that her expression was nothing but composed.

'Were you born in Lannacombe?' he asked, as if they were just making small talk in the most respectable of places

'No, Salisbury. My father's family are from that city. We moved to Looe in Cornwall, where Papa had the living. We did not come to Lannacombe until I was eighteen.'

'Your father was a parson?'

'He was. He died four years ago.'

'I know, and I'm sorry for your loss, Miss Linden.'

'You know?'

'I know something of your brother.'

She nodded. 'I had forgotten.'

'So you live with your mother and your brother?'

'And my three younger sisters.'

'Three!' He smiled. 'Young Tom must be thoroughly hen-pecked by a household of females.'

Francesca smiled at his words. 'Hardly. Tom is rather a head-strong young man, as you may have noticed.' She smiled, and then the smile faded. 'I've known that there's been something going on for weeks. He's been going off at night, supposedly fishing. But he's never fished so late before, and I sensed that he was hiding something. When I tried to speak to him he would have none of it. I knew that something was wrong—that's why I followed him tonight.'

'What were you planning to do? Force him from the boat?'

She shook her head. 'If I could not prevent him boarding then I would have confronted him tomorrow and put an end to this.' She sighed. 'Christmas is coming, Mr Black, and so I can understand Tom's temptation to make some extra money. But this is too dangerous. Were anyone in the village to find out that Tom was working for the Buckleys…' She looked away, suddenly afraid that she had revealed too much.

'It seems to me that you care a great deal for your family,' he said.

She took a deep breath, and this time she did not notice how very close her body was to Mr Black's. 'Yes, I do. And tonight I seem to have made things worse for them.'

'I wouldn't say that.' He looked directly into her eyes. 'After tonight I'll warrant that Tom will have no more dealings with the Buckleys.' In the warm light of the lantern his eyes were kind and slightly teasing.

Francesca could feel the hardness of the deck beneath pressing into her back, and the dampness from the wood stiffening her bones. Her fingers were cold, her toes were cold, even her nose was cold. But it was not the chill winter temperatures that caused Francesca to shiver.

'Are you cold?' He touched his hand to her wrist.

The heat from his fingers seemed to scorch her bare skin.

He shifted closer until their bodies were just touching.

'Mr Black!' exclaimed Francesca in a scandalised tone, and pulled back.

'Miss Linden,' he said, with the patient tone of someone talking to a child, 'I am sharing my warmth with you, nothing else.'

She had to admit that he had felt gloriously warm, but even so… 'It is not seemly,' she muttered in protest. The absurdity of her words struck her. She was lying half-naked next to a strange man aboard a smugglers' boat in the middle of the night. Lord, as if there were a shred of decency about any of it!

He gave a droll laugh as if his thoughts had followed the same path. 'Why not?'

She stared at him as if he had lost his mind. 'I am an unmarried lady, and you are…'

'Yes?' The word resonated with expectation.

'You are a stranger and a smuggler and a *man*, for goodness' sake!' And all that separated their naked skins was the fine lawn of her shift and the barricade of her forearm. But she did not give words to that thought.

He smiled.

'I don't even know you!'

'My name is Jack, and I am six and twenty years old. You know me now.'

'You are incorrigible.'

His smile deepened. 'So I have been told.'

She tilted her face and looked up at him. 'You are still a stranger.'

'I may not be from Lannacombe, but I'm a Devon man all the same.'

She felt surprised at that. 'And you're working with the Buckley gang?'

'I am.'

A dangerous criminal—yet here she was, lying half-clothed by his side, conversing with him. It was preposterous, worse than ridiculous. Her mother would have a blue fit if she knew. But what she saw in his face made her think that he was a different man altogether. Against all rhyme and all reason she trusted him, this stranger, this smuggler.

'Still not enough for you?' he asked.

She levelled her gaze to his and said nothing.

A minute passed before he spoke again. 'I am the worst son that a man might have. I've dishonoured my family name, I've made my father curse, my mother weep and my brothers rue the fact I was ever born. I am a womaniser, a drunkard and a gambler. I do not know the meaning of honour. And if that were not enough I came damn near close to killing my brother. In short, Miss Linden, I am the proverbial blackest of sheep. That is all there is to know of me. Have I shocked you?'

For all his flippant manner she saw something flicker in his eyes before he masked it. She shook her head slowly.

'Even though I readily admit to being bad to the bone?'

'I do not believe you, sir.'

He raised one eyebrow. 'And why might that be? I assure you that all of it is true.'

'For all that I disapprove of your methods, I do believe that you are trying to save my brother's life and mine.'

His eyes met hers, and she could see his torment and his pain. She forgot all about being calm and unswerving and strong. All of those pretences slipped away.

They stared at one another, unmasked. And in that moment it was as if there was a communication, an understanding, a connection.

'A single act of honour might wipe away all of a man's sins,' she said quietly.

Their eyes still held.

'I hope so,' he whispered, and then he looked away and the moment was gone. In its place was thinly veiled surprise and embarrassment. 'We should speak of something else,' he said rather gruffly.

'What subject do you suggest, sir?'

'Politics, religion, the theatre—I do not care, Miss Linden.' There was a touch of the lazy arrogance that she had seen when he had spoken with Mr White.

But Francesca was not fooled. She had seen the truth of him and she knew that, contrary to all impressions, he cared very much.

'Linden, fetch the nets with Ginger and take them up on deck. We'll need them for the transfer.' White sounded irritated.

'But Mr Black…' Tom said, unsure whether their sudden appearance would interfere with Lord Holberton's plan and endanger Francesca.

'Mr Black will be too damn busy with the wench to notice you two clodhoppers.'

Ginger gave a nod and rose from his makeshift seat. 'Come on, lad.'

There was nothing Tom could do other than follow.

The two men walked towards the cabin.

* * *

Footsteps sounded by the door. Before Francesca could even register what was happening Mr Black had rolled on top of her. Despite the material of her shift, she could feel the graze of his chest against hers. Yet she could see that Mr Black had been right: she was in no danger of being crushed, for he was taking the bulk of his weight on his elbows.

Just as he had said he would, he began to kiss her. But this time Francesca knew what to expect.

Someone knocked at the door.

Black pulled back enough to break the kiss, but kept his face down low next to hers. She saw the warning that flashed in his gaze.

The knock came again.

By the time the door opened he was kissing her again. She looked up into the darkness of his eyes and something flowed between them—something that was not play-acting. And then she remembered that she was supposed to be resisting him, and blushed that she had forgotten. Her embarrassment lent strength to her struggle.

'Release me, you fiend!'

In response, Black captured her wrists into his hands and held them above her head.

She could hear the hesitant tread of feet cross the threshold, could hear a man begin to speak. 'Sorry to be botherin' you, sir, but Mr White has sent us to fetch the nets.'

Black glanced behind.

Francesca felt the change in his body, a sudden tension, a coiled stillness that had not been there before, and knew instantly that something was wrong. Yet from where she lay she could see nothing of the man who stood by the door.

'Take them and get out,' Black said coldly. 'Both of you.'

She knew then that there was more than one of them, and was thankful that he was shielding her from them.

'Yes, sir—thank you, sir,' said the same voice.

She heard him hurry across the floor. There was no movement, no sound at all from the second man.

'Come on, lad,' she heard the man whisper urgently.

She felt the ripple of cold foreboding down her spine.

Black rolled off her, making a play of fixing the fall on his breeches.

She clutched the blanket to her and looked across the room. She barely saw the tall ginger-haired man who was struggling to lift the nets. Her eyes widened, and the breath stilled in her throat. For not five paces from the bottom of the coat on which she was lying stood her brother, his face pale, his eyes glinting with a rage she had never before seen.

Jack saw Francesca give her brother a small shake of the head, warning him off, her eyes signalling him to stay calm. But it was too late for that. Tom was beyond logical thought or reasoning. Jack doubted he even remembered the risk to his sister from White. He knew what the boy would do. Tom was acting on instinct—and enraged instinct at that. If Jack did not act quickly Tom would jeopardise everything.

'You bastard!' Tom ran at Jack.

'No!' yelled Francesca. She was scrabbling up, pulling the blanket with her.

'Stay down,' Jack said to her.

Tom's face was now suffused with deep colour. He swung his fist at Jack. 'What are you do—?'

Jack landed a single jab to Tom's throat.

Tom made a suffocated sound and crumpled to his knees, before fainting on to the floor.

Francesca was up and running towards his prone body before Jack's hand caught around her arm, swinging her back. He threw her a warning look, hoping that she was not as foolish as her brother. 'Get back down there!' he barked, knowing that there would soon be an audience at the doorway—if there wasn't one already.

'Take the nets and that fool and get out,' he snapped at Ginger, who was standing gaping as if he could not believe what he had just seen unfold before his eyes.

And then White was there, a look of surprise on his face. 'What the hell is going on in here?' He looked from Jack to Francesca, to Tom's still body upon the floor.

'Young Linden objected to my use of the woman.'

'What in hell has it to do with him? He's been acting strangely all night.'

'Probably been drinking.'

White didn't look convinced.

'By the way, I've finished if you want her.' Jack gestured towards Francesca, ignoring the tug of his heart at her sudden expression of shock and betrayal, and the small clenched fingers that were clutching the blanket like a shield against her.

White's gaze lingered over her, the sight of her bare shoulders and the promise of what was to come distracting him from Tom Linden. 'Not enough time. The contact's in sight. We need to make ready for the transfer.'

'Keep her for the way back. I promise you she's worth it.' Jack picked up his shirt, pulled it lithely over his head and tucked it into his breeches.

'Well, if she's that good, maybe I will,' said White.

Tom gave a groan and began to stir on the floor.

'He's becoming an annoyance,' said White, and delivered a nasty kick to Tom's ankle.

'I agree,' said Jack, praying that Francesca would have the wisdom to remain silent.

'I'll deal with him later,' said White.

Jack gave a small cold smile. 'It might be better to let me do that.' He balled his fist and cracked his knuckles with the other hand. 'You're going to be busy with…other things.' He raised his eyebrows suggestively.

White chuckled. 'Very well.' He turned to the men who were

crowding in the doorway, staring at Francesca. 'Fetch the nets and get up on deck.' When Ginger moved towards Tom, he snapped, 'Leave that buffoon where he is.'

'In here with the woman?' said Ginger.

'She'll be safe enough,' snapped White, 'since he's so keen to play her defender.'

Jack took his coat from the floor, dusted it down and eased himself into it. His actions were smooth and unhurried, almost carefree. And all the while he was aware of Francesca Linden, standing there with her head held high.

He sauntered from the room, following in Mr White's wake. The men had already gone, taking the huge pile of netting with them. His foot was on the first step of the ladder when he stopped and touched a hand to where his shirt gaped open at the neck. 'Neckcloth. Forgotten the damn thing.'

'It doesn't matter. You're supposed to be a bloody fisherman. We're not going to Brooks's,' said White.

Jack raised a single eyebrow and stared at him.

White gave a sigh and rolled his eyes. 'I'll be on deck.'

Jack gave a look as if to say that was better, and meandered back towards the hold. He opened the door and stepped inside, pulling the door behind him but not closing it. Francesca was crouched by her brother's side, her hand to his face. She jumped at his entry, clambering to her feet, staring at him with angry eyes.

'You could have killed him,' she said.

'If I'd wanted to kill him he'd be dead. I had to find some way of silencing him. He was about to give the game away.'

Her expression told him that she knew he was right. But she did not give up her fight so easily. 'You didn't have to hit him so hard.'

'Yes, Francesca, I did. Your brother will have nothing more than a sore throat for a few days, which is a sight better than having it cut from ear to ear.'

'You told White he could have me—you even persuaded him to take me.'

'Rather than have him ask too many questions about Tom, or beat him senseless.'

'True.' She glanced down, and then back up at him. 'But you did say that White would not…'

He closed the distance between them until he was standing so close that the skirts of her dress trailed over the tatty leather of his boots. 'And neither he will.' He had the urge to take her into his arms. 'I shall not lock the door.' He touched his fingers gently to her cheek. 'Have faith, Francesca. All will be well.' Then he moved quickly away, collected his neckcloth and was gone, leaving Francesca Linden standing like a statue, staring after him.

Chapter 3

JACK'S shabby neckcloth was in place and neatly tied by the time he climbed up the ladder and out on to the deck. The night was cold and dark. The December sea was rolling, heads of white foam visible through the darkness. The *Swift* bobbed, but held her own. The wind was bracing, and he could feel the cold damp spray of saltwater upon his cheeks. But it was none of this that caught Jack's attention. He looked instead to the other boat that was some twenty feet away from them.

He made his way over to the bulwarks on port side and came to stand beside White. 'Mr White,' he said, 'it seems we are in business.'

'Crouvier is bringing her round. With the wind as it is the transfer is not going to be easy.'

'Another challenge,' said Jack, and smiled.

The two men stood and watched while the other vessel was brought around. She was smaller than the *Swift*, but sturdy enough. The darkness of the night made it difficult to see details other than the fact there was a body of men busy upon her, their faces pale in the yellowed lights of the lanterns that hung around the deck.

The dark shadow of a flag fluttered to her rear, but it was impossible to see her colours. She drew alongside the *Swift*'s starboard. Grappling hooks were engaged. This was where Weasel and

Ginger's expertise came in. They used the hooks and ropes to slowly, carefully bring the two boats together. In winter seas this was a delicate operation. One mistake would bring the boats crashing together, splintering their wooden bodies, sentencing the men to death in the violence of the freezing waters. It was clear that Weasel and Ginger had done this before…many times.

Jack felt the energy surge through his body. Every muscle was poised ready for action. He could feel the steady thud of his heart in his chest and the race of blood through his veins. He forced himself to control it. Wait. Hold. Steady. Timing was everything. The moment was so close.

He let his gaze wander out into the blackness beyond, to where the roar of the sea was constant. Dark night hid what Jack knew would be there. The cloud cover in the sky was thick, but as he stood there waiting, poised on the precipice of all that he had worked for, a tiny gap opened up, like a tear between the clouds, and through it peeped the moon. Just for a second the thin silver crescent shone its cool light over the water. Jack held his breath and peered harder into the distant darkness. There was the tiniest suggestion of something out there amidst the black.

He thought of what it would mean if the plan went wrong. He thought of Francesca Linden and her fate. His heart skipped a beat, and he knew that he could not let that happen, no matter the cost.

Not one sign of his disquiet showed. He pushed off from the bulwarks and turned almost indifferently to where the men had successfully secured the two boats together.

'We're ready,' said Weasel.

White walked briskly over to the point of joining. The hoist and tackle system was in place on the other boat, which Jack could now see was named *Bien Aimé*, ready to start lifting the barrels. A man from the French boat clambered across the bulwarks, keeping a grip of the securing ropes. Jack watched the man's squat frame, broad and strong from years of physical work, saw the dark woollen cap that hid his head, heard him greet White with sullen tone.

'Monsieur Crouvier.'

Edmund and Crouvier conversed briefly in French. Jack stood by and listened to every word.

A hundred half-ankers of the best French brandy at five shillings a gallon. In England it would be sold on for five times that amount.

The sea was empty. They had seen no one on their way out here. The night was cold and held the promise of bad weather. There would be another shipment in two weeks' time. They agreed on the day after Twelfth Night.

Jack watched while White and the Frenchman exchanged small leather satchels. He knew that the satchels contained the documents at the centre of this whole treacherous debacle. Documents and money. He felt disgust and anger whip through him, but he was careful to keep his face impassive. Then the men began the operation of transferring the brandy from the *Bien Aimé* to the *Swift*. It was a cumbersome process; the wooden tubs were not large, but weighed heavy at more than fifty pounds apiece. On land they were not difficult to handle, with the tub-carriers managing a climb up the steep cliff paths with two half-ankers roped across their chest and shoulders, but the darkness and wind and turbulent water made the transfer between ships more complicated. With the block and tackle transferring four tubs secured within a rope net at a time, the operation ran smoothly enough. Tom's absence did not seem to slow things too much aboard the *Swift*.

Every sense in Jack's body was heightened; he was listening, waiting, primed, conscious of the weight of his pistol against his hip. He thought of Francesca again, of what she had endured this night, of her courage, of her calmness…of the softness of her lips and the sweet scent of her…the feel of her body beneath his. His loins tightened at the memory. He almost laughed at the irony of the situation. He had spent the best part of an hour convincing the company of the *Swift* that he was bedding the girl, creating an illusion, while all the while knowing how much simpler it would have been just to take her. He wanted her, after all. But those days were done, and Jack knew he would make the same choice a thousand times over.

Francesca turned her back on where her brother was sitting and fixed the bodice of her dress back into place as best she could, wrenching her arms into contortions in order to fasten the hooks. Only once she was fully dressed did she go to sit by him.

He touched a tentative hand to his throat and then rubbed at his ankle. 'That bastard!' he said in a strained whisper. 'And what did he do to my ankle? It hurts like hell!'

'Tom!' exclaimed Francesca with a look of outrage. 'There is no need for such language.'

'There's every need,' he croaked, 'when I find him forcing himself upon my sister.'

'He was not forcing himself upon me. It was a play-act contrived to make Mr White believe such a thing. Nothing more.'

His face was white and pinched. 'God in heaven, Francesca, I saw him closing the fall on his breeches.'

'I'm telling you the truth.' She stared into his eyes, willing him to believe her. 'We would both be dead already were it not for Mr Black. Indeed, with your outburst you almost undid all that he had done.'

'What was I supposed to do? Just walk away?'

'Yes!'

'I thought that he was…' His face contorted.

'I know. It was what anyone walking in upon the scene was supposed to think.'

He closed his eyes and leaned his back against the wooden wall of the cabin. 'Lord, Francesca, what are we going to do?'

'We're going to trust that your Mr Black knows what he is doing. There is nothing else we can do.' She forced a smile and tried to reassure her brother. 'In all likelihood we'll be back in Lannacombe tomorrow, preparing for Christmas. And if we're really lucky Mama might never even know that we were gone.' It seemed a forlorn hope.

* * *

The men were working industriously, hauling the tubs over from the *Bien Aimé*. They were almost halfway through the transfer when the naval frigate *Hawk* appeared out of the darkness, swooping in fast towards the two boats.

'Hell's teeth!' White cursed, and looked round savagely at his crew. 'Cut us free, Weasel. Do it now, man!'

There was panic on both boats. Jack could hear shouts and curses in French as well as English. Blades were hacking at the ropes that bound the boats, careless of the grappling hooks that were being left behind. Nothing mattered except the need to escape. But the men's efforts amounted to nothing. The frigate was huge in comparison, and less than fifty feet separated her from her prey. She had moved stealthily, emerging out of the black of night like a great ghost ship.

'Stand to! Drop your weapons!' The captain's voice shouted at them.

'Rot in hell,' White muttered almost to himself. 'Haul off, Weasel. Get us out of here!'

As the two boats separated it looked as if White might just be right. The frigate could not chase two boats at the same time. But on the boats' attempts to flee, lanterns had been lit upon the frigate. Her gun ports were opened, and there was the sound of huge guns being run out.

'Faster, man, faster!' yelled White.

But it was too late. There was the ear-splitting sound of gunpowder exploding, and the almighty splash of a shot hitting the water close perilously close to the *Swift*.

The French boat had turned faster, and looked to have a chance of escape. Another roar, another ball, landing just short of the bow of the French vessel.

'Desist in your efforts!' shouted the naval captain. 'Or we will hit you!'

The French boat ceased her attempted flight. Her flag was lowered.

White saw his chance.

'Keep going, men.'

The *Swift* made her break for freedom. The *Hawk* fired on the leeward, aiming to disable the small boat rather than hole her. Her gunners were good. Jack dived for cover as the shot destroyed a section of the bulwarks, showering the deck in razor sharp shards of wood. Finally the *Swift* ended her flight.

Francesca and Tom heard the almighty roar of the guns even down below in the cabin.

'At last,' Tom rasped. 'We're safe.'

'The Revenue men. But you'll be caught,' she whispered.

'No, not the Revenue. The na—' An explosion ricocheted above their heads cutting off what he would have said. There was a terrible tearing noise and the boat suddenly heaved and shuddered violently.

Francesca was thrown back against the wall. The guns stopped firing. There was only silence.

'Tom, are you hurt?'

'No,' came back his hoarse whisper. 'You?'

'I'm fine,' she said.

'We've been hit.'

She nodded. 'At least they seem to have stopped.'

'For now,' he said. 'White was probably trying to make a run for it. Let's pray we've not been holed. Otherwise we could drown down here before they get to us.'

Her eyes darted to the door. 'Mr Black left the door unlocked for us.'

He looked at her. 'Why didn't you tell me?'

'You didn't give me the chance.'

He gave an exasperated sigh. 'Come on.'

The room beyond was empty, although the lantern had been left burning. They crept across to the ladder.

'Wait here. I'll check up on deck,' said Tom.

But Francesca had no intention of doing any such thing. 'I'm coming with you.'

Tom rolled his eyes but gave no argument. He disappeared up the ladder first, Francesca following behind. Those half-ankers that had already been transferred were stacked nearby. Tom and Francesca crawled out and crouched behind them. Tom turned to whisper to her. In reply she touched a finger to her lips and pointed ahead. There beyond the barrels stood Mr White and Mr Black, and out over the bulwarks loomed a huge naval frigate.

Two cutters had been lowered from the frigate. Jack had watched while the marines climbed down into them. Now he could see the white of their facings even through the darkness. One cutter was still rowing towards the *Bien Aimé*; the other had already reached the *Swift*.

'Looks like the game is up,' said Jack to White.

'Someone must have told them. How else did they know where to find us?'

The marines were climbing up the rope ladders to board, muskets at the ready.

'It must have been that damn boy Linden. Now we know why he's been behaving oddly all night. I'll wring his neck with my bare hands!'

'I wouldn't be too hasty over that, Grosely,' said Jack.

'What the hell are you playing at, using my name?' White turned and scowled at Jack. 'Stick to our pseudonyms. Now, keep quiet and let me do the talking.'

'You've done quite enough talking, sir,' Jack said coldly, and all trace of the bored, lazy rake was gone.

'What?' White's scowl deepened. 'I did you a favour, letting you in on this. I should have kept the brandy and the money to myself.'

'Would that you had kept this country's secrets to yourself, rather than selling them to the French.'

White gaped.

'Or did you think I knew nothing of that?'

'Good God, it was *you*. You're working with the navy. You betrayed us to them.'

'There's only one traitor here, and I'm looking at him.' Jack removed his hand from inside his coat to reveal a pistol aimed at White. 'Drop your stick and put your hands above your head.'

White cursed, but did as he was told. 'I'm making a bit of money from brandy, that's all. If there's anything else going on then it has nothing to do with me.'

'Even as we speak the papers that *you* passed are being retrieved from the *Bien Aimé*. And I'm sure that with some little persuasion Monsieur Crouvier will be only too willing to reveal the identity of his contact.'

'What is this? Some ploy to creep back into your family's favour?'

Jack's face hardened, He felt the rage and guilt exploded within his chest at White's words. His finger tightened against the trigger.

'No!' Both Jack and White turned instinctively towards the voice. There, not six feet away, stood Francesca.

Francesca's heart was pounding wildly, but her voice rang out clearly. Beside her she heard a hoarse exclamation of shock from Tom, before his hand grabbed her arm and tried to pull her away. She dug her heels in and resisted. 'Don't do it, Mr Black.'

'You plead for this villain's life?' Jack was facing White once more and did not look round, just kept the pistol trained ahead and his finger on the trigger. His tone was laced with incredulity.

'It is for the courts to try him. If he's guilty he will hang.'

'You see,' said White, 'even she does not believe you.'

Tom pulled more firmly at her arm. 'Come away, Francesca. You don't know what you're doing. Grosely is guilty as sin.'

She shook Tom off and glared at the man they called Grosely. 'The only reason I plead for your life, sir, is that I would not have Mr Black tried for your murder.'

White smirked, and his pale eyes darted from Francesca to Jack and back again. 'My, my, he must have ploughed you well.'

She felt the heat flush her face.

'On the contrary, Grosely,' said Jack. 'Miss Linden's virtue remains intact.'

'Don't be absurd. I saw you—remember?'

'A fine piece of acting,' said Jack, and loosened his grip on the trigger.

And then the significance of Francesca's name sank into White's brain. 'Linden? She is—'

'Tom Linden's sister.'

'That's why he was so concerned over the wench. Is he in on this with you?'

'I couldn't have done it without him,' said Jack.

Francesca stared at her brother. 'What's going on, Tom?'

'Later, Francesca.'

'I would rather speak of it now,' she said with determination.

'Miss Linden.' Jack's eyes met hers, but what he would have said was never heard, for there was a scuttle of boots against the wooden deck and then a voice.

'Not too late are we, my lord?' A group of marines and their sergeant were standing with muskets at the ready.

'Perfect timing, Sergeant Wilcox,' said Jack. 'He's all yours.'

'Come along quietly, sir. Any trouble and I'll skewer you with a bayonet myself.' The sergeant was a big man, with an expression that told the world he meant every word he said.

White glanced round, and on seeing the sergeant raised his hands higher in the air. His upper lip curled and his mouth contorted to a sneer. 'You haven't heard the last of this, Jack Holberton.' Then he turned to face the marines.

The huge sergeant nodded at two marines and they moved forward to flank White. 'Take him.' Then he looked over at Francesca and Tom.

'Miss Linden and her brother are with me, Sergeant Wilcox,' said Jack.

'Right you are, sir,' said the sergeant. 'Are you ready to leave sir?'

'Thank you, Sergeant Wilcox. We are quite ready.' Then his eyes met Francesca's. 'Miss Linden—Tom.'

Tom took her arm and guided her across to the rope ladder. One of the marines helped her climb over the bulwarks and down the precarious rope ladder into the cutter bobbing on the waves below. The wind nipped at her face and the freezing spray from the waves nigh on soaked her, but Francesca scarcely noticed. The cutter was rowed through the dark tumultuous sea towards the *Hawk*. They were safe. And all Francesca could think was that nothing was as it had seemed.

The *Hawk* did not tarry. Despite the strong Atlantic wind and roughening sea it took a little over an hour to reach Lannacombe Bay, where the smuggled brandy was to be landed. The naval frigate stayed clear of the coast, so that she would not be visible to the watchers on the shoreline—not that the *Swift* would be expected yet.

The arrival of the lugger would bring the men upon the rocky beach not the brandy that they awaited but a party of marines. What he had learned of the Buckleys ensured that Jack wasted no pity on their plight. Smuggling had been a part of life in south Devon for centuries, and with good reason. Many of those involved in the trade were the poor from coastal villages, and relied on smuggling to feed hungry mouths. But the past year had seen the violent Buckley gang dominate the free trade along the Devon coast and put local smugglers out of business. Edmund Grosely had made good use of the Buckleys' greed. Both Lannacombe and Jack would be thankful for the ruffians' demise.

The *Hawk* waited where she was, every light extinguished, invisible through the darkness of the night, until at last the *Swift* arrived. Jack saw the lugger signal two short then two long flashes of a lantern, and watched the reply from the shore. As the *Swift* was manoeuvred in towards the land the *Hawk* silently slipped a cutter into the water and filled it with sturdy seamen, who rowed the path the lugger had led. Jack stood silently on the deck and watched them go, cursing the fact that he could not join them. He waited. Waited. Counted the minutes. Then there was an explosion of men's shouts carrying clear across the water. Behind Jack a man's tread sounded.

'Lieutenant Davies and Sergeant Wilcox will finish what has been started, sir.' The captain stood by Jack's side, scanning the shoreline. Yells and screams and the deafening bangs of musket fire sounded, and small flashes of gunfire speckled the black night like fireworks. Over it all the captain continued to speak. 'When Davies returns with the cutter we'll move to Lannacombe village, in case any of the landers have escaped our shore party. *Hawk*'s too big for the harbour there, but I'll have Miss Linden and her brother rowed over in the jolly boat.'

Jack gave a nod, and although he continued to look landward the action upon the shore now barely registered with him. What occupied Jack's mind was not that Edmund Grosely had been stopped and a traitor caught, nor that a gang of villains had been arrested. Instead he thought of Francesca Linden…and of why he had told her the truth of himself.

Francesca awoke at her usual time in the bed that she shared with two of her sisters. Across the room she could hear the muffled snores and sleepy breathing of her mother and her youngest sister in the second bed. Lydia and Anne lay warm and unmoving beside her.

A week had passed since her misadventure on the *Swift* and, as she and Tom had been fortunate enough that night to sneak back into the cottage undetected, her family remained blissfully unaware of the truth, believing the heavily edited version of events that they'd heard the next day. Francesca's life had gone on just as before, as if that night had never been. And there had not even been the chance to discuss the matter with Tom. Indeed, she was beginning to wonder if she really had been present upon the *Swift* at all.

She did not wonder for long. There were grates to be cleaned and fires to be lit, water to be boiled and porridge to be cooked. She crept from beneath the cosy nest of covers out into the coldness of the room, pulling the curtain back that she might lighten the darkness without waking the others.

Through the window night was beginning to fade, watering down the sky from an inky black to a deep blue. There was just enough light for Francesca to find her way across to the basin of water on the chest of drawers in the corner. Without pausing, she broke the thin layer of ice on top of the water and, stripping off her nightdress, quickly washed. The coldness of the water made her gasp, but soon she was dry and slipping into her dress. She combed her hair, twisted it up and pinned it into place just above the nape of her neck. Then she pulled her shawl about her and moved towards the stairs. From Tom's room came the sound of snoring. Francesca made her way downstairs to begin the day's chores.

By the time the first of her sisters arrived it was to find the candles lit, a fire burning on the hearth, the water cistern filled and heating, a pot of porridge cooking nicely and coffee being brewed. Outside, daylight had not yet crept fully across the sky.

'Morning, Francesca.'

'Morning, Anne.'

'I swear it is cold enough to snow today.'

'Then perhaps we'll have a white Christmas after all,' said Francesca with a smile.

'I hope so.' Anne went to fill the log basket from the pile stacked outside the back door.

Sophy came bounding down the stairs. 'It's Christmas Eve. It's Christmas Eve!' She was the baby of the family and much indulged—as far as that was possible in the Linden household.

Eventually everyone arrived to take their place at the breakfast table before the work of the day began. Mrs Linden sat at the head of the table and Tom at the foot, with the girls in between. The porridge was warming and nourishing, and chased the cold from their bones. They needed it, for although the fire had been lit, the night chill had not yet left the little cottage. Mrs Linden sipped at her coffee, her face pale and fatigued despite her night's sleep. She set the cup down while a coughing fit seized her. The deep hacking sound made Francesca's blood run cold, and her eyes met Tom's across the table. She knew that he was as worried as she.

When the bulk of the chores had been completed, Francesca, Tom, Lydia and Sophy set off for the Portlemouth ferry, leaving Anne and their mother reading by the fire. Francesca and Tom walked together, while Lydia and Sophy rushed in front, impatient to reach the ferry that would take them to Salcombe and the Christmas market.

Francesca glanced ahead to where Lydia and Sophy were walking arm in arm. 'I have been trying to get you alone all week. I wish to speak to you of last week, Tom, and I do not want the girls to overhear.'

'In case they realise that you were present that night?'

'We agreed that no one should know.'

'Relax, Fran. I'm not about to start shouting it from the rooftops. What was it that you wished to speak of?'

'Of you, Tom, and how you came to be in with Lord Holberton and the *Swift*.'

'I knew what I was doing.'

'Acting as Lord Holberton's inside man? Spying on the Buckleys for him? I doubt that most sincerely. You could have been killed— and for what?'

'To help catch a traitor, Francesca, and clear our shore of the Buckleys. With those villains transported maybe there will be a living to be had here for the rest of us again.'

'Even so, you should never have put yourself at such risk. I take it that it was through Lord Holberton that you became involved?'

'He sought me out—said I was the best man for the job.'

'The Marquess of Flete's son?'

'Don't look so surprised, Francesca. I may be only a fisherman, but I have some worth.'

'That's not what I meant.'

'There's nothing to be gained by this discussion,' he said, somewhat sourly. 'We should forget about the *Swift* and Lord Jack Holberton as surely as he has forgotten about us.'

His words stirred a disquiet in her. They were easily enough said, and the most sensible of advice, yet Francesca knew in her heart that she could never do as he advised. What had happened that night was imprinted upon her brain. She could not forget it. It haunted her dreams, and even during the day it seemed that the memory was never far away. And the strangest thing of all was that she felt more affected now than she had been during the actual experience.

'I have not given them a second thought.' She did not meet his eye.

'Then that, at least, is well. Here.'

She looked up to find him thrusting a purse of coins in her direction.

'We'll celebrate Christmas properly for once. I've already ordered the coal, and this should buy more than enough food.'

Francesca peered suspiciously at the bulging purse.

'It's my share of the reward money for catching Grosely,' Tom said. 'Take it. Lord knows, you earned it as much as me.'

Slowly she reached out her hand and took the purse. They walked on in silence towards Portlemouth.

The Christmas market in Salcombe comprised brightly coloured stalls set up in the main street of the town. The crowd was so thick that it was difficult to negotiate from one side of the road to the other. There were pie sellers and jugglers, freshly baked loaves and wooden carved toys.

Francesca left her sisters admiring a stall of pretty baubles while she visited the apothecary to purchase a bottle of cough linctus for her mother. The purse weighed heavy in the pocket of her cloak as she threaded her way through the bustle of people, and turned her thoughts all the more to what had happened aboard the *Swift*…and Lord Holberton.

She passed a stall on which great handfuls of silk and satin ribbons fluttered like rainbow pennants in the wind. She paused and touched a hand to the shiny lengths, thinking that her sisters would dearly love such a gift. Tom's money would have to last, she knew that, but it *was* Christmas and the girls deserved a treat. So Francesca bought the ribbons, and a pretty new cap for her mother, and a scarf for Tom. She paused to admire a fine silver chain to which was attached a tiny silver ship that had the look of the *Swift* about it. Her fingers lingered over the necklace, and she wondered whether it was more than chance that had led her to it. But the necklace was as costly as it was beautiful. One last look, and then she set the little ship back in its box and continued on her way through the market to the place she had left her sisters.

All around delicious aromas wafted, filling her nostrils with roasted chestnuts, baked potatoes and mince pies. The day might be grey and cold and windy, but the busy Christmas market seemed filled with cheer.

Sophy bounded over to her. 'Look, Fran, they're selling chestnuts over there. They smell wonderful, don't they?' Sophy looked over at the chestnut-seller's brazier with longing, but the experience of hardship had taught the thirteen-year-old better than to ask for what she knew they could not afford.

Francesca thought of the purse and the coins within it. 'Would you like some?'

'Can we really?' Sophy's eyes sparkled and her face lit up.

Francesca felt her heart well that so small a thing could bring such delight. She dropped the necessary coins into Sophy's hand. Sophy and Lydia ran off and returned with bags of piping hot chestnuts that burned their fingers and brought billows of steam from their mouths.

Tom appeared, carrying a huge turkey in a sack upon his shoulder. A grin spread across his face. 'Do you think this bird is big enough?'

Sophy and Lydia squealed in surprised delight, and Francesca smiled.

'And I think I spotted a mulled wine stall just over there.' He pointed back in the direction from which he had come.

They made their way through the crowd, smelling the mulled wine stall before they could see it. The air was ripe with the spicy aroma. Francesca slipped some more coins from the purse and bought them all some of the warm red wine. They stood sipping from the edge of their cups, trying not to burn their mouths, tasting the cloves and cinnamon and oranges.

Tom, Lydia and Sophy wandered off to watch a man taking bets on finding the nut beneath the cups. Francesca adjusted the basket against her hip and checked that the purse was secure. She was just about to follow her brother and sisters when something made her glance to the right, to where a gap had opened up. Francesca's heart jumped. She gasped and stared in shock. For there across the street was Jack Holberton, and he was looking right at her.

Chapter 4

A CROWD of bodies passed between them, obscuring Francesca's view. And by the time the street had cleared enough for her to see again, the place where Lord Holberton had stood was occupied by a small rotund man and his lady wife. Francesca peered all around, but of the man she had seen—or rather thought she had seen—there was no sign. She blinked several times and touched her gloved fingers to her forehead, feeling suddenly afraid that she was so affected by that night upon the *Swift* she was imagining Lord Holberton at every turn.

'Are you feeling unwell, Francesca? You look like you've just seen a ghost.' Lydia came over and took her arm, looking at her with a worried expression.

'No, no,' said Francesca reassuringly. 'I'm very well. I was just fixing my basket.'

'You're very pale all of a sudden.'

'I'm cold, that's all.' Francesca forced a smile. 'It's getting late. We should leave now if we're to be home before it's dark.'

'But it's only half past two,' protested Lydia.

'And it will be dark by four,' said Francesca.

'Very well.' Lydia smiled. 'Tom guessed the wrong cup four times and lost his money. Sophy and I were just as bad. That conjurer is very good at making the nut disappear.'

'Then we had best fetch Tom and Sophy before they lose *all* of their money.' Francesca took Lydia's arm within her own, and together they made their way through the crowd towards the conjurer's stall.

They had almost reached the table with the three wooden cups set upside down upon it when Lydia said, 'He's talking to someone—a gentleman.'

Francesca stopped suddenly. She raised her eyes and looked ahead. There, standing beside her brother, was Lord Holberton. His eyes met hers. She forgot to breathe.

Tom glanced round and saw Francesca. He looked slightly embarrassed. 'Lord Holberton, may I introduce you to my sisters?'

Francesca did not want to look. All she could think of was lying beside Jack Holberton, the caress of his hands and the heat of his kiss. Her heart was thumping too fast in her chest, she suddenly felt too warm, and there was the distinct suggestion of a tremble in her legs.

Her sisters were staring eagerly at the gentleman.

She had the urge to run away. But Francesca did not give in to urges. She took a deep breath and, squaring her shoulders, faced Lord Holberton.

'Miss Linden, Miss Lydia Linden, and Miss Sophy Linden,' said Tom. 'Anne is at home with our mother.'

Jack Holberton removed his hat and bowed. 'I'm pleased to meet you, Miss Linden,' he said, as if they were strangers meeting for the first time.

Francesca's cheeks heated. 'Likewise, sir,' she said, and was relieved to hear that at least her voice sounded normal.

'Miss Lydia, Miss Sophy,' he said politely, and made a bow that encompassed them both.

'My lord.' The girls were all wide-eyed surprise. They did not meet many gentlemen—especially gentlemen of Jack Holberton's ilk. They stared at his coat of dark blue superfine, at the way it fitted so snugly across the breadth of his shoulders and his back. Their eyes did not miss his expensive buff-coloured breeches, or the high polish of his fine leather riding boots. Or the neckcloth that was tied as they had never seen.

His dark hair was ruffled by the breeze. He was quite the most devastatingly attractive man Francesca had ever seen, and that thought, along with her reaction to him, quite discomposed her, making her feel defensive and prickly. 'It's getting late. I'm afraid we must leave you; we are to catch the ferry.'

Jack Holberton smiled. 'I'm for the ferry myself.'

Surprise widened her eyes, and her heart spurred to an all-out gallop, but she managed to keep her voice coolly polite. 'Really?'

'Really.' The corners of his mouth curved ever so slightly.

'But Flete is in quite the opposite direction.' She could have kicked herself as soon as the words were out, but there was nothing she could do to recall them.

'You are correct, Miss Linden.' He continued to look at her. 'I'm not going to Flete.'

'Evidently not,' she said, and then, catching sight of the expression on Sophy's face, made an effort to be more congenial. 'Have you been shopping at the market, my lord?'

'I had a few Christmas gifts to buy.' But there was no evidence that he had purchased any goods; his hands were quite empty. She supposed that he had servants to deal with such things, but she could see none in the vicinity.

He glanced down at her bulging basket. 'You appear to have had more success than me. Please allow me, Miss Linden.' He made to take the basket from her.

'Thank you, my lord, but it is not heavy.'

'Even so, as a gentleman...' His hand closed around the basket handle, not so very far from where her own fingers rested.

She tightened her grip. 'I thank you for your offer, but I can manage very well.'

Lord Holberton did not relinquish his hold on the handle.

'My lord,' she said meaningfully, and looked him directly in the eye.

A whisper of amusement played around his eyes and lips. He returned her look, not in the slightest bit put out.

She did not need to glance round to know that Tom and Lydia and Sophy were staring in shocked silence at the ridiculous scene unfolding before their eyes. It seemed that Jack Holberton cared not in the slightest. And then, just when she thought that he would stand there for the rest of the day with his hand wrapped firm around her basket handle, he yielded.

'As you wish, Miss Linden.' His hand dropped back down to his side.

Francesca had won the battle, but victory was not sweet. She was left feeling that she had been both ungracious and unreasonable— especially when she saw her sisters' faces.

'We shall miss the boat if we do not leave now,' said Tom, his gaze shifting from Francesca to Lord Holberton and back again.

'Of course,' said Francesca, and bit at her lip. 'Let us be on our way.'

She did not look again at Lord Holberton, just gathered her sisters to her and began to walk. Never in her life had Francesca behaved in such a way. She forced a deep breath and tried to calm herself. It was all Lord Holberton's fault, of course. But even as she thought it Francesca knew that it was not true. It was her own fault and no one else's. She just did not know why Jack Holberton affected her so.

The journey across the estuary lasted only ten minutes, yet to Francesca it seemed much longer. She was acutely conscious of Lord Holberton, even though it was Tom to whom he spoke. Francesca and her sisters listened while Lord Holberton told Tom that all of the Buckleys had been apprehended and were in prison awaiting trial. The most likely outcome was transportation, although if it could be proved they had any knowledge of the smuggling of British secrets then they would hang. Sophy and Lydia's eyes were like saucers as they hung on Lord Holberton's every word.

When they disembarked at Portlemouth Lord Holberton gestured towards a carriage some distance away. 'I would be happy to take you all home.'

Lydia and Sophy made little exclamations of surprise and grinned excitedly at each another. It had been years since they were in a carriage, and never in one as fine as that which stood across the road.

'That is very kind of you, my lord.' Francesca's pulse was racing, but she looked at him quite calmly. 'But we cannot possibly inconvenience you so.'

'It will be no inconvenience,' said Lord Holberton in his lazy tone. 'Indeed, I insist. Lannacombe is a fair distance from here.'

'A mere three miles, sir,' she replied.

'You have a proper carriage?' asked Sophy. Lydia nudged her.

'A coach and four, warm and well sprung.'

'Oh!' Sophy's mouth gaped.

He was simply here to see Tom, she told herself. Yet it did not stop the fluttering in her stomach or the gallop of her heart. A large drop of rain hit her cheek. Two more landed on her bonnet, and then it began to rain in earnest, great plump raindrops driving into the ground. The other passengers who had crossed from Salcombe picked up their bags and began to run. The ferry disappeared back across the water.

'And did I mention that it is dry?' said Lord Holberton.

The rain fell harder.

'Thank you, my lord, that would be most welcome,' Francesca said in as dignified a manner as she could manage.

They hurried across the street to where the fine carriage and four sat waiting, its coachman at the ready. Lord Holberton and Tom sat on one seat; the girls sat opposite.

During the journey his gaze frequently came to rest on Francesca. And when his eyes met hers she knew that her brother had been wrong in thinking that Jack Holberton had forgotten about either of them.

* * *

The journey in the coach brought such joy to her sisters that it gladdened Francesca's heart. The rain's deluge had eased, and bright light pierced a hole in the thick cloud canopy like a shaft direct from heaven, to paint a rainbow on the dark canvas of the sky. There was a sense of something special about the afternoon. The rich deep browns of the fields and the green of the grass were clear and vivid. Withered leaves still crowded in corners from their autumn fall. The damp cold scent of winter filled the air. Over the rumble of the coach wheels came the song of blackbirds and a robin.

The journey was over too quickly, and it hardly seemed any time before they were drawing up at the little cottage in Lannacombe.

'Won't Mama and Anne be surprised?' said Lydia.

'They won't believe their eyes,' said Sophy.

Francesca was the last to climb down the steps from the carriage.

'Thank you, my lord.' She looked up at him, still ashamed of her previous behaviour, not knowing quite what to say. The eyes that met hers were not black, as she had thought before, but a warm dark velvet brown, and she felt that same strange sensation that had passed between them aboard the *Swift*. It seemed to Francesca that those few seconds stretched to an eternity.

And then Lydia's voice interrupted and the spell was broken. 'Francesca, can his lordship come in for some tea? Mama and Anne would be so happy.'

Lord Holberton looked at Francesca.

There was no other answer that Francesca could give. 'Of course,' she said. 'If he would care to.'

Lord Holberton smiled. 'Thank you,' he said. 'That would be delightful.'

Jack was all politeness when he was introduced to Mrs Linden and the third of Francesca's sisters, Anne. Yet he did not miss the older woman's gaunt frame, or the unhealthy pallor of her cheeks.

'My lord, you are very welcome in our home. Will you take some refreshment? Some tea, perhaps?' Mrs Linden coughed, and the effort racked the poor woman.

Jack saw the worry that dimmed Francesca's face at the harsh hacking sound, and it was as if a hand had reached in and squeezed at his heart. It was a disconcerting feeling. 'Thank you.'

'Let me fetch it, Mama,' said Francesca. She smiled at her mother and disappeared from the room.

Jack perched on the edge of the small armchair to which he had been directed. Mrs Linden sat in the other chair, closest to the fire-place. Francesca's three sisters sat in a row on the sofa, and Tom leaned against the wall by the window. In one sweeping gaze Jack had seen it all: the dampness that crept up the walls, the threadbare rugs and cushions, the shabby furniture, and the valiant way that the room had been decorated with swathes of greenery and mistletoe and holly. A pile of pinecones sat arranged upon the table. Beneath him, the chair's upholstery was sagging so much that Jack dared not relax his full weight into it lest he end up on the floor. The fire that burned on the hearth was small, and threw out little heat. Taking all this into consideration, it was little wonder that Mrs Linden's health was poor.

Sophy and Lydia sat pink-cheeked, excited and tongue-tied. Anne calmly stitched at her needlework.

'Do you go home to celebrate Christmas Day, my lord?' asked Mrs Linden.

'I do. My father's estate is not so distant. The family spend Christmas at Flete every year.'

'I'm sure that your parents will be very glad to have you home,' said Mrs Linden.

Francesca returned with the tea tray. He watched while she poured tea into a cup and passed it first to him. Then cups were produced for her mother, Tom, her sisters, and finally herself.

'My father is holding a ball in three days' time at Holberton House. The cards have been sent, but I thought I may as well mention it as I am here. He would be pleased if you could attend.'

Six surprised faces turned to him.

'All of us?' asked Sophy.

'Yes, all of you,' laughed Jack. 'He is aware of the role that Tom played in bringing those villains to justice,' he said, by way of explanation—although that was not the reason he had asked his father to invite the Lindens to the ball.

Tom could not hide his smile.

'How very kind,' said Mrs Linden, pride and pleasure colouring her cheeks pink. 'We would be delighted to accept.'

Only Francesca said nothing.

He drank his tea to excited chatter about the ball, before making his excuses. 'The hour grows late. Perhaps Miss Linden would be kind enough to see me out to my carriage?'

'Of course,' she said politely.

As the Lindens had no maid, it was Francesca herself who fetched his hat and gloves. And, as he had requested, walked with him down the narrow pathway of the front garden towards the road. Some distance away, his coachman was walking the horses to keep them warm.

Time was running out for the day. Already the sky held the first shadow of night, and the air had cooled to an icy chill.

'I trust you will have a safe journey home.' She pulled her shawl tighter around her.

He could hear the wind stirring the bare branches of the trees and the few leaves that remained in defiance of the weather. From the corner of his eye he could see Francesca's sisters peeking from the window. He stood with Francesca by the gatepost. 'Are you quite recovered from your experience of last week?' His voice was low.

'Yes, thank you, my lord.'

'My name is Jack.'

'I remember,' she said, and then blushed as if that memory brought all the others.

'And you have not had the urge to revisit the harbour?' he asked with a wry smile.

'Certainly not,' she said, but she smiled with the words. 'You should have told me that Tom was working for you...of what was happening that night.'

'Would you have believed me?' He raised an eyebrow suggestively. 'After all, you did think that I was abducting you from the harbour.'

He saw the colour wash deeper in her cheeks. 'That was different.' She glanced away, and when she looked back her expression was quite under control. 'While I have the opportunity I should protest over you recruiting my brother to such a scheme in the first place.'

'Tom was the ideal candidate for the job. As a local and a fisherman he could infiltrate the gang easily enough, and it wasn't difficult for him to inform me of what he learned.'

'It may not have been difficult, but it was downright dangerous.' She paused. 'What was he even doing there that night? You had all the information you needed.'

There was no anger in her voice, and he guessed that she was just trying to make sense of what exactly had happened aboard the boat. He was still trying to do that himself. 'Tom was a regular on the *Swift*. Had he not been present suspicions may have been aroused. White was nervous enough as it was with Buckley's absence.'

'I take it you were behind his disappearance?'

He gave a nod.

There was a small silence, and then she glanced up at him quickly, as if she had been struck by a sudden thought. 'Our meeting in Salcombe was one of chance, was it not, sir?' He saw suspicion flicker in her eyes. 'You did not come to recruit Tom to another of your schemes?'

'I did not.' He laughed. 'Your brother is quite safe, I promise you.' Yet he did not tell her that he had known from Tom that the Lindens would be attending the Christmas market, and that he had waited there much of the day for her arrival.

She smiled. 'I do not know if I am reassured by your promises.'

Her eyes met his, and he was conscious again, as he had been aboard the *Swift*, that Miss Linden was a woman like no other. He was glad that he had decided to seek her out. 'Promises are as gifts at this time of year. They must be kept. I wish you Happy Christmas for tomorrow, Miss Linden.'

'Happy Christmas, Lord Holberton.'

He inclined his head, gave a bow, and walked through the gate to where his carriage waited.

Jack watched from the carriage window until he could see her no more, and even then his thoughts stayed with the girl who stood on the cottage path in the fading light.

That night Francesca could not find sleep. She lay rigid at the edge of the bed and listened to the soft snores and snuffles of her sisters. Thoughts raced through her head, refusing to give her peace. She barely knew Lord Holberton, nor he her. Yet today when she had seen him... She remembered the skitter of her heart when she had spied him across the market, and the shivers of excitement that his presence had caused. No matter that she might wish it otherwise, she could not pretend that she was indifferent to him. His mere presence had her acting all out of sorts. It was ridiculous. He was a womaniser, a drunkard and a gambler. Hadn't he told her as much himself? A man without honour, a man who could only be dangerous to know.

She remembered the role he had played for White—the boldness of his gaze over her body, the lust so blatant in his eyes, the arrogance in his voice. So very convincing, and she could guess why. Lord Holberton was bad through and through, and heaven only knew how many times she had heard talk of such men. But the little voice inside her head whispered that the play-act had ironically saved not only her virtue but her life. Had it not been for Jack... And she could not forget that she had looked into the dark depths of his eyes and seen his pain and felt his torment. A single act of honour might save a man, she had said. And hadn't Jack Holberton done more than that already, with White and the Buckleys and herself?

She should dissuade Mama from accepting the invitation. It would be the right thing to do, given that she seemed to be in danger of developing an unhealthy obsession with the man. Just thinking of him made Francesca's skin tingle, and that could most definitely not be construed as right for any young lady. But the chance of a proper ball, with all that music and dancing and merriment, would be such a treat for Mama and the girls…and, dared she admit it, for herself? She could not deny them that, could she? Even if it meant seeing Lord Holberton again? Surely she was not so silly and missish that she could not conduct herself properly in his presence? Besides, there would be a great crowd of guests present, and Lord Holberton in all probability would not even notice her. The thought did not make Francesca feel any better.

Lord! She almost groaned aloud. What was happening to her? Her mind was a tumble of thoughts. She sighed and, sitting up, slipped quietly from the bed, collected her shawl and padded across the bedchamber to the window. She peeped through the curtain, staring out at the clear night sky with the thickened crescent of the moon and its smattering of stars. Directly in her line of vision was one star that was larger and glittered more brightly than the others. She drew back and touched a finger to the glass, as if she would touch the star itself. And then she remembered that it was Christmas Eve, and recalled all the Christmas Eves that had gone before. Francesca thought about her dear dead papa. She thought about her poor mama, and Tom, and her sisters. She thought about Jack Holberton. And she could not rid herself of the notion that this Christmas would change everything.

'Francesca?' He mother whispered in a sleepy voice through the darkness. 'What is wrong?'

Francesca moved away from the window. 'All's well, Mama. Go back to sleep.' She heard her mother turning over and settling once again beneath the covers. Francesca climbed into her place in the bed across the room, and at last found sleep.

On the day after Boxing Day the carriage drew into a wide gravel driveway, and Francesca and her family collectively sighed in wonder. The house that lay before them was a fine mansion, built in Portland stone. Francesca thought of the little cottage they had left behind, and realised anew how very different Lord Holberton's world was from their own.

There was little time to dwell on the thought, for the carriage soon came to a halt and the Linden family alighted to stand before Holberton House.

Sophy's eyes were wide with wonder. She had never seen such a place. 'This is where Lord Holberton lives?' she asked in disbelief.

'This is the home of his father, the Marquess of Flete,' said Tom.

'It's quite beyond belief,' said Lydia.

If the Lindens had thought the exterior of the house impressive, they were left speechless by its interior. It was furnished in an elaborate style, with gilt and mirrors and heavy gold brocade. The ceiling of the huge hallway had been painted with a host of angels, so that it seemed as if one could stand there and look directly up into heaven.

'Come along, girls. Come along Tom.' Francesca heard the slight change in her mother's voice. It seemed stronger somehow, more confident, as if she was resuming a mantle from long ago. Francesca walked beside Tom at the back of the little family group.

'Well, I'll be damned!' said Tom under his breath.

'Tom!' Francesca gave a scandalised whisper.

'How the other half live.'

There was nothing she could say to that.

They were shown to their rooms. Mrs Linden had the lilac room, all to herself. Lydia and Sophy were sharing the yellow guest chamber. Tom was shown to a small room decorated in gentlemanly shades of brown. Francesca and Anne's room was the furthermost along the corridor of bedchambers. The door swung open to reveal a chamber of cream and rose. The walls had been hung with the most beautiful rolls of paper painted with pink roses. There were pink and cream rugs scattered around the floor. The bed was a four-poster, carved in oak and covered with an ivory-coloured counterpane and pillows embroidered with small pink roses. Pale winter sunshine flooded though the large window, highlighting the crystal sconces that were fixed upon the walls. The room was warm from the fire that blazed on the hearth of the white marble fireplace. All in all it was quite the most beautiful room that Francesca had ever seen.

Out in the corridor she could hear the opening and closing of doors, the scurry of footsteps and the excited lilt of Lydia and Sophy's voices. A knock sounded at the door and a footman delivered their two small travelling bags, which seemed shabby and out of place amidst such surroundings. Anne set about testing the bed, while Francesca sat down in a small pink chair and began to unfasten the ribbons of her bonnet. Dinner and a night of dancing lay ahead. Yet it was not the prospect of those two things that set a tingle down Francesca's spine.

At nine o'clock that evening Francesca stood in the ballroom of Holberton House beside Tom. Mrs Linden sat nearby, with her three youngest daughters. Apart from the Marquess, who had greeted them upon their initial arrival, no one had spoken to them, and the closest the girls had come to dancing was the speculative gazes from certain gentlemen that made Francesca want to box their ears. Of Lord Holberton there was no sign. He had not come down to dinner, nor could she see him anywhere in the ballroom now. She supposed she should be glad of that, at least.

'This could have been the manner of our living, Francesca, had Papa not argued with Grandpapa.' Tom watched the young gentlemen swanking about before them.

'Such speculation is ill advised. Our lives are what they are. Papa always did his best to ensure our happiness.'

'To sentence Mama and us to such poverty can hardly be construed as doing his best.'

'He is dead, Tom. How can you say such a thing?'

'It's nothing less than the truth,' said Tom.

'We know nothing of the details of Papa's disagreement with his family. I'm sure he would not have isolated himself from them lightly. It's not our place to judge.'

Tom did not look convinced, but he said nothing more on the matter. They stood watching the dancers upon the floor, Francesca surreptitiously scanning the crowd.

'He's not here,' said her brother.

'Who do you mean?' Francesca stopped looking around and fixed her gaze upon her brother.

'Lord Holberton.'

'I had not noticed.'

'Don't lie,' said Tom. 'You've been looking for him since we arrived.'

'I most certainly have not.' Francesca flashed him an indignant expression.

'Be careful, Francesca. It is not marriage that he has in mind. Men like Holberton do not marry into families like ours.'

Francesca stared at her brother. 'What nonsense are you talking, Tom?'

'I'm not blind, Francesca. I see the way he looks at you. He wants you in his bed.'

'Tom!' she exclaimed, feeling the heat rush into her cheeks.

'Would you have me say nothing? Just stand by and let him ruin you?'

Francesca's mouth dropped open. Her nostrils flared; her eyes widened. 'I have no intention of having anything remotely to do with Lord Holberton. What do you take me for? Some kind of simpleton?' Her breaths were short and shaky with suppressed emotion.

'I'm just warning you, Francesca, what manner of man Lord Holberton is when it comes to women.'

'I appreciate your concern, Tom, but as I said, there is no need. I have not the slightest—' Francesca broke off what she was saying, suddenly aware that the whispers of a small group of ladies standing close by had grown louder and progressed to titters, and even finger-pointing in her and Tom's direction. 'Perhaps we should finish this discussion later.'

Francesca knew very well what lay behind those unfriendly faces with their arched eyebrows and curled upper lips. She knew that, despite her mother's best efforts, her own clothing and that of her family was worn and outmoded, in stark contrast to the rest of Lord Flete's guests.

'Or somewhere else altogether,' said Tom rather bitterly. 'You see the way they look at us? We don't belong here. We never should have come.'

And in that moment Francesca was forced to agree.

Jack saw Francesca almost the moment that he entered the ballroom, standing over in the corner beside her brother. She was wearing a pale green dress with matching gloves that emphasised her clear complexion and the warm honeyed blonde of her hair. Her hair had been styled in the classical fashion, its curls gathered and pinned up high on the back of her head, with a few stray tendrils dangling on either side of her face. The sight of her stirred a feeling of excitement in Jack. He was glad his journey was done. It had been a long two days, trailing to Salisbury and back, but the trip had been worthwhile, yielding more than he had expected.

He kept Francesca in sight as he threaded his way around the outside of the crowd, uttering replies to the greetings he received and avoiding those he knew would delay him in conversation. It was Francesca to whom he wished to speak.

He saw the expression on her face change, saw the anger and indignation before it was masked. He moved steadily closer towards the couple. It seemed that whatever was being said held both brother and sister's attention completely, for neither noticed his approach. Then she stopped suddenly and glanced towards the women standing not so distant from them. His gaze followed hers, and he saw the disdain on the faces, heard the pretentious little laughs and the whispered remarks.

Something flared inside Jack so that his anger was cold and incisive and determined. He moved quickly away, found those he sought, and spoke a few emphatic words in their ears before returning to Tom and Francesca Linden.

'Ah, Linden,' he said loudly, knowing that his voice would be heard by those around. 'Glad to see you again.' He walked right up to a rather startled-looking Tom, and shook the lad's hand before delivering Francesca a bow. 'Your servant, Miss Linden. Forgive me my absence, I was meeting an old friend in Salisbury last night and am not long returned.'

He caught Sebastian Chortlewate's eye across the room, and signalled to him to come over. Chortlewate first reassured himself that there was no one else behind him at whom Lord Holberton could possibly have been looking, before making his way through the crowd as quickly as a fashionable gentleman could. Jack might have been society's bad boy, but he was held somewhat in awe by many young gentlemen—including Sebastian Chortlewate. So Chortlewate came trotting, just as Jack had known that he would.

Jack smiled in a semblance of friendliness at Chortlewate.

Chortlewate returned the smile, trying, and failing, to hide his eagerness.

'May I introduce you to Tom Linden?'

Tom showed a slightly startled rabbit expression before pulling himself together.

'Mr Linden is a very good friend of mine.' Jack looked at Chortlewate.

Chortlewate paled. 'Beg your pardon, Holberton, I didn't know.' Then he shook Tom's hand. 'How do you do, Mr Linden.'

'Take Tom and introduce him to a few people,' said Jack.

And Chortlewate did.

Jack turned to Francesca. She had not moved. She just stood there with her head held high, her eyes following her brother's departure across the room. And then her gaze turned to him.

'Miss Linden,' he said, aware that the small gaggle of women were positively staring.

'Lord Holberton,' she said smoothly.

The reel that was being danced came to its finish. 'Shall we dance?'

There was a hesitation in which he thought she might refuse him, but then she smiled politely and allowed Jack to lead her out on to the dance floor.

The music began.

Francesca's fingers felt warm within Jack's.

He smiled at her.

'Thank you for that,' she said.

'For what?'

'Introducing Tom.'

'It is what people do at balls—introduce one another and dance. So I introduced, and now I'm dancing. I'm not the only one.' He gestured with his eyes across the dance floor.

Francesca followed his gesture and saw all three of her sisters dancing—even young Sophy. When she looked to where her mother sat, Mrs Linden appeared to be engaged in conversation with none other than Lady Flete. And she knew that Lord Holberton was responsible. The ladies were no longer tittering or chattering. They stood silent, their startled expressions narrowing to jealousy as they looked from her to Lord Holberton.

Francesca could not help herself: she smiled. Lord Holberton was smiling too. They looked into each other's eyes and shared the success of the moment.

The evening passed too quickly, and after a hearty breakfast the next morning, and a delightful walk through the winter gardens in Holberton House, the Lindens departed for home in Lord Holberton's carriage. All the way back Francesca looked out across the bleak winter landscape and felt a strange sense of excitement. One night of dancing. One morning's walk in a garden. Nothing to do with Lord Holberton, she thought. But she smiled all the same.

It was not long after lunchtime the next day when Tom sought her out in the kitchen, where she was scrubbing the soup pot.

The sky was a dull whitened grey. There was a stillness in the air and the temperature seemed impossibly cold. Francesca's hands might be reddened but at least the water in which they were plunged was warm. Steam rose from it to cloud the windows and thaw the air within the little kitchen. Francesca had discarded her shawl, so that it did not become wet from the water, and was scrubbing at the pot with vigour. She was humming a tune beneath her breath and smiling to herself when Tom walked in.

She knew that something was wrong by the way he closed the door behind him. She glanced round and saw the expression upon his face.

'What is it? What's wrong?' she asked, pulling her hands from the water and drying them upon her apron skirts.

'Lord Holberton is here…' He did not say the rest. He did not need to; she could see it in his face. 'Mama has asked if you will make some tea.'

Francesca's pulse jumped, but she gave no sign, just started the tea preparations. 'It would seem that he has taken quite a liking to you, Tom.'

'Would that were the case, Fran. But I suspect that it is not me he has come to see. He danced three times with you at the ball.'

'He did, and he also danced with Anne, Lydia and Sophy.'

'Only once each.'

'And he made a point of introducing you, Tom. By doing what he did he ensured our acceptance. The evening would have been a disaster otherwise.'

Tom shrugged her words away. 'He did not stray from your side during our walk in the gardens of Holberton House yesterday morning.'

'He was our host, he could do little else.'

They looked at one another.

She made the rest of the tea in silence, while Tom looked on. 'Come, we had both best go through to the parlour.'

She unfastened her apron and folded it over the back of one of the chairs by the table. Her heart was beating fast, and she was aware of a small flare of excitement deep within, but Francesca's demeanour appeared as nothing other than its normal self. She smoothed back the loose tendrils that had escaped her chignon, tucking them back in as best she could with fingers that felt all atremble.

'I'm sure you are wrong, Tom,' she said. 'But in the off chance you are not, then I assure you that Lord Holberton is wasting his time.' Francesca lifted the tea tray and walked towards the kitchen door.

Chapter 5

LORD HOLBERTON was warming himself in front of the parlour fire. He had driven himself over to the cottage in his gig and brought with him a huge spiced cake, which was now sitting upon the table.

'There you are, Francesca, with the tea and biscuits.' Mrs Linden smiled. 'May I offer you some, my lord?'

'Thank you,' said Jack.

Mrs Linden filled his cup. 'We had such a lovely time at the ball the other night—didn't we, girls?'

Anne, Lydia and Sophy, who were sitting in a line on the sofa, answered at once and in unison. 'Yes, Mama, delightful.'

Francesca stayed silent.

Lord Holberton took a sip of tea, then raised his gaze to look directly at her. 'And what of you, Miss Linden? Was the evening to your satisfaction?'

Francesca looked into his eyes and wondered if Tom was right—if Lord Holberton was toying with her. She was tempted to tell him that the evening had been tolerable. In truth, the evening had been terrible until Lord Holberton's appearance, and then, contrary to all her expectations, she had enjoyed Lord Holberton's company very much.

'As my sisters said, it was delightful,' she said, but the message in her eyes defied her words.

Jack's smile creased his eyes, as if he found her amusing.

Jack stayed until the light became thick and grey and shadowy.

'How dark it is, and the time is not yet even three o'clock,' said Mrs Linden. Francesca rose to light some candles and collect the cups and saucers on the tea tray, glancing through the window as she did so. 'Oh, dear!' She stopped, and looked again through the window.

Everyone stared.

Mrs Linden struggled to get up.

'No, no, Mama,' Francesca quickly reassured her. 'There's no need for alarm. It's just that it has been snowing—and heavily by the looks of things.'

'Snow!' Sophy bounded off the sofa and rushed to the window. 'Fran's right!' she said with excitement. 'It's completely white out there!'

'Let me see.' Lydia joined her sister at the window. 'My goodness!'

'Perhaps it would be prudent for Lord Holberton to leave before it gets any worse,' said Francesca.

Jack got to his feet.

'I'll fetch your great-coat and things,' said Anne.

'The roads might be too bad for travel. Lord Holberton might be stranded here,' said Sophy.

'I'm sure they'll be fine,' Francesca said.

But they weren't. The entire Linden family stood at the door of their cottage and watched Jack step out on to the path—or at least where the path had been. The snow was a deep, crisp carpet of white. Jack's boots almost disappeared beneath it.

Jack felt the falling snow settle on his cheeks and eyelashes. All the air was filled with a mass of large swirling snowflakes. He could barely see three feet before his eyes, let alone the road that lay somewhere beneath the snow. Overhead the sky was a thick white grey. There would be no abatement. All the landmarks and roads and potholes and rocks were already obscured. Only a fool would travel in such conditions.

'The snow is too bad. You must stay, my lord,' said Mrs Linden. 'I will not hear of you leaving in such weather.' And then she began to cough.

'Mama, go back through to the parlour.' Francesca removed her own shawl and quickly wrapped it around her mother's shoulders. 'The air out here is too cold for you.'

'But Lord Holberton must not—'

'Lord Holberton will, of course, stay with us until it's safe to travel,' soothed Francesca. She looked at Jack, standing outside in the snow. 'Is that not so, my lord?'

'Thank you, Miss Linden. I would prefer to delay my journey until tomorrow morning, if my presence will not be too much of an inconvenience.'

'No inconvenience at all, my lord,' said Mrs Linden between coughs.

Francesca steered her mother into the parlour and sat her down in the chair closest to the fire. The front door banged shut, but no Jack appeared. Francesca looked round in enquiry at her sisters as they trailed back into the parlour, clutching their shawls around them.

Sophy sniffed and wiped a hand across her nose. 'Jack has gone to see to his horse. He said he won't be long.'

'Sophy, use a handkerchief—and it is Lord Holberton, not Jack!' Mrs Linden might still be trying to catch her breath, but she was not about to let her youngest daughter get away with such behaviour.

'He said we were to call him Jack.' Sophy's lip petted.

'Even so, we must remember our manners.'

'Where will he sleep?' Anne asked.

'I know it is Christmas, but we can hardly put him out in the stable,' said Lydia.

Sophy started to giggle.

'I'm sure that Tom will not mind giving up his bed for one night,' said Mrs Linden.

Tom's thoughts on that would never be known, for there was the bang of the back door closing and the stamp of snowy boots against the mat. A few minutes later Lord Holberton appeared.

'Trojan will be comfortable enough in your stable,' Jack said, and began to peel off his outer garments once more. 'Now, who is for a game of whist?' He produced a pack of cards from his pocket. 'Gentlemen versus ladies? Or would that be too unfair, since Tom and I would undoubtedly win?'

'Nonsense!' said Sophy. 'We girls are excellent whist players. We shall beat you fair and square.'

So the rest of the afternoon was taken up with a tournament of whist, which Mrs Linden and Anne won. Francesca left them laughing and arguing and playing while she went to prepare dinner.

It was not until much later on, after the evening meal had been eaten, that Jack had a chance to speak to Francesca alone.

She was in the kitchen, washing the dinner plates in a basin within the sink, when she heard the door open. She glanced round, thinking it was one of her sisters, only to find Jack standing there. Her eyes widened in surprise and she could not prevent a smile. 'What are you doing in here? Go back through to the parlour and I'll bring you some more tea.'

'I've had enough tea to last me a lifetime.' He closed the door behind him and shrugged out of his coat.

'What are you doing?' She stared at him as if he had run mad.

He slipped his coat over the worn wooden back of a chair in the corner and then began to roll up his sleeves. 'I have come to assist you.'

Francesca looked at him in astonishment, and then laughed. 'We are not so hard on our guests, sir. You may return to the parlour in the knowledge that your bed for the night is safe.'

'I have always had a secret desire to fathom the mysteries of the scullery,' he said wryly.

'I assure you they are mysteries that you will be content to leave well alone.'

He laughed, and came to stand beside her. 'I do, of course, draw the line at the wearing of an apron.'

'That is a shame, for I would give much to see Lord Jack Holberton wearing a frilled apron.' She smiled.

'Minx!' he said, and stepped right up to her.

He was standing so close that Francesca felt a sudden shiver ripple through her. She turned quickly away and, dipping her dish brush into a little soap, found the next dirty plate and began to scrub at it.

'What do I do?' he asked.

'You go back through to the parlour, make yourself comfortable by the fire and converse with my brother.'

'I have already informed you of my dishwashing desires,' he said. 'You'll not be rid of me so easily, Francesca.'

'Mama would have a blue fit if she thought that a guest was being set to work in the kitchen.'

'Mrs Linden need not know.' He smiled and picked up a folded dishtowel from the nearby table.

Francesca stared at him in astonishment. 'Put that dish towel down at once.'

'You are sounding very authoritarian, Francesca.'

'I beg your pardon, sir,' she said. '*Please* place the dishtowel down. There is no need for it to be in your hands.'

'I liked the authoritarian tone better.'

'Jack!'

His smile broadened. He flaunted the dishtowel before her and lifted one of the dripping plates from the draining board beside the sink.

'Jack Holberton, if you do not put that plate and dishtowel down I shall…'

'Yes?' Jack smiled again. 'What is it that you're planning to do to me?'

Francesca gave a small sound of exasperation. 'You are quite the most stubborn man that I know.'

Jack shrugged and, placing the dried plate down on the table, began drying another wet one. 'I prefer to think of it as determination.'

Francesca shook her head. 'Is there nothing that will persuade you to retire to the parlour?'

'There is one thing.' His eyes slid to hers, and it seemed that they sparkled with sensuality.

Francesca's heart gave a little somersault.

'Don't you wish to know what it is?' he teased.

'No, I do not.'

He set the plate down on the table, and something of the teasing tone left his voice. 'I wished to speak to you alone, Francesca. I've been trying to do so all day, but there has been no opportunity.'

'Why should you wish to speak to me alone?' she said carefully, and continued with her washing up.

She heard him move across the kitchen to where he had left his coat, and when he returned he had a small black silk-covered box in his hand. 'I wanted to give you this.' The box lay on his palm. He held it out towards her.

She stared at the box. Her heart began to race. Her throat felt suddenly dry. Her teeth bit against her lower lip. She removed her hands from the warm soapy water and dried them against her apron. In all this time she had not yet looked at him. She made no move to touch the box.

'Francesca?' The box was edged a little closer towards her.

She looked up at him then, and there was unease in her eyes. 'I do not wish a gift from you.' At the back of her mind she heard the whisper of Tom's voice. *It is not marriage that he has in mind... I see the way he looks at you...* And now he was giving her a gift. Her cheeks scalded at the implication.

'It's a Christmas gift between friends, Francesca. Nothing more.' His eyes scanned hers, as if he could see what she was thinking. 'Open it.'

'No.'

So Jack opened the box. Inside lay a delicate silver chain, and on the end of the chain hung the ship from the Christmas market.

Her gaze came up to meet his.

His eyes held hers. 'It is the image of the *Swift*.'

She just looked at him, almost not breathing.

'I'll leave it here for you.' He closed the box and sat it on the table.

They heard footsteps from the parlour.

Jack eased back into his coat. By the time the parlour door opened he was gone, and the small black box was hidden inside Francesca's apron pocket.

Jack slept that night on the sofa in the parlour, much to Mrs Linden's shame. He would not turn Tom out of his bed for all of the woman's persuasions. A fire burned on the grate, but the room was still cold and the blankets thin.

Jack thought of Francesca. Her life was one of toil that would have tested the hardiest of matrons. Yet Francesca did not complain. Her common sense and practicality made other ladies appear pathetic by comparison. She was cheerful and bright and quick of mind. It seemed that none of her hardships had quelled her spirit or her self-possession.

He thought of all the night aboard the *Swift* had entailed. Francesca had been frightened, and yet she had striven hard to hide it. He smiled at the memory of the two of them lying side by side on the damp cold deck, and the smile deepened when he remembered the words she had uttered. *You greatly overestimate your appeal, sir.* And then there was the ball, when he had danced with her and they had shared amusement at what he had done. He suspected that they shared very much the same sense of humour.

He smiled as he remembered teasing her in the kitchen, and the fact that he, who had never so much as touched a dirty plate in his life, had helped wash and dry the family's dinner dishes. His father would never have believed it. Jack barely believed it himself. His friends would have laughed and told him to bed her and be done with it. Before last Christmas he probably would have said the very same thing. But Francesca was different, and Jack was no longer the man he had once been. He shifted upon the sofa and, still thinking of Francesca, eventually found sleep.

The next morning the snow was beginning to thaw. Francesca was busy in the kitchen, packing up a basket with food, while her mother sat on a chair pulled close to the fire.

'I'm worried about her, Francesca. She's an old lady, and it isn't right her being on her own.'

'Mama, Mrs Beeley will have it no other way. How many times have you asked her to come and stay with us? She's too proud.'

'So proud that we will find her dead and frozen one of these mornings,' said Mrs Linden.

'When I saw her the other day she was fine. There was firewood chopped, and enough coal. And I put an extra blanket on her bed, just as you said.'

'I cannot help but worry in this weather. What if she goes out to fetch water and…?'

'Ease your worries, Mama. I will take her these provisions and check that she is well.'

'But what of the snow? It's more than a mile to her cottage. And Tom's ankle still pains him.'

'I shall manage very well on my own, Mama.'

Mrs Linden coughed. 'I do not like it. Maybe Anne should go with you.'

Francesca smiled and shook her head. 'Anne has enough to do here.' She wrapped her cloak around her, shoved her hands into a thick pair of woollen mittens and gathered up the basket. 'I'll be back before lunchtime.'

'Good morning.' A deep voice sounded.

Francesca glanced round to find Lord Holberton standing in the doorway.

'Shall I fetch you some tea, my lord?' Mrs Linden made to rise.

'No, thank you, Mrs Linden.' He walked into the kitchen. 'Please do not get up on my account.' His eyes moved to Francesca. 'You are going out, Miss Linden?'

'I am delivering some provisions to a neighbour.' Something in the way he looked at her sent a tingle down her spine. 'If you will excuse me, my lord?' She made to turn away, but his voice stopped her.

'Alone?'

'I bade her take Anne, but she will have none of it,' said Mrs Linden.

'Please allow me to accompany Miss Linden,' said Jack. 'It is the least I can do before I leave.'

'It would set my mind a little more at rest,' said Mrs Linden.

Francesca met his gaze and saw the look that dared her to refuse him. The devil in her made her smile sweetly and say, 'Thank you, Lord Holberton.'

The morning was bright and the air crisp as they walked together through the melting snow.

'I would offer to carry your basket, Miss Linden, but I know how steadfastly you prefer to carry it yourself.'

'If you are referring to the incident in Salcombe, then there was no need to carry my basket.'

'I was merely being polite,' he said.

'And I ill-mannered—as I'm sure you are about to tell me,' she replied.

'I was about to say no such thing.'

She glanced round at him 'But you were implying it.'

'Was I?'

'By pointing out your manners, you were highlighting my lack of them.'

'Or perhaps you are just feeling guilty, Miss Linden?' He glanced across at her.

'Not in the slightest,' she lied.

'Good.'

She cast him a quizzical look.

He laughed.

Francesca found that she was laughing with him. 'Perhaps I was a little forthright in my refusal.'

'Hercules could not have prised that basket from your grip.'

She laughed again. 'I'm stronger than I look.'

'You're quite the strongest woman I know.'

'Then you will admit that there was no need to accompany me on this journey.'

'I desired some fresh air, and to stretch my legs. I feel secure in the knowledge that your superior strength will protect us both.'

Francesca looked at him and shook her head, then smiled. 'Well, if I am doing the protecting, you may do the carrying, Jack Holberton.' She held out the basket towards him.

He grinned and took it.

Together they walked on, leaving behind them two sets of footprints—one large and one small.

Mrs Beeley proved to be in robust health, and she much enjoyed the company of Francesca and her 'young man', as she kept referring to Jack—which embarrassed Francesca and amused Jack.

With the provisions delivered, water fetched and tea made, Francesca and Jack set off to return to the Lindens' cottage. The thaw had opened up gaps in the white blanket that shrouded the countryside, allowing earth and grass to peep through. The sky was clear and pale, and filled with a weak, watery sunlight that found jewels within the melting ice. Great sparkling drops dripped from branches through which there darted a flicker of red: a robin singing its staccato song. From the distance came the caw of crows, and somewhere closer by the alarm call of a startled blackbird. Snow crunched beneath their boots.

They were soon close to Lannacombe, and had almost reached Francesca's home at the edge of the moorland. The burned-out shell of a cottage lay immediately ahead, its usual dark, dismal outline softened by remnants of snow. Opposite the old derelict building was a group of scrubby bushes, their thin twisted branches now more brown than white.

Francesca and Jack had been talking and laughing, but as they neared the ruins there seemed to be a strange silence in the air, as if all of the birds had fallen quiet. Jack slowed his pace and scanned the surrounding landscape.

'Jack?'

He touched his forefinger to his lips in a hushing sign.

There was a prickling across her scalp, and a shiver of foreboding rippled through her. Something was wrong. Francesca just did not know what. Then she saw the figure slip out from behind the dilapidated walls to stand directly in their path. The breath froze in her throat. She stared in horrified disbelief, for there, not four paces before them, was Edmund Grosely, leaning on his cane.

'Ah, Holberton—at last. So noble of you to accompany Miss Linden on her visit to Mrs Beeley.' He glanced at Francesca, 'Your sister was very helpful when I called at your home, looking for my dear friend Jack.'

Grosely had been at her house—had spoken to her sister… Francesca felt her stomach turn over at the thought.

'What the hell are you doing here, Grosely?' asked Jack.

'When I should be rotting in some jail awaiting my execution, you mean?' Grosely raised his eyebrows. 'What did you expect dear Papa to do? Turn up with the rest of the crowd to watch me swing?' Grosely smiled. 'No, we couldn't have me letting the family name down like that, could we? He's contesting your accusations. *You* planted the papers and framed me—didn't you know? Your wickedness was all so clear once my father had greased a few palms. To think what you would do to your own friend in a bid to save yourself. Shocking.'

'You introduced me into smuggling, remember. Not the other way around. And there's plenty that will testify to your actions, Grosely.'

'I think you'll find that your paltry witnesses have all disappeared. Christmas is such a dangerous time of year. Sets tempers alight in the prisons and on the streets outside gentlemen's clubs as well. Dead men cannot take the stand.'

'You always were a bastard,' Jack's eyes were cold and his expression hard.

'Just like you,' said Grosely, and stepped forward.

Jack handed Francesca the basket and gestured her behind him. 'You haven't yet answered my question, Grosely. What are you doing here?'

Grosely smirked. 'I'm sure you know the answer already, dear fellow.' And then his mouth straightened. 'I'm here to kill you—as slowly and painfully as I possibly can.'

Francesca's blood ran cold at the chilling words. 'But if you kill him then you'll rob yourself of a scapegoat,' she said.

'Not necessarily,' said Grosely. 'My father will have it put about that Holberton fled to the continent to avoid arrest. Still ploughing you, is he?' he asked conversationally.

She saw Jack's face pale, the tiny twitch in his jaw and the dangerous glitter in his eyes. Anger and disgust welled in Francesca. 'You are a disgusting and vile excuse for a man!'

Grosely laughed. 'You'll soon be singing a different tune, Miss Linden.'

'This is between you and me,' said Jack. 'Let the girl go.'

'You know I can't do that. She knows too much—her and that brother of hers.' Grosely angled his head to the side and looked at Francesca.

Jack moved so suddenly, so fluidly, so fast, that Francesca jumped. His fist slammed hard into Grosely's jaw. Grosely's head whipped back under the force and he seemed to stagger slightly, so that Francesca thought he would fall in a daze. But Grosely kept his feet. He fumbled with his cane, and then used it to strike at Jack. Francesca heard the whir of the wood as Grosely swung it through the air to land with a sickening thud against Jack's ribs. Grosely drew the cane back, and as he did so Jack kicked at the villain's hand, sending the cane flying off somewhere behind, where it landed with a clatter on top of a crumbling section of wall. Grosely grabbed at Jack, but the hold only brought a series of quick, fast jabs thumping into his body. He stumbled back; Jack pursued him, each punch more brutal than the last, each fist finding its target. But the beating did not stop Grosely. He kicked, and punched, and tried to bite.

The two figures strained backwards and forwards, trampling the grass and the snow flat, unwittingly edging closer to Francesca. She drew back, but she was still close enough to see the blood splatter from each impact of fist against face, to hear the awful thud of flesh and soft tissue and bone. Her heart was thumping so hard she thought she was going to be sick. She had no idea how to help Jack.

The punches rained harder in both directions, but Jack was the stronger, forcing Grosely back towards the wall of the cottage, punch by punch, hit by grinding hit. Francesca clenched her own fists, praying for Jack, willing him on. And it seemed that God heard her prayer, for once at the wall Grosely seemed to collapse, lurching forward and wrapping his arms around Jack, as if clinging on to that support was the only thing that kept him from falling completely. Jack had won.

But Francesca's joy and elation were barely formed when she saw Grosely's hand grope behind him, feeling desperately over the broken stones until it closed upon his cane. His fingers scrabbled with the handle until, she saw with horror, he pulled from the cane a long thin sword. Jack would not see the blade that arced towards his back.

Francesca screamed a warning and ran. Her only thought was to stop Grosely and save Jack. It seemed that time slowed. She could hear her breath loud in her ears, the thudding beat of her heart. All that filled her eyes was the terrible scene before her, and then she was there, and her hands had wrapped around Grosely's wrist, and she was dragging at his hand with all of her strength, stopping it from finding a path to Jack.

But Grosely was strong; that one solitary wrist did not relinquish its weapon, or its deadly intent. And then, just when she thought that he would not yield, that his strength would overcome hers, his hand slid back. She threw all of her weight against it as hard as she could, driving his hand back, pinning it against the wall, holding it there, where the sword still tight in its grip could not strike Jack. Jack landed one last punch, so hard that Francesca felt the reverberation of it through her hold on Grosely's hand. Grosely's head jerked back, hitting hard against the stone wall. There was a grunt, and the hand that Francesca was grasping with such determination went limp. The sword tumbled noiselessly to the ground. She loosed her hold. Grosely slumped to his knees before pitching forward to land face down, his life blood seeping out to stain a crimson arc within the snow. The only sound was the laboured breathing of Francesca and of Jack.

Jack bent and pressed his fingers to the pulse point in Grosely's neck, knowing that the man was dead even before he did so. Blood trickled from Grosely's ear, and from the ragged wound at the base of his skull. The hair which had been silver-blond in life was matted and darkened with blood in death. Jack rose and saw that Francesca had not moved. Her eyes were wide with horror, and she was staring at the gore of Grosely's head.

'Francesca?'

But it seemed that she could not hear him. She still did not move, just stood there staring, with her face as pale as Grosely's and a haunted look in her eyes.

'Look at me, Francesca.' His hands moved to grip her upper arms, pulling her round to him, his fingers were at her chin, tilting her face up to his.

Slowly her eyes raised to his, and he saw in them shock and horror and disbelief. Her breath was ragged. 'Is he dead?'

Jack nodded.

'I thought he would kill you,' she said so quietly that he struggled to hear the words.

'Had it not been for you, he would have.'

'He was so strong…'

'You were stronger.'

She turned her head and looked at the spot on the wall where Grosely's head had struck. Jack's eyes followed, and he saw the pale hair and flesh and blood that marked it.

'Francesca.'

Her gaze dropped and she held her hands out before her, staring at the stains that smeared her palms. 'His blood,' she whispered. 'It's everywhere.'

Jack guided her away from Grosely's body. He bent and gathered clean snow from the ground, rubbing it into her palms. Then he pulled a handkerchief from his pocket and began slowly, ever so gently, to wipe her hands. He wiped methodically, carefully, working in silence until not one speck of blood remained. And then he held her palms up before her face. 'Your hands are clean.'

She stared at her own outstretched palms as if they did not belong to her, and he saw that she was shaking.

'Francesca,' he said again, and closed his hands around her trembling ones.

This time she looked at him. 'Oh, Jack.' Her voice was raw with emotion.

'I'm here.' He pulled her into his arms and held her against him. 'I'll always be here.'

He heard the breath gasping in her throat, felt the sobs rack her body, and knew that she was weeping. He stroked her hair and caressed her back, crooning soft words of comfort in her ear until the sobbing died away, and then he just held her, and knew that he would never let her go. They stood entwined together, and the wind blew and the sun shone, and the snow thawed around them, until at last she drew back and looked up at him. Her eyes were wet and swollen, her nose was pink and her cheeks still blotched from the tears. But, to Jack, Francesca had never been more beautiful.

'We should go home now,' he said, and took her hand in his.

Chapter 6

By the time Francesca reached the cottage she had gathered herself together enough to appear almost her old self. She told her mama only that she and Jack had been attacked, and in the struggle to defend themselves the attacker had been killed. She made no mention of the man's name, or the history that lay between them. The constable arrived and then left to organise collection of Grosely's body. There was no question of Jack leaving that day; the hour was too late and the shock too great.

Everything seemed so normal—as if the nightmare with Grosely had never really happened—but she remembered too well that dead and bloody corpse, and the struggle that had produced it. The scene played again and again in her head as she lay in bed that night, until she thought that she could bear it no more. Then she thought of Jack, and how he had cleansed her hands and held her and made it seem better, and the knot in her stomach loosened. Everything had been stripped bare between them. And she knew what she had known all along, since that night aboard the *Swift*: Jack Holberton was a good man. A mere two weeks ago, and yet it seemed that she had known him a lifetime.

Lydia shifted in the bed beside her. The room was filled with the soft, even breathing and snores of Mama and the girls sleeping.

There would be no sleep for Francesca that night. Her body ached with fatigue, but her mind was alert and racing. What if Grosely's sword had struck home and it had been Jack who had lain there so still and lifeless upon the ground? Just the thought brought a pain that seared through her heart as surely as if Grosely's blade had pierced it. Francesca did not push the rawness of the pain away. Instead she allowed herself to experience every last pulsating bit of it, for she knew quite clearly what it meant. It was a bittersweet revelation that it had taken Grosely's death for Francesca to realise that she loved Jack Holberton.

Outside she heard the soft patter of rain and knew that the morning would bring Jack's departure. 'Jack,' she whispered through the darkness, and knew that she did not want him to go.

It seemed that she lay like that for hours, until at last she could suffer no more and slipped quietly from the bed.

Jack was not sleeping. He lay on his back on the small hard sofa, with his aching ribs, and thought of Francesca and all that she meant to him.

The doorknob turned slowly. Someone was taking care not to waken him. The remnants of the fire still glowed, casting a low shadowed light within the room. The softest of treads, a movement of white, and he saw her.

She stood there in the doorway, as if debating whether to come in.

'Francesca?' he whispered, unable to believe that she was really there, and rolled to a sitting position. He thought for a minute that she would leave. 'Don't go.'

The door closed behind her with a quiet click, and then she was standing before him.

'You couldn't sleep either, then?' Rising, he came to stand before her. 'Little wonder after today.'

'I can't stop seeing him, lying there with the snow dyed red from his blood.'

'It is not a sight to be easily forgotten by any man or woman,' he said.

'Will we be tried for his murder?'

He shook his head. 'You had nothing to do with his death, Francesca. And I acted in self-defence.'

'I smashed his hand against the wall. I held it there.' She shivered.

'You saved my life.' He touched his hand to her. 'Come and sit down. We may as well be comfortable.' He guided her to the sofa, moving aside the blankets that had made up his bed, and sat her down. Then he sat down beside her, and wrapped a blanket around them both.

He could feel her gaze upon him, and then he felt the light touch of her fingers against his bruised cheekbone.

'Does it hurt very much?'

'It looks worse than it is,' he said.

She continued to look at him in silence for some minutes, and then at last said, 'You are not the man that you told me, Jack Holberton.'

'What did I tell you?'

'That you did not know the meaning of honour.'

'It is the truth.'

'No.' Her denial was emphatic. 'It most certainly is not. You have more honour in your little finger than most men have in their entire bodies.'

He gave an ironic laugh, and the truth weighed heavy upon him. Her face was soft and shadowed in the scant light cast from the embers. He reached up his fingers and brushed them against her cheek in the lightest of caresses. 'There is something I should tell you, Francesca. Something that no one save my father and my brother Richard knows.'

'You need not tell me, Jack,' she said softly.

'But I do,' he replied. 'Even if thereafter you can only look on me with contempt. I would have you know the truth of me, Francesca.'

She nodded.

Jack closed his eyes, pushing away the guilt and the shame and the bitterness, and when he opened them again he began to speak. 'It happened not long before Christmas last year, in London. I was called out over an affair with a woman—a pistol duel to be fought two days later, at dawn on Wimbledon Common. Two days later I was not on Wimbledon Common but lying drunk with a woman in my bed—not the same woman, I might add, over whom the duel had arisen. Richard found me, and tried to make me sober and ready, but I would hear none of it. I told him I had no care for reputation and family honour, that London may say what it pleased about my failure to fight. I had no idea what the consequences of my words would be. Unbeknown to me Richard left and took with him some of my clothes. He dressed himself in them and went to Wimbledon Common in my stead. He could not bear the shame my actions would bring. We have something of the same look, and the light was just dawning. His guise was believed. He was shot. The bullet landed in his leg and the wound almost killed him.' All the old pain flooded back. 'He survived, but he walks with a limp.' His whisper was hoarse and filled with anger.

She slid her hand over his in a gesture of comfort. 'Jack…'

He could hear the compassion in her voice and knew that he did not deserve it. 'It should have been me.'

He felt her fingers tighten around his. 'I did not know you then, but I know you now, Jack. You saved my life twice over. You saved Tom's, and the many other lives that Grosely would have betrayed had you not stopped him. I've seen the pain of regret in your eyes.' She reached up and touched her lips to his cheek in a small sweet kiss. 'I still say that you are the most honourable man I know, Jack Holberton.'

He stared at her in wonder. And it seemed that something of the guilt and the pain that had driven Jack for a year began to ease. Beneath the blanket he slid his hand around her waist and pulled her snug against him. She leaned her head against his shoulder and they sat there, side by side, heart by heart, listening to the rain and the ticking of the clock and the collapse of the embers.

It was a comfortable sort of peace that settled upon Francesca—as if she had spent her whole life waiting for this moment with this man, and now that they were together everything was as it should be.

'You do know that I love you, Francesca, don't you? That I have no intention of living my life without you?'

Somewhere inside her was a small part of her that looked on in amazement as she nodded. But it was true. In her heart she knew that he loved her, just as she loved him.

He turned to look at her. She tilted her face up to his, and his lips met hers in a kiss that was gentle and tender and caring. In that kiss she could feel all of his love, all of his longing, and it called out to something deep inside her, so that their mouths clung together as if they could not bear to part. She felt the slide of his hand up her back, the stroke of his fingers against the sensitive skin at the nape of her neck, and the nerves throughout her body tingled in response. The kiss deepened, became more needful, more passionate. She laid her palms against his chest, feeling the hardness of his muscle and the strong, steady beat of his heart. She wanted the moment to last for ever, this kiss that merged them so that she no longer knew where he stopped and she began. She kissed him with all the love that was in her heart, and felt herself immersed in love. His hands caressed her back, slipping down to skim her waist then round to stroke the swell of her hips.

'Francesca,' he whispered against her ear.

His hand slid up to cup her breast through her nightdress. She felt a spurt of pleasure at his touch, and could not help herself from pressing closer to him, driving her breast harder into his hand. He groaned, and his kisses cascaded over her lips, over her chin, down the column of her throat. She arched her neck, dropping her head back, exposing herself to him all the more. The kisses did not stop there. She felt the quiver in his fingers as he untied the top of her nightdress, pulling it open to reveal her bare shoulders. Around her neck hung the silver ship—the *Swift*. He stilled when he saw it, lying there against the pale softness of her skin, and his eyes met hers. And there was only Francesca and Jack and the enormity of their love.

He peeled the nightdress over her head, dropping it forgotten to the floor so that she sat naked before him.

'You're beautiful.' His gaze caressed her.

Then he was kissing her again. Kissing her until she was trembling with desire. She did not notice that he had taken off his clothes until she felt the nakedness of his skin next to hers. He laid her back gently on the blanket on the sofa. His fingers trailed seductively over her stomach before he moved to lie over her. She clung to him as their two bodies became as one, a union of their love, a merging of souls, a bond to last for all eternity. And as they lay together in the aftermath of their loving both knew that they were changed for ever.

Jack woke with a feeling of contentment as the clock struck nine. He remembered what had happened during the night and an overwhelming feeling of happiness flooded him. He opened his eyes. Francesca was gone. Of course she was. It was nine o'clock. She wasn't just going to be lying here beside him for her family to see. A noise sounded from the kitchen: the sound of pouring water, the clank of pots. Francesca. He rose quickly, unmindful of his nakedness.

The room was in darkness. No trace of the fire remained. He moved to the window, pulling open the curtains. Night had faded; the dull light of day lit the sky. He moved to the basin and pitcher that Francesca had left for him upon the table the previous evening. The water was cold enough to chase the last vestiges of sleep from his mind. He washed and quickly dressed. The blankets were a rucked mess on the sofa. He folded them up, seeing the dark stain of blood on one and taking care to hide the mark.

He glanced around the parlour. There was no other evidence of what had happened in the night. Francesca's nightdress had disappeared. Everything was as it had been…save for himself…and Francesca. He buttoned his waistcoat and, raking his hair into some semblance of order, headed for the kitchen. There were things that he and Francesca needed to discuss before he left for Flete. He knocked softly on the kitchen door before opening it to find the entirety of the Linden family seated around the table. Only Francesca was standing, pouring cups of coffee.

'You're awake at last,' chirped Sophy. 'We thought you would sleep for ever. Lucky for you Francesca saved you breakfast— although I'm sure the porridge will be quite thick and horrid by now.'

Jack smiled and closed the door behind him.

The snow had gone, and so had Jack. Francesca had waved him off after breakfast. There had been little opportunity for a private farewell, but she had seen the love in his eyes when he looked at her, and felt the small meaningful press of his hand against hers.

'I'll be back by Twelfth Night,' he had said, 'I promise,' before climbing into the saddle and cantering off down the lane.

She had watched him go, her heart swollen with love for him, but tinged with sadness that he was leaving. He loved her. She loved him. And that love changed everything for Francesca.

She struggled to hide her joy, pretending that everything was the same, when in truth nothing was the same at all. She was dizzy with excitement. The day had never seemed so bright, nor the air so fresh. Jack loved her and their union had sealed that love. He would come back to her. He would marry her, just as he had said, and they would live happily ever after. Francesca hugged the knowledge to herself, and it put a spring in her step.

The days passed and Francesca kept herself busy. She did not mind the dark winter mornings, rising in the cold to light the fire. She did not mind scrubbing the floor or brushing the clothes or boiling the linens. Each morning Francesca awoke with the hope that this day would see Jack's return. But Jack did not return. Not the first day or the second or even the next after that. And with each passing day Francesca's spirit wilted a little. She told herself to be strong until, at last, it was the twelfth and final day of Christmas. She baked the Twelfth Night cake with the last of the flour and eggs, adding in dried fruit and sherry, and decorated it as best she could. And then she waited for Jack to return. A hearty fire blazed in the parlour. All day she listened for the sound of a horse or a carriage, but darkness fell and he still had not come.

She did not sleep that night, but lay restless in the bed, her mind whirling with possible explanations for Jack's absence. What if he had been charged with Grosely's murder? Or Grosely's father had had him killed? What if Grosely had not been dead when they left him that day upon the moor? But she knew the latter supposition to be sheer folly; there had been no doubting Grosely's lifeless corpse. She told herself that her worries were fanciful— that Jack had merely been delayed, that he would arrive tomorrow. But, for all she knew that to be the most likely of explanations, she could not rid herself of the seep of dread that Jack was not coming back.

Her hopes were raised the next day, when a boy brought a prepaid letter to the house. She watched Anne reading the address, her heart beating nineteen to the dozen.

'It is for you, Mama.' Anne passed the letter to her mother.

Francesca hid her disappointment.

The family crowded round while Mrs Linden broke the seal and unfolded the letter. She stood by the window that she might the better read the words penned so neatly upon the paper. She read the letter, and then read it again, and when she had finished she sat back down in her chair and bowed her head and was silent.

'Mama?' Francesca forgot all about her own worries in her concern for her mother. 'What is it? What is wrong?'

Mrs Linden shook her head, and a single tear escaped from her eye. She brushed it away with a work-worn hand.

'Mama?' Sophy stared at her mother with great round eyes.

Mrs Linden took out her handkerchief, dried her eyes and blew her nose. And then, satisfied that she was quite composed, she turned to face her children. 'It is good news,' she said. 'It's just something of a shock to hear it after all this time. The letter is from your papa's brother, George.'

'Lord Sarum?'

'Yes.' Mrs Linden carefully folded the letter. 'It seems that George has lately learned of our whereabouts. He wishes to put the disagreements of the past behind us, and is inviting us to come and stay with him in Salisbury for the month of March.'

'But what of Papa's disagreement with him?' asked Sophy.

'Papa's disagreement was with the late Earl—your grandfather. There was never any argument with his brother, but George was the heir and had no choice but to do as his father said. And your own dear papa was too proud to go back to Salisbury while your grandfather lived.'

'Are we to go to Salisbury?'

'Yes, I believe that we are.' Mrs Linden smiled.

Lydia clapped her hands and danced with Sophy. 'Hurrah!'

'But how came he to learn of our address now, after all this time?' Francesca sat down on the arm of her mother's chair.

'From a mutual friend,' said Mrs Linden, scanning the letter once more.

Francesca remembered Jack's visit to Salisbury, and she had the strangest feeling that he was somehow involved in this.

The weather was dismal—all grey skies and blowing gales and rain. A week had passed since Twelfth Night, and Tom and Francesca set out alone for the market at Salcombe, leaving their mother and sisters to stay warm and dry at home.

After days of fretting Francesca knew she had to do something. So she phrased her question as nonchalantly as she could. 'I wondered if you had heard aught of Lord Holberton of late?'

Tom cast her a look that had shades of both puzzlement and suspicion. 'I've heard nothing,' he said. 'Why do you ask?'

'Curiosity,' she said calmly, and forced a smile to her face. 'What other reason could there be?'

'I can think of one.'

She felt her heart somersault, but she did not stop walking. She did not even look round at Tom, lest he see the truth written all over her face. Instead she adjusted the basket on her arm and smoothed some imaginary strands of hair back from her face.

'Sophy seems to be under the impression that you are sweet on him. Is it true?'

'Sophy is young and prone to fanciful impressions,' said Francesca, and knew that she was being unfair to her sister.

They walked in silence for a few moments.

'If he has done anything that he should not—'

'He has done nothing,' Francesca said before he had even finished the question. 'Why should you even think such a thing?'

'Because of how happy you were when he was here and how unhappy you now seem.'

'You are imagining things.' She forced a laugh.

'Perhaps. You know that he has something of a reputation, don't you?'

'A man may change for the better.'

'Not him,' said Tom succinctly.

She remembered what Jack had told her of how his brother came to be shot.

'He is a rake, Fran. He seduces women and abandons them, with no notion of honour or dishonour.'

'Tom!'

'I did try to warn you.'

She kept going somehow, one foot in front of the other, maintaining her face in a mask of normality. *He seduces women and abandons them.* She heard the words over and over again. Just as he had seduced and abandoned her. It could not be true. He had asked her to marry him; he had to come back. But she thought again of that night when they had shared their love, and it seemed that she heard the whisper of the words he had said: *You do know that I love you, Francesca, don't you? That I have no intention of living my life without you?* And she realised for the first time that he had not actually proposed marriage to her at all.

A dreadful chill was spreading through her. He had loved her and he had left. In almost two weeks he had not come back. There had been no letter—not even the smallest scrawl of a note. The evidence was damning. Francesca knew that either she had been ruined by the most beguiling of rakes, or that something terrible had happened to Jack. Neither was an option in which she wished to believe, and yet if she must choose she would take the former a hundred times over.

She wanted to weep and cry aloud. She wanted to run away and keep on running. She walked on, the empty basket over her arm, her purse and Tom's coins in her pocket. Walking and walking. Tom was still talking, but she did not hear his words. She was concentrating on locking all her hurt away, on being strong and calm and capable. There was food to be bought and dinners to be cooked, a house to be kept, a family to be cared for. There was no time to dwell on the darkness of probability.

Francesca and Tom were returning home from the market with their basket filled with supplies. The rain had been falling constantly for the last hour, soaking into their clothes until they grew damp and heavy. Francesca's bonnet was limp and bedraggled, her cloak was so wet as to be clinging to her, and the bottom of her skirts were sodden and muddy. Tom was little better. They made their way down the lane towards home, their feet slopping and rubbing in the wetness of their boots.

The front door opened and Anne ushered them in. 'You're soaked through to the skin!'

'We'd better go round to the back door,' said Francesca, 'or we'll leave a trail of mud and water throughout.'

'No, no,' Anne insisted, 'Come in quickly.'

Francesca was too cold and miserable to notice the excitement in her sister's tone. She hurried after Tom through to the kitchen, and began to peel off her wet clothing.

'We've got a visitor,' said Anne.

'Who is it?' Tom pulled off his muddy boots and stockings.

Francesca stopped, her cloak hanging heavy in her hand, rain-water dripping on to the floor.

'Lord Holberton.' Anne smiled.

Francesca grabbed for the table and leant heavily upon it until the lightness in her head subsided.

'What's wrong, Francesca?' Anne stared at her sister with concern.

'Nothing at all. I'm fine.'

'Go and change. I'll wring out your clothes and hang them up to dry.'

'Thank you.' Francesca squeezed her sister's arm and hurried up to the bedchamber with wet bare feet. She stripped off the remainder of her clothing and pulled on a plain grey dress that was made of warm wool. She rubbed her hair with a towel until it no longer dripped water, then combed it out and pinned it, still wet, in a roll at the nape of her neck. She found clean stockings and a pair of slippers, and finally stood ready, but she made no move other than to sit down upon her bed.

Jack was downstairs, and she did not know what to think. Her heart was bruised from the long wait and the worst of imaginings. He was down there, and a part of her lit with joy at the knowledge, and the other part was scared of seeing him again. There was so much risk in loving, so much vulnerability, so much potential to be hurt…and yet joy too vast to be measured. She touched her fingers to her chest and felt the small bump of the *Swift* that lay beneath the layers of clothing. She thought of all that had happened since that night aboard the boat. She thought and she thought, and then she took a deep breath and, rising from the bed, walked towards the bedchamber door.

* * *

Jack thought Francesca was paler than he remembered, and there was a slightly strained look about her eyes. He worried that she had been working too hard and not eating enough.

'Lord Holberton has come to visit us,' said Mrs Linden. 'Lydia, pour Francesca some tea,' she directed. 'It should still be warm.' She peered at Francesca. 'You look rather pale.'

'She's coming down with a chill,' supplied Anne. 'She almost fainted in the kitchen.'

Everyone looked at Francesca.

'You exaggerate, Anne. I'm quite well,' said Francesca.

Jack stood up from his chair by the fire. 'Take my seat, Francesca.'

'I'm fine where I am, thank you, my lord.' She stayed seated on the wooden chair by the door.

'I insist.' He rose and walked over to her, reaching his hand down towards hers.

He could feel all eyes of the Linden family upon him, but he did not care. He took her hand in his, feeling the tremor within it, and guided her over to the armchair by the fireside. Her face was still pale, but two pink patches had now appeared on her cheeks. When she was seated he took the cup of tea from a gawking Lydia and passed it into Francesca's hands. She was trembling so much he could hear the slight chink of china as the cup rattled against the saucer.

Everyone stared. No one spoke. Francesca sipped her tea in silence.

'I was wondering,' he said, 'if I might be allowed a few moments to speak to Francesca.' He looked meaningfully at Mrs Linden. 'It will not take long.'

Tom looked at him suspiciously, but Mrs Linden was on her feet. 'Come along, Tom. Bring the tea tray, Anne. We shall retire to the kitchen for a little while.' Her cheeks had turned very pink. 'Sophy, Lydia.' Mrs Linden shooed them all out before her.

The parlour door shut. He could hear them trailing through to the kitchen, their voices murmuring, raised in quiet, questioning tones, and Mrs Linden hushing them before the firm closing of the kitchen door.

He came to her then. Crouched down and took both her hands in his. 'I'm here at last.'

'Yes.' Her voice was so soft that the word was barely more than a whisper.

'Francesca…'

She looked directly into his eyes. 'Where have you been, Jack?'

'London.' His brow furrowed in perplexity. 'There were affairs to be set straight with regard to Grosely. His father was causing difficulties. I told you all in my letter.'

'I received no such letter.'

Jack frowned; the reason for Francesca's pallor was now apparent. 'Then you know nothing of my journey and must have thought the worst of my absence.'

'I feared that something, or someone, had beset you.'

'Not that I had abandoned you?'

'Perhaps the thought crossed my mind.'

'I told you once before that promises made at Christmastime are as gifts and must be kept.' He stroked his thumbs across her fingers.

She bowed her head briefly and he could see then that she was holding back the tears. He knew that she had suffered in the time he had been away.

'You are here now and that is all that matters.' She glanced up at him and smiled.

'I took advantage of my trip to London to sort out certain other matters.' He slipped his hand into his pocket and produced a folded piece of paper, which he handed to her. 'Read it.'

She opened the paper out and stared at it.

'A trifle presumptuous of me, I admit.' He raised an eyebrow. 'But then the last time I was here you did lead to me believe that you would not be too averse to having me as a husband. And, as my patience will not stretch to the reading of banns, a special marriage licence seemed the obvious solution.'

She laughed, and slowly the tears began to roll down her cheeks.

'Will you marry me, Francesca?'

'I will gladly marry you, Jack Holberton.' She was laughing and crying both at once. He pulled her to him and she wrapped her arms around his neck. His mouth found hers and he kissed her deeply, passionately, with all the love in the world.

Francesca lay in bed and watched the sleeping form of her husband; a month had passed since she had been able to call him thus. Somewhere in the house a clock struck ten, and morning light was peeping through the thick red velvet of the curtains. She stretched out in the warm luxury and marvelled again at the man by her side. His face was boyish and innocent in repose; a far cry from the truth, she thought, considering that in which they had been indulging for a good part of the previous night. She leaned over and, gently sweeping his hair back, dropped a light kiss on his forehead. He gave a contented sigh and curled his arm around her.

Outside there was the sound of feet skipping down the gravel driveway, of laughter and a girl's squeals, followed by a shout. 'Tell him, Mama. He's pulling my pigtails again!'

Jack gave a groan. 'I feel a visit to Salisbury coming on.' He opened one eye to watch her reaction. 'Sarum seems to be taking his time over redecorating the old parsonage. Might need to paste the paper on to the walls myself to speed the matter.'

'Jack Holberton!' Francesca pushed at his chest playfully. 'You know Uncle George just wants everything perfect for Mama.'

'And rightly so.' He chuckled and pulled her closer. 'I'm only teasing. I love having your family to stay—even if they do get up at such an ungodly hour. Is it even daylight yet?'

'It's ten o'clock.' She laughed. 'Well past time we were up.' As she made to move, a shaft of sunlight made its way past the curtains to land upon the silver necklace that still hung around her neck. The

Swift seemed to sparkle and glint. Francesca watched Jack reach out to gently capture the tiny ship and bring it to rest upon his fingers.

'The tale of that December night will be told in taverns throughout Devon for years to come,' he mused.

'A smuggler's tale of how Lord Jack Holberton captured a traitor as well as the notorious Buckley gang,' said Francesca.

His eyes met hers. 'I was thinking more about how a brave and beautiful woman captured his heart.'

'You are incorrigible.' She smiled, and teased her fingers along his cheek.

He released the *Swift* and captured her fingers instead, kissing each one in turn. 'So I've been told,' he said. Then he pulled her back down against him and began to kiss her in earnest, and for Francesca it was as if the magic of a Christmas night had never ended.

* * * * *

THE SAILOR'S BRIDE

Miranda Jarrett

Author Note

I've always believed that Christmas was more about family and the spirit of the season than commercial excess. That's the feeling I wanted for the hero and heroine of *The Sailor's Bride*. Both Abigail and James are far from not only home, but also far from any traditional English Christmas celebration. Yet it is their shared memories of past holidays that help bring them closer together, and cement the joy of their love for one another.

Of course, I didn't make things particularly easy for Abbie and James, by setting them down in the middle of one of the more exciting incidents of the Napoleonic Wars. Many readers will recognize Lord Nelson and Lady Hamilton, here just beginning their doomed love affair. Sir William's famous collection of antiquities, the Battle of the Nile, the well-planned escape of the Neapolitan royal family before Napoleon's troops, even the freakish Christmas Eve snow storm and the eruption of Mt. Vesuvius are all historical fact. Abbie and James live only in this story—though I like to think they *could* have been real.

Wherever your Christmas may find you this year, I wish you and your family every happiness and all the best for the coming New Year.

Miranda

For Abby Zidle, with much affection and thanks for your wise editing, and the best of wishes for all your new endeavors!

Chapter 1

Naples, Kingdom of Two Sicilies, September, 1798

WITH both hands Abigail Layton clung to the wicker sides of the little donkey cart as it jostled and bounced up the narrow street. After nearly two months at sea, on the voyage from England, she'd grown so accustomed to the rocking of the ship against the waves that when she'd disembarked this morning it had seemed as if the ground had lurched beneath her feet. Riding in this cart over the cobbles was even worse—the feeling so unfamiliar that she feared she'd be as seasick—or land-sick, if such a thing were possible—as she'd been when she'd first set sail from Gravesend.

'The house of the British ambassador, *signorina*,' the driver said, pointing his whip farther up the hill.

'The British embassy, you say?' Abigail said faintly, tugging the brim of her hat a bit lower to shield her eyes as she squinted into the sun. 'Thank you.'

The embassy was large and grand, high on the hill overlooking the sea, and to her eyes looked more a palace than a home. Abigail forced herself to *observe* the house the way Father had taught her—to study it intellectually so that she'd forget her uneasy stomach. Twelve tall windows to each floor, a long gallery of white columns in the classical style: yes, focus on them, and not on the way the sweat was trickling down her spine beneath her too-heavy woollen mourning gown. When she'd left her home in Oxford summer had already ended, but here in Naples the heat was still blazing away.

For reassurance she touched her fingers to the little gold heart she always wore around her neck, a gift from Father the last Christmas they'd had together. How strange to think she'd spend this Christmas beneath sunshine and palm trees instead of holly boughs, at least she would if the ambassador decided to keep her.

'Here, *signorina*.' The driver drew the cart before the house, the jingling bells on the donkey's harness tinkling incongruously before the row of steps that swept up to the ambassador's imposing door. The man hopped down to the pavement, lifted out her single trunk to the steps, and held his hand out to her.

'Yes, of course.' Abigail began searching through her pocket for coins for the fare, but that wasn't what the man had intended.

'No, no, *signorina*.' The driver swept his arm low in a courtly bow before he held out his hand again, making it clear he'd meant to help her from the cart. 'First I am the servant of the beautiful English lady, yes?'

Abigail flushed. She'd been warned that every Italian man fancied himself a gallant, and here was the proof. She hadn't journeyed all this way for flirtation; she was here on business, serious business. Pointedly she pressed the coins into the man's outstretched hand, and climbed down to the pavement unassisted. She smoothed her skirts, took a deep breath to settle her nerves, and resolutely climbed the steps to knock on the ambassador's door.

The tall footman who answered didn't bother to hide his disdain as he stared down at her from beneath his tall powdered wig. 'What name, *signorina*?'

'Miss Layton,' Abigail said, handing him one of her father's cards. 'Miss A.R. Layton. Sir William is expecting me.'

The footman hesitated, making it clear that he doubted very much the ambassador had any such expectation. Abigail could understand his reluctance. She *did* look shabby. Despite her best efforts, the hem of her black mourning gown was blotched with white salt-stains from the sea-spray, and the inexpensive wool had faded to a rusty brown. But Father deserved her respect, no matter how weary that mourning had become, and besides, it was all she'd brought. Given the grandeur of this doorway alone, she doubted the footman let anyone through who was dressed as sorrily as she.

Yet still she stood her ground, determined to be admitted. She *was* here by the ambassador's invitation. She had his letter in her pocket to prove it. And anyway, she'd no money left for the passage back to England.

'Please tell Sir William I am here,' she said, striving to make her voice sound genteel, not begging or desperate. 'I wouldn't wish to tell him that I'd been delayed on his own doorstep.'

'I'll see if Sir William is in.' Finally the footman stepped to one side and opened the door for her. He motioned towards one of the stiff little receiving chairs near the door, and left her. The hall was long, with a high ceiling that made it cooler after the bright sun outside, and with a little sigh Abigail sat on the edge of the first chair while the driver dumped her trunk unceremoniously at her feet. She was exhausted and frustrated, and her stomach was still uneasy, but—like any other tradesman—she'd have to await the ambassador's whim. She had no choice.

Servants came and went, walking by her as if she didn't exist. From somewhere inside she heard a clock chiming away the quarter-hours. As the morning passed, the sunbeams that filtered through the fanlight over the front door shifted across the floor. Still she waited, and waited.

Finally she heard footsteps and voices bustling towards her. An older gentleman in a richly embroidered coat came down the steps, surrounded by a clerk and two footmen carrying his cloak and his sword. Another footman hurried forward to open the door, showing the carriage waiting outside.

Abigail rose and expectantly stepped forward. She was sure this must be Sir William Hamilton, and though it wasn't proper to address him first, she wasn't going to let him escape without seeing her.

'Forgive me, Sir William,' she began, and he stopped abruptly, two stairs above her, so she had to look up. 'I have come at your express invitation, and I've been waiting since this morning to see you, and—'

'You're English, ma'am,' he declared with obvious surprise. 'You're English, yet I've kept you waiting? Carter, why was I not told this lady was here to see me?'

The clerk bustled forward, his hands clasped. 'I believe Thompson informed you of her arrival, Sir William, and presented her card. Sir William—Miss, ah, Miss Layton.'

The ambassador's eyes widened with surprise. 'But A. R. Layton—'

'Was my father, Sir William,' Abigail finished quickly. 'We have—*had*—the same initials, you see. I have assumed his trade since his death last year, and if you could but spare me a few moments, I can assure you that my scholarship is equal in—'

'In here, Miss Layton.' Brusquely he motioned towards the nearest parlour, off the hall. 'I don't have any moments to spare, but clearly this matter must be settled directly.'

'Thank you, Sir William.' Her head high and her heart thumping with anxiety, Abigail entered the room first, stopping before the fireplace while Sir William closed the door. He *had* to accept her in Father's place; he couldn't possibly refuse her services, not after she'd come this far.

The ambassador cleared his throat. He was older than she'd expected, a tall, grandfatherly gentleman. She prayed he was as kind as he looked.

'I am sorry for the loss of your father, Miss Layton,' he began uneasily, 'but I'm afraid that—'

'Please listen, Sir William—oh, please, before you judge me!' she cried. 'My father trained me in his scholarship and knowledge from a very early age. I can vow with every confidence that I will catalogue your collection and prepare it for shipping with all the thoroughness that it deserves, Sir William, and that you will never find anyone else more skilled, more careful, at preparing your precious antiquities for their return to England!'

He cleared his throat again. 'You speak with great passion for my old pots, Miss Layton. Especially for a young lady.'

'They're a good deal more than old pots, Sir William,' protested Abigail. 'Your collection of antiquates is reputed to be the most exquisite in all the Continent. And of course I have made myself entirely familiar with the catalogue made for you by the Baron d'Hancarville.'

'You have seen that?' he asked with surprise.

'I have seen it, sir, and read it in its entirety,' she said confidently. And she had, though in her opinion the Baron's enormous work wasn't entirely without flaws. 'To be able to work with such a magnificent collection would be the greatest honour imaginable.'

Sir William smiled, obviously pleased by her comments, yet it was also clear that his reluctance remained.

'It's not so simple as that, Miss Layton,' he said, 'nor a question of your qualifications. How can I ask you to remain here in my employment and put yourself in the possible path of growing hostilities? Surely even at sea you must have heard of the great battle fought by His Majesty's Navy against Bonaparte's forces?'

'I've heard no such news, Sir William.' As the only female passenger on board the merchant ship that had brought her to Naples, she'd kept to herself and eaten her meals alone. The few times she'd ventured on the deck, the hands had whistled and taunted her with names that were so rude she couldn't have begun to understand them. Even the captain had been a rough, ill-mannered man, and she'd wanted no more part of him or his crew than they'd wanted of her.

'A very great battle, Miss Layton, and a great victory for Admiral Nelson, too, at the mouth of the Nile River. Not so far from here, you know—just across the Mediterranean.' The ambassador smiled proudly. 'We expect the English fleet to appear here in Naples for repairs and refurbishing any day now.'

Abigail tried to smile. Just what she least wished: more sailors, and fighting ones at that. 'Then the danger has passed, Sir William?'

'Oh, not at all!' His hollow-cheeked face grew studiously grim. 'We might have struck Bonaparte's navy, but what that shall do is inflame his armies to the north all the more. We must remain vigilant, Miss Layton, at constant readiness—which is why I'd hoped to engage your father's services. The last thing I'd wish is to see my collection fall into the hands of those ravening French devils.'

'How fortunate it is, then, that I'm able to attend to your collection in my father's stead,' she said, and for the first time she couldn't keep the desperation from creeping into her voice. 'Test me, Sir William. That's all I ask. Grant me but one day to demonstrate my skill and my knowledge, and I'll prove my worth.'

He frowned again, but she could sense that he was considering her offer. The expertise she could offer would be rare so far from London. What choice did he have?

'I won't make any exceptions because of your sex, you know,' he warned. 'You will lodge here in the house as our guest, but I'll expect the same work from you as I would from your father.'

'I will not disappoint you, Sir William.' He was going to let her stay; she was sure of it now. Relief washed over her like a wave, so strongly that she felt dizzy. She'd been too uneasy to eat breakfast, and she'd not been offered so much as a glass of water while she'd been waiting for the ambassador. 'I can begin as soon as…as soon as…'

She caught the edge of the mantelpiece to steady herself.

'Miss Layton?' Sir William's voice sounded distant, echoing oddly in her ears. 'My dear, are you unwell?'

'I am…fine,' she mumbled. She felt herself slipping down, gently, as if her legs were melting away beneath her, and then she felt nothing more.

* * *

'You've not visited Naples before, Lieutenant, have you?' The admiral didn't turn, continuing to gaze towards the faint shadow of the coastline with the spyglass set at his one good eye. His wispy hair fluttered beneath the bandage around his head, his black cocked hat still set defiantly over the wound across his forehead. He was weak and pale, and though he stubbornly insisted otherwise, every other officer on the quarterdeck stood ready to catch him if he faltered. 'It's a beautiful city, a marvellous city. You will be enchanted.'

'Yes, sir.' Of course Lieutenant Lord James Richardson agreed. He'd signed on as a midshipman in His Majesty's Navy as a boy of thirteen, and now, risen to the rank of first lieutenant after ten years in the service, he would have agreed even if Admiral Nelson had said there'd be pink bulls and green monkeys floating in the sky over Naples. But in this James agreed with his heart as well as his duty. He wanted to be enchanted by Naples.

No, more than that: he *needed* to. He'd fought in many battles, and seen many men, good and bad, die in horrible ways, but the scale of carnage—nearly two thousand lost on both sides, with all but one of the French ships destroyed at the mouth of the Nile River—had been beyond anything he or the rest of the English fleet had ever experienced. James was one of the lucky ones—alive and unharmed. But while the horror of battle was never forgotten, the memory could certainly be eased. In the officers' mess, there'd been much discussion of the beauty of the Neapolitan women, and their eagerness to welcome the English naval heroes.

James had listened, and prayed they were right. With any luck they'd be stationed in the bay at least until Twelfth Night to make their repairs, perhaps longer. How much better it would be to hear the sweet sighs of a willing partner than the screams of the dying that still filled his head. Better, far better, to lose himself in the pleasures of the flesh instead of remembering how easily a man's face could be blown away into blood and bone.

'Ah, here comes the first committee for hospitality.' The admiral smiled wryly as he lowered his spyglass. The English warships had been spotted from shore, and already a group of small vessels and fishing boats were sailing out from the bay to greet them. Bright pennants flickered among their sails, and here and there a mast sported the familiar British red, white and blue. 'No boarding, Captain Hardy. I'd rather we didn't appear in port as a floating brothel, but made a seemly entrance. There will be time enough for the men to enjoy the fair sex, eh?'

The *Vanguard*'s captain and the other officers laughed together, as Admiral Nelson had meant them to, but all James did was smile, and smooth the snowy cuffs of his dress uniform coat one more time. In recognition of his courage and resourcefulness during the battle—and because he could speak Italian—the admiral had invited him to join his party when they called formally on Sir William Hamilton and his wife at their home, as soon as they'd landed.

It was also assumed that, as the youngest son of the Earl of Carrington, James would know how to behave in genteel company. But it had been a long time since he'd dined ashore, and longer still since he'd dined in genteel company, with rows of crystal wine glasses and silver forks to navigate with each course, and well-bred ladies—*ladies*!—who'd expect him to make conversation. The sad truth was that the prospect of dining in the ambassador's home worried James far more than facing the French ships-of-the-line.

The *Vanguard* was making its way past the island of Capri. Off the starboard, James could see the smoke-shrouded volcano Vesuvius, and in the distance ahead the city of Naples, with the white villas of the wealthy scattered along the coast. One of them must belong to Sir William, where Lady Hamilton's servants were doubtless laying out her linens and silver on the dining table, like so many traps for him and his career.

But he'd conquer them. Just as he'd conquered everything else that had stood in his path. And when he had, then there'd be the merry girls of the tavernas waiting to welcome him.

'Ah, yes, Naples,' the admiral said again, more to himself than anyone else. 'Our orders—and the movements of the French army—should keep us here through the holidays, and a good thing, too. Naples, Naples, surely there's no more magical place on earth.'

Abigail had never before fainted, nor felt as mortified as when she wakened on the floor with Sir William's silver-buckled shoes before her nose. She tried to explain that it had only been the heat, exhaustion, surprise, that had made her crumple like a wilted flower, but Sir William insisted that she be helped by his servants to her room, fed weak tea and a dry toast, and put to bed with the curtains drawn like the sorriest invalid.

She protested as vehemently as she could, yet as soon as she laid her head on the pillow she fell into the deepest sleep she'd had since she'd left home months ago.

By the time she finally awakened, the sun had set and the windows were dark, though she could still hear voices and laughter elsewhere in the house. Disorientated with sleep, she fumbled for her father's pocket watch on the table beside her, squinting at the face as she tried to make out the numbers.

Seven o'clock! Oh, how had she slept so long? Swiftly she sat upright and threw back the coverlet. How could she prove to Sir William that she was worthy of his regard by lying about like this? She lit a candlestick, dressed quickly in a fresh gown, found a journal for notes in the bottom of her trunk, and hurried out into the hall.

A maidservant—a Neapolitan woman with glossy black hair and plump cheeks—was using a long taper to light the candles in the chandeliers.

'Excuse me.' Abigail smiled warmly, praying the maid spoke English. 'Might you show me to the room where Sir William keeps his collection of antiquities?'

'No one's permitted in there, signorina.' She sniffed for extra emphasis, making it clear that Abigail's status, while not exactly that of a servant, wasn't that of an honoured guest, either. 'Not even to tidy. Sir William's orders.'

'But it's his wish that I catalogue his collection,' Abigail said. 'That's why I'm here. If you'd ask him, I'm sure—'

'Lady Hamilton and Sir William are with the admiral now, signorina, and cannot be disturbed,' the maid said. 'Can't you hear them downstairs, signorina? The house is full of officers from the navy ships, here to call and take supper.'

Now that Abigail listened more closely, she could tell that the voices she heard in the distance had a distinctly male rumble. 'But surely you could at least show me to the collection?'

The maid sighed with irritation. 'I'll show you to Sir William's chambers, signorina, on my way downstairs,' she said. 'But I'll not go in with you. I've duties of my own, signorina.'

Abigail followed her down the stairs and along another hall, to stop before the furthest door.

'That's it, signorina,' the maid said, already backing away. 'That's the door to Sir William's rooms, and as far as I go. I've no wish to risk my place by disobeying him, and if he asks I'll swear I've told nothing to you.'

'Thank you,' Abigail said, but the girl had already fled. Abigail took a deep breath. She wasn't going to back down now; this was why she'd come all this way, wasn't it? She turned the latch, pushed open the door, and stepped inside.

She raised her candle high, and caught her breath in wonder. Tall shelves and cabinets lined the walls, each filled with more treasures than she could ever have imagined. Exquisitely painted vases and plates, marble sculpture fragments and bronzes: every manner of ancient artefact crowded into a single room. Her scholar's heart leaped with excitement at the sight of so many rare and beautiful things, and her only sorrow came from knowing Father hadn't lived to see them, too.

She stepped closer to the shelf to set her candlestick down, and the light washed over a small marble relief: the Three Graces, carved with such infinite care and loveliness that she sighed with pleasure. Remembering the maid's warning, she touched the nearest figure with the lightest possible fingers. The snowy marble was smooth and cool. A Roman copy of a lost Greek original, she thought automatically, already beginning to catalogue in her head. First century, second at the latest, and—

'Ah, forgive me, miss,' a man's voice said gruffly. 'Didn't intend to intrude.'

'You didn't.' Quickly she turned back towards the door that had opened again behind her. With the brighter light from the hall spilling around him, the man's fair hair appeared golden, like a halo, yet his face was in shadow. 'That is, it's not my room, so you could hardly intrude.'

'No, miss.' From his speech she realised he must be English, too, a relief in this foreign place. 'But perhaps you might oblige me, and set me on the proper course to Lady Hamilton's parlour?'

He took a step forward, into the ring of her candle's glow. He was younger than she'd first guessed from his voice, close to her own age, yet already a navy officer, his dark blue uniform coat glittering with gold buttons and lacing that seemed as bright as his hair, with more gold still on the hilt and scabbard of his dress sword. And, oh, he was perfectly, effortlessly handsome in that navy coat and those spotless white breeches, his smile wide and even in his sun-browned face, his eyes an impossible blue despite the candlelight.

'The proper course. I see.' She nodded, and gulped, ordering her head to think, *think*, and herself to stop being such a scatter-brained ninny. Yes, of course, the man was handsome—appallingly handsome—but he'd also just caught her in Sir William's collection gallery, touching these priceless artefacts in exactly the way she'd been warned not to do.

And, to her horror, this officer was now doing it too.

'I say, what a lot of old things,' he said, picking up a small clay statue of Apollo and turning it upside down, as if looking for a price marked on the bottom. 'I'd heard Sir William was a collector, but this is rather like my auntie's attic. Ha—look, this poor old fellow's even broken. Mark the crack—there, across his arm. What's the point of keeping one that's been winged like that, anyway?'

'Because that "poor old fellow" is nearly two thousand years old, that's why.' She hurried forward and took the little Apollo from him as carefully as she could, cradling it in her arms like a baby. 'Because he's beautiful and rare and can never, ever be replaced.'

'You're young, miss,' he said, forgetting the statue entirely. 'You sounded old, there in the dark, but you're—you're not.'

She'd next to no experience with handsome gentlemen, and she'd no notion at all of how she was supposed to respond to such a statement. She raised her chin, hugging the rescued statue to her chest.

'I am twenty-one years of age, sir, and if—'

'The same as I, but two,' he said. 'I'm twenty-three.'

Still recovering from being interrupted, Abigail nodded before she doggedly continued. 'If I sounded older, sir, then I suppose that's on account of having spent so much time exclusively in my father's company, sharing his scholarship. Yes, that must be— Oh, please, sir, watch yourself!'

He'd turned, and to her horror the scabbard of his dress-sword swung against a tall pot on the floor, rocking it sideways on its rim. She lunged forward to save the pot, somehow keeping hold of the little Apollo as well, but managing to smack squarely into the man's chest.

'Steady now, miss, steady,' he said, protective as he clasped her gently by the shoulders. 'No need to crash about, eh?'

'No need!' she exclaimed, too horrified by how close she'd come to genuine disaster to realise that he was still holding her. 'You very nearly broke this Attic black-figured vase, sir!'

'Like a great lumbering bull, I am,' he agreed ruefully. 'But didn't I say all this rubbish belonged in a dusty attic?'

'No, no, *no!*' she cried, turning her face up towards his. 'I meant the vase was made in Attica, the region surrounding ancient Athens, not—not—'

How could she think, let alone speak, when he insisted on smiling down at her like that, his hands still resting on her shoulders and only all those gold buttons and the little statue between them? She forgot Attica, and Athens, and the Apollo in her arms, and thought only of how she'd never stood so close to a gentleman like this before, nor realised quite how confusing it could be. Confusing, and unseemly, too. And by the single candle's light she felt her cheeks grow hot.

'Forgive me, sir, for prattling on so,' she said, her voice oddly breathless. 'I shouldn't presume that you've any interest in antiquities. Most people don't.'

'If you're interested, miss,' he declared gallantly. 'Then so am I.'

She felt her flush deepen more. If he wasn't going to end this foolishness, then she must. 'That is very—very kind of you, sir. But I must ask you to release me so that I can—'

'Oh, aye—aye, miss. Forgive me.' Chagrined, he took a step back from her, his hands flying from her shoulders as if they'd been burned. 'I should know better than that. It's been so long since I've been in the company of an English lady that I've forgotten how to behave, haven't I?'

He began to bow again, putting another tall standing pot behind him into peril.

'Oh, sir, don't!' She darted around him to catch and save the pot. 'I am sorry, sir, but I'm afraid that I must ask you to leave, before any damage occurs to Sir William's collection.'

'I never intended—'

'No, sir,' she said quickly. She had to be firm. She had to be resolute, to remember how important cataloguing Sir William's collection had been to Father, and forget how charmingly this officer had smiled at her. 'I believe if you proceed down this hallway to your left, you'll find Her Ladyship's parlour. You need only follow the voices of the other guests to find it, sir.'

'Which is exactly what I could have done in the beginning, couldn't I?' He grinned, and held his crooked arm out to her. 'You will join me, miss?'

But Abigail only shook her head, clutching the Apollo more tightly, as if to keep her hands from betraying her. 'I'm sorry, sir, but I'm not Lady Hamilton's guest. I'm employed by Sir William as a scholar to catalogue his collection—or rather, I hope to be, if he finds me satisfactory.'

'Satisfactory, miss?' His grin turned endearingly lop-sided. 'Ah, miss, how could he not find you so?'

'He could,' she said, too unsure to acknowledge the compliment. 'He could indeed.'

'But he won't. Not if he's any sense.' He lowered his arm to his side, and began to back slowly towards the open door. 'Scholar or guest, I will see you again.'

It wasn't a question, but a statement, and bold enough to make her blush all over again. 'I cannot say, sir.'

'I can, miss,' he said softly, pausing in the open door. 'I can, and I assure you I will.'

Chapter 2

JAMES stood on the tavern's narrow balcony, gazing out over the tiled rooftops of Naples to the villas that loomed ghostly pale over the water. This wasn't where he'd planned to spend his first night in port—not at all—but after what had happened earlier in the evening, at the house, he found he no longer had any interest in those grand, gaudy plans. Now the wine was bland, the food indifferent, and, though the company in the room he'd just left included two of his closest friends on this earth, he wasn't in the mood for their bawdy good humour, or the girls that they'd bought with the wine.

He drew out his pocket watch to check the time. It was barely midnight; they weren't due back on board the ship for another four hours, in time for him to take the first watch.

'Why the devil are you skulking about alone out here, Richardson?' demanded his friend and fellow lieutenant John Beattie who reeled out onto the balcony to join him. 'Why disappoint the ladies, I ask you?'

James glanced past him to the three laughing young women sprawled across the benches in the private dining room. 'They're hardly ladies, Beattie.'

'But they are *willing*,' Beattie said earnestly. 'What else have we been speaking of these last weeks, eh?'

James shrugged, unwilling to explain what he didn't entirely understand himself. 'Some other night.'

'"Some other night"?' Beattie frowned. 'What's this about? Are you daft? Did you eat something dicey at Sir William's table?'

'Don't *you* be daft,' scoffed James. 'We ate the same, side by side, didn't we?'

'Not quite.' Beattie slung his arm across James's shoulder. 'I should've guessed you'd found another amusement when you disappeared before dinner. A parlourmaid, was she? Or a serving girl?'

'Hardly.' James slipped free of his friend's arm and turned to face him. 'Not that I'm about to tell you one word further about the lady.

'A lady?' Beattie asked, clearly mystified. 'There weren't any ladies in the house tonight save Sir William's own—and even she's not exactly a thoroughbred.'

'No.' Despite her demurring about not being a guest, the dark-haired girl he'd met among the statues was ten times the lady that Lady Hamilton could ever be. It was no secret that Sir William's much younger wife had first been the cast-off mistress of his nephew, and before that had toiled both in a brothel and as an artist's model. 'The lady I met was in mourning—which was likely why she wasn't at dinner, even though she's English.'

'An English widow?' At once Beattie's round face grew sombre. England had been at war off and on for as long as either of them could remember, and young widows had become far too common. 'Was her husband an officer, then?'

'I didn't ask.' He wouldn't have, either; such things were better left for a lady to volunteer. He'd taken care to be respectful, considerate of her sorrow, even as he'd noted that her black dress was so faded that her grief couldn't be fresh, either.

But, widow or not, there had been something about the girl that had affected him, affected him strongly. He couldn't say exactly what it had been: how her blue eyes had widened when she'd looked up at him, or the way she'd managed to be both shy and forthright, or how she'd defended Sir William's musty old rubbish as determinedly as any ship-of-the-line? Perhaps it had simply been her very Englishness that had reminded him of the home he hadn't seen for years, yet still risked his life to defend.

No, he wasn't good at explaining such things. Never had been. Yet, whatever the reason, he'd been unable to put the girl from his thoughts ever since he'd left her in that cluttered storeroom.

Nor, really, did he want to.

Noisily Beattie cleared his throat, making it clear that James had, in Beattie's opinion, taken longer to reply than was decent between friends.

'Well, now,' he said heartily, 'I can understand why such a lady would distract you, but there's no point in letting her spoil your sport, is there?'

'You stay,' James said. 'I'll hire a boat to carry me back to the ship.'

'You would leave these pretty little doxies for a widow you may never see again?'

'I'll see her.' James was confident of that, even though to his chagrin he realised he'd never asked the girl so much as her name. 'I'll see her again, and soon.'

'But not tonight.' Beattie waved his hand towards the women waiting inside. 'Recall what the wise man said about a bird in the hand, Richardson. I've heard these Neapolitan doxies do tricks with their tongues that can make a man weep.'

'Then I'll leave it to you to discover the truth.' James set his tumbler with the unfinished wine on a nearby chair, and placed his hat back on his head to leave. 'I'll have to contain my curiosity until you can tell me in the morning.'

'*If* you're there on board,' Beattie said. 'More likely you'll be with the admiral, hauled ashore once again and back to Sir William's for breakfast.'

James frowned. He was the *Vanguard*'s first lieutenant now, and the admiral had as much as told him he was next in line for a command of his own. His place in the morning should be back among the other officers on board, overseeing the repairs to the fleet. Yet if he *were* again accompanying the admiral, then he'd have another opportunity to find the little widow. 'What are you saying?'

'I don't have to *say* a blessed thing,' Beattie said. 'We both saw what we saw with our own eyes, didn't we? Lady Hamilton throwing herself at the admiral, brazen enough to shame her poor old husband? Not that the admiral minded, did he?'

'No.' There was no point in denying it. Every man on board had witnessed Lady Hamilton's hysterical welcome. Nelson was a genius at sea, and as close to a bonafide hero as James had ever served beneath, but the man was so scarred and frail that it was hard to imagine him fascinating the still-beautiful Lady Hamilton. It hadn't mattered, either, that the admiral had a wife waiting for him in England—much as Lady Hamilton had had Sir William beside her. 'She did make her interest known.'

'In a manner, aye.' Beattie retrieved James's half-full wine glass from where he'd abandoned it, holding it up to the light before he emptied the contents himself. 'No wonder he wants us to stay in this harbour until after Christmas, with her ladyship offering so much cheer.'

'We've seen far worse harbours,' James said, glancing out over the nodding palm trees and the calm waters of the bay beyond: hardly the sort of snowy Christmas scene he remembered from his boyhood in Devon, but he'd take peace and calm waters over ice and snow any day. 'If this is what comes of her ladyship's Christmas cheer, than so be it.'

'Oh, aye, her *cheer*.' Beattie snorted with amusement. 'They say the admiral took her fancy years ago, back when he had two eyes and she weren't so blowsy, but it's still more'n I want to consider. Cupid's a peculiar little fellow, ain't he?'

'Deuced peculiar,' James said, even as he thought again of how the fierce little widow with the candle in her hand was worth more than all the doxies waiting inside. 'Take care that Cupid doesn't send his arrows towards you while you're in this place, mind?'

Beattie laughed. 'No question of that,' he said with a wink. 'But watch yourself, Richardson. Who knows what might happen with your little widow at the Hamiltons' between now and Christmas?'

James laughed, too, but his mood was less raucous. 'Who knows?' he said softly. 'Who knows, indeed?'

With a pair of silver tongs, Abigail carefully placed a slice of toasted bread onto her plate, then turned to find a place for breakfast. She had her choice: though the long mahogany table was beautifully set, with a fine linen cloth and silver baskets filled with fruit, not one of the two dozen chairs was taken. Nor were there any signs of the house's other occupants appearing. Given how the laughing voices and the music from the parlour had continued long into the night, Abigail was not surprised. A maidservant had informed her that her presence was requested at breakfast at half-past seven, but clearly in Naples half-past seven meant something different than it did in Oxford.

Tentatively Abigail sat at the far end of the table, near the armchair that must belong to Sir William's lady. She'd stayed up most of the night herself as well, writing a proposal for Sir William based on what she'd seen in his gallery, and now all she could do was wait for his final decision.

She might have no company, but at least the view from the tall windows before her as she nibbled her toast was breathtaking: framed by the red-flowered vines curling over the balcony's rail, the deep blue bay was bright in the morning sun, with the city curled around it and Mount Vesuvius with its mist-shrouded crown in the distance.

A beautiful view, even a romantic view, and for the first time in her life she let herself imagine sharing such a small pleasure with a gentleman. An officer in the King's service, a lieutenant like the golden-haired one who'd surprised her last night, caught her when she'd stumbled, and—

No. She closed her eyes against the seductive view and the memory of the officer. *That* was not why she'd come this far. She was here to carry on her father's work, not to engage in a—a *flirtation* with a man who'd sail away without a second thought. Likely he was already gone. Likely she'd never see him again.

And foolishly, she wished it weren't so.

'Miss Layton?' The lady entered the room as if she were coming onto a stage, her face raised and her hands held out from her sides, palms turned up, so her elegant Kashmir shawl drifted dramatically behind her. She was tall and plump, and past her first youth, but a breathtaking beauty still, with flawless creamy skin and masses of chestnut hair, and her smile was so genuine that Abigail seemed to feel its warmth like the sunshine on her skin.

'I am Lady Hamilton,' she said as she came towards Abigail. 'I feel perfectly dreadful for not welcomin' you myself last night. Are you feelin' better? Your room suits you?'

Hurriedly Abigail rose and curtseyed. Lady Hamilton looked like a lady, and her welcome was as warm as her smile, yet to Abigail's confusion her voice was a dreadful low-born squawk, her accent more fitted to a fishwife than an ambassador's lady.

'Yes, my lady,' Abigail said. 'That is, I am entirely well, and the room—the room is perfect.'

'Good.' Her ladyship sat, motioning for Abigail to sit, too. At once a servant set a plate of shirred eggs, sweet rolls, cheese and grilled white sausages before Lady Hamilton, who began to eat with robust appetite. 'I know you're here to work with Sir William, but I hope you'll spare a little time for pleasure, too. Might I offer my condolences on your sorrow an' loss?'

'Thank you, my lady,' Abigail said. 'I mourn my father, whose work I hope to continue here. He died a year ago last August.'

'So long ago?' Lady Hamilton asked, her mouth full of eggs. 'It's not my place, I know, but it's past time for you to set aside that mourning, miss, an' dress yourself gay. The house will be full o' handsome young officers, ready to ogle a pretty young lady like you!'

Abigail flushed, instantly recalling the officer from last night.

'I fear my responsibilities will allow little time for—for idleness, my lady.'

'Oh, pish,' Lady Hamilton said. 'Sir William don't expect anything o' the sort from you, an' you know your father wouldn't, neither.'

Without thinking Abigail touched the gold locket around her throat. Her ladyship's guess was right; Father had always worried that she'd devoted too much time to his scholarship and to tending him through his last illness, and not enough to finding a husband, as other girls her age did.

'There now, I'd no wish to make you sorrowful.' Her ladyship reached over the table to pat Abigail's arm gently. 'And I know what it's like not to have the blunt to pay for gowns an' ribbons an' such. I'll send up a few things to your room, an' you can see if anything suits. Besides, you'll be more at ease if you dress for Naples an' not London, an'— Oh, here is England's own darling hero!'

She jumped from her chair and rushed towards the doorway. And if Lady Hamilton didn't fit Abigail's ideal of a lady, then neither did Admiral Nelson resemble her notion of a war hero. He was slight, almost frail, with wispy white hair poking out from beneath a thick bandage wrapped around his forehead. His right arm was gone, lost to a long-ago battle, his empty sleeve pinned to the chest of his uniform coat, yet his one good eye seemed to fair glow with joy as Lady Hamilton dropped to her knees to kiss his hand, rubbing her cheek against it in a shamelessly, scandalously dramatic display.

'Enough of that, my lady,' he said, bending slightly to help raise her back to her feet. 'No need for such demonstrations, eh?'

But as the admiral leaned forward Abigail saw the officer standing behind him: her golden-haired lieutenant from the night before. As her gaze met his, he bowed slightly in recognition, his expression solemn. Abigail's cheeks flamed, and hastily she stared down at the half-eaten toast on her plate.

She'd done nothing wrong, she told herself fiercely. She'd no reason to blush simply because a gentleman had nodded her way.

But how could he possibly be more handsome by the morning light than he'd been last night? And what twist of fate had made him appear again here, now, to take her so thoroughly by surprise?

'Might I present Miss Abigail Layton?' Lady Hamilton was saying. 'She is here to tally up Sir William's collection o' rarities. Admiral Nelson, Miss Layton.'

Hurriedly Abigail rose to make her curtsey while the admiral smiled indulgently.

'Lieutenant Lord James Richardson, Miss Layton,' Lady Hamilton continued. 'His father's the Earl o' Carrington, you know, but here he's honoured to serve our glorious hero.'

'Miss Layton,' the lieutenant said. 'Your servant.'

'Your servant, my lord,' Abigail murmured, her cheeks hot yet again. He wasn't just a sailor, nor even just an officer, but an attendant to the admiral and the son of an earl, and he was smiling at her now with the oddest expression of bewildered curiosity. And his name was James: a name she'd always liked. *James.*

'Ah, Miss Layton, here you are!' Sir William came striding into the room, holding a long fragment of marble in his arms. 'I have read the papers you sent to me this morning, and I'm impressed. Most impressed! But I thought I'd give you one more test, if you will.'

He set the heavy fragment on the dining table beside her plate and stepped back, folding his arms over his chest. 'There, now, Miss Layton. Tell me what you can about this fellow.'

'Oh, Sir William, really!' Lady Hamilton protested. 'Let the poor girl eat her breakfast!'

'If you please, my lady, it's no trouble,' Abigail said, already studying the fragment—a long panel showing a prancing satyr. As such tests went, this one wasn't hard at all. 'The stone is marble, of course, most likely all that remains of a stele. From the carving, I should guess it's Ionic, from the fifth century BC—certainly no later.'

Sir William leaned closer, his expression shrewd. 'But for what purpose, eh?'

'Purpose, Sir William?' Abigail asked, not wanting to blunder by misinterpreting his question.

'Yes, the purpose,' he repeated. 'Where would it have been originally situated?'

'Forgive me, Sir William, but I cannot see how that should possibly matter,' interrupted the lieutenant gallantly. 'The lady has already answered your question.'

Abigail stared at him, horrified that he was trying to defend her when clearly no defence was wanted, or even needed. Didn't he realise how he could spoil everything by making her seem ignorant?

'On the contrary, my lord,' she said swiftly, 'I haven't answered the question at all.'

The lieutenant's smile was dazzling in its kindness, but still wrong-minded. 'No one expects you to, Miss Layton. Not really.'

'*I* do,' she said. 'Because I *can*.'

She turned back to the ambassador, determined not to let herself be distracted by the lieutenant. 'While most steles of this period were used for funerary displays, I should venture that, because the subject is a satyr holding a wine cup, this example was more likely part of a temple to Dionysus, or perhaps commissioned for the pleasure garden of a private patron.'

Abigail knew she was right, that not even her father could have given a better answer, yet Sir William didn't reply. His expression was unchanging, and it felt as if everyone in the room was holding their breath with her.

'Is there anything else I might answer, Sir William?' she asked at last, unable to bear it any longer. 'Another question?'

'Another, Miss Layton?' Sir William laughed. 'Only how soon you might begin!'

Abigail smiled as relief swept over her. 'At once, Sir William, at once!'

She nodded eagerly, reaching for the heavy marble stele to take it back to the rest of the collection. But as she strained to pick it up, the lieutenant reached down and intercepted it.

'Pray, permit me, Miss Layton,' he said. 'That's more than a lady should have to hoist.'

Abigail opened her mouth to protest that she was perfectly capable, but Lady Hamilton answered first.

'What an excellent idea, Lieutenant!' she said cheerfully. 'Miss Layton, you can show him the way back to the galleries.'

'It *is* an excellent idea, my lady,' the admiral agreed. 'In addition to Lord Richardson's exemplary bravery, he also has a knack for arranging things. He could certainly offer a sailor's perspective on stowing your collection so it arrives safely in London, Sir William.'

'That is most generous of you, Admiral,' Sir William said, beaming with pleasure. 'But I couldn't presume to claim your lieutenant's time for my humble—'

'Oh, not at all, not at all,' the admiral said. 'Consider his expertise a return for your hospitality, Sir William.'

'Then the lieutenant must stay here on land with you, Admiral, as our guest,' Lady Hamilton cried happily. 'Though I must warn you both, this house will be a merry place in the Christmas season.'

'Forgive me, my lady,' Richardson said quickly, 'but I've responsibilities to my men that must make me refuse—'

'Not at all, Richardson, not at all,' the admiral said, with just enough edge to his voice to make it an order. 'There's plenty of others to look after the *Vanguard*. And surely you cannot object to working beside this fair young lady, can you?'

'No, sir,' the lieutenant said, and he took the stele into his arms. 'Miss Layton?'

Knowing that it was the only answer he could give was not flattering, but then she couldn't exactly protest, either. Instead she nodded curtly, bowed to the others, and led the way from the room and into the hall.

'Why do you wear mourning if you're not a widow?' he demanded, as soon as they were out of hearing from the others.

'I wear mourning for my *father*.' Abruptly Abigail stopped to face him. 'Why didn't you tell me you were a—a *lord*?'

'Because it's not the most important thing to know about me!' he exclaimed indignantly. 'I care to be judged upon my own merit, rather than for my family's name.'

'Well, then, my mourning my father isn't the most important thing to know about me, either.' She turned away and began walking—no, marching—towards the ambassador's gallery.

'Hold now, Miss Layton, one moment.' With three long steps he was in front of her, blocking her path. 'It's not my choice that we work together.'

'Nor mine, my lord,' she said quickly. 'Especially not after you tried to make me seem like a perfect ninny before Sir William.'

'The hell I— That is, I most certainly did not!' he exclaimed. 'Miss Layton, all I intended to do was to deflect Sir William's criticism.'

She gasped. '*Deflect* Sir William?'

'Aye, deflect him,' he repeated. 'Because I thought he was challenging you in a way no gentleman should challenge a lady. I thought I was defending you, Miss Layton, but I see my concern was unwelcome.'

'Of course it was unwelcome!' Abigail cried. 'Would I have journeyed all this way if I couldn't answer such simple questions? Would I have suffered the expense and discomfort of that voyage if I couldn't offer Sir William the benefit of my knowledge and learning?'

He frowned, clearly still unconvinced, and looked down at the marble stele in his arms. 'I've never known a learned lady. My sisters—all they care for is how many admirers they can dangle at a time.'

'Then surely from your own position as the son of a peer—'

'A *younger* son,' he said quickly. 'I was made a midshipman the week of my thirteenth birthday, and sent off to sea. I'd never a head for schooling, anyway. Never saw the point to it.'

'The point to knowledge of the ancients?' she repeated, shocked. 'The point to classical studies?'

He shrugged carelessly, a lock of his golden hair slipping across his forehead. 'Aye, that's it. Nothing useful, by my lights. I'd far rather be able to bring a ship safe into port with a westerly wind, or know how to bear the long guns to rake the masts of a French frigate, than study a pack of dusty old philosophers. Not that I mean to slander you, Miss Layton. Not at all.'

It occurred to her that he'd just done exactly that. Yet she'd have to admit that there had been no malice to his words, only ignorance, and if she were truly being honest she'd have to admit she was just as mystified by his westerly winds and long guns.

'Then please, my lord,' she began solemnly, 'if you find so little use in my studies, might I ask why you bothered to defend me before Sir William?'

'Why?' He grinned, his smile as wide as that of the carved satyr in his arms. 'That's easy enough to answer, miss. I had to do it, Miss Layton, because you are the finest lady I've met in ages. Truth to tell, maybe ever.'

'Oh,' she said—all she could think to reply under the circumstances. No gentleman had ever said such a thing to her. Not one. *'Oh.'*

'Aye.' He cleared his throat self-consciously, and shifted the satyr from one arm to another. 'I wouldn't have said it, Miss Layton, if it weren't true.'

'I suppose not, my lord.' She swallowed, as if her throat needed clearing, too, determined to put aside this foolish confusion she was feeling and return to her usual practical self. 'If we are to finish this task before Christmas, as Sir William wishes, then we should begin at once.'

'Aye, Miss Layton, Christmas,' he said softly. 'Then we haven't a moment to waste.'

Chapter 3

'YOU can say whatever you please, Miss Layton, but I'm here to tell you that *that* won't work.'

Abigail shoved her hair back from her face and stared crossly at Lieutenant Lord Richardson. Her black wool gown was sticking to her back and arms in the warm afternoon, her head ached from concentrating so hard on making proper identifications, and her fingers were sore from writing so many notes. While she and the lieutenant had begun the morning granting one another a certain polite deference, born more of shyness than anything else, as the day had progressed that politeness had begun to disintegrate as each had realised the limits of the other's knowledge—or, more correctly, Abigail had decided, how wretchedly ignorant *he* was of how Sir William's priceless artefacts should be preserved.

'Each century's pieces must be packed together, my lord,' she explained, for what seemed the hundredth time. 'Else they'll be far too difficult to sort again in London. There must be hundreds—thousands!—of pieces in the collection. The fourth-century Roman bronzes must be near the fourth-century vases, and so on.'

He began shaking his head even before she'd finished. 'If you put bronze *anything* next to that crockery, all you'll have in London is a pile of smashed rubbish.'

'That, my lord, is why everything is to be wrapped in woollen batting for safe-keeping.'

'A ship's hold is a powerfully damp place,' he explained. 'Your wool will soak up every drop of it, and rot what you've wrapped it round besides. If you came on board the *Vanguard* I'd take you deep down in the hold, and you'd see it all for yourself.'

She straightened to confront him, her hands squared at her waist. 'I've been on board a ship before, thank you,' she said, remembering how awful her voyage from England had been. 'I've seen quite enough.'

'Some low, slovenly merchantman's not the *Vanguard*,' he said, with open admiration and affection. 'She's a little battered and torn about now, but she's still one of the neatest, fastest vessels in the fleet.'

'You sound as if you're speaking of a—a person,' she said, surprised by the intensity of his feeling. 'Not just a boat.'

'A first-rate ship, miss, not a boat,' he corrected gently, smiling. 'And, aye, to sailors a ship does become like a person over time, I suppose.'

Earlier in the day he'd asked her permission to remove his heavy uniform coat, and she'd granted it, not seeing any reason to refuse. But as the day had warmed he'd also rolled the sleeves of his shirt back to his elbows, and the sight of his bare wrists and muscular forearms dusted over with golden hair had been more distracting than she'd dreamed possible.

'When she's sailing under full canvas and a brisk wind, the waves crashing against her bow and the lines singing taut and sharp, why, then she *does* seem alive,' he continued. 'To stand on her deck on a sunny morn, with the wind and spray dancing all around—*ahh*, there's nothing finer in this life, Miss Layton. Nothing at all.'

But to Abigail there was nothing finer than how glorious he looked, standing there smiling before her, in his white breeches and shirt, with the Neapolitan sunlight streaming around him. She might not comprehend his devotion to the sea or his ship, but she did understand the kind of passion that glowed in his face. She felt the same when she studied a particularly beautiful statue or carving—which was why, in a way, she was so determined that Sir William's collection be given the care it deserved.

'That speed and unease of a ship through the waves is exactly why I must insist on the woollen batting to protect the artefacts, my lord,' she said, forcing herself to concentrate on her work instead of his handsomely distracting self. 'For the safety of fragile objects, wool is always best.'

'You'll do far better with wood shavings, Miss Layton,' he insisted. 'That will keep things snug, even in a stormy sea.'

Steadfastly she looked back to his face. 'What would be even better, my lord, would be if your captain could keep better control of his ship within the waves, so that the passage would be less taxing.'

He sighed with exasperation. 'Why not ask me to pour a great vat of oil upon the seas and calm them clear to Portsmouth for transporting your bric-a-brac?'

'Why not, indeed, my lord?' she answered tartly, 'Since every other request I make seems to strike you as so unreasonable that you—'

'Unreasonable, Miss Layton?' Lady Hamilton swept into the room. 'I cannot believe this handsome gentleman would ever be unreasonable.'

'It was a slight difference of opinion, my lady,' the lieutenant said quickly. 'No more.'

'No more, my lady,' Abigail agreed, just as quickly. She wasn't sure if he believed what he'd said, or if he was simply being gallant again, but he'd saved her before Lady Hamilton, and for that she must be grateful. 'You may assure Sir William that we are making excellent progress.'

'I'm glad to hear it,' she said, smiling, 'because I intend to put an end to your work for today, so that you might prepare for the ball.'

'The ball, my lady?' asked the lieutenant, his voice carefully non-committal.

'Yes, yes!' exclaimed Lady Hamilton. 'I've only a week for the planning, but I'll have it ready. In honor o' dear Admiral Nelson's birthday, o' course.'

Abigail's brows rose in dismay. She'd never attended a ball, nor did she wish to go to one now, either. 'Forgive me, my lady, but I must beg to be excused, seeing that my work here has only—'

'Oh, no, you're not to be excused,' Lady Hamilton said cheerfully, waving an outsized ivory fan before her face. 'We'll need every pretty English lady we can muster.'

'Then I shall leave you ladies to, ah, make your plans,' the lieutenant said, bowing even as he eagerly grabbed his coat from the back of a chair. 'It's high time I returned to my duties on the *Vanguard*.'

'Only if you swear to me you'll be one o' my guests at the ball, my lord,' Lady Hamilton said. 'The admiral will expect you there with him, I know.'

The lieutenant winced, his expression so wretched that Abigail might have laughed if she hadn't been feeling exactly the same way.

'Forgive me, my lady,' he began, 'but my duty—'

'It's your duty to come and pay our hero homage, my lord, an' to dance with the ladies, too.' Lady Hamilton tucked Abigail's hand into the crook of her arm so at least *she* couldn't escape. 'Now, come with me, Miss Layton. As our sailing friends say, I must "rig you out proper".'

Abigail's last glimpse of the lieutenant was over Lady Hamilton's rounded shoulder as she drew her through the door. His expression was one of such mournful sympathy that Abigail could almost—almost—forgive him his stubbornness about the woollen batting.

But first she'd have to cope with Lady Hamilton, now steering her briskly up the stairs. 'While I appreciate your interest, my lady, I'm afraid I'm not, ah, the sort of lady to invite to a ball.'

'Nonsense.' Lady Hamilton led her into her sitting room, with her bedchamber just beyond. Windows ran along one wall, open to the breathtaking view of the harbour, dotted with tall English warships. Three Italian women curtseyed to them as they entered: a mantua-maker in an extravagant organdy bonnet and, flanking her, two assistant seamstresses. 'Once we've put aside that dreary mourning, why, you'll look as pretty as a princess. Prettier, considering the homely state of the princesses at this court.'

Bewildered, Abigail watched the three women begin displaying lengths of embroidered muslin and silk ribbon and Venetian lace for her consideration. She could only imagine the beauty of the gowns they'd create, and the exorbitant cost of them, too. Why, she could squander half of what she'd earn here on a single gown!

'I am sorry, my lady,' she began, 'but I can't begin to afford to—'

'More nonsense,' her ladyship said, holding a pink ribbon beside Abigail's cheek. 'It be on my reckoning, and that's an end to it. I cannot bear to see you shrouded away like a little crow, and I'd wager your father would say the same, wouldn't he?'

Tears sprang to Abigail's eyes, and she pressed her hand over her mouth, struggling to keep them back. Father *had* always wanted her to be more light-hearted and merry, like the other girls on their street, but there'd never been extra money for fancy gowns or dancing masters, nor had Abigail wished to leave Father's side after he'd become ill.

'There, now, no more tears,' Lady Hamilton said softly, patting her arm. 'I 'spect you've shed more'n enough of those by now. Let's be more cheery, eh? Signora Teresa, something cheery for the young lady!'

But nothing Abigail had known in her life had prepared her for how Signora Teresa and her assistants seemed to pounce upon her, measuring and marking and draping her in drifts of sheer Indian muslin and shining silk, and tucking plumes and ribbons into her hair. The ambassador's wife oversaw it all with the same unquestionable assurance that Admiral Nelson must have shown at the Nile.

'Here, now, the final touch.' As the seamstresses packed their baskets to leave, Lady Hamilton took a length of white ribbon, woven with blue flourishes, and tied it in a bow around the high waist of Abigail's old black mourning gown. 'You can at least wear this until the rest is ready, day after tomorrow.'

Overwhelmed, Abigail shook her head. 'I do not mean to be ungrateful, my lady, but this is too much for me to accept. My father was a university scholar, not a true gentleman, and to make me out to be a lady like this cannot be right.'

'Hush,' Lady Hamilton said, smoothing the ribbon bow until the other women had left them alone and the door had closed. She gave the bow a final pat and stepped back, twisting her hands in the ends of her shawl.

'Let me explain, Miss Layton, and please mind what I say.' All the earlier levity was gone from her lovely face, replaced by something harder, more determined, and far, far more serious. 'I wish to see you happy, yes, and dressed as you should be. And if you and that handsome lieutenant can amuse one another while you're my guests, all the better. I do love lovers, an' always will.'

Abigail blushed—something she felt she'd done almost without stopping since she'd come to this house. 'You are very kind, my lady, but I've come here to work.'

'Perhaps you have,' she answered. 'But now that you're here, you're part o' something else altogether. Has your lord lieutenant spoken much o' the battle to you?'

'Not at all,' Abigail said. 'He'd didn't speak a single word of brave deeds and glory.'

'And he won't, Miss Layton,' Lady Hamilton said with a sad smile. 'That's the way o' these officers. The worse the war is for them, the less they speak of it. And from what I've heard from Sir William, the Nile was very, very bad indeed.'

'But the English won, didn't they?'

'They did, aye, but at a terrible mortal cost,' Lady Hamilton said sorrowfully. 'Over two thousand men killed between the two sides, and many died most horribly when one of the French ships exploded. Hundreds of burned and dying men floatin' about in the waves—the ones that survive don't forget that, no matter if they be French nor English. Once the wounded are brought ashore tomorrow I'll go and call upon them myself, though the sight will fair break my tender heart.'

Horrified, Abigail could not imagine the carnage the other woman was describing. How could the lieutenant smile at all after fighting in such a battle? Though England and France had been at war as long as she could remember, the reality had never touched them at Oxford, not like this. Her version of war had come from Homer and other ancient poets, full of idealised glory and noble causes, no real pain or death.

'So that is why you are having this party for the admiral's birthday, my lady?' she asked. 'To help him and his men forget?'

'Would that that were all!' Lady Hamilton's laugh held little humour. 'No, Miss Layton, we're all of us in the war far deeper than that. Our great navy won the day at the Nile, but Bonaparte's armies on land remain as strong as ever and ready to claim all o' Italy if we let them.'

'Italy?' Abigail repeated faintly. 'Not Naples, too?'

'Oh, yes, Naples, too,' Lady Hamilton answered firmly. 'My husband would never have knowingly asked you, as a woman, to risk yourself by coming here at this perilous time. But now that you are here, you must know of the danger.'

'Thank you, my lady.' Abigail tried to sound brave. It was a bravery she didn't feel. To be trapped in the path of the French army, here in a place that was already so foreign—oh, *why* hadn't she stayed in Oxford, where she'd been safe? 'I suppose it is better to know than not.'

'It is indeed better!' Lady Hamilton exclaimed. 'Now you understand why it's so important to Sir William to have his treasures and you shipped home as soon as can be.'

'Yes, my lady,' Abigail said, no longer even trying for bravery. 'That—that will make for a very different sort of Christmas for us this year, won't it?'

'It will if the French army comes, which we don't want at all,' Lady Hamilton warned. 'That's the true reason you and I and all the other English folk here must make a great, brave show of the admiral and the rest of his men, and of the King and Queen o' Naples, too. French spies are everywhere, and we must take care they carry only tales of how strong and proud and clever we English are.'

Lady Hamilton raised the end of the ribbon tied around Abigail's waist, tracing the monogram with one finger. 'Here you see two letter Ns: one for the Nile, and one for Nelson. Everyone in the house will be wearing this ribbon at the ball. It's the least we can do. For them, and for England.'

'For England.' Abigail looked down at the ribbon that now seemed so much more than a mere length of costly silk.

Her reasons for being so ill-tempered earlier with Lieutenant Lord Richardson had likewise changed, and now seemed selfishly insignificant, enough to make her thoroughly ashamed. He deserved far more than that from her, and as soon as she saw him again she meant to apologise. And she'd do it: she'd do it just as she would be as strong and brave and clever as Lady Hamilton had said she must be.

For what choice, really, did she have?

Chapter 4

THE next morning, James made sure he was in Sir William's gallery first, before Abigail arrived and almost before the sun rose. Though they'd both been included at dinner last night, he hadn't found a chance to talk with her alone, and afterwards she retreated to her room before the other ladies rejoined the gentlemen in the drawing room.

He caught his reflection in the bull's-eye mirror over the fireplace, and quickly smoothed the front of his hair back again, over the cowlick that always made it fall forward. As he'd lain awake late last night it had crossed his mind that Abigail might be avoiding him on purpose—hardly a pleasing or flattering possibility. Not that he could blame her, either. Not after he'd been so insistent about the method of packing. The more he thought of it, the more he realised, to his considerable remorse, that he'd been as bad as any bully, expecting her to obey his orders as if she were a new crewman, not a lady.

He was determined to make it up to her today. He'd explain his reasons, not just order her around. And he'd brought flowers, too: flowers could solve almost any dispute with a lady. At least, he remembered flowers doing the trick with his sisters when they'd had fallings-out with gentlemen. He studied the bunch of flowers he'd bought earlier in the market: exotic, star-shaped white blossoms, and scraps of greenery tied up with a red ribbon. Tentatively he lifted them to his nose to sniff the fragrance. It wasn't often he had the chance to smell anything very sweet at sea, especially not when—

'My lord.' She paused in the doorway, clearly surprised to find him here first. 'Good day to you, my lord. Are you keeping rooster's hours, too?'

He jerked his face up from the bouquet, feeling more like some damned donkey caught nibbling in a flowerpot than a rooster. 'Ah, no, Miss Layton. That is, sailor's hours aren't much different from a rooster's. These are for you.'

He thrust the flowers out to her, and she smiled with unabashed pleasure. The way her dark hair was sleeked back beneath her plain cap only made the rosiness of her cheeks all the more apparent as she came towards him, and he grinned back, glad he'd earned that reward from her.

But instead of taking the flowers she looked past them, then lower, and frowned.

'Oh, dear, no,' she said, shaking her head even as she continued to smile. 'Forgive me, my lord, but you're dusted all over with pollen.'

He looked down. The front of his dark blue uniform coat was dusted with yellow pollen from the flowers, even to a faint film over the brass buttons.

He could think of nothing, absolutely nothing, to say that was acceptable before a lady.

'Here, now, we'll dust that away directly,' she said, drawing her handkerchief from her pocket. With quick, brisk strokes she flicked the pollen from his coat, resting her hand lightly on his chest to hold the fabric taut. He held his breath to keep from shifting, and prayed she wouldn't feel how fast his heart was beating so close to her touch.

'That's the worst of it.' She gave his chest one final pat before she looked up at him. 'No lasting harm, my lord, not that— Oh, no, it's on your nose, too!'

Before he could stop her she'd reached up and dabbed the end of his nose with the handkerchief, as if she were his nursemaid. He jerked back, and once again held out the flowers that had already brought him so much sorrow.

'These are for you, Miss Layton,' he said again. 'To show I meant no ill yesterday.'

'How kind of you, my lord,' she said, smiling shyly as she took the flowers, though he noted how she held them away from her own dark clothes. 'Though if anyone should be making amends it should be I. You were trying to help, and I reacted by being a disagreeable shrew, and—'

'Not at all,' he said firmly. 'I was the one at fault, giving you orders as I did.'

'You didn't mean it,' she said quickly. 'I knew that.'

'Well, at the time I did.' He cleared his throat, glad she'd stayed so close to him and hadn't backed away. 'But I give you my word that I won't again. Since we're to work here together, as mates—'

'As mates?' she repeated, her blue eyes opening wide. *'Mates?'*

'I don't intend the word like landsmen do,' he said hastily. 'At sea a mate's your friend—one who shares your mess and your watch. The fellow sitting at the next place at meals or in battle, the one you'd trust with your life. *That's* what I meant.'

'Ahh,' she said softly, and looked down at the flowers in her hands. 'Forgive me for not understanding, but I've never had anyone like that. I've never worked beside anyone else save my father.'

'A sister, then,' he said. 'I'd consider my brothers as mates, too, even though we all fought like blazes when we were boys.'

She shook her head, still gazing down at the flowers. She had extraordinary lashes, dark and thick and brushing over her cheeks. 'No brothers, no sisters. I cannot recall my mother, either, she died so long ago. 'Twas always Father and me and no one else.'

Abruptly she turned away, as if she'd realised too late she'd volunteered more than she'd meant to. 'I'll have to ask one of the servants for water for these.'

'They won't have far to look. There's more than enough old vases around in here,' he said heartily, hoping that would be enough to make her turn towards him with her usual indignant fire. But instead she kept her back to him, her shoulders so taut he knew she was upset. Blast. What had he done now?

'Now, now,' he said softly, resting one hand lightly on her shoulder. 'I told you before, miss, I'd be honoured to serve as your mate.'

At last she turned back to him. 'You don't have to say that,' she said quickly. 'I know you're just trying to make me feel better.'

'No, I'm not,' he said, too quickly himself, before he'd thought it through. 'That is, I want you to feel better, but that wasn't my reason for speaking as I did. I don't say things I don't mean. Wouldn't be honourable.'

That made her smile, though he still had the uneasy suspicion that she remained close to tears. 'And you are a most honourable gentleman, my lord, aren't you?'

'I try to be, aye,' he said, hoping that her tears wouldn't spill over. He'd had enough grief and sorrow already for the rest of this life, and the next with it. 'I would always be honourable with a mate.'

'Then I shall promise the same, and mean it, too.' Her smile widened, brighter than the sun that was just rising over the harbour. 'I'd venture we'll both be needing a good mate or two before we're done here in Naples, my lord.'

He grinned with her, pleased to hear her speak of him as a 'mate' like that. 'Here, now, if we're going to be mates, then you must leave off using my title. In this room, between us, I'd rather be no more than James Richardson.'

'Oh, my lord, I couldn't do that, not with you the son of a peer!' The look on her face was so deliciously scandalised that he wanted to laugh. 'It wouldn't be proper, my lord!'

'Would you do it if I called you by your Christian name, too?' he asked. 'That's proper, between mates.'

She paused, considering, likely balancing propriety against his proposal. Then she nodded—a swift, decisive dip of her chin.

'You are right, James,' she said. 'Such familiarity would be proper between—between *mates*, James.'

'So it would, Abigail.' After these last grim months of war and death, how much he enjoyed the uncomplicated pleasure of hearing his given name spoken by a pretty girl! 'Abigail it shall be.'

'I'm glad.' Suddenly shy, she hurried across the room with the flowers. Earlier a servant had brought a large silver water pitcher with a teatray for James, and Abigail carefully settled the flowers' stems inside it, spreading the greenery to fill the pitcher's spout. 'There. That's handsome enough, isn't it?'

'It's not the only thing I brought you, either.' He turned to show her the large barrel standing beside him, thumping the wooden top like a drum. 'Instead of explaining what I intended yesterday, I have decided to show you.'

She returned to his side as he prised open the top of the barrel. 'What's inside?'

'Only this.' He plunged his arm into the wood shavings and brought out a handful for her to see. The wooden curls were fresh and fragrant, and to his mind far sweeter and less hazardous than the flowers had been. 'You can't do better than this for packing anything of value for a long voyage. Perhaps a light swaddling of linen and this would be all you'd need.'

Abigail touched the shavings in his hand, her fingers grazing his palm with just enough of a touch to make him feel like some over-eager schoolboy. What the devil was wrong with him, anyway?

'I suppose this would work,' she was saying, fortunately unaware of his thoughts. 'And so much air amongst the shavings would keep the damp from collecting, the way it would with wool. As you said yesterday, my lor—that is, James.'

'Exactly,' he said, dropping the shavings back into the barrel. 'I may not be able to recite much about old Caesar and his ilk, the way you can, but I do know how to stow a hold.'

'You should, it being your chosen profession in life.' She drew herself up very straight, clasping her hands at her waist. 'I was wrong to show such disrespect for your knowledge and experience yesterday, and I'm sorry for behaving like such a—such a shrew. I hope you'll forgive me. There. Now that I've said that, we can be proper mates.'

'I never thought you were a shrew,' he protested. 'Not for a moment.'

'But I was, which is why I'm offering my apology to you now.' She slipped her work apron over her head, briskly tying the strings around her waist. 'You're an officer of the King, and a hero, too.'

That stopped him cold. 'I never claimed that. Not for myself.'

'You didn't have to. Lady Hamilton told me.' She smiled, her blue eyes innocent of what she was saying. 'She said that while the ball next week is mostly for Admiral Nelson's birthday, it's also to honour all the heroic gentlemen who won the glorious victory at Aboukir Bay. Including you.'

He stared at her without seeing, his thoughts sliding backwards against his will. They'd won against the French, aye, but how it had happened wasn't glorious, and he wasn't a hero. The battle had been bloody and unpredictable and filled with fire—more fire than he'd ever seen. And more death and suffering, too. He'd never experienced anything like the explosion of the French flagship. A column of fire and thunder, and a thousand men dead in an instant, scattered to heaven and hell. Throughout it all he'd simply been following orders, doing his duty, clinging to discipline, fighting and clawing to stay alive one more day, one more hour, one more minute. *That* was the way war was: no glory, and no heroes.

'James?' she asked softly. 'My lord? Are you—are you quite well?'

He stared at her. Damnation, how long had it been since he'd spoken last? How long had he left her there to think the worst of him? And why, when he needed words most, could he think of absolutely nothing fit to say to a lady?

She touched her fingers to his arm, as light as could be. 'You don't have to tell me anything if you don't wish to. Lady Hamilton said that, too.'

'Did she?' he said, his voice sounding flat even to his own ears. 'What else did she say to you?'

'That if you'd no wish to speak of the war I should ask you instead about Christmas.'

'Christmas?' he asked, uncomprehending. *'Christmas?'*

'Yes.' She felt around her throat until she found the fine gold chain, drawing it forward so he could see the tiny gold heart that hung there. 'My father gave this to me our last Christmas together. I suppose that should make me feel sad, because he died before the next Christmas, but it doesn't. Instead it cheers me, and reminds me of the happy time we did have together.'

Struggling to focus on anything other than the horror of Aboukir, James looked down at the little gold heart, dangling there on the chain between her fingers. A father's last gift to his only daughter, a symbol of his lasting love, engraved with her swirling initials.

'For once Father and I had decided to leave Oxford for Christmas,' she continued, her voice soft, almost husky with remembrance. 'We travelled by stage to London, and stayed in a lodging house near the centre. We walked in St James's Park and watched the skaters on the canal. We saw the menagerie in the Tower, and watched puppet plays in the market. On Christmas Day it snowed, but we went to hear the choir in Westminster, and dined on the goose and chestnuts our landlady had roasted. The day before we had to return home, on Twelfth Night, Father gave me this necklace. I've not taken it off since.'

He couldn't look away from the little heart. 'I've not been home for Christmas in years,' he said hoarsely. 'Last year, when we were stationed off Gibraltar, my little sister Elisabeth was wed the day after Christmas. I've not even met the fellow she married, and now she's written to say that she's carrying the rascal's child and heir.'

'But there were other Christmases, weren't there?' Abigail asked. 'When you were a boy, before you went to sea?'

'Oh, aye,' he said, remembering it all. 'We'd be down in Devon, of course, at Carrington Woods, and on Christmas Eve Mother would have the house filled with greenery. The balls would go on most every night until Twelfth Night. The whole county was invited, it seemed, and no matter how young we were, we were allowed to stay up as long as we could manage to. It was the only time of the year that Mother would wear her jewels in the country, and the only time she'd consent to dance jigs with Father, too, kicking her skirts high like a serving girl instead of a countess, with the dogs barking all around her.'

He laughed in spite of himself, the memory of those long-ago balls wonderfully fresh. 'Now I realise they'd all had too much of Father's special punch, even Mother, but then I thought it was just Christmas making everyone merry.'

'Was there snow?' she asked eagerly, letting the heart fall back against her chest.

'Oh, always,' he said. 'And an enormous log hauled in for the great hall's fire.'

'Were your brothers there, too, along with Elisabeth?'

'Oh, aye—down from school and up for mischief,' he said, thinking of how cheerfully miserable the four sons of the Earl of Carrington must have made the lives of the cook and the kitchen maids. 'Mind, I'm the fourth and last of us boys. Henry's the eldest, then Michael, then Marcus, and me. Then there's the girls. Maryanne, Barbara and Elisabeth. Quite a crew of mates, eh?'

'Oh, you are so fortunate,' Abigail cried wistfully. 'I always wanted brothers and sisters. Those must have been merry Christmases indeed.'

'They were,' he said, reluctant to let the memories slip away just yet. 'The happiest of days.'

'They still are,' she said, 'so long as you keep them safe within you.'

He frowned down at her, unwilling to let her see the depth of his own emotions. 'Did Lady Hamilton tell you that, too?'

She shook her head, self-consciously smoothing a loose strand of hair back beneath her small linen cap. 'It's my own little thought, nothing more. I never dreamed I'd spend a Christmas here in Naples, with palm trees, a volcano, and half the English navy in my sight. But so long as I can recall that last Christmas with Father, and the happiness it gave me, then I'll find joy in this Christmas, too.'

'Then do you believe the same of me?' he asked, striving to keep his voice lighter than he felt. 'So long as I can recall my mother's jigs and my brothers shoving one another face-first in the snow, I should be happy this Christmas, too?'

Her cheeks pinkened, but she did not break her gaze from his, and he wondered if she were even aware that she'd once again touched her fingertips to the gold heart at her throat.

'I—I wouldn't dare presume,' she said softly. 'You must decide such a thing for yourself, my lord.'

'James,' he said. 'Not "my lord". James.'

'James,' she repeated, scarce more than a whisper. 'James.'

She was standing close to him, so close that he could count every one of her lashes if he'd a mind to. Her lips were parted, her breath quickening. He'd thought her eyes were blue, but now he saw that the blue was flecked with tiny bits of silver, as rare and captivating as she was herself.

What would she do if he took her into his arms? Would she push him away or come to him, her body soft and willing against his? Would she understand why he wanted to hold her? Understand how he felt when he couldn't explain it himself? Understand that it was not just bold-faced desire driving him, but something more, something finer, something that was a jumble of what she'd said about Christmas, and Aboukir Bay, and happiness, and her?

And *her*.

'James?' she said now, his name a breathless question on her lips. 'James?'

'It's time we turned to work,' he said gruffly, forcing himself to break away from the temptation she so innocently offered. 'If Sir William wants all this bound for England by Christmas, we've no time to waste.'

* * *

'Ah, so it's Lieutenant Lord Richardson,' the admiral said. 'Come, be seated here, so we might speak in confidence.'

'Thank you, sir.' James took the offered armchair beside the admiral's bed.

The room was almost dark, the curtains drawn and the shutters closed against the bright afternoon sunlight. The admiral's remaining good eye was still sensitive, and his wounds from the battle, while healing, continued to plague him more than he wished it to be known to the Neapolitans or, more importantly, to the French. While he made a brave show of going about the city with the Hamiltons as his guide, he retreated here to his rooms—the most luxurious guest rooms in the embassy—when the headaches became too much. Tonight he'd have to endure the exhausting celebration of a ball for his birthday.

With concern James noted how frail Nelson appeared, lying in the centre of the oversized bed, looking far older than his age. England couldn't afford to lose him—not and continue winning against the French at sea.

'So tell me, lieutenant,' the admiral said, lifting the chilled cloth from his brow to look at James. 'How do you find your duty here, eh? As pleasant as I predicted?'

'Yes, sir,' James said. 'Most pleasant, sir.'

The admiral chuckled, his smile showing the gaps of lost teeth. 'I thought you'd find it so, given your station. Of all of my lieutenants, you would appreciate the hospitality of such a fine house. I trust you've had the chance to write to your father by now?'

'Yes, sir,' James said proudly. 'I gave him every detail of the victory. He is a great admirer of the navy, sir, and you can be sure he will share my letter with his acquaintance in the House.'

'I thank you for that.' It was common knowledge that the admiral longed for a title, and hoped fervently that Parliament would offer him at least an earldom as a reward for winning such an important battle. 'I also trust you likewise weren't overly modest in your own achievements, lieutenant?'

'I gave credit where it was properly due, sir,' James said modestly. 'I also wrote how Lady Hamilton and Sir William have been kindness itself.'

'Indeed.' The admiral smiled, and James suspected it was likely the mention of Lady Hamilton that had done it. The gossip he'd heard about Lady Hamilton and the admiral on board the *Vanguard* was nothing compared to what he'd seen between them here in her house: the way she cut his food and fed him the tenderest morsels at the dinner table, how she'd sit so close to him in the carriage she was practically in his lap, how openly she came to visit him while he lay abed—and everything done with Sir William's apparent blessing and the ignorance of poor Mrs Nelson back in England. From loyalty to his admiral James had carefully omitted those particular details from his letter home; if Lady Hamilton's attentions could ease the burden such a great leader carried on his narrow shoulders, then so be it.

'The hospitality of this house,' Nelson continued, 'and the loyalty of its inhabitants to the Crown, are unrivalled. Which is why I have assigned you to oversee the preparation of Sir William's collections for return to England. You are making progress?'

'Yes, sir,' James said. 'With Miss Layton's assistance, I—'

'Has that girl any useful knowledge at all?' interrupted the admiral impatiently. 'I know Sir William claims to put faith in her, but I suspect that's more because of the chit's pretty face than any brains behind it.'

'Miss Layton is most knowledgeable, sir,' he said, scarcely able to bite back the sort of retort that no officer could afford to make to his superior. 'Sir William's collection could not be in more able hands.'

'She'll find a good deal more of Sir William in her hands if she's not careful,' the admiral said. 'Make certain there's no loitering. She must make everything ready as soon as possible. I've promised Sir William that the navy will do its best for his collection in return for seeing we've had a haven here in Naples.'

'I believe Miss Layton feels her work will be done by Christmas.' He'd thought much of Christmas after their conversation: not only of the past Christmases of his boyhood, but of how much he'd like to make Abigail happy for this coming Christmas as well. They'd spoken of it often as they'd worked side by side these last days, and it had become part of the growing bond between them.

'Christmas!' the admiral groaned, settling the cloth back over his face. 'Given the news from the north, it had better be done before that. The last thing I want is to have those infernal treasures of Sir William's fall into French hands. I'd never hear the end of it.'

'But Christmas is three months away, sir,' James said. It seemed at once an eternity stretching before him and Abigail, yet far too short as well. 'Surely the French won't come far into Italy before spring, if at all?'

'The French are already in Rome,' the admiral said bluntly. 'Our goal here is to force the Neapolitans to abandon their cowardly neutrality and throw their lot in with England. Then it will be our duty to aid them as is necessary in retaking Rome, if they display a modicum of initiative, or help them defend Naples if they don't and the French attack here first. Those are our orders, Lieutenant, at least as far as you need know them. The sooner you get Sir William's valuables out of the way of the French, the better.'

'What of Miss Layton, sir?' James asked, all thoughts of a frivolously happy Christmas forgotten. He'd seen enough of war to know the grim fate of women left in the path of an invading army, and he'd never abandon Abigail to that. 'Surely her safe passage back to England must be considered along with Sir William's collection?'

'Then urge her to finish her assignment and return.'

'Forgive me, sir, but the merchant vessels won't—'

'Merchant vessels are not my affair.' The admiral grunted. 'Don't let your pleasure in the girl's company blind you to the fact that she's a civilian, Lieutenant, and that she is here in Naples by her own choice. His Majesty's ships have more important responsibilities than to ferry Miss Layton about the Mediterranean.'

'But, sir, Miss Layton cannot—'

'That is all, Lieutenant,' the admiral said curtly. 'That is all.'

But for James it was only the beginning.

Chapter 5

WITH bits of wood clinging to her black sleeves, Abigail plunged her hand again deep into the froth of shavings, searching desperately for the tiny bundle she knew must be tucked deep inside.

'Hurry, miss, hurry!' urged the footman. 'Sir William's determined to present that medal to Admiral Nelson tonight, before the King and Queen!'

'Are you certain he asked for that particular medallion?' Abigail asked. 'I don't understand why he'd set it aside as one of those to pack, only to ask me to retrieve it now.'

'It's not our place to question Sir William,' said the footman, drawing his lips together with prim disapproval. 'He told me to wait until you found it, and wait I shall until you do.'

Abigail muttered an unladylike expression under her breath as she shoved her hair back from her forehead and began hunting through the next packed barrel. She'd already been late leaving the gallery when the footman had come with his order from the ambassador, and now she was doubly so. She should have gone to her room to wash and dress for the ball—her first ball!—three hours ago. She'd been hearing the carriages of the dinner guests as they arrived since before the sun had set, and now those who'd been invited only to the ball were beginning to come, too. Yet here she remained, hot and sticky and covered with sawdust, until she found that infernal—

'Here it is.' She knew it was the one by touch alone as she unwrapped the strips of protective linen, but still she held it up to the candle to be sure, turning it over between her fingers. She recognised the medal well enough, having just completed the catalogue entry on it the day before. 'Julius Caesar, in all his glory.'

'Give that to me.' The footman snatched the medallion and ran from the room—back to wherever it was that Sir William waited. Just as quickly, Abigail grabbed the candlestick and the key, locked the gallery's door, and hurried down the hall and up the stairs to her own room. Sounds of laughter and music drifted up from the ballroom; they'd already begun the dancing, then. She'd asked James to look for her, never dreaming she'd be so late. Was he hunting for her still? Or had he given up and begun to dance with another lady?

'Signorina.' The waiting maidservant jumped up and curtseyed as soon as Abigail threw open the door. 'Her ladyship sent me to attend you, signorina. Your bath, your gown, your hair.'

She stepped to one side, gesturing towards the round wooden tub before the fire. Flower petals floated on the water's surface, and as with both hands the maid lifted the kettle from the fire, to pour hot water into the tub to warm it further, fragrant steam hissed from the surface. At any other time Abigail would have relished such unimaginable luxury, but now all she could think of was James in the ballroom below.

'I'm already late,' Abigail said, as she began unfastening her gown without waiting for the woman's help. 'Help me hurry, please!'

The maid understood—or perhaps she, too, wished to join the others downstairs. With brisk efficiency she helped Abigail scrub away the day's dust and grit, and brushed her hair dry before the fire, artfully curling the ends with tongs heated over the coals. At last she dressed Abigail in the new chemise and gown, and the stockings and slippers which had that same afternoon been delivered by the mantua-maker. Everything was pale and ethereal and *new*, and after over a year of nothing but black, she felt almost like a butterfly freed from her chrysalis. Only her gold locket was familiar, and she touched it again, as if begging pardon from her father for giving up her mourning.

With a deep breath to steady her anxiety, she finally turned towards her reflection in the long glass in the maid's hands.

'Oh, gracious,' she whispered, stunned by the elegant figure staring back at her. 'I've never looked like this before.'

'You are a beautiful lady, *signorina*,' said the maid, smiling at Abigail's surprise. 'You will break many hearts tonight, yes?'

At once Abigail thought of James. That was the only heart she'd consider. She'd never want to break his, of course, just…just please it. That was all: please his heart, and please him.

With her own heart racing with anticipation and worry, Abigail grabbed her gloves and fan from the bed and hurried towards the ballroom, smoothing the long kid gloves over her arms as she ran down the stairs. She didn't join the line of important guests waiting to be announced, but instead slipped into the ballroom through one of the side doorways.

Hundreds and hundreds and *hundreds* of people, she thought with dismay. Yet the only one who mattered was nowhere to be seen. Already other gentlemen were glancing her way, preening as they tried to catch her eye and appraising her from head to toe with embarrassingly frank admiration, and she set her face in a stern expression, determined to discourage them. She'd only wanted to look this way for James, but where, *where* could he be?

With a small cry of frustration, she ducked her head and plunged resolutely into the crowd.

Standing beside one of the open doors to the gardens, James once again scanned the crowded ballroom. He'd heard that nearly two thousand guests had come here to the embassy tonight, to honour Admiral Nelson's fortieth birthday, and to celebrate their victory at Aboukir Bay.

On a makeshift dais at one end of the room sat His Majesty King

Ferdinand and his wife Queen Maria. Beside them stood Sir William and Lady Hamilton, and in a smaller armchair nearby sat Admiral Nelson, by special favour of King Ferdinand. The admiral looked happy and pleased, and why shouldn't he? Pinned to his breast was some new honour from His Majesty, and around his neck hung the rare ancient medallion given to him earlier by Sir William. The room was draped with banners singing the praises of Nelson and the Nile, and every lady wore ribbons embroidered with twin Ns in his honour. This was even more considering how the majority of the guests were Neapolitans and, beyond James's fellow officers, precious few English faces were to be found in the ballroom's noisy crush.

Which, for James, made Abigail Layton's absence all the more obvious.

He'd been seated with a group of Neapolitan officers and their wives at dinner, whose conversation had been limited by their determined efforts to speak English. He'd searched the dining room in vain for Abigail then, too, though she'd asked him that very afternoon to look for her. She'd been so charmingly shy about the invitation that he'd never doubted she'd be here, but it was now nearly ten, and he'd yet to find her. Could she have changed her mind or, worse, been swept away by some Neapolitan gallant?

Again James scanned the room. His eyesight from the masthead had always been as keen at spotting distant ships as any foretopman, yet tonight he couldn't seem to spot a sensible young woman dressed in mourning in this gaudy, spangled crowd and—

'Lieutenant—my lord. My lord—here!'

He'd know her voice anywhere, and eagerly he turned. But instead of the sombre, black-clad Miss Layton he'd been working beside all this week, he found someone else so radically, radiantly different that it knocked him speechless.

She was dressed in a silvery pale high-waisted gown so delicate and insubstantial that it seemed to drift around her like a scrap of morning mist. The gown had tiny sleeves and a low neckline that revealed more than it hid—more lovely creamy skin than he'd ever dared imagine. She wore no jewels or ornaments beyond the little gold heart at her throat, nor did she need any. But threaded through her hair—such hair as he'd never imagined she possessed, either— dark chestnut hair piled high on the back of her head in fat, shining curls—was a thin blue ribbon the exact colour of her eyes.

She laughed with delight. 'Did I truly surprise you?'

'How could you not?' he asked, still unable to look away. 'It's not that you were plain before, but I'd never guessed you could be— well, like this.'

She laughed again, a sound he knew he'd never weary of hearing, and other men turned towards her with an eagerness that James didn't care for. Swiftly he reached for her hand, claiming her as his, and without hesitation her fingers curled into his.

'It's all Lady Hamilton's doing, you know,' she said. 'She told me it was time I put aside my mourning, and though I hesitated I knew Father would have wished it, too.'

'How would he not?' He still couldn't believe the change in her—the new lightness that seemed to glow from her face. Yet still she remained the same Abigail whose spirit and intelligence had already charmed him beyond measure as they'd worked together.

The Abigail that he'd now have to send away, or else put her life in jeopardy.

'But you like it as well, don't you?' she asked, too sincere and anxious ever to be a ballroom coquette. 'I've never had a gown as fine as this. It's only because of Lady Hamilton that I have one now. But I wanted to look as if—as if I were worthy of being with you tonight.'

'Oh, Abigail,' he said softly, smiling. 'You're so beautiful. How could I not want you always at my side?'

'I?' Her laughter faded, her eyes filling with amazement. 'You cannot truly believe that, James, can you? It's a pretty sentiment, yes, but surely—'

'I believe it,' he said firmly, 'because it is true.'

'Oh, my,' she said, her smile wobbling. 'That is— Oh, excuse me, *Signor*! *Mi scusi!*'

The man who'd jostled into her back bowed and leered, his face flushed with drink and his voice thick. '*Ah, ma bellissima donna. Sei piu bella d'un angelo!*'

'Shove off, *signor*,' growled James possessively, drawing Abigail closer and slipping his arm around her waist for good measure. 'This lady is with me. Come, Miss Layton. This is our dance.'

Before the man could react, James pulled Abigail away, guiding her before him through the crowd.

'What did that man call me?' Abigail asked, twisting around to look back. 'He was so fuddled, I couldn't make out his words. What did he say?'

'He said you were beautiful—more beautiful than an angel,' James said grimly. There were certain Italian phrases that every English sailor had learned; that was one of the few that were civil. 'He'd no right saying that to you. That is, you *are* more beautiful than an angel, but I'd rather I were the only one saying it to you. Come, I'll claim that dance now.'

'Oh, James, no,' she said, stopping abruptly. 'Please.'

'Why in blazes not?' he asked, still irritated with the man who'd bumped her. 'You're always telling me about Christmas dances.'

Her eyes were wide, almost panicking, for no reason that he could see. '*You* spoke of those dances, James. I never did.'

'Well, then, I'll give you something to speak of now.' He might dread dinners, but his whole family loved to dance, and there was precious little chance for officers at sea. He'd been looking forward to dancing with Abigail, to guiding her through the steps and moving together in time to the music. 'Hah—they're calling an *allemande*.'

'Please, no.' She pulled her hand away from his, folding her arms for good measure. 'I'm sorry, but I—I cannot dance, James. Father thought dancing was idle foolishness, a waste of time and money. I never learned how, and I've no wish to blunder in such fine company, to shame you as well as myself.'

Without a word, he reclaimed her hand and led her not towards the gathering dancers but back through the garden doors to the courtyard, and then to the farthest corner away from the ballroom, near the balustrade. The evening was warm—the air tangy with the scent of the sea, the sky filled with stars and a quarter-moon—and while other couples lingered in the shadows, they had this side of the courtyard to themselves.

'I told you, James, I'm sorry,' she said again, turning defensive. 'But I'll not make a fool of myself trying to do something I can't or—'

'Hush,' he said. 'Do you really believe I'd expect you to do that?'

Her chin rose. 'I don't know what you'd do.'

'Oh, yes, you do,' he said. 'Leastways you should, considering all the time we've spent together. I wanted to dance with you, not shame you. We can do that well enough out here, where we can still hear the music. Here—stand before me.'

'James, please!'

'Stand there, Abigail, and listen to the music,' he said. 'I'll count to four, and on four we'll step to the right. Follow me, and the music.'

She let him take both her hands, yet still fussed with uncertainty. 'James, I've no gift for this, and I've never—'

'Any lady who's clever enough to parse Greek and Latin like you can dance an *allemande*,' he said. 'Steady, now. One, two, three, *step*.'

'James, please,' she protested, yet she stepped to the side as he'd ordered. She stumbled on the next two steps, unable to follow his lead, then tried to pull away. 'You see—I told you. I am hopeless, *hopeless*!'

'No, you're not,' he said calmly. 'Not at all. It's not that hard, truly. Stop looking at your feet, and look at me instead.'

'Look at *you*?' she repeated crossly, staring at him with such a fixed look of concentration it was a wonder she could move at all.

But this time she mirrored his steps, and when they repeated the pattern again she could do it without hesitation.

'There you are,' he said. 'I knew you could do it. Now, bend forward when you turn, there, and slip beneath my arm. Duck, else you'll strike your head.'

She followed him with surprising grace—surprising to her as well as to him.

'Hah, not so clumsy after all, am I?' she declared, and followed the music to repeat the turn. Her eyes were bright now, challenging him. 'It *is* easy, just as you say.'

He laughed at her sudden confidence. 'It's easy because you have such an excellent partner,' he teased. 'You wouldn't feel the same if I had to hand you to the next gentleman in our set. One of those rascally Neapolitan gentlemen, say.'

'Gracious, no,' she said quickly. 'But I'm doing well enough for a ball like one of your mother's at Christmas, aren't I?'

'Oh, aye, more than well enough,' he said, but her unwitting comment struck hard at his merriment. Neither of them would be attending his mother's Christmas ball. Not this year, or likely any other, either. If he followed his conscience, he should be telling her what the admiral had said about the French. He should be telling her to book passage on any ship that she could, bound for England. He should be sending her home as soon as was possible, away from the danger and the war.

And, of course, from him.

'The guests at the Christmas balls are generally so far into their cups that they'd never venture anything so nimble as this,' he said instead, forcing his tone to remain light. 'Jigs and hornpipes and other country dances: those are the order of the day.'

'You'll have to teach me those next,' she said, still concentrating on her steps. 'Lady Hamilton has promised another ball at Christmas, and I wish to be ready. Though I imagine it shall be a great deal more lavish. Everything in Naples is.'

Tell her she must leave before then. She's given you the perfect chance to explain. Tell her, for her own good. You'll be a selfish bastard if you don't.

'Everything that Lady Hamilton oversees in Naples is always more lavish than any place else on earth.' He *was* a selfish bastard— and, worse, a coward. But he couldn't give her up, nor the peace she brought to him. Not yet. 'She's second only to the Queen here.'

Unaware of his thoughts, Abigail laughed, her face bathed in moonlight. Suddenly the music stopped, the dance done, and she stopped, too.

'I curtsey now, yes?' she asked breathlessly, dipping before him with her skirts spread, and unwittingly granting him a glimpse of the sweet curves of her breasts above the gown's low-cut neckline. 'Thank you for that dance, my lord.'

'And I thank you, Miss Layton,' he said, making an elegant leg. 'I'm honoured to have been your tutor.'

'Are you?' Her smile faded and her expression turned serious, her lips parting in an unconscious invitation that he was finding increasingly hard to resist.

'I am,' he said, lowering his voice. 'And if we truly were at a Christmas ball by now I'd be contriving a way to coax you beneath the mistletoe.'

'But it's not Christmas.' Her eyes widened, more with interest than wariness, and she didn't draw back. 'And there is no mistletoe in Naples.'

'Then I must jury-rig matters to suit, like any good sailor worth his salt.' He shrugged out of his dress coat and settled it around her shoulders. 'There now, Abigail. Don't want you catching a chill. The snow here in Devon is fierce this year.'

At once she understood his game. She grinned, and feigned a shiver, drawing his coat more closely about her shoulders like an oversized cape. 'The snow's so deep by now, James, that the roads will surely be closed. We'll be forced to spend Christmas here by the fire.'

'I'd say we've no choice.' He'd already decided he was going to kiss her, but he couldn't tell if she'd realised it, too. He reached up and snapped a tiny sprig of pine from the tree growing in the courtyard, and held it over her head. 'At least we have plenty of mistletoe.'

She looked up at the sprig, then at him. 'Should I wish you joy of the season, my lord?' she asked in a husky whisper. 'A merry Christmas?'

'The merriest,' he said. 'That's what mistletoe's for, you know.'

'I've heard that, yes,' she said softly, and as she smiled she licked her lips.

Just as he read the sky for the weather, he'd take that to mean she was willing—or at least that she wouldn't object. Before he thought about it overmuch, he pulled her close and kissed her.

She was soft and warm and willing, curling her arm around the back of his neck to steady herself. The substitute sprig of mistletoe dropped from his fingers as he drew her closer, and neither of them noticed or cared. When he slanted his mouth to deepen the kiss, she parted her lips for him with a fluttering little sigh and an eagerness that matched his own. He'd never kissed another woman like this, but then he'd never met a woman as desirable as Abigail Layton, either.

'Oh, my, James,' she whispered, breathless when at last he broke the kiss. 'When you said you wished to keep me warm against the snows, I'd no notion *that* was what you meant.'

He laughed. 'Not at all, Abbie.'

'Abbie?' she repeated, her blissfully dazed expression doubtless a reflection of his own face. 'No gentleman's ever called me Abbie.'

'No lady's ever kissed me like that, either,' he said, brushing his fingers lightly over her velvety cheek and along the line of her jaw.

This time she shivered with pleasure at his touch, not at the pretend snow. 'It must be the mistletoe.'

'Or the dancing.'

'Or my dancing master.' Shyly she tipped her face towards his, her lips parted and waiting. 'Perhaps we need to try a bit harder to discover the truth.'

'Merry Christmas, Abbie,' he said as he bent to kiss her again.
'Merry, merry—'

'Miss Layton—Lieutenant Lord Richardson.' The liveried
footman bowed, unperturbed by what he'd interrupted so long as he
delivered his message. 'Lady Hamilton wishes your attendance
directly.'

'We must go, James,' Abigail said hurriedly, slipping free from
his embrace. 'I should have gone to her first, I know, but I looked
for you instead, and now she'll know. She'll *know*.'

'And what if she does?' James took back his coat from her shoulders, watching as she smoothed her skirts and her hair. It didn't
matter what she did: she looked like a woman who'd been kissed,
and who had kissed in return. Her face was flushed in the moonlight, her lips ripe. She was right: Lady Hamilton *would* know. She
and all the others would see the change in Abigail in a moment.
'There's no sin in kissing.'

'But I didn't come to Naples to—'

'Stay here with me, Abbie,' he said, his voice rough with urgency,
catching her arm to pull her back. 'Another five minutes, that is all.
They won't notice—not among so many others.'

She hesitated, and it pleased him that she was considering. 'I
can't,' she said softly, sadly. '*We* can't. You know it as well as I.'

He groaned, because he did. If the navy had taught him anything,
it was to obey orders and respect his duty, to behave in an honourable
way, even if those same orders and duty and honour would take him
away from Abigail in the moonlight.

She smoothed the front of his coat, running her palms over his
chest—a small bit of female housekeeping that struck him as impossibly seductive for being so unconscious.

'There,' she said. 'You look respectable again. Now, come with
me…'

He caught one of her hands, lifting and turning it so he could
brush his lips across her open palm, his gaze holding hers prisoner.
'I will see you again?'

'Of course you will,' she said breathlessly. 'Tomorrow in Sir William's gallery, when we—'

'I meant alone, Abbie,' he said, determined to make her understand what he was only just beginning to understand himself. 'You and me and no one else. This isn't just a single kiss at a ball, sweet. I'm not going to let you slip away from me. Tomorrow, aye, and tomorrow, and tomorrow after that, Abbie. This is only the beginning.'

'Oh, James, yes,' she whispered, and reached up to kiss him again. *'Yes.'*

Chapter 6

WITH no surprise, Abigail found herself the only one at breakfast the next morning. The ball had been ending when Lady Hamilton had permitted Abigail to leave. It had been soon after midnight, but when she'd tried to sleep it had seemed to Abigail that the festivities had lasted much later than that. Now the embassy seemed silent as only a house exhausted by too much celebration could be, and as Abigail sipped her tea alone, she wondered how many aching heads would not lift from their pillows at all today.

But she was surprised not to see James. He'd left the ball even earlier than she, pleading some sort of navy errand. Surely he shouldn't still be feeling the effects of too much strong drink? She'd seen him take scarcely a single glass of wine the entire night. And after how he'd kissed her, and what he'd said—why, she wouldn't have slept much even if the revellers hadn't kept her awake.

Finally she pushed her plate aside and rose. Likely he was still following orders or another duty. She couldn't imagine he'd keep away on his own—or at least she hoped he wouldn't. But, with James or without, she could still make plenty of progress cataloguing.

'Good day, Miss Layton.' Sir William entered, and with him James, their expressions uncharacteristically sombre. 'I'm glad to see you've finished your breakfast, for we've great need of your services downstairs directly.'

'My services, Sir William?' It was not often a classical scholar was called on an emergency. 'Should I fetch my notebook from the gallery?'

'Yes, at once.' Sir William glanced at James. 'I must return below. Please bring Miss Layton as soon as you can.'

'What has happened, James?' Abigail asked. 'Is something wrong? Are the French—?'

'The French are not here, Abigail,' he said. 'That much I can tell you, but little else.'

She'd never seen his face set like this—all grim, almost ruthless, full of seriousness—and she realised enough to ask no more. This must be how he was at sea, she thought, her fingers shaking a little as she unlocked the gallery. This was the side of him that belonged not to her, but to the navy.

'You'll want your apron, too,' he said, his eyes sweeping over her white muslin gown as she found her notebook. 'Next time you'll want to wear your old mourning, but there's no time now for you to change.'

He led her not down the embassy's main staircase, but down the servants' stairs, narrow and twisting, and then down further still, into cellars she hadn't known existed. Although there were lanterns hung along the passage, the murky twilight made Abigail shrink against James, and he slipped his arm around her waist to guide her.

She didn't like dark places, particularly dark places under the earth that harboured mice and rats and spiders, and this hall, she decided with dismal certainty, was sure to be full of all three. The stucco walls curved into a crude arch overhead, so low that James had to bend his shoulders to keep from striking his head, and so narrow that Abigail had to pull her skirts close to keep the fabric from snagging on the rough, dirty plaster.

Finally they could hear muffled voices, and more light glowed before them. They turned a corner in the passage and entered a much larger space, clearly used for the storage of crates and barrels much like the ones upstairs. Sir William was there already, supervising two of the embassy's footmen in prising open one of the crates. As soon as it popped open Sir William reached inside and drew out a large gold goblet, richly enhanced with fantastic engraving and rubies around the stem.

'Here you are at last, Miss Layton.' He smiled, buffing the polished side of the goblet with his cuff before he handed it to Abigail. 'Precious treasure, yes, Lieutenant? Have you ever seen the like, Miss Layton?'

Abigail frowned at her reflection in the gold. 'Forgive me, Sir William, but this is unlike anything else in your collection. I should venture it's of a much later date, perhaps of the fifteenth or sixteenth century, and the work of a master goldsmith.'

'You can write it up like the rest, can't you?' asked Sir William. 'A catalogue to match what's upstairs?'

'Yes, Sir William, of course,' Abigail said, glancing past him. 'But to include what lies here with the rest will double my time.'

'And will double your reward,' Sir William said. 'That is understood. What concerns me is the time involved.'

Abigail shook her head, turning the goblet in her hands. 'To do all this justice, Sir William, I could not possibly complete before the spring.'

'I'm afraid it must be done sooner, Miss Layton,' said the ambassador. 'What if I were to triple, even quadruple your fee?'

But Abigail wasn't listening. 'This engraving—here. That is the mark of the royal family, is it not?'

'Tell her the truth, Sir William,' James said curtly. 'She has a right to know, and to refuse.'

'I see you have a champion, Miss Layton.' Sir William smiled. 'Very well, then. These crates contain personal treasures belonging to the royal family. They are being brought here for safekeeping by night, through the tunnels in these hills. A few pieces at a time, you see, so no one will notice their absence in the palace. To stop anyone from questioning, they are to be temporarily absorbed into my own collection.'

'A favour in return for the King letting us moor and refit in his harbour,' James said. 'Another favour for the Two Sicilies slanting their neutrality towards England.'

'Something like that, yes,' Sir William admitted. 'Though it's Queen Maria Carolina who is especially concerned about not letting any royal belongings fall into Napoleon's hands. Her sister was King Louis's queen, you know, and it's taken all of Lady Hamilton's charm to win her over to us. A tidy solution, you must agree?'

But Abigail's thoughts had already raced on to the next conclusion. 'And if the French should invade Naples, then an English ship could safely carry off the royal treasures with your own.'

'By Christmas everything must be settled, Miss Layton.' His smile now was far from reassuring. 'That is why I urge your compliance, and your haste.'

'You have the right to refuse, Miss Layton,' James said, his voice harsh with urgency. 'This is far beyond your original understanding. You can request to return to England now, before the danger grows any greater here. Sir William could find you safe passage.'

'No!' Abigail cried, stunned by the prospect of having to leave him, even if it were for her own good. 'That is, my lord, I have an obligation to complete the task my father agreed to. My professional reputation would be ruined if I did not.'

'Nor, I fear, would a safe passage be possible to obtain,' the ambassador said, without a hint of regret. 'With Spain having allied herself with France against England, we've only Austria and Russia left to call friends. I can guarantee nothing.'

'You should have sent her home before this, Sir William,' James said, his frustration bursting into anger. 'Damnation, you should have placed her welfare before your wretched collection!'

'My lord, you forget yourself,' Sir William said mildly. 'Better you should pray that the lady completes her task well enough that your admiral considers her sufficiently valuable to merit passage on one of his blessed navy ships.'

'I accept, Sir William,' Abigail said quickly. 'I'll do as you ask, as fast as can be managed.'

She looked down at the goblet in her hands, at her face distorted in the gold and the damp ovals her anxious fingertips had left. She understood everything now: she'd been caught in the middle of a war that had nothing to do with her, and even if she did as Sir William wished, she still had no guarantee that she'd ever see England again. She knew that James cared for her, exactly as he'd claimed in the moonlight—cared enough that he'd challenge Sir William in her defence, cared so much that he'd do anything for her.

Beside her, she felt him tense. 'Miss Layton, you need not—'

'But I do,' she said, and tried to smile at him so she would not weep. 'For what choice, really, do I have? Now, come. If I'm to finish by Christmas, I must begin at once.'

'Well said, Miss Layton, that's the spirit,' the ambassador said and, satisfied, returned to inspecting the open barrel with his servants.

'Christmas, Abbie,' said James bitterly. 'What kind of Christmas will this possibly be?'

'For us, the merriest,' she said softly, and let her hand steal over his while Sir William's back was turned. 'So long as we stay together, then it will be the best Christmas ever.'

'There they are, Abbie,' James said as they stood at the window and looked down at the English ships making ready in the bay. 'They'll sail with the morning tide, and I won't be with them.'

'They'll sail away, James, but not for long.' She leaned closer into his side, her body soft beneath his arm as she shared his warmth. It was early November now, and even Naples had grown cooler in the evening. 'They've only to deposit King Ferdinand's army at Leghorn, and back they'll come. You'll scarce miss them.'

'Likely not,' he admitted. 'But it's still going to feel deuced odd to see them clear Naples without me.'

But then, to James, nothing about these last weeks had felt normal. Finally bowing to the arguments of the Hamiltons and Admiral Nelson, King Ferdinand had abandoned his cautious neutrality and agreed to retake Rome from the French. Overnight the city had blossomed into a frenzy of military patriotism, and tomorrow the English warships were to carry King Ferdinand and much of the Neapolitan army north, where they would be led by a more experienced Austrian general before they attacked.

But if the English navy was reduced to little more than a transport convoy, then James himself was no better. Instead of the fearless warrior, the first to volunteer for the most daring raids or to hurl himself into any hand-to-hand combat, he'd been relegated to watching over Abigail Layton—ostensibly as her assistant, but really as her bodyguard. It was the longest time he'd been on shore in years, and the longest time he'd spent in the company of a single woman who wasn't related to him by blood.

And, to his bewilderment, he'd never felt more honourably employed.

It was hardly the lark his fellow officers imagined, teasing him mercilessly the few times he returned to the *Vanguard*. The reality was far more work, and far less salaciousness. With Christmas as her deadline, Abigail worked furiously between Sir William's collection and the boxes that appeared in the embassy's cellar each night from the palace. James did whatever she asked—which was mainly urging the Neapolitan servants to carry the barrels and crates at less than a snail's pace.

But he also watched over Abigail herself, never going far from her side. In addition to the knife he always wore, he now kept pistols tucked into his belt. War and the army's departure would only serve to heighten the instability in the city, which held so many insurgents that more and more bodies were found in the streets every morning. Allies or not, Englishmen were foreigners, and no foreigners ventured out alone. If anyone learned what Abigail was doing—how she was working towards a possible escape for the royal family—then she, too, would be in peril, from both Neapolitans and French spies.

And what would become of them both when her work was done? That was something neither wanted to consider.

'Look,' Abigail said, pointing across the harbour to the uneven cone of Mount Vesuvius in the distance. 'The volcano's glowing tonight, like improperly banked coals. Lady Hamilton says it will shoot sparks and fire like skyrockets for a holiday, as if it somehow knows it's a special day.'

'Now, that I should like to see,' he declared. 'A sympathetic volcano. Maybe it will co-operate for Christmas.'

'That reminds me,' she said, slipping free to go back inside. When she returned, she carried a small package that she handed to James. 'As soon as I saw this, I thought of you. Consider it part of our Christmas.'

He frowned as he untied the ribbon. 'You didn't go to the shops alone, did you?'

'You know I didn't.' She pressed her hands together in anticipation, eager for his reaction. 'A pedlar came to the kitchen door and Cook let him in.'

'Cook would let in Bonaparte himself if he were selling something.' Out of the paper came a small wooden box, beautifully inlaid. 'That's a handsome trinket.'

'It's a music box, James!' she exclaimed with excitement. 'The key's beneath, and once it's wound you must lift the lid to hear it.'

Dutifully he wound the box, and set it on the wide sill. 'I hope it plays "Roast Beef of Old England", and not "La Marseillaise".'

'Neither,' she declared. 'Now, listen. *Listen!*'

Only a few notes, but he recognised the very English tune at once: 'Greensleeves.'

'We can pretend we're at Carrington Woods,' she said, 'at one of your mother's Christmas balls. Though I don't believe there are volcanoes in Devon.'

'There aren't.' Her gift touched him deeply. It was something only Abigail could have given him. No one else knew this was his favourite song, one he always associated with Christmas. 'Mother wouldn't allow it, anyway.'

'But she has hired the small group of musicians for tonight, who've come despite the snow outside. They're playing "Green-sleeves" first, at your mother's special request, for her brave officer son, a hero of the Nile, and home on leave from the war.' She grinned, and curtseyed to him. 'May I have this dance, my lord?'

'You're a saucy jade, asking gentlemen to dance,' he teased gently as he took her hands. They hadn't danced since Admiral Nelson's birthday; there'd been neither music, nor opportunity. 'Do you remember how? Should I count?'

'I remember,' she said, concentrating to match her steps to his with more accuracy than he'd expected. Gradually the music box ran down, the song slowing and their steps with it, drawing them closer until, when the last note sounded, they stood in one another's arms. She looked up at him, her eyes bright.

'I remember,' she said again, little more than a husky whisper as she raised her mouth to him. 'I'll never forget.'

Instinctively her mouth found his, turning the exact distance for their lips to meet and meld, and for James to remember everything else he'd so loved about kissing her: how eagerly she sighed as her lips parted for him, how warm her mouth could be, how she seemed to melt against him, as if making her body touch his in as many ways as she could, how she tasted and smelled and felt and *loved*—yes, loved—him in return. They kissed, and it was as if there were no war. They kissed, and everything in life seemed once again possible, as long as she was there to share it with him.

He deepened the kiss, his hands sliding along her sides to pull her hips closer to his own, to let her feel the hard proof of how much he wanted her, how much he needed her.

'Ah, Abbie, Abbie,' he murmured, threading his fingers into her hair to hold her face before him. Lightly he feathered kisses over her cheeks, along the curve of her jaw and the throat that he'd learned was most sensitive. 'My own lass.'

With a shuddering sigh, she gently twisted her face away from his lips, drawing far enough from him to study his face. Her lips were wet and parted, her breathing rapid, leaving no doubt in his mind that she'd relished their kiss as much as he. Yet her eyes were enormous with uncertainty, their confusion punctuated by the spiky shadows of her lashes falling across her cheeks.

'I remember, Abbie,' he whispered, running his hand up and down her back, hoping the caress would comfort and reassure her, as well as remind her of the pleasure in what they had been doing before she'd pulled away. 'I remember how you looked in the moonlight before, and how—'

'No, no, *no*,' she cried plaintively. 'That's not what I intended, James, not at all. I thought with the music box I could kiss you and think ahead to Christmas, to us together and happy, and—and, God help me, I cannot. What if all we'll have is the past, James? What if there's nothing more for us than memories of what's already done?'

She pulled away from his embrace and with trembling fingers rewound the music box.

'Abbie,' he said softly, looping his arms around her waist as he brushed his lips across the nape of her neck. 'Abbie, please. I know I cannot change whatever fate is set for us, but I'll do everything in my power to make a future for us—because I love you.'

She went very quiet as music spilled from the little box in her hands.

'I love you, Abbie,' he said again, his voice rough with urgency, with his desire to make certain she understood. 'You're the only woman I've ever said that to, and I mean for it to stay that way. I love you, Abbie, and, whatever else may happen to us in this life, that will never change.'

'Oh, I love you too, James,' she said, her voice breaking with a sob as she flung her arms around his shoulders and pressed her face against his shoulder, clinging to him as if she'd never let go. 'I love you more than anything!'

He held her like that, just held her, and when the music box ran down again they let the dying notes play around them into the night, and claimed the silence as their own.

Chapter 7

'THERE,' said Abigail, dropping her pen with an exaggerated flourish as she pushed her chair back from the long work table. The once crowded shelves of Sir William's gallery were clear, the walls echoing with emptiness. 'Everything's counted, and recorded, and packed away. Only the final loading remains to be done before the *Colossus* can sail for London.'

'Why, Miss Layton, you're practically crowing,' said James, though in truth he was as pleased as she that they'd accomplished so much in such a short time. 'Mind you, we still have those last bits and pieces coming into the cellars each night.'

'Oh, but that is next to nothing,' she said, coming round the table to join him. 'The hardest part was always Sir William's collection, as you know perfectly, perfectly well. But I've finished it all, James—and with nearly a fortnight to spare before Christmas!'

'I never expected less from you, sweet,' he said, pulling her onto his knee so she could claim an enthusiastic congratulatory kiss.

This wasn't the only good news to celebrate: as commander-in-chief at the Battle of the Nile, Admiral Nelson had been made Baron Nelson, and given a pension to go with his new title. Another grand ball was planned in his honour, this one to be given by Selim III, the Sultan of Turkey, who intended to lavish more honours and rewards on the new Lord Nelson.

The news from the north had been wondrous indeed, too, with King Ferdinand's troops having taken the French by surprise and driven them so completely from Rome that they'd retaken the city and invited the Pope to return. Naples had gone wild with joy and pride. With the help of their English allies, anything now seemed possible.

And so it seemed for James, too. Lord Nelson had assured him he would also soon benefit from their victory on the Nile—perhaps even be made a captain in his own right. James didn't care what manner of vessel he was given; all he'd ever wished was a command and a crew of his own to prove himself, and to serve England. But now there was more. Captains were permitted to bring their wives to sea with them. Few did, for it was a hard, dangerous life for a woman, but then few wives were women as brave, as clever, as resourceful as Abigail Layton. He hadn't said anything to her yet, for nothing was as unpredictable as navy promotions, but it was his dearest dream, and his goal, too. Could there be a better Christmas surprise for them both?

For now, he'd planned another surprise—not quite so grand, but he hoped a fit reward for Abigail.

He pointed back towards her closed notebook. 'What's that scrap of paper poking out from your book, eh? You can't consider yourself righteously done with that kind of untidiness.'

'I've no idea what that is,' she said, hopping from his knee to go and investigate. 'You know I'm not messy like that, not with my records.'

He covered his mouth with his hand to hide his smile as she pulled the folded paper from the notebook, opened it, and read. She read it again, and her eyes widened as she looked back to him.

'You wish to surprise me with a rare adventure this Sunday?' she asked. 'Pray, what exactly does that mean, James?'

He shrugged. 'If I told you then it wouldn't be a surprise.'

She raised her chin, folding her arms over her chest. 'But if you do not tell me I may not agree to go with you.'

'If you don't agree,' he said, 'then I'll have to abduct you, and carry you off like a Turk. I've already asked for leave from his lordship. I'm not going to change my mind simply because you refuse to oblige.'

She narrowed her eyes. 'If you dare try such a dirty trick—'

'Oh, you know I'd never mean you harm,' he said, laughing. 'I'll tell you only that it will bring the greatest pleasure to us both.'

'Now, that *does* sound like a Turk!'

He laughed again, and reached out to pull her back into his lap. The feel of her there—her soft, rounded bottom pressing against the front of his breeches, the fullness of her breast against his chest— was sweet torment indeed. He wanted her—wanted her badly—and the ardent way she responded to his kisses and light caresses made him certain she felt the same for him.

They were always careful to be discreet before the others—a good deal more discreet than Lord Nelson and Lady Hamilton were—but the embassy was such a public place, for business as well as entertaining, that the times when he'd been confident of their privacy had been precious few. More than once he'd considered inviting himself to her bedchamber, but decided against that, too. When she finally became his, he wanted to be able to make it special for them both, not to worry that they'd be interrupted by some nosey footman. His Abbie deserved better than that.

'It's meant to be a treat, sweet, not torture,' he said gently, letting her nestle more comfortably against him. 'I haven't forgotten what you said about us not being able to look forward, only back. I wanted to give you something to anticipate.'

'Oh, James.' She gazed up at him, tears glistening in her eyes. 'You remembered that?'

'I did,' he said, kissing her lightly on her forehead. 'These have not been the best circumstances for making you happy, but because I love you so much I'm trying my damnedest.'

'I love you, too,' she whispered. 'You still won't tell me the secret?'

'All I'll say is that it's almost Christmas,' he said. 'That's more than enough.'

'Christmas with *you*,' she repeated softly. 'And that, my love, will be more than enough for me.'

'Miss Layton! A word with you, if you please!'

Abigail turned, and stopped on the steps of the little Protestant church to wait for Lady Hamilton. She hadn't expected to see the ambassador's wife here, not this early in the day.

'A splendid service, wasn't it?' the older woman said as she joined her. She lifted the veil from her face, tucking it onto the wide brim of her blue velvet hat. 'Poor Rev'nd Dowling don't have the same flock he once had, now that all the English gentlemen an' ladies have fled home to London from fear o' the French.'

'Yes, my lady,' Abigail murmured, her thoughts far from the near-empty church. Riding in the carriage with the house servants, she'd come to the earliest service so she could meet James and spend the rest of the day with him. He'd refused to relent about keeping his plans secret, and now she could scarcely wait to learn where they'd be going, what they'd be doing.

'O'course, if the navy gentlemen had come, then we would have had a full house,' Lady Hamilton was saying, 'but they will keep the Sabbath on their ships, with their men. Will you ride with me back to the house, my dear?'

'Thank you, my lady,' Abigail said, surprised to be asked. 'I'm honoured.'

'So am I, Miss Layton,' Lady Hamilton said. 'Your company's precious dear these days, isn't it? Here's the carriage now.'

Climbing into the carriage after Lady Hamilton, Abigail wondered uneasily what she'd meant. She hadn't long to wait: before the carriage had even begun moving, Lady Hamilton turned on the leather seat so she could look directly at Abigail.

'So, how attached are you to Richardson?' she asked bluntly. 'There's never a time when I don't see the pair o' you together— why, there's plenty o' couples courtin' serious that don't play the lovebirds like you two.'

'Forgive me, my lady, I—I do not know what to say,' Abigail stammered, her cheeks flaming. True, she *was* almost always in James's company, though not in any unseemly way before the others. But she'd tried to remain professional whenever she was with the Hamiltons—a scholar first, and not once, she'd hoped, a 'lovebird'.

'If I have disappointed in any way,' she began, 'if I've failed to live up to the expectations that your husband's trust has put in me and my scholarship, why—'

'Oh, nonsense,' said Lady Hamilton, sweeping her gloved hand through the air, as if sweeping aside Abigail's objections. 'There's not one tiny fault with your blessed scholarship, an' you know it. Sir William finds you the very soul o' accomplishment. Which makes your entanglement with Richardson all the more troubling to me.'

'It's not an entanglement, my lady, but a rare friendship and regard,' Abigail said, as firmly as she could—which wasn't very firmly at all. 'I have the highest regard for him, and he for me.'

'And *that*, Miss Layton, is a peck o' spoiled fish,' Lady Hamilton said succinctly. 'I've seen how the two o' you gaze at one another, an' worse. How he watches you with that hungry man's look in his eyes. An idle flirtation's well an' good, but that—ah, that makes me fear for you, Miss Layton.'

'But I'm not frightened, my lady, not at all,' Abigail said, and just the thought of how he called her Abbie, how he brushed her hair back from her forehead, how he kissed her and told her he loved her—ah, it was enough to make her smile again. 'Why should you be?'

'Because, as clever as you are in book matters, Miss Layton, you're as innocent an' as ignorant as a new babe in more worldly ones,' Lady Hamilton said. 'You're smiling now, imaginin' his handsome face, aren't you?'

'And why not?' Abigail said defensively. How could Lady Hamilton speak to her like this when she herself seemed to be conducting an intrigue with Admiral Nelson? 'Lieutenant Lord Richardson is a gentleman, an officer of the King, who puts honour first among all things.'

'First o' all things he is a man, an' you are a woman, a very pretty young woman.' She leaned closer, resting her hand on Abigail's knee. 'Your lieutenant may be handsome as the day, an' gallant as they come, but he's also a peer's son. He'll dally where he pleases, then wed where his papa says. No matter what he tells you, he won't wed you. He'll love you now, an' tell you you're his world, but soon enough he'll sail away without a care, an' leave you with his brat in your belly. An' all the Greek an' Latin you know won't help you then, Miss Layton. It won't help you at all.'

Abigail flushed again. 'But Lieutenant Lord Richardson is different, my lady. I can tell. He wouldn't treat me with such—such disregard.'

'Do not believe it, Miss Layton. Or him,' she said sternly. 'You are the most clever girl ever I've met, an' I'd not want to see you turn foolish now. When I was far younger than you—long before I met Sir William—I believed a gentleman who promised me everything, an' the sum o' what I had from him was his bastard daughter.'

'Oh, my lady, how sad!' exclaimed Abigail softly, shocked. Of course she'd heard of girls who'd been deceived by false lovers—girls who'd been ruined and seemed to vanish into the air—but she'd never heard the tragedy from a girl herself, now grown and wed and received by a queen. 'I am so sorry for you!'

'I don't want your sorrow or your sympathy, Miss Layton,' Lady Hamilton said, her smile tight. 'I want you to know the price o' love before you risk everything for it, an' listen to your head before your heart. Will you promise me that, Miss Layton?'

'No, my lady, I will not,' Abigail said slowly, looking down into her lap. 'I will not, because I won't make a promise to you that I cannot keep.'

'Oh, lamb, please—'

'Forgive me, my lady, but I must speak,' Abigail said, her words tumbling in a rush directly from her heart. 'I love him—yes, love him with every bit of my soul and my heart. How could I do otherwise, with the world overrun with madness and Frenchmen? What if this is my one chance in my life to love, and be loved in return? What if I were to drown as I returned to England, or be shot dead by a Frenchman's gun, and never knew the joy of love?'

'Then I am too late.' With a groan, Lady Hamilton dropped back against the seat. 'I wouldn't ever wish my fate upon you, Miss Layton. But if ever you need another, in sorrow or in joy, I will be that friend to you.'

'I'll always thank you for that, my lady.' Abigail didn't try to hide her tears, letting them slide down her cheeks. 'You've never shown me anything but kindness, my lady, yet I wouldn't change a thing. I didn't come to Naples to fall in love, but I did, and I won't regret it—or James.'

'There he is now,' Lady Hamilton said softly. 'Ah, no wonder you love him so!'

The carriage had slowed as it drew up before the embassy, and from the window Abigail spotted James at once, waiting beside a small hired carriage decked gaily with ribbons and tiny bells. James was grinning and waving, and melting her heart with the joy he so obviously felt in seeing her again. James, the one man on this earth she was meant to love.

'Ah, so fine a gentleman puts all promises to shame, don't he?' Lady Hamilton smiled wearily. 'But no matter how sweet, remember the price o' love, an' be sure. Be *sure*.'

Abigail sat in the stern of the little boat, the wind tossing her hair inside the brim of her bonnet and rippling the fringe on her shawl. Spray scattered like diamonds in the sunlight as the boat cut across the blue water, and she laughed with pure delight as the white-winged gulls danced across the cloudless sky overhead. She'd never been in a small boat before—so different from the ancient, lumbering merchantman that had carried her from England—and she marvelled at how James could send them flying across the bay with no more than a single sail and the tiller in his hand.

'How do you know how to *do* that, James?' she asked, holding the ribbons on her bonnet so it wouldn't blow away. 'To bend the wind to your will like this?'

Now he laughed, too. 'Those are things a sailor must know, sweet,' he said, raising his voice over the sounds of the taut canvas and the wind singing in the lines. 'If I cannot manage a neat little craft like this, how could I possibly manage a frigate?'

'It's a mystery to me, that's all,' she said, marvelling as much at how handsome he looked, with his golden hair blowing back in the wind, as at his talents as a sailor. Instead of his glittering dress uniform, he'd dressed like the common sailors today, in a billowing white shirt and short jacket, his wide-legged trousers rolled at the hem over his bare legs and feet—and all of it was vastly becoming. She wished he'd not felt the need for his pistols today, but she knew the reason for it, and why it could not be helped. 'There seems to be so much to learn.'

'That is how I felt when you began spouting Homer to make a point to Sir William,' he said. 'And in the original Greek, too. How's a poor sailor boy to cope with that?'

'I'll show you how to cope, you poor lord sailor boy,' she said, reaching over the side to flick a handful of water at him.

'Don't begin that game, madam,' he warned. 'Not unless you can swim.'

'You know I can't,' she said warily, grabbing the side of the boat just in case. They were almost at an empty beach in a small inlet, and she guessed she could likely wade from here to shore if she had to. 'James, please, don't jest about that.'

'You began it,' he said, running the boat in until they were almost ashore. He furled the sail, then hopped out into the water, taking care to keep his pistols and powder clear. Wavelets lapped his knees as he tied the boat to one of the old timbers jutting from the water—all that remained of a wharf. Then he turned back towards her with arms outstretched.

'Come along, then,' he said. 'I'll not wait for you all the day long.'

She frowned, looking from him to the water and back, then swiftly stripped off her own stockings and slippers. Bunching her skirts over her knees, she swung her leg over the side and into the water, shrieking at the unexpected chill.

'You didn't have to do that, Abbie,' he said with dismay. 'I would've carried you.'

'You could've dropped me, too,' she called over her shoulder, laughing as she hurried clumsily through the water towards the beach. As hard as she tried to run, she knew he'd catch her, and he did, seizing her around the waist.

'Are you that eager for your surprise, then?' he asked, laughing too, taking her hand. 'You don't even know where you're bound.'

But *he* did, leading her away from the beach and up a narrow, sandy path between scrubby bushes and large vine-covered rocks until, at last, he turned into a small clearing overlooking the sea. Overgrown thickets of trees shielded and shaded the space, almost as if it were a private room outdoors. Abbie gasped, and forgot her waterlogged skirts as she pressed her hand over her mouth in amazement.

A red coverlet had been spread over the grass, with striped pillows piled invitingly. A wicker hamper of food stood waiting to be unpacked, with plates and glasses already arranged on the coverlet. Festive red ribbons had been tied into extravagant bows around the branches and trunks of the trees, and a score of small brass bells had been hung from the branches, where they'd chime in the breezes from the water.

'Well, now,' James said, more sheepish than amazed. 'I paid to have this rigged out like Christmas at home, but I'm afraid it's more gaudy old Naples than merry old Devon.'

'It's perfect, James,' Abigail said with awe. 'To think that you would do this for me! Oh, it's the most perfect, perfect surprise ever.'

'It will be in a moment, anyway.' He opened the hamper and drew out the music box she'd given him, winding the key. 'It's cold tonight, I know, and that wind is blowing something fierce. We'll have snow up to the sills by morning.'

'Then we'd best begin the Christmas ball at once, my lord, to help us keep warm.' She smiled, and held her damp skirts out in a curtsey as the first notes of 'Greensleeves' thrummed to life. 'Will you honour me, my lord?'

He took her by the hand, drawing her close. 'You honour *me*, love,' he whispered, his voice rough with longing as he trailed his lips across her cheek and along her jaw, in small, teasing kisses that made her shiver. 'You always have, and you always, always will.'

'Always,' she murmured in return. She thought of what she'd told Lady Hamilton, and wondered how she'd even dared consider anything that felt this fine, this *right*. Tenderly she pressed her lips to the hollow at the base of James's throat, silently pledging herself again to the heart that beat so strongly there. They'd come this far together, and she wouldn't be the one to halt now.

Together: yes, that was the keystone, wasn't it? What she and James had done—what they were doing even now—had been done together, two as one. They belonged to each other, seamlessly, as lovers equal and true. She had trusted James with her life, and now her heart. All that was left to give him was her body, and with a sweet shudder of resignation she sank with him onto the red coverlet.

He lay half atop her, his kisses salty from the sea and so heady that she could well have been floating, as they had in the little boat. She slipped her hands inside his shirt, restlessly running her hands along the broad muscles of his back. For all that he was so much larger, she didn't feel trapped beneath his body. Instead her own body seemed to relish the weight of his upon her, and as they kissed she stretched and wriggled languorously beneath him, her movements an unconscious amplification of his mouth over hers.

'God in heaven, Abbie,' he groaned, and she froze. Perhaps what she found pleasurable was not so to him? Perhaps to be agreeable she shouldn't move, but lie still?

'Forgive me, James,' she said anxiously, 'if I've acted wrongly or—'

'Nay, love, not wrong.' He brushed his lips across her cheek to reassure her. 'Nothing wrong, and everything right.'

As if to prove it, he shifted more heavily across her, and she sighed with the *rightness* of it. He slid his hand over her breast, tugging aside the muslin and linen until he reached her skin. Now it was her turn to gasp as his palm teased her nipple into a tight, hot bud of longing. Impatiently she arched against his hand, seeking more, and she felt the deep rumble of his chuckle at her eagerness.

As distracted as she was by his caress, chuckling did register as better than a groan, and boldly she returned the caress. His skin was hot, burning, as if he'd been too long in the summer sun, and her touch was enough to make him groan again.

With another little sigh she whispered her legs apart and let James's body settle there, between, and at once that little sigh changed into a startled gasp. Even though she was still protected by layers of her shift and his trousers, she could feel the rigid heat of that most masculine part of him, pressing hard against the place where she was most a woman.

But instead of retreating, her body longed to be closer still to him. She felt soft and warm and aching, her own heartbeat now concentrated in that same place between her legs, and instinctively she drew her bare legs up higher around his hips to draw him closer.

'Damnation, Abbie,' he rasped, with a desperation of his own, his breath as laboured as if he'd run from town. 'You'll unman me if you keep doing that.'

'Then love me,' she said in a rush, not sure of anything else. 'Just—just love me.'

'I love you already, lass,' said James, and kissed her hard, his lips demanding enough to steal her breath and maybe her soul with it.

She felt him pull her skirts higher, into a mass of crushed muslin at her waist, and then he was sliding between her legs, touching her, telling her how beautiful she was, how much he wanted her, and stroking that warm, secret place at the top of her thighs until she realised that the low, animal sound was coming from herself. Her body was tightening, coiling strangely inside, and then suddenly he was inside her, too, filling her in a way that she hadn't realised was possible, but felt impossibly perfect.

He gasped her name, and shifted, and suddenly the pleasure was even more breathtaking, and both of them were half-laughing and half-weeping as they moved together, together, *yes*, until they found the joy that would bind their love together.

And when they lay together afterwards, a long, long time afterwards—after they'd loved one another twice more, after they'd eaten the sweet Italian cake that stood in for Lady Carrington's Christmas plum pudding, after James had given her her Christmas present, a gold-rimmed cameo of an angel holding a wreath that the local carver had sworn was holly, after James had fastened the chain around her neck to wear beside her father's gold heart, enough to make her weep—after all of that, content and exhausted, Abigail drowsily decided there was no better Christmas to be had in this life than to be here, now, with James's chest against her back and his arm around her waist and his heart beating in time with hers.

They returned far later than James had intended. The wind had changed, too, blowing cold against them the way a real December wind would in the north, and by the time they'd reached the public docks it was after dark and well after the time when English men and women with any sense had left Naples to the Neapolitans.

But there was more than just the hour that felt wrong to him. His instincts sensed danger. Like the wind, the temper of the city seemed changed, agitated and restless. There were too many voices in the streets, too many lights at too many windows.

'What's happened, eh?' he asked the driver of the hackney he'd hired to carry them back to the embassy. He spoke softly in Italian, almost in a whisper, so he wouldn't alarm Abigail, drowsy beside him. 'What's wrong?'

'You haven't heard the news, *signor*?' The driver shook his head with doleful resignation. 'The French have retaken Rome and are headed towards Naples—and may God have mercy on our miserable souls.'

Chapter 8

THEY went directly to the ambassador's library as soon as they returned. The Hamiltons were there, of course, and Lord Nelson, and several other captains from the fleet. Every face was so grim, the tension so thick, that Abigail knew the news James had told her in the hackney must be true.

'High time you showed your face, Richardson.' The admiral glared at James, tipping his head to focus his displeasure through his single good eye. 'You have heard, then?'

'That Rome has fallen,' James said calmly, still holding Abigail's hand, 'and the Neapolitans are in retreat.'

'The damned Neapolitans are running and yipping with their tails between their legs,' Lord Nelson said, biting off each word with disgust. 'That fat fool Ferdinand is running the fastest—hiding himself in peasant's clothing instead of leading like a man, let alone a king. His officers haven't lost much honour, God knows they'd but little to lose, but they most certainly have lost all they had. What the devil is *she* doing here?'

It took Abigail a long, awful moment to realise the admiral meant her. 'My lord,' she said, dropping a belated curtsey in her bedraggled gown. 'I am here because I have an interest in—'

'Miss Layton is with me,' James said, as if this were the answer to everything.

'Miss Layton's presence here is o' no importance compared to saving the lives o' Ferdinand and his family,' Lady Hamilton said, and automatically everyone's attention swung away from Abigail. 'As soon as Ferdinand returns, they must all be carried to safety, away from the French.'

'The poor Queen is terrified,' Sir William said, 'and who can blame her? I've heard the French army travels with a guillotine in their baggage cart, ready to put the infernal machine to use whenever they can.'

Her fear growing, Abigail's fingers tightened into James's for reassurance. How had one single day brought her the greatest happiness she'd ever known and now the very real threat of Jacobins with guillotines?

'It's not the French army that's worryin' me,' Lady Hamilton said bluntly. 'It's the King an' Queen's own subjects. If the people o' Naples see the royal family leavin', they'll tear them to pieces like wolves. There won't be nothing left but scraps for the French and their wicked guillotine.'

'Well said, my dear, well said.' Sir William glanced fondly at his wife. 'Emma is entirely right. The royal family must be moved to safety with the greatest discretion.'

Irritably Lord Nelson leaned forward over the table. 'But you say it's not just the King and Queen and their pack of children. I must also haul their entire court and servants. Why, there won't be room to turn about between decks, there are so blasted many of them.'

'Yes, my lord,' Lady Hamilton said. 'Unless you wish to have their blood on your hands.'

'A plague on them all,' the admiral grumbled. 'If they'd defended Rome with any courage, matters wouldn't have come to this.'

'But they have, Lord Nelson,' Lady Hamilton said with surprising patience. 'Which is why we've made our plans to fall in the middle o' the Sultan's party. We'll each o' us slip away one by one to the tunnels, to where your boats are waitin' to take everyone to the ships and then to Palermo. The trick will be to leave the ball without any show or fuss, so that no one suspects.'

Abigail listened, her fear growing. Palermo was on the island of Sicily—the other half of Ferdinand's kingdom. An island was the safest place of refuge for the royal family, for the French wouldn't dare challenge the English navy and their guns, but what would become of the rest of them? What would become of *her*?

'We must be the last to leave the ball,' the admiral was saying. 'Sir William and his lady and I will then return directly to the *Vanguard*. Richardson, you will wait for our signal on board the *Colossus*.'

'Yes, sir,' James said. 'The *Colossus*, sir?'

'Of course, Richardson, you were not here earlier, when this was discussed,' the admiral said, and one of the other captains handed James a sealed packet of orders. 'I congratulate you, sir. In honour of your heroic actions and initiative at Aboukir, you have been made Captain. You are to sail for England at once on board the *Colossus*, my lord, to Portsmouth, where you will receive further orders regarding a command.'

Abigail caught her breath with joy for him, wishing she could shout and whoop and throw her arms around James's neck. But there was no place for such public rejoicing over personal achievement now, with so much else at stake.

All James himself did was release her hand to step forward and bow, and take the packet of orders without once looking her way. He broke the seal, scanning the pages quickly.

But there was no smile for her, no shared pleasure in his achievement.

Surely he was only being stoic, behaving as a new officer should? Her hand felt cold and bereft without his around it. *Surely he didn't mean to scorn her, or to abandon her now, when she'd need him most?*

'Thank you, my lord,' he said, the picture of official restraint. 'I am deeply honoured.'

'You should be, Richardson.' The admiral allowed himself a smile. 'The honour is well earned, and deserved.'

'Thank you, my lord,' James said again. 'I should like to ask that Miss Layton be permitted to accompany me to Portsmouth.'

Stunned, Abigail could say nothing. Relief washed over her so completely that she feared she might faint from it.

'Miss Layton?' said the admiral incredulously. 'On board the *Colossus*? This—this woman? I am sorry, my lord, but such an indulgence is absolutely out of the question. You know my beliefs regarding women on board ships of war.'

'I know that women in general are forbidden on board, my lord,' James said. 'But captains are permitted to be accompanied by their wives.'

At last he turned back towards Abigail, and took her hand as he knelt on one knee before her—before the world. 'Miss Layton, will you do me the greatest of honours and be my wife?'

'No, no, Richardson—no!' the admiral exclaimed, appalled. 'I won't let you do this. You are the son of a peer, an officer with every advantage for the future. I will not let you harm yourself by such a connection. Your father would never forgive me if I did!'

But all Abigail heard was James's proposal, and all she saw was the love in his face.

'Marry me, Abbie,' he said. 'Marry me, and be mine for ever.'

'Yes,' she said, the only answer her heart would ever give. 'Oh, yes.'

Now he was the one who caught her in his arms, holding her as if he'd never let her go. 'My own Abbie,' he whispered into her hair. 'My own love!'

'There's no time now for banns and a wedding. Not even a shameful wedding such as this,' the admiral protested. 'Not with the French bearing down hard upon us.'

'Dear sir, there is plenty o' time,' Lady Hamilton said firmly, coming to stand beside Abbie and James. 'Not for a landsman's wedding, no. But if the captain o' the *Colossus* keeps a cleric on board, then he can marry them as soon as they come aboard, as a special case. War changes everything, you know. No one will protest if the banns or licences or whatever come later.'

'Then it shall fall to Captain Peters to decide,' the admiral grumbled. 'God knows, he's sentimental enough to do it, and I know for a fact that he sails with a chaplain in his company. But a wedding—on this night of all others! I still believe the thing should not be allowed—not with a young gentleman of such promise.'

'And I, Lord Nelson,' countered Lady Hamilton, 'will not allow it to be otherwise. Every young gentleman o' promise needs a wife with cleverness an' beauty to steady him, else he'll not amount to nothing.'

'As a clever woman with beauty yourself, my lady, I suppose you should know.' The admiral gazed towards the heavens in silent appeal, and then sighed with resignation. 'Go then, Richardson. Marry your sweetheart and find joy with her.'

Beaming with satisfaction, Lady Hamilton kissed Abigail on the cheek. 'I told you I'd be your friend when you needed one, Miss Layton,' she whispered, for Abigail alone to hear. 'An' I was.'

'Thank you, my lady,' Abigail said. 'For everything.'

'Hah, it was you that was wise enough to trust your man when I said otherwise!' She laughed, and patted Abigail's arm with genuine fondness. 'Besides, there aren't many ladies who'll wake to find such a fine new husband beside them on Christmas morn.'

James chuckled, his arm still curled possessively around Abigail's waist. 'I told you I'd surprise you, Abbie, didn't I?'

'You did,' she whispered happily. 'Oh, yes, you *did*.'

On any other night Abigail would have delighted in the spectacle of the Sultan's ball. Dressed, to her eye, like paintings of the Three Wise Men, the Sultan and his attendants wore magnificently rich robes and turbans, silks and brocades thick with gold and silver thread. At their waists they wore fantastic curving swords—even here, to the ball—and there were jewels glittering everywhere on their persons, from the rings on their fingers to their swords' scabbards, even within the elaborately wrapped folds of their turbans.

More wonderful still was the sight of the Sultan formally presenting Admiral Nelson both with one of the curved swords—a scimitar with a gilded hilt in the shape of a crouching crocodile, to symbolise the Nile—and a jewel of his own.

Lady Hamilton had told Abigail the jewel was called a *chelengk*, the highest award for valour granted by the Turks: a huge Brazilian diamond, surrounded with a hundred more diamonds set like the rays of the sun, and a bow beneath that rotated by means of a tiny clockwork inside. Because Nelson wore no turban of his own, the Sultan pinned the *chelengk* to the front of the admiral's cocked hat, where it turned and spun like some sparkling demon eye for the rest of the evening.

Yet despite so much gaudy spectacle, rich food and drink, and an orchestra for dancing, Abigail could take no real pleasure in the ball. The realisation of what so much gaiety was serving to mask was never far from her thoughts. At James's side, she noted it as each royal face vanished from the crowd, and worried that others were noticing, too.

'You're nervous as a cat tonight, love,' James said as he brought her a glass of punch. 'You're not having second thoughts about wedding me, are you?'

'Oh, no!' she said. 'It's—it's the other part.'

'Don't fuss over that,' he said easily, his gaze sweeping the crowded room. 'It's all going as well as can be expected. Even better, perhaps, for I believe that all who needed to leave are gone.'

'I'll feel better once we're safely away, too,' she said in an anxious whisper. 'I'm not as accustomed to these sorts of—of evenings as you are.'

He laughed. 'Adventure is good for the constitution, sweet. I recommend it most highly.'

She sighed, unable to relax. The truth was he *did* seem to be enjoying himself—as if he'd magically transformed the danger they must all be in into an invigorating excitement. 'Is this how you are before a battle, James?'

'I suppose I must be,' he said, amused that she'd noticed. 'I never feel more alive than when there's a risk I might die.'

'Don't speak so,' she said, troubled. 'That's ill luck—and on our wedding night, too.'

'I've hardly forgotten.' He bent to kiss her, his lips tasting of punch and excitement. 'Not with having you as my wife in my bed as my reward. Ah, the admiral is making his farewells, and so are the Hamiltons.'

'I wish we could say goodbye to them again ourselves,' she said wistfully. 'Who knows when or even if we'll see them again?'

'They've been good friends to us, aye,' he said, 'and our best friends with come through our lives again and again. Come, sweet, dance with me, and then it will be our turn to leave.'

She set the still-full cup of punch on the tray of a passing footman. 'I don't think I can dance, James. I'm too uneasy.'

'Then dancing will show the world how brave you are,' he said easily, taking her hand to lead her to the floor. 'That's what Lady James would do. Make everyone recall when she was here, but not the time she left. She's vastly clever that way.'

She frowned. 'Lady James?'

'That's you, my dear goose,' he said. 'Or at least it will be later this evening.'

'I suppose it will,' she said, and finally grinned back at him. 'I'd not realised that. Lady James Richardson! How grand!'

'Soon to be Captain Lady James Richardson,' he said. 'Though to me you'll always be my Abbie, wading barefoot to shore without a thought for your gown.'

'Oh, James,' she said. 'How I do love you!'

'And I you,' he said over his shoulder. 'Now, come, dance with me, and let everyone here remember you as the most beautiful lady here tonight. It's almost Christmas, you know, and this will make for good practice before you dance at my mother's.'

And, with her head high, Abigail danced, gloriously buoyed by his love for her and hers for him. When the dance was done, he tipped her back into the crook of his arm and kissed her again, with such passion that afterwards her head spun, and others around them applauded with amused appreciation.

'Surely they won't forget us after that?' she said, still deliciously wobbly as she followed him through the room.

He smiled down at her, and winked. 'I don't care if they do or not, Abbie,' he said. 'I did that for us.'

They hurried to the cellar stairs, gathering their cloaks and his pistols from where they'd hidden them earlier, and made their way through the shadowy tunnels beneath the house. They were the last to leave, and the candles in some of the lanterns had already guttered out. There would—or should—be one more boat waiting for them on the beach, ready to ferry them to the Vanguard. It seemed easy enough, yet still Abigail was sure the entire world must hear the thumping of her heart, and not even James's hand in hers was enough to calm her.

At last they came to the door, old and worn with rusted locks. Cautiously James drew a pistol and cocked it, his ear close to the door as he listened before opening it. Satisfied, he pulled it ajar, looked again, and beckoned to Abigail to follow. Once again he took her hand, and together they crossed out onto the sand, already churned that night by dozens of footsteps before theirs.

'The boat should be waiting behind those rocks,' he told her softly. 'Almost there, love.'

'You there—halt!' The order in crude Italian came from behind them, in a rough voice that meant to be obeyed. 'Halt, or I'll shoot!'

At once James stopped, and Abigail stopped, too. 'I'm Lieutenant Lord Richardson of the *Vanguard*, and this is my wife,' he announced in Italian, without turning. 'We are bound for the *Colossus*, there in the harbour, and for England. We mean no harm to you, or anyone else.'

'Toss your gun in the sand to your left,' the man ordered. 'As far as you can—and no tricks.'

James obeyed. 'No tricks.'

'Turn about, both of you. Slowly, slowly.'

Again James obeyed, and Abigail did as well. Over the last months her Italian had improved dramatically, but even if she'd been unable to understand the man's words she'd have been in no doubt of the danger they were in. It was almost as palpable as the salt in the sea air—and if she'd been frightened before, it was nothing to the blinding terror she felt now.

This man must be one of the few soldiers left behind to guard the city, or possibly even a deserter—his uniform was shabby and his hair dishevelled. But the musket in his hands glinted cruelly in the moonlight, and Abigail didn't doubt for a minute that he'd use it. He'd never be caught if he did, and nor would anyone care—not in this lawless place.

But their lives couldn't end here on this empty beach. Not before she and James had fairly begun. It couldn't end before they were married, or had returned to England, or he'd become a captain and she'd become a mother, and, oh, a thousand, thousand other things she still wished for them both.

It couldn't end before she told him she loved him at least one more time—not tonight, not before Christmas…

The man stepped closer, squinting at them. 'If everything is as you say, then why are you skulking about here at night? Why not go by day, like a gentleman would?'

James sighed. 'Very well, if you must know the truth, this lady is not yet my wife. She is a high-born lady, and we are eloping against her father's wishes.'

Unprepared for the audacity of his lie, Abigail gasped, and without thinking touched the two charms she wore around her neck.

'A lady, you say?' Greedily his gaze followed her hand. 'Then you're wearing jewels, aren't you, signorina? A necklace of diamonds or pearls?'

He took another step closer, and Abigail shrank away. Neither the gold heart nor the new cameo that James had given her were of sufficient value to please a thief, but to her they were priceless. Desperately she tried to think of a way out—something to say or do that would let them escape.

'Leave her alone,' James ordered. 'She's nothing of value.'

The man laughed. 'Oh, yes? That's a sure sign of the opposite. Give me what's round your throat, hussy, before I take it for myself.'

'No!' she cried in Italian, pulling away before she dropped to her knees in the sand. 'Oh, no—not my ring! Oh, James, I've dropped my ring—the diamond betrothal ring you gave me!'

Frantically she pretended to search for the non-existent ring in the sand, hoping both that the man would understand her words and that James would play along.

He did. 'That ring was my mother's, Abigail, and worth five thousand if it was worth a farthing. You can't have lost it.'

'But I have!' she wailed. 'I had it on my finger, and when the man startled me it slipped off and into the sand!'

'A diamond worth five thousand, you say?' The man's greed overcame his sense, and he bent down beside Abigail to hunt for the ring.

At once Abigail threw her handfuls of sand into his eyes, and the man yelped with pain and surprise. James grabbed the musket from his hands and struck the back of his head with the butt, knocking him face-first into the sand at Abigail's feet. Groggily he struggled to rise, then pitched forward and lay still.

'Are you unhurt, Abbie?' James asked, without turning away from the soldier to look for himself. 'You're all to rights?'

'Of course I am,' she said, and strangely she was. Perhaps James had been right about excitement being good for the constitution, for now that they'd outwitted the thief she felt strangely exhilarated. She ran across the sand to retrieve James's pistol from where he'd tossed it, and returned holding the gun gingerly with both hands. 'Here's your gun.'

'You *are* a brave lass,' he said with admiring approval. 'Brave and clever, truly. You deserve a real diamond ring worth five thousand for such inspiration. I should tell the admiral that I'm worried about being worthy of you, not the other way round.'

'Don't be,' she said, staring down at the unconscious man. 'I was more frightened than I've ever been.'

'But that's what real bravery is,' he said, standing beside her. 'Only an idiot doesn't know fear. Bravery's no more than knowing where you're weak and how you're strong, when to stand alone and when you need another by your side.'

'Like love, then,' she said softly. Over her shoulder, she could see the longboat pulling towards the shore, ready to carry them out to the *Colossus* and, at last, their wedding. 'At least how love is for us.'

He laughed, a deep, warm sound that she knew she'd never tire of hearing. 'Then surely we're the bravest lovers of all time. And I can swear to you, Abbie, that I wouldn't wish it otherwise.'

The captain of the *Colossus* proved to be every bit as sentimental as Admiral Nelson had predicted. With a white bridal cockade pinned to his coat, Captain Peters served as cheerful witness as his chaplain married them by candlelight that night. He toasted them at supper afterwards—with wine captured from a French smuggler—and had even, at short notice, had his cook concoct a passable English wedding cake with candied fruit. But, most generous of all, he'd shifted his belongings from his cabin and given it over to them for their wedding night—or, more accurately by then, their wedding morn.

Morning or night, they still managed to put the swinging cot to most excellent use, celebrating their marriage in the way only they could.

It was still dark when Abigail woke. Beside her James slept still, his arm curled endearingly around her waist. She clung to that pleasant state between sleep and waking as long as she could, cosy beneath the coverlets with her husband. Her husband James: ah, how she liked the sound of that, and how well she loved him!

'James,' she whispered softly. 'My own dear, perfect husband.'

Like all sailors, he woke at once, and leaned over to kiss her. 'Good morning, Lady James.'

'Not just any morning, but Christmas—and already it's a merry one at that,' she said, smiling up at him. 'Listen! I hear the bells!'

'Those are the bells to mark the watch, goose, not Christmas bells,' he teased. 'But perhaps today they mark Christmas as well.'

'I say Christmas,' she said, then stared at the curving stern window across the cabin. 'Oh, James, it cannot *be*!'

She slid from the bunk, wrapping herself in one of the coverlets, and padded across the deck in her bare feet to peer through the glass. By the light of the stern lantern there was no mistaking what she saw.

'Look, James, *look*,' she said with awe. 'It's Christmas, and it's *snowing*.'

He chuckled, his head propped on his elbow as he watched her from the bunk. 'A pretty fancy for the day, sweet, but I know it never snows in Naples.'

'I'm not fancying,' she insisted, watching the fat flakes spin and fall. 'It's Christmas, and we're still in Naples, and it *is* snowing.'

'Oh, love,' he said, sliding from the bunk to join her. 'I know we've pretended it's Christmas between us all along, but now— Damnation, it's *snowing*!'

'And more than that, James,' she said slowly. 'Look over there, at Vesuvius.'

Through the swirling snow, the crown of the volcano's black silhouette glowed orange in the early-dawn sky, lit by shooting flames and sparks as spectacularly bright as any skyrockets.

'Fireworks and snowflakes and you to love as my husband on Christmas Day,' she said, turning her face up to his. 'Why should I ever have to pretend again when my life is so glorious as this?'

'I told you I'd surprise you,' James said, and kissed her warmly, passionately, perfectly. 'And I don't ever mean to stop. Merry Christmas, my love. Merry Christmas!'

* * * * *

SPECIAL EDITION™

**brings you a heartwarming
new McKettrick's story from**

NEW YORK TIMES BESTSELLING AUTHOR

LINDA LAEL MILLER

THE McKETTRICK
Way

Meg McKettrick is surprised to be reunited
with her high school flame, Brad O'Ballivan,
who has returned home to his family's
neighboring ranch. After seeing Meg again,
Brad realizes he still loves her. But the pride
of both manage to interfere with love...until
an unexpected matchmaker gets involved.

—— McKettrick Women ——

Available December wherever you buy books.

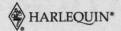

REQUEST YOUR FREE BOOKS!

 **Harlequin® Historical**
Historical Romantic Adventure!

2 FREE NOVELS PLUS 2 FREE GIFTS!

YES! Please send me 2 FREE Harlequin® Historical novels and my 2 FREE gifts. After receiving them, if I don't wish to receive any more books, I can return the shipping statement marked "cancel." If I don't cancel, I will receive 6 brand-new novels every month and be billed just $4.69 per book in the U.S., or $5.24 per book in Canada, plus 25¢ shipping and handling per book and applicable taxes, if any*. That's a savings of close to 15% off the cover price! I understand that accepting the 2 free books and gifts places me under no obligation to buy anything. I can always return a shipment and cancel at any time. Even if I never buy another book from Harlequin, the two free books and gifts are mine to keep forever.

246 HDN EEWW   349 HDN EEW9

Name _____ (PLEASE PRINT) _____

Address _____ Apt. # _____

City _____ State/Prov. _____ Zip/Postal Code _____

Signature (if under 18, a parent or guardian must sign) _____

Mail to the **Harlequin Reader Service®:**
IN U.S.A.: P.O. Box 1867, Buffalo, NY 14240-1867
IN CANADA: P.O. Box 609, Fort Erie, Ontario L2A 5X3

Not valid to current Harlequin Historical subscribers.

Want to try two free books from another line?
Call 1-800-873-8635 or visit www.morefreebooks.com.

* Terms and prices subject to change without notice. NY residents add applicable sales tax. Canadian residents will be charged applicable provincial taxes and GST. This offer is limited to one order per household. All orders subject to approval. Credit or debit balances in a customer's account(s) may be offset by any other outstanding balance owed by or to the customer. Please allow 4 to 6 weeks for delivery.

Your Privacy: Harlequin is committed to protecting your privacy. Our Privacy Policy is available online at www.eHarlequin.com or upon request from the Reader Service. From time to time we make our lists of customers available to reputable firms who may have a product or service of interest to you. If you would prefer we not share your name and address, please check here. ☐

HH07

HARLEQUIN *Presents*

IN Bed WITH THE Boss

Chosen by him for business,
taken by him for pleasure...

A classic collection of office romances from
Harlequin Presents by your favorite authors

ITALIAN BOSS, HOUSEKEEPER BRIDE
by Sharon Kendrick

Book #2687

Raffael needs a fiancée—and he's chosen his mousy
housekeeper Natasha! They have to pretend to be
engaged, but neither has to fake the explosive
attraction between them....

Available December 2007 wherever you buy books.

Look out for more sexy bosses,
coming soon in Harlequin Presents!

www.eHarlequin.com

HP12687

Get ready to meet

THREE WISE WOMEN

with stories by

DONNA BIRDSELL, LISA CHILDS

and

SUSAN CROSBY.

Don't miss these three unforgettable stories
about modern-day women and the love
and new lives they find on Christmas.

Look for *Three Wise Women*
Available December wherever you buy books.

TheNextNovel.com

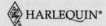

EVERLASTING LOVE™

Every great love has a story to tell™

Martin Collins was the man
Keti Whitechapen had always loved but
just couldn't marry. But one Christmas Eve
Keti finds a dog she names Marley.
That night she has a dream about
Christmas past. And Christmas present—
and future. A future that could include the
man she's continued to love.

Look for

A Spirit of Christmas

by

Margot Early

Available December wherever you buy books.